THE FESTIVAL OF VISION AND FIRE

LOGAN MIEHL

Published by Touchwood Publishing.
Visit www.loganmiehl.com for more information about the author, updates, or new books.

Cover by Jenny Zemanek at Seedlings Design Studio
Editing by Catherine Jones Payne at Quill Pen Editorial Services
Book Layout ©2017 BookDesignTemplates.com

The Festival of Vision and Fire by Logan Miehl – 1st ed.
ISBN 978-1-0809830-0-1

To every wandering soul—for all that is lost,
and all that is found.

Natalia,
Enjoy the next
adventure!

Faeries, come take me out of this dull world,
For I would ride with you upon the wind,
Run on the top of the dishevelled tide,
And dance upon the mountains like a flame!

THE LAND OF HEART'S DESIRE BY WILLIAM BUTLER YEATS

PRONUNCIATION GUIDE

Róisín	row-*Sheen*
Cináed	kin-*Ay*-juh
Naoise	*Nee*-sha
Aimsir	*I'm*-shur
Lughnasa	*Loo*-ness-ah
Eirwen	*Air*-win
Aisling	*Ash*-ling
Eimear	*Ee*-mer
Caitriona	kah-*Tree*-nah
Aibreann	ah-*Brawn*
Pádraig	*Paw*-drig
Tuatha	*Too*-ah
Sorcha	*Sir*-uh-kah

{ 1 }

I lean low across Sona's back, his maroon coat glistening as we race against the golden sun. Everything, from the open sky to the emerald hills scattered with colorful will-ó-the-wisps, is bursting with life.

I am alive.

A pink sunset fades into the blood-orange clouds gathered on the distant horizon. The smell of a summer storm fills my lungs just before the first raindrops pelt my exposed head, neck, and arms.

I look at the transformed sky that grows darker by the minute. I'm about to tell Sona to turn around when I peer ahead, into a film of heavy mist. And that's when I see him.

Naoise.

His shadowy form waits for me, predicting my next move as he always does. Dread crushes me as I realize there is no escape.

My scream makes Sona rear onto his hind legs. With a startled cry, I fall to the sodden earth.

The remaining air in my lungs gets knocked from my chest as I hit the cold linoleum floor of the apartment. I detangle myself from my bedding, wheezing as I try to breathe.

It was just a nightmare. It was just a nightmare. It was just a nightmare.

I half-crawl to the bathroom, blinking against the soft afternoon light slanting through the closed blinds. As I wash my face in the sink, I avoid looking in the mirror. I don't need to be reminded of how haggard I've grown in the last several weeks.

But it's a small price to pay for safely returning home from the Otherworld. These days, the worst demons only exist in my dreams.

At least for now, anyway.

I lean against the bathroom wall, using a breathing technique I learned last month to help with anxiety.

If only Google could tell me how to purge Naoise from my mind for good. Killing him—however necessary it was at the time—came with an unexpected consequence: his lingering presence, haunting me, punishing me for what I did.

The heater turns on, startling me into a crouch, my fists raised. I quickly recover, glad for once that I live alone so that no one witnessed me almost attack a heat duct.

A glance at the alarm clock tells me it's time to catch a bus to the Robertses'—Darren's adoptive parents. Since I prefer to sleep fully dressed, just in case, I tighten my ponytail and call it good. Then I grab my coat and lock the door on my way out.

As small as this studio apartment is, it's the most space I've ever had to myself. The faerie suite I stayed in last summer never felt like *mine*. A golden cage is still a cage.

But as I trudge through slushy snow toward the downtown skyline, I smother a stubborn pang of loneliness in my chest.

This is the first time I've lived alone. I couldn't leave foster care until I turned eighteen this winter. And while independence is all I've ever wanted, I'm still finding my stride as an adult.

It helps that Darren and the Robertses live a quick bus ride away. When they offered to pay my rent until I got a better job, I wanted to say no. Allowing them to do that was one of the hardest choices I've ever made. I've never been good at taking handouts.

But Darren's happiness outweighs my pride. We grew up in separate foster homes, and I'd dreamed of the day I'd live close to him again. Since we returned from the Otherworld, everything I've been waiting for has fallen into place.

The cold air is sharp in my lungs. I slow my pace as I round the corner of a building. City faeries like to hang out in innocent-looking places to play pranks on passing humans—

who are completely unaware that they coexist with an entire race of invisible creatures. Faeries use their brand of magic, *glamour*, to hide from humans. This gives the fae free rein to do whatever they want without consequence.

What these faeries don't know is that Darren and I have the Sight. We see and hear everything they do. Which makes ignoring them almost impossible. But we *have* to ignore them—pretend like we're normal, oblivious humans. Our safety depends on it.

I spot a large fae-hound around the corner, sniffing a pile of trash. The ashen beast is supposed to be invisible to me, and I have to behave accordingly. It bares its fangs as I pass by. I stare at the sidewalk, keeping my pace normal. All the while I'm praying it finds something worth eating in that garbage so it won't hunt me instead.

When it returns to the trash, I can't help but jog the rest of the way to the bus stop. I arrive out of breath, drenched in a cold sweat.

Another day turned into a waking nightmare. As if I needed another reminder of why I hate faeries.

Well, not *all* faeries. It just so happens that every faery I care about lives in the Otherworld.

Without preamble, Cináed's face appears in my mind. Startled, I close out of the thought like it's a pop-up ad on a computer.

You left him—you left all of them—because you belong with humans. With Darren.

Returning to the human realm, however, wasn't at all what I expected either. No matter how many weeks pass, forgetting about Ireland, the summer festival, and the fae is made impossible by the Sight.

Some days I don't know what's worse—having my eyes opened to their invisible world or knowing that it's existed all along and I lived seventeen years in ignorance. I shudder and pull my coat more tightly around me.

I glance up the street, but instead of the bus rumbling my way, I see a lone female faery. With practiced casualness, I scan over her as if I'm watching for the bus, making sure I keep my gaze distant and unfocused.

This is a daily routine for me now. Invisible faeries approach, and I ignore them like a blind human. Most faeries ignore me too. I have yet to encounter one willing to do more than pinch my arm or hackle some foul-mouthed phrase in my ear.

After witnessing more serious harassment, however, I know better than to think I'm untouchable.

Just last week, I looked out the bus window to see a jogger being trailed by a pack of winged monsters akin to the demon faery—the Sluagh—who stalked me last summer. The bus turned the corner before I could decide whether to risk my own skin or not. When I got home, I vomited my dinner into the sink.

If the jogger survived, I'll never know. I do know that my unlucky day will come, and unlike other humans, I'll be ready for it.

As the faery approaches, I feel for the iron pocketknife tucked into a secret zipper along my collarbone. I also have pepper spray in my purse, but I don't know if that works against the fae. Iron, though . . . is poison to them.

A bird chitters, and my eyes trail up toward it, using the chance to take another look at the faery.

She's beautiful, but most fae are. Even if their skin is sickly green or they have sharp fangs and a tail, all of them possess a captivating glow that beckons me closer. And at the same time, their careless—often malicious—actions keep me on edge.

I blink away the snow settling on my eyelashes and step under the overhang, thinking she'll stroll right past me.

But the closer she gets, the more I realize she's not using glamour to turn herself invisible. She's using it to make herself look *human*.

I've never seen anyone do that except Cináed. Her confident stride and alluring smile make me squirm. Instead of walking around the overhang, she stops beside me, facing the empty street.

Of all the days for the bus to be late.

I focus my gaze straight ahead, clenching my hands inside my coat pockets, keenly aware of the absence of a knife in my empty fist.

Do I make small talk to show I believe she's human? Or do I say nothing and ignore how close she's standing to me?

"Hello."

The sound makes me jump. I glance at her with a tight smile.

"Hi."

She's dressed in a white cloak laced in fur. Actually, that's what she's wearing *underneath* the glamour. Her "human" self is wearing a modern coat buttoned down to her thighs. Her irises are nearly white, like glittering crystal. Thick locks of white-blonde hair frame her pale face. My eyes come to rest on her full, red lips. She's hiding her actual lip color with glamour as well—a wise choice seeing as they're frost-bitten blue.

"Waiting for the bus?" Her voice is modulated and slightly husky.

A group of blue-skinned, sharply jointed fae are walking down the other side of the street. One of them pushes a passing human and shrieks in delight when he falls to the ground.

I keep my eyes on the human. To anyone else, it looks like the man slipped in the snow. But they can't see the leering faery, its sharp teeth inches from the man's face.

My jaw tightens. There's absolutely nothing I can do. But it doesn't make watching it any easier on my conscience.

Snow-faery is observing me, her eyes sparkling with interest. She can see the scene across the street, but it doesn't seem to faze her at all.

I respond at last to her question with a nod.

"I thought as much," she says.

The throng of blue faeries shuffles away and leaves the man alone. I suppress a sigh of relief. Then I see the bus creaking around the corner. As it grinds to a stop and the door swings open, snow-faery says, "Have a blessed evening . . ."

Her words trail off, and I know she's fishing for my name. Telling her *that* seems like the worst thing I could do. The fact that she's showing interest in me has set off every internal alarm system I have.

"Yeah, nice to meet you."

Her smile stops my heart. "Eirwen."

The bus driver calls out to me, and I race up the steps. After apologizing to the driver, I glance out the window and see a deserted sidewalk where the faery and I were standing.

If she wasn't waiting to catch a bus, that means she was standing there, pretending to be human, just to talk to me.

{2}

It's been a long day—a long week, actually—and I'm excited to spend the upcoming three-day weekend with Darren. Even if it means letting Juliana hover over me like a fussy mother hen, and enduring awkward conversation with Howard, who I know is still wary of me. Both of the Robertses are, and who could blame them?

After Darren and I went missing for nearly four months, only to wash up in the Boston airport like a couple of bruised and bandaged ragamuffins . . . it's a miracle they even let me step foot inside their house.

I can't take any credit for that, though. That magic was all Darren. We had gone over our cover story on the plane home from Ireland, and while I hated how dumb our lies seemed, I resigned myself to them simply because I couldn't think of anything else.

Even I—a practiced liar—couldn't formulate an excuse as to why Darren and I had vanished from August to November.

But the moment the Robertses arrived at the airport, rushing toward us—well, toward Darren—my shell-shocked little brother, who had survived faerie imprisonment and countless other traumas, became the epitome of collected composure. He told his would-be parents the best-crafted lie I've ever heard.

Talk about a proud big sister moment.

Plus, his lie totally saved me. Without it, I'd have been blamed—as the kidnapper, the bad example, the one who led Darren away to who-knows-where. Which is exactly how I felt inside.

Through tears and hugs and Juliana holding Darren's face in her hands like he was made of glass, my brother told the Robertses he'd been scared they would change their minds about adopting him. That when I showed up to visit, he'd tried to convince me to run away with him.

When I'd refused, he'd taken off alone. And me, being the good sister I am, had chased him down to bring him back. He'd stowed away on a cargo ship, and I'd gone after him. But the ship had left port with us onboard, sailing for months with no way to contact anyone. By the time the ship docked, Darren had realized it was wrong to leave like that, and we'd purchased plane tickets and flown home as soon as we could.

Even now, I can't help but shake my head at the memory. The way they bought into his explanation seemed too good to be true. And it was. When I talked to Darren afterward, he told me he thinks he used glamour on the Robertses to help them believe our story.

As I expected, the Robertses had been working with local authorities on our search investigation. In the weeks that followed, Darren continued to flex his newfound glamour abilities, and he taught me a few tricks for when I was interrogated. The two of us told our "glammed up" story until every party involved had been placated.

Neither of us are sure what all of this means—if the spell will stick, if there are unseen consequences to manipulating people's minds—but thankfully, Darren is a cautious kid. I doubt he'll abuse that skill for stupid things, the way I would if our roles were switched.

Not anymore. Everything is different now. I'm different.

The bus stops, and I hop down the stairs, my boots crunching through the hardened snow. The Robertses' house is nestled between equally grand homes, its brick face and shuttered windows cast in a golden glow from the inside out.

I catch sight of Juliana carrying a steaming bowl to the table. With a little sigh, I knock on the door with a gloved hand, shrugging my shoulders to shed the snow gathering on my coat.

In two seconds, the door swings wide open, and Juliana's ruby lips part in a beaming grin.

"Hellooouu!" she croons, taking my arm and guiding me inside. "Come in, come in! It's quite the blizzard outside, isn't it? Next time Howard will pick you up so you don't have to walk in the cold. Speaking of, we should go boot shopping. I've misplaced my only waterproof pair, and yours won't last through the winter. How about next Tuesday?"

As Juliana rambles on, I let her lead me to a barstool along the marble counter separating the kitchen from the dining area. I twist my mouth into what I hope looks like a genuine smile, nodding and mumbling something about how I actually took the bus here and only walked from the corner.

But Juliana doesn't hear me. Either that or she brushes my comments aside like she often does. She's not trying to be rude. During the time I've spent here, I've realized that

Juliana simply has a lot to say. It makes talking with her easy because she expects little reciprocation from her audience.

She tasks me with sprinkling paprika onto a plate of deviled eggs and tells me about Darren's upcoming mathlete tournament. I smile and nod at all the right places, taking mental note of the tournament date. I'll have to ask for a shift change at the coffee shop, but with all the extra shifts I've been taking, I'm confident I can find a replacement in time.

Darren emerges from his room down the hall. He snatches an egg and pops it in his mouth while Juliana's back is turned. I shove his shoulder but make no verbal protest. He smirks through his mouthful and gives me a side hug. That's when Juliana sees him, and while it should be humanly impossible, her smile grows even bigger.

"Darren, honey, can you set the table?"

"Sure." He takes the stack of four plates from her and heads to the table, but not before swiping another egg.

I glance at him as he walks behind me, noticing just how much he's grown in the last several weeks. Soon enough, he'll surpass me in height and no longer be my little brother in both size and years. A surge of emotion tugs on my gut at the thought.

The garage door closes in the laundry room, followed by the sound of Howard's footfalls and Juliana's sing-song *hello* to him. He appears, smiling at each of us and carrying his shoes in hand.

I curse under my breath. I forgot to take my shoes off at the door. Again.

Even with the best of intentions to fit in here, it's a steep learning curve. Three weeks ago, I arrived late for family dinner and forgot to give my condolences to Howard—on behalf of his mother's death that morning—until I was halfway through my plate of lasagna.

While Howard and Juliana share their greeting in the kitchen, I sneak to the door and peel my boots off. I hear the warbling blend of voices as Darren gets pulled into the group hug.

I hesitate in the shadow of the entryway until their private moment passes. Then I return to sprinkling paprika on the eggs.

While Juliana and Howard discuss the day, I go searching for Darren, who's managed to sneak off again.

I knock on his bedroom door. When I hear something hit the ground with a *thump*, I don't wait for his approval before swinging the door open and barreling into the room.

"Darren—Darren what's—"

My panic blurs my vision until I find him. Darren, kneeling by his bookshelf, hurriedly shoving fallen books into place.

If not for the touch of fear on his face, I might have played this off as my own overreaction. Ever since the Otherworld, I've become what most would call an overly protective big sister. Or what Darren calls *bossy* and *annoying*.

"Uh, *privacy*?" He stacks the last few books on the shelf.

"Sorry." But I don't backtrack toward the door. Instead, I visually dissect the room for danger.

Darren stands, taking in my momma-bear stance, and rolls his eyes. "Nothing's wrong, Raisin." He rolls his swivel chair over from the desk. When he sits in front of the bookshelf, crossing his arms with exaggerated coolness, I almost roll my eyes back at him.

"Clearly," I say.

"Well, nothing's wrong with *me*. You, though, are delusional."

Delusional. I frown. Yet another word for my paranoia.

But I'm not giving up so easily. He's hiding something in that bookshelf, and I'm not leaving this house until I figure out what it is.

"So, what's going on?"

While his baby face remains impassive, I notice his eyes flicker to the shelves. "I don't know what you're talking about."

"Alright. Well, Howard was looking for you."

He stands from the chair but doesn't move to leave.

"Don't worry—I'll leave your room alone."

I walk out first to prove it, and he follows behind me. When he closes the door, I turn and step into the bathroom. I stand in there, listening by the closed door until I hear Darren walk down the hallway. Then I peek into the empty hall and dart into his room. The door closes soundlessly behind me.

The chair rests in front of the unassuming little shelf, and I roll it aside before I start pulling down books one by one.

When the top shelf reveals only sci-fi and fantasy novels, I start working on the second shelf.

Halfway through a section of illustrated encyclopedias, I begin pulling on the next book and meet some resistance. I tug again, but the book isn't budging from the shelf. I crouch down, using both hands, and the book unsticks and falls into my lap.

Along with a large, brown toad.

The creature blinks up at me from where it landed on top of the book. We both shriek, and I flip the book and toad from my lap, scurrying backward on my hands. The open book lands on top of the creature, and I hear a pathetic *squeak* from beneath the pages.

The bedroom door flies open, and Darren rushes in. I imagine his wide-eyed expression mirrors my own.

"What did you do?" he hisses, closing and locking the door.

I point at the book, and Darren swears. He kneels down, blocking my view of the smashed toad. After a second, I begin to crawl closer, listening as Darren murmurs apologies over and over again.

I open my mouth but realize he's not talking to me. Peering over his shoulder, I see Darren gingerly lift the book. The toad stirs and blinks at the ceiling, and then its beady eyes find mine.

"May Dagda's cauldron boil the flesh from your soul."

Darren inhales sharply. I just stare, slow to accept that an amphibian told me to go to hell.

My brother begins another string of apologies, lowering a hand toward the toad. It slaps at one of his fingers and stands on its own, cutting Darren off as it growls at me with its small but surprisingly powerful voice.

"Explain yourself girl! Why did you try to destroy my home?"

"No, Thomas, she didn't mean it—"

Thomas—who looks like a tiny man with the face and limbs of a freckled frog—holds up a three-fingered hand, silencing Darren.

"I wish to hear an explanation from *her*."

Darren opens his mouth, but no sound comes out. He looks at me, eyes bulging. I turn to the angry toad with increased interest, realizing that my apology might get Darren his voice back.

"I—I had no idea you were living behind the book. I—" I glance at Darren again, feeling sheepish. "I thought Darren was hiding porn or something."

Darren's face turns beet red, and he throws his head back with a soundless groan. I honestly *had* been hoping Darren's secrets would be normal teenage stuff. My worst-case scenario was something to do with faeries, and I hate that I was right to be paranoid.

Thomas places his hands on his wide hips. "*Humph.* I sense you speak the truth. But if you cross me again, girl, you will know my wrath."

It takes less than a second to size up such a small creature. But I bite back my smirk and only nod. "Won't happen again."

Thomas then looks at Darren and seems to remember stealing his voice. “Oh.” He snaps two of his long fingers. “There you go, Master Darren.”

“I didn’t know brownies could do that,” Darren says, hand on his throat.

Thomas smooths his palms over his tiny trousers and buttoned shirt, both shades of brown. “We have many tricks, Master Darren.” Then Thomas glowers in my direction. “Our tricks benefit those we serve as long as we are not provoked or harmed.”

I hesitate, but curiosity gets the better of me. “Why are you called a brownie?”

Thomas’s black eyes stare at me. “Why are insolent girls—who try to destroy what they do not understand—called humans?”

I bite my lip again, this time scolded into a willing silence despite the questions dancing on my tongue.

Juliana calls from the kitchen, telling us dinner is ready. Thomas steps onto Darren’s lowered hand and is lifted onto the shelf, where he has to turn sideways to squish himself between the books.

I follow Darren out the door, and as soon as it closes, I grab his arm and make him face me. “What in the world was that?” I whisper.

He wipes a hand across his face, glaring at me. “It’s a brownie, Raisin. And, thanks to you, he almost turned into a boggart.”

“Translation for the non-nerd, please?”

"Brownies are a type of faery. They like to serve, and are extremely loyal."

"Hence the *Master* Darren."

Darren ignores my smirk and continues talking like an audible definition taken straight off the internet.

"But if you do something wrong, like thank them or give them new clothes or, you know, *smash them with a book*"—he shoots me an icy glare—"they transform into a boggart, their shadow side."

"And what do they do then? Claw your eyes out with their frog fingers?"

"Just don't do anything stupid to make him mad again, okay?"

"What's he doing here, besides being grumpy?"

"He showed up a few days ago and pledged himself to me." Darren shrugs. "Said he'd protect me from harm."

Protect Darren? My eyebrows form a hard line. "He stole your voice and threatened to do worse if we cross him."

Darren mirrors my scowl. "Only 'cause *you* attacked him." His mouth softens as he glances at the closed door. "Besides, I don't mind having him here."

The subtext is written all over his face. Darren copes with the Sight much better than I do. But I know he still gets scared. And I see now that, to him, the brownie represents safety.

Which is not at all what it represents to me.

"Come on," Darren says. "Mom hates—I mean, Juliana hates it when dinner gets cold."

I smile at the correction. It's not the first time he's stumbled over what to call Juliana and Howard since the adoption. I imagine I'd have done the same if I'd ever been adopted.

But my frown returns as I follow him down the hall, my mind spinning.

The brownie's been here a few days. Darren has been tiptoeing around me—avoiding me by hiding in his room—for weeks now.

Could Darren be hiding something else—something more significant than a talking toad?

{ 3 }

"So, Róisín," Howard says a few minutes into the meal as he dishes salad onto his plate, "how's the job treating you?"

"Good," I say in the same affirmative tone I use whenever I'm asked anything about work, school, the apartment, or my life in general.

"And the studio?" Juliana's fork of green beans hovers in front of her keen expression. "Do you feel safe at night?"

"Jules," Howard interjects, "it's in one of the safest neighborhoods."

"Well, then, are you at least warm enough?" she continues, undeterred. "We can send you home with another quilt for the bed."

I swallow a piece of buttered role. "The studio is perfect."

I almost begin to thank them but stop myself. My verbal gratitude is a daily thing, but it never satisfies the imbalance between myself and the Robertses. The only way to truly express my thanks is through my actions. By working, studying hard, and repaying them when I can.

You sound like a faery. Faeries always prefer actions to verbal appreciation.

To change the subject, I make a passive comment about the three-day weekend coming up. I turn to pluck another roll from the basket and sense the sudden tension around the table.

When I turn back, everyone seems to be looking at anything but me.

Juliana glances at Darren. "Well, um, we were actually waiting until Dare-bear had the chance to tell you first."

"Mo-om," Darren mutters, but I'm not sure if he's objecting to the ridiculous nickname or to telling me . . . something.

I softly set my fork down and turn toward Darren, who's sitting beside me. Whenever I'm in the Robertses' house, I try to appear to have good table manners. I was never taught etiquette and never cared to learn. But, for some reason, I want them to think I'm the kind of person who has social graces.

Darren sighs, his gaze shifting from me to his adopted parents and finally to his plate.

"I was going to tell you after dinner," he begins slowly, only aggravating the churning dread inside me. "Juliana was offered a new job. In Maine."

When he doesn't continue, Juliana adds, "We want to take a road trip to look at houses in the area."

"This weekend," Darren finishes.

"Oh."

I think I try to smile, but my face doesn't seem capable of anything but blank surprise.

Howard, never one for confrontation, digs into his food with renewed interest.

Darren picks at a roll.

Juliana rallies, maintaining her positive tone as she explains. When the job offer first came, she almost turned it down. But with the recent passing of Howard's mother, they realized they had no ties here. The more they explored the idea, the more sense it made for her to accept the offer and for them to move.

"Howard can work from home, which he's wanted to do for years. And we are very excited about the private high school in the area."

I nod but can't force myself to make a sound. Not when I hear no mention of my place in all this change.

I somehow survive dinner. When Howard starts clearing plates, I excuse myself, claiming I need to check on a school assignment on my phone, and escape onto the porch for some alone time.

Darren is leaving. Darren is leaving, and he didn't invite me to come. Darren is leaving without me.

I feel displaced, uprooted like a weed and tossed into the garbage. The sense of belonging I've been cultivating, stripped away in a single moment.

No ties here. That's what Juliana said.

I'd symbolically photoshopped my face into the Robertses' family portrait. I'd convinced myself that they were accepting me into their lives . . . and now I feel so utterly stupid.

But that's not what hurts the most. After all the years Darren and I spent apart, fighting to be closer—I thought he would fight for me.

I sit on the porch stairs and hug my knees to my chest with a sigh. My nose tingles, and I angrily wipe a sleeve across my watery eyes. The door opens, spilling yellow light around me.

I glance over. It's Darren, so I dismiss the forced smile I was about to summon. I'll always want to shield my true self from the Robertses. But Darren knows me well enough to see through my masks. Which sucks during moments like this.

"Hey," he says, sitting beside me.

He's wearing a coat and socks but no shoes. I'm reminded of that night that feels like a lifetime ago, when I chased down a demon and traded my sneaker for my kidnapped brother. A small scar on his neck is the only proof it ever happened.

When I don't say anything, Darren continues. His prepubescent voice cracks, and he speaks in an urgent, pleading voice. "Raisin, you have to believe I was going to tell you."

"When? After the moving truck arrived?"

The venom I wanted to inject into the words is missing. Maybe it left with the last of my pride when I was rejected by my only kin.

"I thought maybe I could contact Cináed first, to find out when he's coming back."

Hearing that name out loud ignites a chain reaction in my body. My stomach flutters, and my face flames despite the cold.

"What does he have to do with this?"

A pause, then desperation infuses Darren's voice. "Only that, if he's coming soon, I don't want you to miss him."

My brow furrows, and I finally look at my brother. "Miss him?" I growl. "Me living here has nothing to do with him."

Darren winces. "Yeah, but when he does come back—"

"If he does, he can come find me. I'm not waiting around for whenever that might happen."

Knowing how crazy fae time can be, I could wait—*waste*—years of my life before Goldilocks decides to return. And for what? A short visit that will only remind me we can never work because we belong in different worlds?

"But . . ." Darren pauses again, his button nose scrunched in confusion. "But I thought . . ."

"What?" I ask, though a squirming feeling tells me I already know what he's going to say.

"I thought you'd want to go back with him. To the Otherworld."

I'm shaking my head before he's finished talking, and I stand to pace in front of the stairs. The heat in my face has bloomed through my entire body, fueling me with agitation. "Neither of us are ever going back. That place nearly killed us."

"But it didn't," comes the muttered response.

"Don't you remember all those humans, trapped in the Otherworld because they can't cross through the portal anymore?"

It's a stupid question. He would remember those poor souls better than anyone—he was the one imprisoned with them in the dungeons.

But I keep going, like a train picking up speed. "We got out while we still could. The others weren't so lucky. Why would I ever go back, even for a day, and risk ending up like them?"

"Because you won't get trapped. You're not just a human."

I halt mid-stride, turning to stare at Darren. We've hardly spoken about the realization that he and I could be half-breeds—part faery and part human.

It hasn't ever mattered who our parents were. My whole life, I've assumed they were dead. I see no reason to change that—or to go digging into our past—based on some theory.

My mind flutters toward our experiments with glamour. But I shoo away the confusing memories.

"We don't know that," I say, my throat tight.

"Well, I thought you'd want to know for sure. I thought you were waiting for Cináed so you could go find out the truth."

I cross my arms. "And what makes you think I'd want to do that?"

He looks away, picking at his wool sock. "You remember more."

By that he means I have more memories of our childhood. But that's hardly true. I've retained fragments of distant memories that lead me nowhere. I can't remember the important stuff: our parents' names, physical descriptions, or where they went the night they disappeared.

Darren continues, "I don't think you can move on until you know."

"And you can?"

A smile touches his brown eyes that are a shade darker than my own. "I'm happy with Juliana and Howard."

Well, I'm happy with you, I want to say, but bite my lip instead. He needs the Robertses, and it's becoming clearer and clearer that he might not need me. At least not anymore.

"And that's all I want—for you to be happy," I say at last.

His smile holds as he stands to hug me. My chin no longer reaches above his head, and I get a mouthful of shampoo-scented hair before he pulls away.

"I have more bad news." A sheepish grin threatens to burst across his face.

I quirk an eyebrow, steeling myself for another blow.

"Howard made his famous cream pies, and I already ate most of yours."

I ruffle my hand through his hair, tacking on a smile. "Well, you'd better get after it before I hoard the rest."

I convince him to go inside without me, making some excuse about answering an email. He pretends to believe me and heads for the door, shooting me a smile before returning to his place at a table I thought had room for me too.

The January night greets me with a frozen kiss. My nostrils inhale the smell of moonlight and stale snow. I zip my coat up to my chin, pull on my hood, and start walking.

Silence presses against my ears, contrasting with the tumult of thoughts screaming in my mind.

I can't imagine Darren leaving without me. It would be ironic, really. Bitterly, horribly, painfully ironic.

And it would serve you right, after what you did to him.

One of my darkest memories resurfaces like a sleeping monster. I remember it like it was yesterday, but that doesn't mean I don't try my best to suppress it from my conscious mind as much as possible.

When Darren and I lived in foster home #2, I left four-year-old Darren behind and joined a group of foster kids making their own way. Even though I eventually gave up my freedom and returned, I had permanently marked my record as an "unruly child," and we were separated from there on out—for Darren's safety.

And now—after I thought I'd finally redeemed myself by bringing us together again—he's leaving me behind.

I push my feet faster, trying to leave the worst of my thoughts in my wake. By now, I've passed the nearest bus stop. I'd rather keep moving than wait in the cold.

I'm walking so fast that, when I round the corner, I don't see the hole in the sidewalk until I'm falling. A strangled shout escapes me, and my arms flail, fingers clawing at dirt until I land in a heap at the bottom of the hole.

The strong scent of earth fills my nose, as powerful as the pounding in my head. I stir, groaning. My right arm is pinned beneath me, and nausea crashes through me when I realize I've lost the ability to move my hand.

I assess the rest of my body before slowly sitting up. Besides my throbbing arm, tingling hand, and aching skull, I think I'm okay.

I blink up from the bottom of a tunnel of earth. It's as if I plummeted down an abandoned well. Either that, or an unmarked construction project in the middle of the sidewalk.

Gritting my teeth, I scoot across the flat ground shaped into a circle no bigger than a bathroom rug, and lean against the wall of solid earth. I stare out the hole that must be at least twice my height. No distinct handholds in the sides. Meaning that, unless someone finds me down here, I'm not getting out.

A quick check of my phone confirms my growing fears. *No Service*. I stretch my arm up and wait, praying the service status changes before my battery dies.

I open my mouth, which is caked in dirt like the rest of me, and holler the loudest shout I can muster. In the empty silence that follows—as I peer at the sky and will someone to appear—I notice something is . . . *off*.

What was once a blank canvas of stars becomes a canopy of tree branches. And the silence. Cars should be driving this street, and people should be walking by, chatting on their way to and from the bars and shops.

Instead, the only sound I hear is my own heartbeat and the distant rattling of bare branches in the wind.

My throat closes, and the edges of my vision turn black. I force my lungs to keep working as I mentally retrace my steps.

Was I so consumed in my thoughts that I took a wrong turn? I remember seeing the familiar red lights of an *open* sign and parked cars lining the street.

I shrug my bruised shoulder, shaking off the numbness so I can attempt to climb the wall. At least I can move my hand now.

As the silence stretches on, interrupted only by my cries for help, any remaining assurance crumbles at my feet.

I don't know where I am. And I don't know how I'll get out.

{ 4 }

When my throat is raw from screaming—fingernails aching from all the dirt shoved into them as I try and fail to scale the wall—I finally hear something.

Footsteps. A lot of them.

I watch the sky, ignoring the strain in my neck from having held this position for so long. As I pace the muddy floor, I imagine I resemble a caged animal. With a wicked scowl plastered across my dirty face, I make a silent vow to enact swift, sweet revenge on my captors.

At this point, I'm positive I've been kidnapped by faeries. Who else could create the illusion of a downtown street to lure me into this hole located in some remote, forested spot where no one can hear me?

My muscles spasm with adrenaline, aching to be set loose on whoever dares show their faery face to me. I'm so consumed in my molten rage that when the head of a buffalo peers down at me, it takes a few seconds to register the creature's face.

"Manny?" I croak, hardly believing it's him.

"Hold on, Róisín."

Manny speaks to someone I can't see. Then he lowers a rope and tells me in his deep, commanding voice to climb.

I grip the rope in both hands, and despite the slight numbness in my right arm and the sharp pain in my ribs, I manage to scurry up the rope, digging my boots into the dirt to propel me.

Manny passes the rope off to someone behind him, kneels, and takes ahold of me by my coat. In one motion, he lifts me the rest of the way, launching me onto a frozen lawn. A streetlight blinds me, and I blink hard as my surroundings come into focus.

I've been on the edge of a public park this entire time. Mere yards from the familiar streets of downtown.

Embarrassment at my overreaction and renewed anger that no one heard my shouts are set aside as I take in my rescue party.

Other than Manny, a minotaur and Cináed's first mate, I also recognize a stubby green goblin—another sailor on Cináed's ship. There are three faeries standing close together wearing identical, silken gray cloaks. A female with a waterfall of ice-blue hair is the first to offer me a hand. I hesitate a second before accepting it, standing with a wince as I clutch my side with my good arm.

"What's going on?" I ask the group.

"This is the girl?" a male with ink-black skin addresses Manny, ignoring my question.

Manny snorts steam from his wide, buffalo nose. "Aye."

"Then we shall return as swiftly as possible," the male says in his steady voice. "Her Sovereign will wish to speak to both of you."

The cloaked trio turn and begin crossing the lawn of the shadowy park. Manny guides me with a gentle but sturdy hand pressing on my back. Again, I try to ask what's going on, but he silences me with a warning.

"Our words are not safe here," he grunts.

"But Darren," I protest under my breath. "Is he safe?"

A curt nod from Manny calms the worst of my fears. I'll stay silent for now, but I'm going to unleash a long list of questions as soon as I get the green light.

We stick to the sections of the park that have no trails or light posts. Aside from Manny, my rescuers have all donned glamour, turning themselves invisible to the human world. Manny plucks something from a satchel at his waist and pops it in his mouth. Moments later, he fades like the invisible faeries.

It's not long before I see clusters of faeries, in all shapes, sizes, and colors, enjoying the otherwise-empty park at what must be the early hours of the morning. Before sunrise invites the dog-walkers and joggers to the scene.

It's not just the diverse array of creatures that makes it hard to tear my eyes away. It's the dancing, the way their strange, beautiful bodies seem to breathe starlight and exude shadow. Midnight itself on visual display.

Manny never allows a gap between us, keeping his arm around me. I'm glad for the stability, the reminder to keep moving. I have no doubt that if I were alone, the lure of the music would intoxicate me.

As if on cue, I see a man just older than me, wrapped in the gossamer arms of a faery lover. The guy is human, clearly drugged by the magic of the moment. He doesn't seem to notice how faeries throng him, pressing against him, how one faery with razor-sharp wings is leaving cuts all along his bare arms and legs. I press a hand against my mouth as the winged faery licks away a trickle of blood with a pointed tongue.

I break my silence, whispering just loudly enough for Manny to hear.

"We have to do something!"

Manny's bearded head turns toward the dance. We're cresting a hill, leaving the helpless man behind.

The minotaur's tone is rough, like a page being torn in two. "The human cannot be saved."

"Can't we at least try?"

"He has seen too much. He won't be released."

I turn away from the man and clench my teeth until my head throbs. For all I know, he's the victim I might have become if Manny hadn't rescued me. The man's laughter turns to screams as we pass over the hill and leave the park.

We travel for another hour. After I urge Manny to explain some basic details—that I was captured by the faeries dancing in the park and the Sovereign of Winter sanctioned my rescue—I let myself fall into a stunned silence.

At least Darren is safe, I tell myself. Although nothing can quell the sharp guilt I feel that I was rescued while the other human got left behind.

I send Darren a text to tell him I'm okay. With my battery on its last breath, I debate whether to call him now or wait until I have more information. Then my phone shows *No Service* again.

The other three faeries walk ahead of us, their cloaks catching the morning breeze in rivulets of gray. The goblin grunts like an old man with every labored step, and sweat glistens on his swarthy, green face.

"Bins," Manny addresses the goblin, "you will stand watch outside."

The goblin's rough voice grates on my tattered nerves. "But they have their own watch, surely."

"It is not wise for all three of us to enter without a pair of eyes we can trust on the outside," Manny says.

"Even this building?" Bins says, and we all look at the structure we're approaching—the old chapel I hadn't thought to notice until now.

At first glance, it seems there's nothing out of the ordinary here. It's not until I refocus that I can see—or *sense*—a pulsing glow around the building.

We step through this wall of what I assume is glamour, and the barren ground, peeling white paint, and decaying steeple fade, replaced by a simple but lush lawn, a fresh coat of paint that glitters as if it's imbued with diamond dust, and a statue where the steeple once stood.

The cloaked faeries enter the chapel doors as we reach the stairs. I stare up at the statue, outlined in yellow by the rising sun, and see that it's a woman carved from white stone. Her steely expression and commanding stance belong to a warrior.

I pass between two faerie guards, their ogre-esque bodies decorated in silver armor and belts glinting with weapons. I almost feel bad for Bins, holding his tiny dagger and eyeing the ogres from a yard away. When I follow Manny into the chapel, however, every thought is whisked away.

It's as if I've left all semblance of reality behind and entered a world that belongs in a snow globe.

Instead of wooden church benches and carpeted floors, I see walls, floors, and beams along the arched ceiling, all made of solid ice. Frost blankets every surface in intricate swirls. I recognize the raised design on the floor as a Celtic knot. My boots have crushed the edge of one swirl, and I remove my foot only to watch as frost sprouts like blades of grass, refilling my footprint in a second.

With this much ice, I expect the temperature to drop as Manny and I step through the doors. Although I can see my breath dancing in front of my face, there is no familiar sting of cold. Instead, my stiff limbs tingle from the unexpected warmth after being outside all night.

Faeries line the walls—the majority dressed in extravagant hues of gray, blue, and white and wearing ringlets of silver on their heads. Conversations continue around us, but the words blur together in hushed whispers.

The cloaked trio pauses in front of a rounding staircase near the back of the chapel, where I can almost see the faint outline of an altar beneath the glamour. But holding onto the "normal" view of this place makes my headache worse, so I let the human details slip away and focus instead on surviving this new group of faeries.

Manny follows a step behind me, and for once I don't notice my own indelicate way of walking. The buffalo's hooves create ripples through the room, rattling the ice furniture and the chandelier high above us, which looks like a captured snowstorm strung from the ceiling.

When we reach the staircase and Manny stills, an audible sigh blankets the room. One female seems to have been trying to save the delicate glassware from falling off a nearby table by encircling the dishes with her arms. I catch her eye as she gives me an exasperated look, and I refrain from snorting.

A real-life bull-in-a-china-shop situation. On a less hellish day, I might have laughed.

It's then that I notice the girl's legs are covered in tawny fur from her exposed navel to her hoofed feet. Several similar creatures dot the room, each holding trays of berry-red drinks in frosted glasses.

The word *faun* springs to mind—although I'd need Darren's expert eye to really know. My focus has been on managing our lives with the Sight, not on learning the countless species of magical beings.

Manny's furry hand reminds me to start climbing the stairs, and soon we leave the lower floor behind us. My eyes become level with the upper floor, and with each step I enter what is probably the attic of the chapel, used to store hymnals and dust bunnies. But like before, that image fades under a spell of glamour.

There is a notable difference, though. If the first room felt like a snow globe, this room is a cozy winter cabin. The rich, earthy colors of the plush furniture and wooden floors bring warmth to the space.

And sitting at the center—on a throne of ice that somehow hasn't melted despite its proximity to the crackling fireplace—is the mysterious snow-faery.

Eirwen.

{ 5 }

Eirwen's white-blond hair is gathered in a loose bun that frames her face. A silver crown with frosted rubies rests above her pointed ears, and a single line of silver earrings drips to her shoulders.

Again, she's dressed in a fur cloak—rich amber instead of white. And unlike the day we met, she makes no attempt at hiding her pale blue lips, which are curved into an intrigued half-smile.

I stand a few paces from her throne. Manny's heavy breathing hits my back, along with a rush of renewed confusion and anger.

How is Manny involved with this faery? Am I being framed, blackmailed, tricked?

I dig my nails into my palms and balance on the balls of my feet, poised to run at the slightest sign of a trap.

Manny sidesteps around me and bows his head, and Eirwen redirects her attention to the beast who can barely stand upright without hitting the low ceiling.

"Greetings, Your Grace," Manny says.

Eirwen nods, her smile falling into a hard line. "I was told there was no interference during the girl's retrieval. The distraction I sent must have been sufficient."

Distraction?

I look at Manny. He tries to hide his scowl from me with a blank expression, but it's too late. He made the same disapproving face earlier, in the park.

Had the man being mauled by faeries been used as a pawn in my rescue? I clutch my stomach and battle a surge of nausea.

Manny clears his throat. "Aye, my lady." He gestures to me. "She is of great importance to my captain, and I assure you he will repay the favor."

Eirwen sits back, crossing a leg beneath the heavy cloak. "Cináed owes me nothing. His role as liaison between our lands has proven invaluable to us these many years."

Her clear gaze settles on me. Me, the girl of supposed importance. Eirwen brushes aside a human sacrifice with less emotion than someone choosing a kitchen rug.

How dare she call a life a mere distraction?

This isn't a trick—it's a murder disguised as a rescue. All I want is to be gone from here. Which reminds me of the one reason I haven't yet fled.

"Darren," I address Manny, "you said he's safe, but for how long? Are the faeries who captured me going to come after him?"

Manny shifts his stance as I speak, angling so that both Eirwen and I can see his face. "That is a complicated question, Róisín."

It's the first time since we entered the chapel that he's called me by name. Eirwen notices it too. The wine glass dangling lazily in her hand gets set aside as she sits straighter in her throne.

I look into Manny's dark eyes. "Everything about the fae is complicated. Just tell me if Darren is in danger."

Manny and Eirwen share a glance. Manny sighs, his wide shoulders sagging. "We believe you are being stalked by faeries from the Unseelie Court. Whether Darren is a target is still unknown."

"Shadow faeries," I say, my voice snagging on the words. Both the Sluagh and Naoise were shadow faeries, members of the Unseelie Court.

"Not exclusively," Eirwen says. "Your would-be abductors are as diverse as they are unpredictable. What we wish to know is their motive."

I almost want to laugh at her.

I'll give you a motive: faeries suck.

Instead, I say, "While you guys figure that one out, how do we protect Darren?"

It's a question I purposefully turn into an order. I make eye contact with both of them and cross my arms—my stubbornness on full display.

I have no limits to my determination when it comes to Darren's safety. I competed against some of the Otherworld's best—a reckless, senseless move on my part—to get Darren back home. And I'd do it all again in a heartbeat.

Eirwen's eyebrows arch as she sips her wine. Manny seems to sense my frustration and counters it with his own demanding stance and tone. Which, granted, is far more frightening than mine.

"You wish to protect Darren? Help us find out why you are being hunted. Until we know this, you have no hope of surviving the human realm. Cináed sent me to offer you protection within the Otherworld, but these threats could follow you anywhere."

I want to ask why Cináed didn't come himself. But the idea of him sending Manny as his messenger hurts more than I want to admit.

"What if Darren moved?" My voice sounds foreign to my burning ears. "What if he moved hundreds of miles away?"

"Without you?" Manny asks.

The words crush my heart to rubble. I nod, holding my breath.

"Because no threats have been made against Darren thus far, it is possible this journey could lead him to safety. You would remain behind, isolating both yourself and the variables surrounding the threat . . ." Manny's voice trails off like he's thinking out loud.

Eirwen's stare is locked on me. When I meet her eyes, I almost think I see a blur of emotion swimming in them. "You would do this? Sacrifice for your kin?"

I'm barely able to keep my own emotions in check. "I'd do anything for him."

Eirwen nods, appearing to be lost in her own thoughts. She turns to the third member of the cloaked trio—a female with milky-white skin and cropped hair—and whispers something I don't catch.

I'm distracted by the male who enters from the stairs and steps between Manny and me to stand before the throne. When he kneels, the dove-gray cloak settles around him, contrasting with the dark skin of his shaved head.

"My Sovereign," he says, "a group of winter nymphs have vandalized the Sovereign of Spring's personal orchard."

"Again?" Eirwen frowns, sounding annoyed. She looks at Manny and me in turn. "You will have to excuse me while I tidy up this mess. Please enjoy the delicacies below. I shouldn't be more than an hour."

She gives her cloaked messenger a pointed look as if to say, *It had better not take that long.*

Without another word, Manny and I retreat to the stairs. On our way down, I mutter to Manny to meet me outside where we can talk in private. I'm not waiting another hour for answers.

I reach the bottom and start for the exit, expecting Manny to follow. I'm aware of the rush of stillness settling behind me, but all it does is spur me on faster.

As I near the closed doors, two guards lower their swords, creating an *X* of blades between me and my escape.

{ 6 }

I stand in front of the guards, their silver swords mirroring fragments of my face and coat. I'm breathing hard, feeling the entirety of the room behind me slicing me to shreds with their luminous eyes.

"Drink, miss?"

I turn my head to the right and see the girl with animal legs and hooves. She's holding a tray of wine glasses in her hand. It takes a moment to register that she wants me to take a glass. I do, and she and I both pretend my whole arm isn't shaking like a naked branch in the wind.

I clutch the frosted glass in both hands. The girl offers me a seat several paces from the doors. Again, I process her quiet gestures with the mind of a slug.

Maybe spending the night in a dirt hole is getting to me. Or maybe it's the wasted hours that have passed since—waiting for critical information that could drastically alter my life.

I let the nice female guide me to an empty, frozen chair. The couple sitting nearest are watching me like they're two terrified rabbits and I'm an unwanted hawk. Actually, scratch that. They're staring at me like I'm covered in mud and clearly don't belong here—both of which are true.

These faeries aren't afraid of me. They're disgusted by me.

What else is new? I received the same sneering welcome when I first arrived at King Rauri's castle last summer. Right before I was thrown in the dungeon.

Slowly, like a frozen lake thawing, the room resumes its chatter, and the music strikes up again. The couple across from me returns to their whispered conversation, touching and eyeing each other like two slices of strawberry tart.

Public displays of affection are nothing to gawk at. Just visit the nearest high school between classes, and you'll experience plenty of it. But no mushy teenager could hold a candle to these beautiful creatures. I blush when one of them catches me staring.

A hairy leg enters my line of sight. I'm expecting the goat-girl, but instead, I have to crane my neck as I take in Manny's huge form.

I stand, letting his body block the stares from the crowd, and hiss, "What are we doing here? Why can't I leave?"

A grunt stirs my hair, frazzled and filthy but somehow still contained in a secure ponytail.

"We cannot discuss this here."

His words carry. Maybe he's incapable of using his "inside voice."

"So, we just wait until Her Majesty has time to chat?"

Another grunt. It dawns on me that maybe he is equally aware of his booming voice. Less words—less disruption.

"Fine. But answer me one thing. Will my brother be okay while we're stuck here?"

"If he remains indoors as instructed, the two sentries I left to guard him and the brownie he somehow procured on his own will protect him from harm."

Maybe temperamental Thomas will earn his keep after all.

I release a tentative sigh. Darren is responsible. If he was told to stay inside, he will. As if he would ever tempt dangerous faeries, anyway.

That's more my specialty.

"This is hardly the place to talk," Manny says in his best attempt at a whisper, "but I sailed here with orders I intend to obey. To ask if either you or your brother would like to return to the Otherworld with me."

My mouth works, but before I can respond, he continues.

"I agree that Darren should stay in the human realm but journey far from here. As for you"—he looks down at me and snorts—"I will not promise protection as Cináed might. But the offer remains. We sail at dawn."

"I'll pass."

Darren might be safer without me, but there's no guarantee I'll be any safer in the Otherworld. Manny said these threats could follow me anywhere.

I've made enough mistakes to last a lifetime, but I'm not stupid. I can't seek sanctuary from wolves by hiding in their den.

Manny stares at me, so I repeat my answer.

"I'm not going back. And tell Cináed I don't want him sending you or any other messenger again."

What feels like hours later—when my backside aches from sitting on solid ice and my temper has chilled into a chunk of iron in my gut—one of Eirwen's gray-cloaked messengers approaches and tells me the Winter Sovereign is expecting me.

I follow warily, wishing I'd seen where Manny disappeared to earlier. I'm hoping he's with Eirwen, but when I enter the small side room, Eirwen waits for me alone.

"You are dismissed," she says to the cloaked faery. When it's just the two of us, she nods to the empty armchair across from her.

"Róisín, is it?"

She pours a cup of dark, steaming liquid as I sit on the edge of the chair. This room matches the decor of the attic. The brown leather armchairs are draped in furs, and a thick rug cushions my boots. The single window is coated in perfectly frosted snowflakes—another glamour trick, I assume. Real snow would slide down the glass in clumps of wet slush.

"Where's Manny?" I accept the brimming teacup but set it aside, untouched.

"His business here is finished. He left to prepare to sail in the morning."

I'm startled into silence. When I turned down his offer, I didn't think he was leaving right away. Before I can press for more information, she changes the subject.

"You wear your fae heritage like a natural. I, of course, noticed it straightaway when I saw you on the street. But to a lesser eye, you are as dull as any common human."

Is this what I've waited hours for? A cup of tea served with unsolicited criticism?

I stare at her, chewing on a selection of snarky replies. I decide to refrain—out of indecision, not politeness. Ironically, my comebacks all sound so *human* to me now.

Eirwen drops a cube of sugar into her cup, seemingly oblivious to my growing frown. "You hide nothing beneath glamour. At least, nothing as obvious as most fae."

I can't help but trace my gaze across her flawless face. The glamour that once masked her true features is gone, and the full force of her beauty is enough to make me shift uncomfortably in my chair.

"But there is a certain *something* . . ."

Her voice trails off, and her crystal eyes glint as she leans closer. The look she's giving me is verging on inappropriate, like she's undressing me with her eyes. I sit back and clear my throat.

"Don't tell me," I drawl with forced humor, "I just grew a tail." We're still practically strangers. Just because Manny and Cináed know her doesn't mean I should trust her.

As if remembering to act decently, she straightens and crosses a leg. "No. But you do carry a unique aura. An undeniable *glow*, if you will."

My mind returns to the moments after I entered the Otherworld. How one of the flying lightbulbs called will-ó-the-wisps told me I was glowing. I never knew what to make of it.

"How come I can't see this *aura*?"

"Perhaps you were not looking for it. It is rare and elusive. If you don't search for it, you are blind to it."

"Okay . . ." I swallow a groan, wishing for a condensed version of this conversation. I should be returning to Darren, making sure he's okay. "Let's say I do have a *glow.* What does that really mean? Will it make it impossible to hide my Sight from other faeries?"

Her bottom lip pokes out as she seems to mull the thought over. "Potentially. It could also hint at your untapped glamour potential. The stronger your glamour, the more you can hide. Even from the fae."

She smiles as she raises the teacup to her blue lips. I get the sense she believes she's doing me a favor. Informing me of her valuable opinions with her precious time. And she expects me to be grateful for every second of it.

"Do you know who your fae parent is?" she asks.

I start to laugh, then try to hide it with a series of coughs. The faery lifts a single eyebrow, as slender and delicate as the rest of her. The question seems so ridiculous that I can't even respond. So I just shake my head, and she continues.

"Do you have any other relatives?"

"Just my brother."

"Interesting. Has he displayed any signs of being half-fae?"

I shake my head. Not because he's excluded from this weirdness—he did confess to using glamour against the Robertses and others. But Eirwen already knows too much about my brother.

She hums under her breath, tucking a lock of white-blond hair behind her bejeweled ear. "I believe one of your parents could be high fae."

High fae. I recognize the term. Cináed and the other noble faeries who live in the castle are from the High Court, which is comprised of high fae.

"And what does that mean, exactly?"

"It means you had best be careful. Countless lesser fae would pay a generous sum for a half-breed with relations in the High Court."

"But why? What makes high fae different from anyone else?"

"Power, and the wealth that comes with it. Or perhaps it's the other way around." She leans back with a distressed sigh. But her eyes glitter with impish delight. As royalty, she must be high fae.

Despite my experience with faeries, I have yet to grasp their politics. I've had no reason to learn the complicated details. Faeries already stole enough from me, and I don't want to waste another second on their drama. But if given good reason—like my safety, or Darren's—I'm all ears.

Begrudgingly, of course.

Eirwen continues, "If you are the child of a powerful, wealthy faery, you could be held for ransom. It would explain why faeries from the Unseelie Court captured you last night. You likely herald from our opponents, the Seelie Court."

It takes half a second to repeat her words in my head.

Our opponents.

I feel the blood draining from my face. *Manny ditched me in Unseelie territory!* I clench my trembling hands until they ache, unwilling to show how afraid I am.

My tongue swells, fat and dry in my clamped mouth. A sip of tea might tempt me. But now I have good reason to suspect it's laced with poison.

"If I was captured by your court," I begin, as slow and cautious as a mouse tiptoeing down the spine of a cat, "why get involved in my rescue?"

Her shoulders shrug beneath the cloak of amber furs. "Curiosity. Even queens are subject to boredom, Róisín." A coy smile tugs on her blue lips. She lifts her cup, drinking with her pinkie extended.

How dare she spin this web of terrors in front of me and then smile as if the idea of me being hunted is funny. Like we're all game pieces for her to play with.

Which is exactly how she treated the human, the distraction, who took your place on the chessboard.

"What of your Sight?" she asks. "Has it been constant?"

I'm a hot second away from storming out of here, Unseelie Court be damned. But her question surprises me, and I decide to answer. I guess she's not the only curious cat in the room.

"I've noticed strange things my whole life. Small stuff that I ignored. It wasn't until last summer that the fae became . . . unavoidable. *Real.*"

Like, demon-stalker real.

I watch as her mind works something over. The clear blue of her eyes shifts with the silent significance of an ice cap fracturing and tumbling into the dark ocean. I shiver and look away.

She responds after a moment, face softened, sultry voice hardened with sincerity. "I saved your life today and expect nothing in return except that you listen to me now."

I pause, wary but intrigued. When I nod, she continues, placing a solid hand on my arm.

"Journey to the Otherworld, Róisín. Your past is not as it seems. Much clarity awaits you there."

I look at her hand on my skin. The only thing keeping me from shaking it off and walking away is what she just said herself—I owe her my life.

"I'm not going back." *And I'm sick and tired of everyone thinking I should.*

She must sense my agitation because she removes her hand. "Why do you resist?"

"My parents are dead to me." I swallow, fighting to keep my emotions from weakening my firm tone. "I've been waiting in plain sight for nearly eleven years. There's nothing for me in the Otherworld."

Cináed's face looms in the corner of my mind, but I flick it aside like a golden-winged butterfly. He said he would come for me, but he sent Manny instead. Besides, it never would have worked between us, anyway.

When I meet Eirwen's gaze, I'm surprised by the pinched skin between her white brows. It's the first sign of empathy I've seen from her.

"You are afraid." Her voice is distant, barely above a whisper. "I can sense it—your fear of opening your heart only to be abandoned a second time."

"You don't know anything about me."

I stand to leave. But her response hits me in the back like an icy gust of wind.

"If you do not return to the Otherworld, you will become a subject under my rule."

I turn to see her steely expression. She softens her next words with a smile, but her eyes remain unflinching.

"It is the only way to ensure your protection."

She would keep me here, imprisoned for my own safety. Another faerie cage.

I unclench my jaw enough to ask, "Why do you care if I'm protected?"

Her blue lips part, then close again. I wasn't expecting to catch her off guard.

So the flawless crystal ornament has a chip, a weak spot.

An anxious thrill pricks my skin. I face her fully and set my hands on my hips, ready to wait her out.

She sighs through flared nostrils. "As Sovereign of Winter, few details evade me. Someone is willing to pay dearly for you. I want to know who."

A faery's petty arrogance. That's what saved my skin last night. Eirwen's need to know everything, to foil the plans of anyone who tries to keep her in the dark.

Silence fills the tense space between us. The rebel in me is already swinging punches, ready to fight until I'm free.

But the part of me I've been nurturing these past weeks—the one who takes responsibility, who sacrifices for Darren at any cost—already knows I've been defeated.

As if sensing my submission, Eirwen's kind smile returns. "One more thing, Róisín. If you return to the Otherworld, be careful who you trust." Her lip curls into a sneer. "Those who claim to serve the crown are often the ones who lust for it most. Naoise of the Western Moors might be gone"—she smirks at me, as if in appraisal—"but he left Orla the Gray in his shadow."

I blink, taken aback. She's warning me about *Orla*? I've given little thought to the pious, insufferable faery since she threatened me, telling me to leave the Otherworld the night of Naoise's death.

Eirwen's slitted eyes make me shift in my boots. "Be watchful. I sense your perils are only beginning."

{ 7 }

I descend the stairs and wind down a small hallway of ice until I find the back door of the chapel. It's propped open, and as I rush outside, I see two guards talking on the step. Maybe if I ignore them, they'll ignore me.

But it's the cloaked faery with blue hair who gestures for the guards to stand down. I don't waste time ducking between them and crossing the small patch of grass. When I get too close to the shimmering barrier surrounding the property like a translucent bubble, the cloaked faery clears her throat and shakes her head at me.

I feel like a dog on a leash as I scowl and retreat a step. The three sentries continue their conversation while my mind spins with an overload of information.

I hate Sovereign Snowlady and her intrusive questions, her flaunted arrogance. But I'm unsure what I hate more: her, or the unsettling feeling her words provoke in me.

One thing I do know is that I won't be her pawn. Naoise imprisoned me with chains of fear and manipulation. I'd rather die than allow anyone to control me like that again.

I take out my phone as I turn away from the guards and the cloaked faery. A shrub shields me from their gaze.

No Service.

I hold my arm closer to the barrier, poking my hand through the intangible glamour, and grin when a single bar appears. I ignore the two texts from work and open the voicemail from Darren.

He says he and Howard are having a *Lord of the Rings* marathon, so the two of them are posted up in front of the TV all morning.

I hit the *call back* button and hold the overheating phone to my ear. Darren answers on the third ring. It's not until I hear his voice—unstrained and seemingly fine—that I really let myself believe he's okay.

He tells me to hang on, and I can hear him ask Howard to pause the movie. A few shuffles and a closed door later, his voice reappears. "Okay, I can talk now."

We dive into details, each asking the other to confirm what happened from the moment I left the Robertses' house after dinner until now. He tells me that Manny, the goblin, and the sentries showed up about an hour after I took off. Darren was in his room, texting me to see where I'd gone, when the brownie burst out of the bookshelf and started going crazy.

"He locked the door and turned off the light and ordered me to stay quiet."

"He can jump high enough to lock the door, and you're sure he's not a frog?" I ask.

I can almost hear Darren roll his eyes. "Anyway, Thomas is on the windowsill peeking out of the closed blinds, and then he asks me if I'm expecting any visitors. I look out the window, and that's when I see Manny in the backyard."

Darren explains how he hid the brownie in his coat and met Manny in the corner of the yard beneath the trees. Manny told him he'd come to make sure he and I were okay. When

Darren said I'd taken off, Manny offered to find me, leaving behind a pair of trained warriors as guards over the house.

"He said something about the full moon and how faeries get extra wild or something," Darren says.

I want to laugh, but nothing about last night was funny. So I fill him in on my side of the story, leaving out the scariest details.

"The thing is . . ." I hesitate as I battle with what I'm about to say. "Until we figure out who tried to capture me, I can't be around you. In fact, the sooner you move to Maine, the better."

His worried voice rises in pitch. "What? You mean you can't even say goodbye before our road trip?"

My heart caves. If Darren wants to say goodbye, I'll make it happen.

I glance at the faeries behind me. Even though they appear to be in casual conversation, I know I'll be chased down if I step through the barrier.

"When do you leave?" I ask.

He pauses long enough that I think I lost the call. "Today. When Juliana is done buying car snacks."

"So, like, an hour or something?"

"Yeah." We're both silent for a moment. "Can you make it here by then?"

If the road-trip announcement knocked me like a leaf from its branch, Darren's anxious words just now—knowing he wants to see me—lift my heavy spirits in an instant.

Despite all I've been through in less than twenty-four hours, I find myself smiling as I say, "I'll do whatever I can to make it there in time."

I begin planning my escape. If one of the guards catches me, they won't hurt me, right? What's the point in Eirwen protecting me if I get killed for trying to leave?

Then, again, I'm dealing with the fae here. Who knows what secret agendas are going on beneath the convoluted bullcrap.

I'm so absorbed in my calculations that I almost miss Darren's next words.

"You're leaving with him, right?"

"Um, what? Who?"

"Manny. You're leaving with him when he goes back to the Otherworld."

This time he doesn't say it as a question. It lacks the confidence of an outright statement, but it's still not a question.

I'm silent too long, too deflated to respond, and Darren stutters like he's trying to backtrack.

"It's not like you *have* to go with First Mate Manny or anything. I just thought you'd want to. You hate it here—you've always hated it. And Manny told me that Cináed said—"

"If Cináed had something to say, he should have sailed here and told me himself."

"Well, yeah, but Manny said he couldn't 'cause—"

"Hey, Darren, I gotta go, okay? My battery is about to die. I'll see you soon."

I hang up and shove the phone into my pocket. My ear is hot and itchy. It's true my phone has been on the verge of death since I fell into that pit—as have I—but that's not the only reason I ended the conversation.

I won't let Cináed influence this decision. If I'm going to return, it has to be on my terms.

I tug my ponytail tighter and grind my teeth as I refocus on the glamour bubble shimmering like the surface of a rose-gold pool.

Then I turn to the guards behind me.

"Hey," I shout across the lawn, "I'm leaving now, so you can either escort me to keep me from being captured again or stay here and tell Eirwen I've left alone."

The three of them share a look, and the cloaked female says with a smirk, "Why not relay the message to the Winter Sovereign yourself? You cannot step through the glamour barrier unharmed without her consent."

My muscles tense as one of the guards snickers at me. I glance at the barrier, remembering how easily I popped my hand through it just moments ago. I take a deep breath, close my eyes, and take two steps in the direction of the shield.

When I open my eyes again, I'm standing on the other side.

"Wait!"

I turn to see one of the guards race inside, probably to inform Eirwen of my disobedience. The cloaked faery is holding out an arm toward me, her eyes wide. "Wait, my lady. We will escort you wherever you wish to go."

"I have to make a visit," I say as I continue walking.

The blue-haired faery travels fast, matching my stride as the other guard hurries to catch up. I'll be honest, I feel much safer with the two of them beside me. Traveling alone—when unknown threats might be waiting to recapture me—is not my idea of a good time.

We've walked for an hour when I sense we're being followed.

The cloaked faery and the armored guard haven't spoken since we left Eirwen's safe house. But at my frequent glances behind us, the female turns to follow my gaze.

"Hounds," she says, nostrils flared like she can smell the beasts from here. "And not our own."

"Are they tracking us?" I ask, pulse quickening at the thought of being hunted by faerie dogs.

Her lips thin, and she shares a look with the guard before facing me. "They will not give chase unless we run, but by visiting your friend, I fear we risk leading these hounds straight to their next meal."

I feel myself paling. "You mean, they might not hunt me, but they'll hunt him?"

A howl pierces the winter air. My skin prickles with goosebumps at the haunting sound. Tucked between two distant buildings, I spot the shrouded form of a large, ashen dog. Its glowing gaze tracks us until we round a bend in the road.

"That depends on how hungry they are," the faery replies.

My dirty fingernails claw into my palms. "Then we won't chance it." I pivot to the left, veering down another street, away from the Robertses' house.

When another minute has passed, I ask if the hounds are still following us. A curt nod is the only response.

The cloudy sky darkens into a starless evening as we reach the water. After speed walking to keep up with my escorts—they sustain a fast pace much better than I can—slowing to a normal walk feels strange. My sore lungs are glad for the break, but my legs and feet tingle, and I become aware of fresh blisters burning my ankles.

True to the female's word, the hounds have kept their distance. But their presence has been enough to push me through both my physical and emotional pain.

"Why have you brought us here?" the guard asks. With his head shielded in a helmet and his face hidden beneath a blond beard, only his eyes are visible. This is the first time he's spoken directly to me.

"To see a buffalo about a boat." I've been heading in the direction of the first place I met Cináed, which is where I also saw his ship later that same day.

Walking along the familiar storefronts, smelling the crisp scent of salt water, my thoughts are transported to that day. The image of Cináed's golden curls bursting from the ocean after he dove in to save me, his dimpled grin that both terrified and transfixed me, the way his wet shirt clung to his torso . . .

"Lady?"

I blink, and the images melt into the frozen skyline. The female is pointing toward the docks at the looming structure of *Branna*—the faerie vessel named after Cináed's lost lover.

The vessel that's about to set sail for the Otherworld. The place I promised I'd never step foot in again.

That was before. Things change.

I lean into my raw heels and heave every drop of air from my tight chest. When I changed course from the Robertses' house, I wasn't thinking about an alternate destination. I wasn't planning my next move, just focusing on keeping Darren safe.

But as I walked, I realized that each step I put between me and my brother adds insurance to his protection.

I inhale deeply, clearing my head with frozen salt air.

I also realize that Eirwen was right about one thing: I have to return to the Otherworld. Not for the reasons she gave, however.

Until my ties to the fae are severed—until I figure out why I'm being targeted and put an end to it—I cannot be in Darren's life. I can't have any life at all.

I toss my reply over a shoulder as I start toward the ship. "Here she is—the noblest vessel of the sea."

Seeing the ship renews my keen longing for Darren. If I'd known last night would be our last night together indefinitely . . . I sniff against the moisture cresting my eyelashes.

I've already texted him, telling him I won't make it in time before they leave on the road trip. I also told him I'm leaving with Manny and that I'll try contacting him once we land in Ireland.

Seconds after I sent the message, my screen went black. If he responds, I won't know until I can recharge my battery. Which will be impossible aboard an ancient sea vessel.

Ocean foam froths between the layers of waves lapping at the ship. With my escorts waiting behind me, I cup my hands and call out. Almost immediately, a furry head pops over the deck railing.

"In the name of Goddess Aine," Jarlath squeaks, "is that you, lassie?"

A hint of a smile pulls on my mouth. I think maybe I've missed rat-face.

"Let me up, and I'll prove it's me," I shout back.

The plank lowers until my hand catches it, and I guide it the rest of the way to the dock. Jarlath has disappeared, and I don't recognize the faery holding the plank steady.

I hesitate, thinking about all of the things I wish I'd packed for the trip. Thinking about Darren in the back seat of the Robertses' SUV, well on his way to their new house, their new life.

Jarlath appears on top of the plank. He waves his little paw and gives me one of his signature toothy grins.

Darren's voice resounds in my head, echoing through my bones.

You're leaving.

Not a question. Not a statement. A suggestion. A gentle but hopeful push.

The cloaked faery clears her throat. I turn to look at her. She eyes the rat, who's waving and squeaking at me in his strange vernacular.

"This vessel sails for the Otherworld?" she asks.

I nod.

"The Sovereign of Winter will welcome you if you wish to return with us."

Her ultimatum is clear. I can either walk this plank or hike back to Eirwen's frosted chapel. Who knows how long snow-queen would keep me on her leash—for curiosity's sake as much as to protect me.

Even more importantly—this is the best chance I have to give Darren the life he deserves.

Because I couldn't be the sister he deserves.

I leave Eirwen's escort behind me as I cross the plank, boarding the ship full of monsters sailing for the Otherworld.

This is a necessary evil, I tell myself, burying the words deep in my being. I'm not running away—I'm running to the source.

I'm going spelunking in the wolves' den.

{ 8 }

The midday sun beats against my back, and a line of sweat darkens my shirt. I give it another hour before this rare warmth gets swallowed by grim cloud cover. Compared with the last few days of frigid temperatures, I prefer the heat.

Shouts from the lower deck pull my tired eyes from the wood. Manny has me searching for barnacles and sea gunk along the crevice where the floorboards meet the railing.

My neck protests as I lift my head, but the commotion is out of sight from where I'm kneeling on the upper deck. So I stand with a groan, deciding now is as good a time as any to give my aching fingers a break.

I shrug my shoulders and wince when my arm seizes in pain. While I can still work through my injuries, I find myself favoring my right side that took the brunt of the impact of landing in that hole. There's a cut on my upper arm that has yet to mend on its own like the other scrapes. I clutch that spot through my shirt, hoping I didn't just reopen the wound.

The upper deck is a third the size of the lower deck, and it provides refuge from the chaos below. I think it's because the upper deck houses the ship's helm, and the hallway leading to the captain's quarters is right behind that.

Regardless, I make an effort to hang out here as much as possible. The crew hasn't made any moves toward me, but their jeers and catcalls, along with their strange and horrifying appearances, give me plenty of reasons to avoid them as a whole.

Except Jarlath, of course. He dutifully brings a tray of food every morning and night and chats with me whenever he drops down from the riggings to check on my tasks. Bins and the other goblins don't talk much—at least not with me.

Then there's Manny, the first mate and stand-in captain of the ship. When he's not at the helm, he's usually tucked away in his room right beside Cináed's. I know because the night I stepped foot on the boat, Jarlath brought me to Manny's room. It mirrors Cináed's in every way but one—the furniture is three times bigger. Which leaves no space for visitors.

That night, I stood just inside the doorway, Jarlath behind me in the hall. Jarlath didn't listen when I said I didn't want to see Manny—at the time I was still pissed he'd left me in Eirwen's Unseelie grasp. Manny sat at a desk littered with papers. Flickering candles lined the table, and the window provided enough light to see the shock pass over Manny's features.

I have a hunch he'd rushed out of Eirwen's to avoid that exact moment—me changing my mind about tagging along.

Once he recovered from the sight of me, Manny gave me a list of chores, assigned Jarlath as my supervisor, and told me to sleep in Cináed's room.

It wasn't until the next morning that I realized why.

I'd thought the crew members were unruly and frightening on my first voyage. But without their charismatic captain on board, the small semblance of decency they might have possessed has been tossed into the waves.

Putting me in Cináed's quarters is Manny's best effort to separate me from the monsters.

So, I've come to expect the daily brawls between crew members. Which is why, when I cross the upper deck and peer out at the scene below, my surprise is twofold. Not only am I shocked at what's happening, I also can't believe these creatures can take me off guard when I thought I'd seen it all.

A large, potbellied creature that resembles an ogre has another faery suspended above his head. The image of Donkey Kong heaving wooden crates at Mario flashes in my mind—a distant memory from an old video game I played with the other kids in foster home #2.

When I wasn't hiding in the neighbor's greenhouse, that is.

Despite the mob pressing around the ogre, I locate the true instigator within seconds. The corpse-blue faery named Pryctic, with his jagged elbows and knee joints, and cheekbones that could puncture a lung. He's standing just outside the fray, on top of a crate, with a smug look pinching his sharp face. I'm still unsure of the different faerie subspecies, but these blue faeries seem to have a special talent for trouble.

The crew's chants reach a crescendo as the ogre suspends the trapped faery above the railing and over the churning water below. I catch sight of a torn wing and hear the faery's strangled cries.

"Stop!"

The word flies from my mouth before I can reel it back in. But over the commotion below, no one seems to hear me. Jarlath and Manny are nowhere in sight. If I don't intervene, the faery will get thrown overboard. But the moment I enter the scene, I could get tossed over too.

My hesitation lasts mere seconds, but I'm painfully aware of the way each one drags itself into the next.

Pounding footfalls shake the floor beneath my feet. I turn and watch as Manny thunders down the stairs, crosses the lower deck, and parts the crowd.

At Manny's command, the ogre turns from the railing and lowers the faery to the deck.

I don't stay to watch the rest. Instead, I stumble to my room and lock the door behind me. Then I sink onto the mattress and stare at the ceiling.

I let it control me again. I kept silent—did nothing—because of fear.

You have a right to be afraid, my logic chimes in. *The fae have given you every reason to run.*

A shudder racks my body, and I lean against the wall for support. Naoise's face takes shape in my mind. The metallic tang of blood fills my senses, made sickly sweet by his scent: wild honeysuckle and moonlight on the moors.

I swallow the bile in my throat and suppress the terror clinging to my guts like hardened sap.

He's dead. You killed him yourself.

I manage another shaky breath, force myself to stand, and get back to cleaning the deck.

{9}

That night, I toss for hours until I finally give up on sleep and crawl out of bed to light a couple candles and peruse the bookshelf.

Almost everything is written in a language I can't read. I find two books in English—a well-used dictionary dated 1963 and a tattered copy of *Grimm's Fairy Tales*. I skim over a few stories but put the book away after reading a version of Hansel and Gretel that makes me sick to my stomach.

Clearing a pile of papers on the desk reveals the map Cináed used to explain our route to the Otherworld. My eyes zero in on the spot where our hands touched. I hide the map with the papers and climb back in bed.

But, of course, that doesn't help anything. *Me, in Cináed's bed.* The pestering emotions I've kept at arm's length resurface with a vengeance, leaving me flustered and sleepless for new reasons.

In the couple of hours I manage to doze off, I dream I'm running after the Robertses' SUV with Darren locked inside. He pounds on the windows, calling my name.

When I wake, a dust of frost and fog covers the small window. Early-morning light casts long shadows around the small space. Soon enough, the sun will appear over the horizon and erase the chilling darkness.

Even then, I doubt anything could banish the heavy gloom lingering beneath my skin. If I were to cut open a vein, I'd probably bleed gray.

Shoving the covers aside, I wince as my arm protests. Wanting to inspect the wound, I lift my black, long-sleeved shirt over my head right when the door swings open.

"Ooohhhhh, good morrow, good morrow, good mo—" Jarlath's song is cut short by my shout as I hug my shirt to my chest.

"Apologies, lassie!" he says, beady eyes trained on the ground. "Only meant to cheer up your morning, you see."

His tiny paws are holding a tray of breakfast. Once he sets the tray on the ground, he pauses in the doorway, staring at my bare arm.

"Sakes alive, lassie." He points a finger. "I's be seeing infection bloomin' on ye arm."

Still holding my shirt to my torso, I twist to take a look at the cut. Sure enough, the scabbing gash is infected with gross yellow pus. I wrinkle my nose and look away.

"You guys don't happen to have any disinfectant lying around?" I ask, though I already know the answer. This boat is as archaic as the Otherworld, which means no modern medicine.

Jarlath chitters a *tsk tsk* sound. "You must be seeing Eimear the druid. Eat a morsel or two, then find her below deck."

"Below deck?" Now it's my turn to squeak. Cináed told Darren and I that anything below the deck was off-limits. I was never tempted to ask why.

“Aye, lassie.” Jarlath waddles out the door, and before I can say another word, I hear his cheery morning song strike up again.

After the simple breakfast of human food, I pull my hood over my ponytail and step outside.

I want to know the exact location of the druid so I can get in and out as fast as possible. But Jarlath is nowhere to be seen. I find the darkened stairs leading below deck, and I don’t hesitate long, knowing how easily I could talk myself out of this.

A crisp breeze follows me as I duck my head and trade a ceiling of clouds for the dank underbelly of the ship. Bits of light peek through the floorboards above me, and my boots stick to an unseen substance on the floor.

“*Bleh.*”

I sidestep and collide with a passing creature in the tangible darkness. What looks like the ogre grunts at me, and I hide behind a wooden pillar until he passes. My pulse knocks against my skull as I catch my breath. I see a goblin’s green skin appear between two beams and disappear into the shadows. With another short inhale through my mouth—the smell down here is barbaric—I follow the goblin.

He should know where the druid is. I’d rather not fumble around in the dark until something with an appetite for humans snatches me up.

I hide behind a pile of crates as a couple of crew members pass, headed for the stairs. One of them is laughing, and by the sound of it, it's at the second faery's expense. Something about dealing a bad hand of cards.

They leave, and I turn to see where the goblin went. Something grabs my hood and rips it back, pinning me in place. In a single motion, I unzip the coat, shrug it off, and spin around to slash my knife at the assailant.

The blade slices through my coat but nothing more. The hood got caught on a nail. I work my jaw and scan the shadows for what I swore was a monster trying to grab me.

I'm fine. It was nothing.

The relief I know I should feel doesn't come. Instead, I sense the unused adrenaline thrashing inside me, searching for an outlet. Searching for something, someone, to fight off.

"I suggest you hide that blade before someone sees it."

I jolt, startled by the cool voice speaking from around the beam. I look toward the source and find a pair of eyes staring at me from beneath a cloak. In the dark, I'm forced to go on tone alone when I guess that this feminine voice belongs to the druid.

"Eimear?" I ask.

"We are the only two females on this ship," she says, her voice spiced with humor. "I would think it would be obvious."

I want to say that no one told me we were the only females. But I'm not in the mood to explain myself. I extract my knife from the shredded layers of fabric, tug the hood free from the nail, and hide the blade inside it.

I honestly don't care about the coat. I learned long ago not to get attached to material possessions because they usually got repossessed or lost during the move to the next foster home.

I'm upset because I'm traveling abroad in late January with just the clothes I'm wearing. And I've managed to gouge a hole through the best protective layer I have.

"Come," Eimear says.

I stick close to the tails of her long cloak, not wanting to get lost as we take turn after turn, winding deeper beneath the ship. The one creature who passes us nods to the druid, ignores me, and continues on.

We enter a slender hallway filled with closed doors, illuminated by a single candle sconce on the wall. I follow Eimear into one of the rooms, and she closes the door behind me.

The dank odor remains trapped outside, allowing the fresh herbal aromas in the room to calm my stinging nose. It's a small, windowless space, lit by the glow of a will-ó-the-wisp the color of spring grass. At our arrival, the will-ó-the-wisp darts into the far corner.

Eimear steps around me, lowering her hood to reveal a head of flaming red hair and a pair of bright blue eyes.

"Sit wherever you wish."

She waves a hand toward a cluster of chairs, all nailed to the warped floorboards that creak under my weight. I choose a chair and sit. The far wall is lined with two sets of tall bunk beds. A tapestry hangs on the wall by the door, but I can't make out much of it in the low lighting.

The will-ó-the-wisp zooms closer to Eimear, who stands beside one of the beds. I catch sight of the faery who almost got thrown overboard. His bandaged wings jut from his back, and he moans a little as he lifts himself up on his forearms.

"There, there, Leif," Eimear says, cradling a cup to his lips. "This should lessen the pain as your sinews begin to fill the tears."

Leif's throaty response is barely audible above the humming of the glowing orb. "Tell me truthfully—will I fly again?"

Eimear's soothing tone grows stern. "Aye, if you rest and drink the tonics, your wings should return to their original state. But you'd be wise to stay out of trouble. Cináed took a chance on your obsession with gambling when he hired you. You owe it to him to behave."

Eimear leaves the bedside and stands by a counter blanketed in a tasseled covering. She lifts a hand to a group of hanging baskets, stretching on her bare toes to pluck out a glass bottle. She holds the vial to the light of the will-ó-the-wisp and frowns.

"Nope."

When she reaches for the basket again, I stand up. "I can help."

Eimear's blue eyes rove over me, and she nods. "Tall for a human female, are you not?"

I guess 5'7" is kinda tall. I'm definitely taller than Eimear, who stands just above my shoulder.

"Which one are you looking for?" I tip a basket full of bottles toward the light, peeking at the cursive-lettered white labels.

"It should read *cleansing blend*."

I find the bottle and remove it. The liquid is goopy and green. I hand it over, and she ushers me to a chair.

"Where is the wound?"

"Oh." I wasn't expecting her to already know about my cut.

"Jarlath told me about it when he stopped by this morning for his monthly teeth clean. So, where's the wound?"

Monthly? I shudder but push aside that thought as I point to my upper arm. Despite our size difference, I feel a bit like a child visiting the school nurse.

"Remove your shirt, then."

I stare at her, glance at the supposedly unconscious Leif, and look back at Eimear's expectant face.

Oh, what the hell.

My shirt comes off, and I hold it to my torso while Eimear gets to work cleaning the cut. I grit my teeth to keep quiet. After a moment, I feel her dabbing the liquid over my arm. The subtle sting that follows feels nice, at least compared to the cleaning of the wound.

"So, where and why did you acquire that iron blade?"

Her tone warns me to proceed with caution. She knows as well as I that iron is poison to the fae.

"I got it back home. For protection." True.

"Protection from whom?"

"Everyone," I mutter. She seems to be done with my arm, so I pull my shirt back on. I gesture to the bandaged cut, now hidden beneath my shirt.

"Payment?" I wish I could mutter a quick *thanks* and get out of here, but faeries hate verbal gratitude almost as much as the sight of an iron knife.

She shakes her head, shifting her thick red locks around her cloaked shoulders, and stands beside me. Her words are tense, clipped. "The captain pays my wages. All I ask is that you toss that wretched blade into the ocean." She points to the bundle of coat in my arms that conceals the knife. "Only a fae-hating human would ever use a weapon like that."

She pauses, piercing my soul with her blue-eyed gaze. Seeing as we just met, she easily could have branded me a *fae-hating human* when she saw my knife. Instead, she's making a point to warn me. *Why?*

When I make no comment, she tips her chin with a little huff—a domineering gesture like an animal that knows it won the fight. She returns to her counter, tossing the last words over her shoulder. "And if you ever use it, even your importance to the captain will not save you."

I'm speechless, thoroughly schooled. I sit forward in my chair, glad the dim lighting hides my blush.

I doubt the majority of the crew would lay a finger on me, but one of them might. And I've been burned too many times to walk around weaponless.

That said, I know Eimear's right. I need to be more discreet with my knife if I don't want my carelessness to get me into trouble. Or, should I say, *more* trouble.

And her comment about Cináed . . . my blush lingers on my flushed cheeks. Every day, we sail closer to the Otherworld—closer to him.

I'd finally started to move on from the idea that I would ever see him again. Now my life has flipped upside down. In a matter of days, we could be standing in the same room. The mounting anticipation is frustrating at best and all-consuming at worst.

I pause by the druid's closed door, realizing I have no idea how to retrace my steps out of this acrid-smelling, beast-infested maze of shadows.

Eimear must sense my hesitation. She whistles, and the will-ó-the-wisp descends from the ceiling to hover beside her head. "Lead her to the main deck," she instructs the green orb.

I meet the druid's bright gaze, and as I step out the door behind the floating beacon, she calls, "Return again tomorrow. And this time, keep your wits about you."

{ 10 }

I shudder deeper into my coat and wipe the ocean spray from my stinging cheeks. The afternoon chill seems spiteful today—like it's trying to prove a point by freezing us where we stand. Last night's frost still glistens on the deck below.

From where I'm sitting, I have a full view of both decks. Jarlath somehow convinced me to climb to the lowest landing on the front mast. It's half the height of the landing that I foolishly climbed to the day I tried to win Cináed over. The day I almost got myself killed.

Being up here, a couple of stories from the deck, is plenty reminder that I prefer my feet on the ground. Even the constant sway of the boat makes me uneasy. Not seasick—*thank all the fae gods*—but eager to make contact with solid earth again.

"At this rate, lassie, you'll be finished before our noon-time pandy," Jarlath says.

I look down at the pile of ropes in my lap. This is the third time he's tasked me with repairing a section of rigging. By now, my fingers have settled into the monotony.

It reminds me of the cat lady I lived with in foster home #4. She made me knit with her once, as a punishment for sneaking out. At first, I agreed to learn so I could knit a phallic symbol just to spite the old lady. But I ended up enjoying the mindlessness of making something with my hands. It distracted me from my tumultuous emotions when all I wanted was to pick fights with a world that had screwed me over.

"Let me guess," I say, glancing at Jarlath's own sizable pile of mended ropes, "does the noon-time pandy include sardines?"

His short snout lifts as he grins, revealing all of his dirty little teeth. I hold my breath before he opens his mouth. "Aye, lassie. Same as always."

It sure is. Every day, just after midday, Jarlath removes a can of sardines from his overalls pocket, cracks it open, and downs the contents in a disgusting, delighted slurp. Hence why I've made it a point to finish my work and be as far away from him as possible before then.

I genuinely like Jarlath. His hygiene, however, makes me gag.

I set the completed ropes aside and scoot closer to the rim of the landing. In order to reach the deck, I have to climb down a series of ropes and slender beams. The support of my boots and my callousing hands actually make the journey enjoyable. Being suspended in the air, with an endless expanse of ocean in all directions, gives me a little thrill.

Jarlath bids me farewell. I turn back to him, watching him swing his rat legs off the ledge like a kid on a park bench.

"Hey, Jarlath?"

"Aye, lassie?"

"Does everyone on this ship owe Cináed? I mean, is that why they're here? Working for him?"

He pauses before answering. “In a sense. But I’s be guessin’ some repaid their debts long ago. I sail for the captain because his is a true heart. His is a worthy cause.”

“What cause is that?”

Jarlath looks up from the two ropes he’s retying. The sun glints off his maroon eyes. “He’s believing we are more than the wars and fighting. We are more than our fears.”

I let the words play over in my mind. “Fear of what, exactly?”

What does Cináed—what do all of the misfit creatures aboard this ship—have to be afraid of?

The rat turns to stare at the place where water and sky overlap like two sections of rope tied together.

“We’s be fearing the unknown. The frightful outs”—he points toward the horizon—

“and ins.” He places his paw on his chest.

We’re silent for a while, both watching the distant waves roll closer. I tell Jarlath to enjoy his sardines, and then I descend the rope ladder.

I clutch the neckline of my shirt over my nose as I duck below the ship. Besides the groans from the wooden beams and the subtle drip of condensation, it’s quiet beneath the deck. The unexpected stillness—paired with more light thanks to the bright rays of sunshine crawling through the cracks in the floorboards—makes this place seem a lot less horrifying than it was yesterday.

That said, I don't want to search for Eimear's room. There are still a few turns I'm not sure about.

I lift my face from my shirt and whistle a note like the one Eimear used to call the will-ó-the-wisp. Sure enough, within seconds the green orb floats around a beam and pauses a yard away.

"Um, hey." I step forward but stop when the light retreats a little. "Wait, I'm here to see Eimear. Do you mind bringing me to her room?"

The will-ó-the-wisp bobs as if nodding, and I follow its lead as it floats into the darkness.

We reach Eimear's door, and when I open it, the orb darts inside, casting temporary light on Leif, the injured faery, who's sitting on the top bunk.

He meets my eyes and gives a tired smile. I take in his heart-shaped face and small, wiry frame. His purple seraph wings splay out behind him, taped with white gauze.

"If you're here to see the druid, she left to fetch something. She'll return soon."

I nod, standing in the doorway. Without Eimear here, I feel like this is more of a bedroom than an office. I'd rather wait outside until she arrives.

"Come in and sit," Leif says. "Unlike some of the other sailors, I don't bite. Usually." His wan smile broadens into a grin, and he winks at me.

The wink reminds me of Cináed, and for a moment, I'm disoriented by it, lost in a pool of short-lived memories that grow dimmer by the week. Memories that eventually would have died of natural causes. Now . . . who knows what will happen?

I step inside the room and sit down, folding my hands in my lap.

"Róisín, right?"

I look at the faery. "Yeah?"

His eyebrows disappear beneath his dark, scraggly bangs. "I do not mean to offend. It's only that meeting you in person is an honor." He ducks his pointed chin. "If I had known it was *you* here yesterday, seeing me in that shameful state . . ."

I blanch, taken aback. I hadn't meant to sound rude—my mind was caught up in a mess of mixed emotions about Cináed.

"Oh." I swallow. "I mean, what? You must have me confused with someone else." Meeting me, an *honor*? I stifle a snort.

He stares at the ceiling as someone's heavy footfalls cross the deck above us. "You are the Róisín the captain speaks of, are you not? The one we sailed the ocean in search of, at his order?"

I open my mouth but am unable to summon a response. I guess Leif isn't wrong. It's just, when you put it that way, it sounds so . . . *romantic.* Which, of course, it isn't.

Solid argument, Róisín. You should have joined the debate team.

I nod mutely to affirm my identity. Leif beams, seeming to have forgotten his prior embarrassment.

"I should add that I knew of you before Cináed hired me. After Lughnasa and the summer games, your name has done a fair share of traveling."

I make a face, picking at the hole worn into my jeans from kneeling on the deck to scrape barnacles.

Being known for my connection to Cináed is hard to swallow. Being known for what happened with Naoise at the summer games . . .

Shivers dance across my skin. I close my eyes and breathe deep until the nausea subsides.

"Are you well, lady?"

I open my eyes. Leif is sitting forward on the top bunk, eyes pinched in concern.

I nod and clear my throat. "What, uh, what exactly is being said? About that?" I'm hoping he'll sense my discomfort and avoid the dirty details.

He stares at me for a second before smirking. "A bit of everything, to be honest. Some say you possess the God Lugh's golden spear. My favorite spin of the tale"—he pauses to take a breath, voice rising in pitch and energy—"is that *you* are Lugh's soul reincarnated. After all, it didn't rain during the festival until you killed Naoise. I'd bet this year's wages that's a sign from the gods."

I feel like all the blood in my body has pooled in my feet. Leif continues, totally unaware.

"Overall, the most consistent legend tells the story of a girl who saved Rauri's kingdom from imminent downfall and then disappeared just as mysteriously as she arrived." The last phrase drops to a dramatic whisper. He even wiggles his fingers in the air.

"Oh," I say, regretting I asked for more information.

"Róisín, the rose who slew the shadow with a single thorn."

The door opens, and Eimear enters. I don't think I've ever been more grateful to see anyone in my life. She carries a bundle of something, and a tray of food that she hands to Leif.

"Greetings, Róisín," she calls over her shoulder while she removes the contents of the bundle and begins organizing them on her counter. "I trust Leif didn't bother you with too many questions in my absence."

Leif ducks behind his bowl of food. I stand and turn to show Eimear my arm—before returning today, I forced the long sleeve up to my shoulder to avoid undressing again. I don't bother answering Eimear's question. I'm not in the mood for small talk after what I've just been told.

That I'm a low-key faerie celebrity.

"The cut is healing. No signs of infection. All the same, we'll reapply the ointment to be safe."

I observe the wound, visible now that she's peeled back the bandage. She's right, it is healing. Faster than should be possible. A memory flashes in my mind.

It was my first voyage to the Otherworld. With Cináed's guidance, Darren was at the helm, steering the ship. I was checking Darren's fresh wounds from the Sluagh. And what I found beneath the bandages was a miracle. His gash had nearly healed in a matter of hours. I learned a druid was responsible.

"How long have you worked on this ship?" I ask Eimear.

She shrugs as she organizes bottles. "In human time? A couple of years."

Unexpected emotion stings my nose and eyes. The druid was *her*.

On that day, I reacted to Darren's rapid healing with protective rage. Some creature had laid a hand on my brother, put magical ointments on him, without my consent.

I see now just how flippant and annoying I must have been. No wonder Cináed threatened to throw me overboard.

Eimear interrupts my trip to the past. "How are you feeling otherwise? Malnourished?"

"I'm fine." The food here isn't anything to get excited about, but I'm not going hungry.

"Overworked?"

"Nope." Jarlath keeps me busy, but I prefer the distraction that the chores give me.

She finally faces me, staring so intently that I squirm.

"How are you sleeping?" she asks at last.

My hesitation seems to satisfy her question. Her teeth pull on her bottom lip as she stretches onto her tiptoes and sifts through one of the baskets.

"I will brew you a sleeping draught," she says.

"No." It's nearly a shout. Leif jumps, and Eimear looks at me, curiosity lifting her brow.

"It will only take a moment—"

"Thanks, but I'm fine." I quiet the fear in my voice, trying to project force and strength.

Eimear clicks her tongue and lowers her empty hand from the basket. “Then reapply the ointment, and be on your way.”

I take the bottle from her and sit in a chair. She busies herself at her counter, seeming to ignore me. But I sense I’ve piqued her interest with my refusal. I hope she’ll let this drop. The last thing I need is her sneaking a sleeping draught into my cup.

When I’m done, I set the bottle on the counter. “Can I go now?”

Eimear is fussing over Leif’s wings and barely glances at me as I head for the door. When she whistles for the will-ó-the-wisp to escort me, I decline the offer.

“I finally learned the route.”

She nods, and Leif gives a small wave. “Farewell, Shadowslayer.”

Eimear rolls her eyes, and I leave to the sound of her reprimand. “Let her be. She will be bombarded with enough of that once we reach the Otherworld.”

When I reemerge onto the main deck, I’m surprised to find a tumultuous sky swirling with gray and lavender clouds. Instead of escaping to my room, I linger near the railing and untie the coat from around my waist. I pull it on with a sigh as I’m reminded of the gaping hole in the back.

I’ll have to borrow a sewing kit from Juliana, or maybe from Howard. Asking Juliana would lead to a string of follow-up questions, and if she learns about the hole, she’ll consider the coat ruined and insist we go shopping for a new one.

My hands curl around the edge of the railing, and I sigh again. None of that is ever going to happen. At least not for a long time—until I'm sure the threats won't follow me home.

By then, the Robertses will be gone, along with Darren. Who knows if or when I'll be invited back into his life.

Before my tender emotions can resurface, I try rephrasing my reality. *I might be alone, but I'll be free to live how I choose.*

The past week has helped me remember how much I've always hated school. What I thought was me acting more mature was actually me feeling obligated to finish school because the Robertses were paying for it. Even now, thinking about the assignments that won't get turned in during my absence—realizing that I'll probably fail my classes—I feel only relief.

I wish I'd thought to tell Darren in my final text to donate or sell my stuff and end the contract on the apartment. My old possessions were given to me by foster families and the new stuff was from the Robertses. I have a few things I purchased on my own. Maybe a couple of stolen items from my thieving phase.

Whenever I return home, I want to have a clean slate. Nothing left over from my past.

My lungs expand with sea air, and lightning flickers in the distance. For the first time in what feels like an eternity, I release my grip on all my worries. Impressing the Dread Parent Robertses. Darren's desire to live separate lives. Even the news about my name being spread through the Otherworld.

"Enjoying the last night of open ocean, I see."

I turn to watch Manny approaching. He's also staring at the sky, and for a moment, we gaze at the oncoming storm in silence.

We haven't spoken in a couple days, since I told him I owe him big time for securing my brother's safety and for rescuing me from that pit. He might only be here on Cináed's orders, but I couldn't let his help go overlooked.

"Can I ask you something?" I say at last.

"It appears you already have."

I shoot him a glance, wishing he used more facial expressions so I could get a better grip on his sense of humor, if he even has one. His cow ears twitch, and I take that as my sign to proceed.

"Second question, then. Why didn't Cináed come with you?" I almost add that I want an honest answer, but from what I've observed of Manny, he's fluent in the language of bluntness.

"It's as I told Darren." The words rumble from deep in his throat. "Cináed remained behind to deal with matters of the kingdom. More specifically, he has been visiting Rauri's sister, Queen Caitriona of the northern kingdom, to persuade one of her children to accept the high throne."

I let that settle in my mind, deciding that's the most I want to push for answers about Cináed—at least for now.

"When I was here before, the throne was like a grand prize. Why do Caitriona's kids need convincing?"

Now it's Manny's turn to shoot me a glance. "There is a growing superstition that anyone who attempts to rule the southern kingdom will be murdered."

Oh.

I swallow hard and lean against the railing, mortified that Naoise's death had such a widespread impact.

"Which is why the search for a ruler is more urgent than ever," Manny continues. "We must find a worthy ruler before corrupt alternatives can use the kingdom's fear to their advantage and seize the throne for personal gain."

"Sounds familiar," I mutter.

This is the exact problem the kingdom faced last summer. I thought killing Naoise would end it. But today I'm learning that if everyone were a marker, Naoise would be the permanent kind.

Manny's gaze doesn't break from the horizon. "And may I also ask you something?"

"Sure."

"What inspired your return to the Otherworld?"

I shrug, not in the mood to dig up what I just decided to bury. "I think going to the Otherworld is my best chance to fix things." I shake my head as I mutter my thoughts aloud. "If Darren heard that, he wouldn't believe I'm his sister. Not when I've been saying for months that faeries ruined our lives."

Low thunder rattles my bones. Lightning slivers across the horizon.

"Retire to your quarters," Manny says, eyes tracking the expanding indigo clouds. "You will want to be safely stowed away when we sail through this storm tonight."

His curt, dismissive tone clues me in to my mistake. It's one thing to inwardly resent my situation. It's another to spell it out right to Manny's face.

Manny turns to leave, and I struggle to explain myself.

"Manny, I-I didn't mean it like that—"

He lifts an arm. "I had my doubts when Cináed asked me to lead this voyage. But he assured me you were not like other humans—that you were worth the journey. Now I see clearly who was right."

Another round of thunder accompanies Manny as he turns and walks away.

I stand there for another five seconds—face burning like I've been slapped—until my legs can carry me to my room. I bolt the door and prepare to wait out the oncoming storm.

{ 11 }

I wake to inky-blue darkness as I'm thrown off the bed. I land with a *splash* on the floor. An inch of standing water floods the room.

Lightning flashes outside the window, briefly illuminating the storm clouds that have consumed the ship. I scramble onto the bed, dripping wet and trying to regain some sense of reality.

The ship jolts, and I go flying toward the nearest wall. My hands reach out and soften my blow with a *smack* that shoots pain through my wrists. Just as I right myself again, the room pivots the other way, and I cry out as I tumble into the desk.

I claw at the furniture to keep my footing. My hip throbs from colliding with the blunt edge. Papers scatter, floating on the water like the ghosts of lily pads.

Water spills into the room from beneath the closed door. The sound of crashing waves and booming thunder rattles my teeth. My stomach lurches, anticipating the next wave.

I can't do this all night. If I'm going to be tossed around by this storm, I'd rather be on deck, helping the crew keep us afloat.

Before the next wave hits, I crawl to the door and open it. More water rushes in, but I grip the doorway and surge past it into the hall. I use my memory to navigate the narrow hallway in the darkness.

When I step onto the upper deck, the sight of the ship provokes a cry of terror from my lips.

Grotesque monsters that belong in the unreachable depths of the ocean are clambering over each other, trying to get on the ship.

Two of them are scaling the main mast, and through dark sheets of rain I catch sight of Jarlath swinging from a rope while one sea monster grabs at him.

Manny is at the helm, his strong legs braced against the pull of the waves as he fights to control the wheel. I hear him shouting something above the storm.

"There's another! Starboard side!"

Sure enough, to my right I see two webbed hands gripping the railing, followed by the matted head of a red-eyed bull.

A shout comes from my left, and all three goblins race for the monster. One goblin stabs the bull's hand with a spear, and the monster screeches before tumbling into the water.

The goblins' collective cheer is lost in the crack of thunder and blinding flash of lightning. Another wave hits, and I see stars as I tumble out of the hallway toward the helm.

A rack of weapons is bolted to the railing that separates the upper and lower decks. I let the next wave guide my slipping feet in that direction and take one of the wooden spears in both hands.

The familiar weight of the weapon injects panic into my veins. I swallow the fear down with a tall glass of determination. Traumatic flashbacks from the faerie games will have to wait until after I fight the sea monsters.

Something hits the wall below me on the lower deck. I see the druid, red hair slick and darkened with rain, in a wrestling match with a sea monster. I run along the railing and tumble down the stairs.

When I reach Eimear, she's just been pinned by the full weight of the monster. I use the force of my momentum to sink the spear into the creature's slimy back. It howls and flails, then topples to the side. Eimear scrambles to her feet, eyes bulging.

This *thing* has the head of a long-horned goat and the tail of a brown-scaled mermaid. Its torso is a gross blend of fish and goat, now coated in sticky blood that looks like tar and smells worse than Jarlath's sardine breath.

Eimear holds onto my arm, and we find an alcove beneath the stairs as the chaos continues around us.

"What the hell are these things?" I shout, wishing I could wipe away the goopy blood that clings to the end of my spear.

"Merrows!"

I don't ask her to elaborate. Another pair of ruby-red eyes peers over the side of the ship. A wave rocks the boat, and a winged creature tumbles right into the monster's webbed hands.

Leif.

Eimear shrieks as Leif clings to the wet railing, fighting to stay aboard. I tell myself to move—to go save him. But panic seizes my chest, paralyzing my freezing muscles.

Then a clear thought pierces my mind: *this is my chance to show fear who's boss.*

I set my jaw and grip my spear. Leaping to my feet, I spring headlong through the rain, screaming a guttural cry from deep in my core.

"Help!" Leif yells, kicking his foot at the cow's face. The monster *moos* in frustration, flashing its razor teeth.

I get close enough to strike the merrow with my spear, but at the last moment, the cow releases its grip on Leif and latches onto my arm.

My spear slashes its side, spilling a stream of thick blood onto the deck. But its webbed grip only tightens on me.

The deck rocks, and we tip toward the blackened water. My boots lose their footing, and I scramble to find leverage. The ship groans. Something cracks as the waves force the vessel to a near-vertical angle.

For a breathless moment, I'm caught in a free fall, tangled with the bodies of Leif and the sea monster. Then the deck disappears, and I hit the water, sinking like a pebble in a depthless ocean.

A touch of seraph wings brushes my arm, and the scaled texture of the merrow rubs against my legs. My limbs kick and pump as I battle against the dark waves piling on top of me.

Red eyes flash from below as webbed hands try to keep me submerged. I kick until I hit something. The sea cow relinquishes its grip, and my head bursts from the water.

Heaving and choking, I struggle to draw breath. I've already drifted too far from the ship, and I doubt I'll be able to swim fast enough to reach it. I see no sign of Leif or any sea monsters.

Wooden crates and a torn sail float around me. I chase after a crate before the ocean can steal it away. Relief floods me as my arms close around it. The security of the crate keeping me afloat allows me to focus again on the ship.

I blink against the rain pelting my face. Something dark looms near the ship. A wave swells and blocks my vision. I cling to the crate and kick hard, somehow managing to keep my head above water. As I rise on another wave, the horizon reappears and the darkness takes the shape of a jagged outcrop of rocks.

I'm so intent on the rocks that I miss the wave cresting behind me. As the water opens its mouth to swallow me, the deafening sound of splintering wood cracks in my ears. I catch sight of the ship as rocks pierce its underbelly and it grinds to a stop.

Then the wave curls around me, and I tumble into the darkness. Bubbles and foam swarm me, and I fight for the surface, lungs already screaming for air. But blackness presses around me from all sides. I don't know which direction to swim to break free.

A pair of red eyes interrupts the endless blue. I sense they're swimming closer, and my empty hands long for the spear I don't remember dropping.

My knife! I tug it from my coat pocket. The monster's scaled hands reach for me. I plunge the blade into the beast's hairy neck.

I realize I can hear the full impact of the sea monster's injured screech, which means we've resurfaced. I lap up the air like a starved animal. The monster swims away, leaving me alone again.

I tuck the knife into my pocket, hating how it feels in my hand. The lingering sensation of stabbing through flesh courses through my arm as I search for the ship. The image of my spear puncturing Naoise's gut flashes in my mind.

I find the ship's defeated outline, blending into a backdrop of rocks and thick fog. I wipe the moisture from my face, squinting at the shades of brown and green visible behind the mist.

Have we reached Ireland?

I decide to swim around the rocks and the half-sunken ship, toward what I hope is a beach. If I can avoid running into any more merrows, I'm sure I can swim that far.

The incessant downpour has lessened into a gray drizzle. The enormous waves calm enough for me to stay afloat. While I know the freezing water must be hard on my body, I can't feel much beyond the adrenaline pushing me to swim faster.

But my numbed muscles spasm after another fifteen minutes. I'm breathing hard and shivering harder. I turn my head toward the ship, and then something tugs on my foot.

Before I can hold my breath, I'm pulled under. Salt burns my open throat. I'm reaching for the blade in my pocket when another attacker latches onto my back, pinning my arms behind me with clawed fingers that cut into my wrists. We continue to sink into the deep blue. My ears ring, and my aching head screams with a new level of pain.

My mind begins to play a strange tune. It echoes within and seems to somehow exist outside of me, too. Suddenly, the weight pulling me down disappears, and my limp arms are freed.

But I'm too tired to swim anymore. I've swallowed so much water. All that's left is to be swallowed in return.

As my consciousness succumbs to oblivion, a pair of strong arms wraps beneath my shoulders from behind.

My last thought is of Cináed, on the day I tried to lower the sails. I remember how his arms lifted me onto the safety of the landing. And I remember how he held me, my back resting against his chest, for a very long time.

{ 12 }

I slowly become aware of the smell of decaying seaweed, followed by the grit of dried sand and salt caked in my mouth. My eyelids flutter open only to squeeze shut against the direct sunlight. I roll over and listen to the steady *whoosh* of the ocean as I try to orient myself.

My trembling arms lift me to a seated position. I squint at the lapping waves eating away the rocky shoreline, just a few yards from where I've been passed out on a bed of gray sand.

Something catches my eye—a blurred shape to my left. At first, I assume it's an illusion created by heat waves on the horizon. Then I recognize the strange shape as *Branna*, the half-sunken ship that's been glamoured to appear invisible to humans.

This sudden clarity invites the rest of my memories to the surface.

We were attacked by sea monsters. I nearly drowned as I tried to swim for the shore.

But I didn't drown. Something—some*one*—saved me.

The memory of my rescue takes the longest to form, and even still, it's as fuzzy as the distant ship. I grasp at random sensory details that float around in my head like dust particles caught in a ray of light.

First, there was that eerie, captivating melody—a blend of tinkling chimes and echoing voices. Then the feeling of solid hands wrapped under my arms and the pressure of being pulled through the water. I remember the sound of myself coughing and the taste of salt and stomach acid on my tongue.

And finally, the image of someone's bare back, the curvature of their spine, and the hiss of velvet scales dragging across the sand before the creature's fish tail disappeared beneath the waves.

If my throat wasn't so raw, I'd be tempted to laugh out loud.

Call me Prince Eric, because I think I was just saved by a mermaid.

I know I need to get moving. Not only to find water but to search for surviving crew members. Leif's face appears in my mind. I don't let myself think about how many lives might have been lost.

Every inch of me is coated in sand and dried sea grime. I smack my cracked lips, willing my tongue to salivate enough to spit. I doubt anything but guzzling glasses of clean water will rid the fishy taste from my mouth.

Making tracks in the sand seems unsafe considering last night's attack, so I walk atop the dark boulders veining the beach. I move toward the ship, maintaining a keen lookout for danger.

After what feels like days—but judging by the length of my shadow is probably an hour—I see small footprints trailing from the ocean. I crouch to get a closer look. If I'm not mistaken, these tracks belong to Jarlath's rat feet. They lead to a hill of sand and long, yellow grass. I follow it, scanning the hillside and surrounding rock clusters for movement.

"Jarlath," I whisper. "Jarlath, are you here?"

I reach the top of the hill, and my eyes rove the other side. The paw tracks stop mid-climb where the grass grows thicker. I'm about to turn back and retrace my steps when I hear something.

"Get down from there before you get us all killed!" a voice hisses.

I spot a tendril of red hair through the grass. Eimear glares at me beneath the shadow of her green cloak that blends into the scenery surprisingly well. If I'd kept walking, I might have stepped on her.

I duck and scoot downhill toward her. "Eimear, what's going on? Where is everyone?"

She shushes me and eases down the slope's shaded side. I follow her lead, wishing I'd learned stealth mode in nature instead of the city. Eimear's movements sound like nothing more than wind rustling the grass, but my boots crunch along behind her with the grace of a lumbering moose.

The hill slopes into a cluster of trees and heavy underbrush, and Eimear and I stand and enter the grove. Branches sway with brown moss. And Manny and Jarlath are here. My breath whooshes from my lips as I smile.

They look disheveled and exhausted, their hairy coats matted with dried blood and sand. But they're here—and alive.

Manny catches my eye first, and he jumps to his feet at the sight of me. He takes a half step in my direction, then halts.

"Róisín," he grunts, sounding relieved. I can't help but hope this means he's forgiven my rudeness.

"Lassie!" Jarlath waddles to my side. "They's been sayin' you were lost to the sea"—he shakes his head, scattering sand at our feet—"but I's be knowin' better. She's a fighter, this one."

Eimear shoots me a sheepish look, silently admitting she's the culprit who thought I'd drowned.

"Where are the others?" I ask.

Manny's weary tone matches his demeanor. "Several just left."

He trails off, head lifting toward the unseen ocean, no doubt envisioning Cináed's wrecked ship.

"Left? To go where?"

Eimear answers in a hushed tone, glancing at Manny. "To find employment elsewhere. Pryctic convinced them that they"—she drops her voice to a whisper—"that they cannot serve a fallen vessel."

Pryctic. The corpse-blue faery. Of course he's the ringleader of the deserters.

"Several lives were lost." Eimear speaks with the gentleness of spring buds. "Cináed would want the survivors to go their own way after all they sacrificed to save his ship."

Jarlath places a paw against the mousy coat of his chest. "And I's stayin' with the rest to safeguard *Branna*. We's be few but fierce."

"We are not leaving you here," Eimear says, pushing loose strands of hair underneath her hood. "Cináed would never ask that of you"—I catch her glance again in Manny's direction—"so neither will we."

Manny, avoiding eye contact with all of us, folds his thick arms. "If Jarlath and the goblins wish to remain behind, that is their choice."

"But what about the merrows? It's too dangerous here—"

Manny tosses a hand in the air. "Let them stay. We need eyes watching the ship for whenever the orchestrator arrives. Whoever it is will want to see the extent of the damage."

My brow furrows in confusion. "So those monsters have a boss? I mean, a ruler?"

Manny doesn't answer. Instead, he begins transferring some of the contents of a brown pack into Jarlath's tiny arms. I lower my gaze, shifting in my soggy boots. Maybe I'm not forgiven after all.

Eimear turns to me with a loud sigh. "Manny doubts the merrows had enough motive for such a siege. They would need an instigator to make it worth their while."

"But why?" I press, taking the break to peel my boots off and scrape the wet sand from the soles.

A frigid winter breeze snakes through the grove, sprouting goosebumps on my arms and legs. I'm wearing all the clothes I have, but they're still damp from my night swim. Eimear shudders against the chill and rubs her hands together. I stave off a wave of jealousy as she curls into her warm, dry clothes.

"The Wanderer has sailed the world over." She shrugs. "I'm sure he made an enemy or two along the way."

Now it's Manny who interjects, swinging his pack over a shoulder. "We will not speak ill of the captain. Only he knows if this was a staged attack and, if so, who might have planned it."

Eimear and I share a look. It's clear the first mate isn't himself, and understandably so. The weight of this lands on him—he's the one who has to report the news to Cináed.

Manny and Jarlath share parting words, and I whisper to Eimear under my breath, "Does this mean we're going to find Cináed?"

She quirks an eyebrow but keeps her voice equally quiet. "Where did you think we were heading?"

I shrug and sit to retie my boots, cheeks flushed. Of course we're going to find Cináed. The real question is whether I'm ready to face him again.

Manny addresses the group, staring ahead at nothing, his voice rote. "We are a half-day's journey from the nearest doorway into the Otherworld. Walk quickly, stay close, and"—he pauses, locking eyes with me—"are you trained in the use of glamour?"

I look away, hands picking at the sand beneath my nails. I haven't attempted to use glamour in weeks. Every time I'd thought about trying it again, I couldn't make myself do it.

"I—I used it a couple times," I stutter.

"To turn yourself invisible?"

"No."

"So you cannot turn yourself invisible." His coldness fills me with hot shame. He says it like I was expected to master glamour already. As if I had nothing better to do with my life.

When I shake my head, Manny grunts and directs his next command to Eimear. "If you detect the slightest sign of humans, use glamour to conceal both of you."

"And what of you?" Eimear tightens her hood to frame her freckled face.

"I have one remaining pill that should last until we reach the doorway. I will take it before leaving these trees."

I want to ask why Manny needs pills while Eimear and Cináed can turn themselves invisible through magic. But Jarlath smiles up at me, the tips of his ears reaching my knees.

I crouch. My voice is surprisingly thick. "I'll see you again, right?" I hesitate. A hug feels too personal. If Darren were here, though, he'd be the first to wrap his arms around Jarlath in a sardine-scented embrace.

Jarlath's mouth splits into two layers of tiny, sharp teeth. "Aye, lassie. If the gods be willin'." He extends his paw, placing it on my hand.

"Be safe," I say as I stand.

Jarlath nods and starts toward the sloped hillside and the wrecked ship beyond it. I discreetly wipe my eyes on my tattered sleeve. Manny huffs a breath that settles in the air like a little cloud. Then he turns and marches in the opposite direction. Eimear extends her hand to me, and I stare at it.

"We must walk under an open sky," she says. "We will use glamour until we reach the next trees."

Of course. Because I can't use glamour to make myself invisible, I'll mooch off Eimear's instead. For that, we have to be touching.

Cináed once turned Darren and I invisible in the same way, when we were trespassing the docks at night.

It wasn't the first or last time Cináed put himself on the line to help me. He cares—his actions prove it. But past experiences can only carry a relationship so far. We're creatures of different realms. The odds were stacked against us from the start.

I take Eimear's offered hand, and we trail behind Manny, traveling inland into Ireland.

{ 13 }

"I don't think this is any better."

I'm standing on a gentle hill, looking down at the winding country road nestled between mossy, crumbling stone walls. The road leads to a small town whose name I didn't even try to pronounce when I saw it written on the sign.

Eimear heaves a sigh and rolls her blue eyes toward the patches of gray sky above us. Sparse foliage exposes us to winter's unforgiving embrace. My teeth chatter so hard I fear I'll chip a molar.

"You could wear whatever you wish if you'd only try—"

"I'm not using glamour," I say with a touch of venom. After spending hours walking beside her, holding hands half the time, I'm learning Eimear won't listen unless someone shakes her hard enough.

I've only used glamour out of pure desperation. This situation is far from that level of urgency.

The druid shrugs. "Then you have no other choice but to wear my cloak into town."

With her cloak around me, Eimear stands in a homemade shawl and a long brown skirt that brushes the ground. Both the hem and her boots are splattered with mud. My pant legs and boots are no better, but the cloak shields them from view. I look at what's left of my coat, tossed on the nearest boulder in a damp heap.

"I have two choices, actually."

Eimear's pink lips curl into a grimace. "Not with that hole you cut through it. Wear that, and you'll attract more attention than Manny running down the road."

Now I roll my eyes. "Don't take this the wrong way," I drawl as I unfasten her cloak from my shoulders, already missing its warmth, "but a druid from the Otherworld isn't qualified to give advice when it comes to humans. I'm wearing my coat."

If Manny hadn't left to scout ahead, his input would have been appreciated. He's spent significant time in the human realm. Eimear might have sailed a few missions with the others, but she told me herself she rarely steps foot off the boat.

I toss the cloak at Eimear, and she snatches it. I ignore her scowl and repeat the plan. "I'll follow the wall until I reach the nearest shop that sells food."

Convincing her I should get the food was easier than I expected. Manny was, of course, not a viable option. He left us here with instructions to find food, probably assuming Eimear and I would go to town together. Thankfully, Eimear seems more than happy to avoid human interaction and didn't argue when I insisted I go alone.

She wraps her cloak around her and nods to the pack Manny has been carrying. "You will find the coin you need in a small satchel."

I dig through the pack, my anxiety growing as I imagine trying to pay for food with fae gold. "Right—because whipping out a coin satchel won't make me stick out at all," I mutter to myself. "I'll just tell the locals I'm an elf on a quest. The cloak can complete the ensemble."

Eimear's brow wrinkles. "Why in the name of Dea would you say you're an elf? You might not be a full faery, but you're far from an elf."

She sits on the boulder beside my coat, avoiding it like it's a dead animal. I briefly wonder if this is because of the coat's general filth or because it's the most human-looking item I have. Maybe both.

I'm so hung up on her allusion to my faery ancestry that I don't bother explaining my sarcasm. I find the satchel and peek inside to see a wad of paper that looks like human, Irish money. My gut unclenches as I sigh through my nose.

Did Cináed give Manny this money?

I brush aside thoughts of Cináed as I shrug on my stiff coat. "I should be back within two hours," I say. "I'll meet you guys here."

"Wait." Eimear removes a slender, smooth stick from her skirt pocket. "At least let me try to dry you off."

I stare at the stick with renewed interest. "How?"

"With a spell, of course." She stands up from the boulder, a focused determination in her posture.

I stumble back a step and hold my arms in front of me. "Hold on!" I call out, defensive and startled. "Faeries have magic wands? I thought that was a witch thing."

Eimear's hand drops, and she huffs a breath, the cloud of air lifting one of her curls from her cheek. "Dear gods, you are simple." She uses a tone meant for teaching a child as she says, "Yes, Róisín. Druids have wands. I was recently gifted this one, after I completed my introductory training."

I stare at her, then the wand, then back at her. "You just finished introductory training, and you expect me to trust you with *that*?" I point at the wand and sidestep out of its path.

A frown dimples her small chin. She also looks at the wand, conflicting emotions storming in her blue eyes. At last, she tucks the stick into her cloak and scowls at me.

"After the day we've had, I'm not in the mood for casting spells, anyway."

Before I can reply, she spins on her heel and marches into the trees, green cloak flapping behind her.

Way to go. I sigh through my chattering teeth. *Now I've offended both my travel companions.*

After thirty minutes, the stone walls end, and the road widens into two lanes. A cluster of one-story, gray-toned buildings crop up, separated by hedges and stubby trees. I stick to the little sidewalk, reading the signs in search of a grocery store or a restaurant that offers takeout.

A stout building of weathered brown stone catches my eye. A lady exits, carrying two paper bags loaded with food.

Bingo.

I wait for a blue car to pass before I cross the street and enter the store. As the door closes behind me and my eyes adjust to the dim lighting, I second-guess myself. This isn't the typical corner market I was expecting. But it has food. A few wooden shelves are stacked with dry goods, and there's a floor freezer near the doorway.

"*Dia duit!*"

I bend at the waist to peer around a shelf and see an old man waving at me from behind a counter. I nod and disappear between the shelves before he says something else I don't understand.

My stomach gurgles as I load my arms with items I hope I have the money for. A box of crackers. Some wafer cookies. A block of cheese and slices of ham wrapped in wax paper. I reach the counter and pile the goods by the register. It's the old kind with manual buttons and a tray that pops out.

The man makes some comment about the weather, and I nod. If I don't speak, he won't hear my foreign accent and ask questions.

When he tells me the total price, I hand him the correct amount, careful to keep the hefty wad of cash concealed. His leathered hand takes the money and fingers through the bills. He glances up at me with a twinkle of humor in his bright eyes, hidden within wisps of gray hair that frame his sideburns and soft beard.

"Might I ask where yer from?" he says in his kind, gravelly voice.

While I want to get going as soon as possible, it feels wrong to ignore a direct question.

"Just passing through," I say, sliding the brown bag into my arms. This will be a bit awkward to carry on the long walk through the forest. But definitely worth it.

His overgrown eyebrows lift, wrinkling his forehead in deep creases.

"An American!" he says cheerfully. "Here on holiday?"

If you call being chased from your home—twice in one year—a holiday.

I nod once, securing the bag in my arms. He winks and taps the counter as he says, "Whatever you do, don't go wandering to the clootie tree. The good people are going about their dancing and feasting from now through Imbolc."

"The good people?" I ask, wondering what kind of group could earn such a title.

His bushy eyebrows arch even higher. "You don't know? Well, it is unwise to speak of them"—he leans a bit closer over the counter and glances around the empty shop—"so don't go repeating this."

Curious, I set the groceries down and wait for his response.

"The good people. The blessed ones. The keepers of the hills. It is what we call the faeries."

I can't help it. I snort right in the old man's face. The fact that humans would call the fae those nice things—out of respect or fear or whatever—is ridiculous.

Well, there are a few exceptions. Cináed has a good heart—sometimes too good, actually. Then there's the three faeries who were assigned to wait on me during Lughnasa—Fodla, Lana, and Hafwin. And Aimsir, the bard who inspired me to share my own history during the storytelling competition. Oh, and Sona, of course. Is a horse considered a faery because he lives in the Otherworld?

The old man's brows disappear into his wispy hair as he rocks back on his heels. I mutter a quick apology, seeing that I just offended a faerie worshipper, and head for the door with my bag.

"American, were you?"

I pause at the entrance and turn to nod.

He straightens and taps his fingers on the counter again. "I always tell tourist kids to stop by Mary's place down the street. She owns one of those smartphones if you want to give yer ma' and da' a call."

I bite my lip. I have to try to contact Darren. When will I have another chance to make sure he's okay?

Besides, what's the worst that could happen? *That he doesn't answer.* I can handle that, right?

"I can use her phone to call someone in the U.S.?"

He scratches at his beard. "So I've been told. I don't quite understand these smartphones. Have no use for one."

I let myself imagine how good it would feel to hear Darren's voice again. My empty stomach does a somersault as excitement overtakes me.

"Thanks!" I call as I sprint out the door.

{ 14 }

Mary's place is down the street, just as the old man said. I have to duck under the doorway as I step inside. I could touch the low ceiling if I raised a hand above my head.

Booths line the right wall, and to the left I see a bar counter where two guys are sipping beers and watching the television in the corner.

I cross to the bar and set my bag on a stool. "Is Mary here?" I ask one of the men.

Both their gazes unfix from the television and rove over to me. One of them nods, and they return to staring at the screen.

Before I can press for more information, a woman in her forties steps out from the door behind the counter. Her wiry, sandy-blond hair matches the color of her stained apron. She smiles warmly at me.

"Hey sweetie," she says in a bright voice. "Did ol' Fergus send you over?"

I nod as she refills one of the men's drinks from the tap that reads *Guinness* in gold letters.

She disappears behind the door and comes back with a phone in her hand. I follow as she leads me to a booth. When I make it clear I've never made an international call before, she gives me simple instructions on what I can and can't use—yes to anything that uses WiFi, no to anything that uses data.

I thank her as she turns to leave. With my stomach in anxious knots and my hands trembling, I log into my social feed and search for Darren's name.

If calling him doesn't work, I can at least DM him and let him know where I'm at, that I'm okay. I just hope he sees the message before I have to leave. More than anything, I need to know he's protected. That the brownie and the guards are keeping a vigilant watch.

And maybe, just maybe, he'll ask when I'm coming home. I know it's dumb, unfair even, to want that from him. What matters is that he's safe. And right now, he's safer without me.

I send Darren a message that says I'll try calling him in three minutes. Then I go to his account page and scroll to the most recent post. It's a selfie of the three of them—him, Juliana, and Howard. Their faces are squished together, and you can tell Howard's arm is stretched to fit all of them in the shot.

The look on Darren's face captures me. The photo caught him mid-laugh. His eyes and button nose are scrunched, his mouth parted. The caption is Juliana's:

Our first family road trip with my favorite guys! Can't wait to see our new home in Maine!

I keep scrolling and find a dozen other images from their trip. One photo is of them standing at some historical site. Another shows their hands holding mugs of hot chocolate.

"Any luck?" Mary asks, setting a soda on the table. Its dark bubbles froth, and the glass perspires invitingly.

"I'm about to find out," I say with a wan smile, sipping the soda.

She places her hands on her hips and gives me what looks like a sympathetic smile. "Being away from them must be difficult. I can only imagine, seeing as I've rarely traveled outside Doohoma."

So, that's how you pronounce it.

Mary returns to the bar. I click over to my messages, but Darren hasn't responded. I brace myself and press the *call* button, listening as it rings once, twice, three times . . . then cuts off.

I suck in a breath, thinking he's answered. But the phone is silent. I remove it from my ear and read the words: *Darren is not available.*

Staring at the white screen, I take a long pull from the straw. My eyes and nose tingle, and not just from the carbonation.

I give it five more minutes before calling again. Nothing. I send another message explaining that I have to go and that he shouldn't call back. I'll try reaching out again when I can.

Which, heaven forbid, could be months from now in human time.

I log out of the app, wipe a hand across my face, and leave a bill with the number 20 on it by my half-empty glass. Then I walk to the bar counter.

Mary's smile sinks when she sees me. I set the phone on the counter and readjust the grocery bag in my arms. Strange—not fifteen minutes ago, I wanted to singlehandedly scarf down all this food. Now my stomach feels like a rock, and all I want is to disappear.

Before my emotions get the better of me, I thank Mary and leave.

Manny and Eimear await me at the edge of the trees. Eimear has been doodling strange images in the dirt with her wand. She stands at the sight of me, and Manny turns, ears alert.

I mutter curt answers to their questions about town, and soon enough they catch on to the rain cloud above my head and leave me alone. After a quick lunch, we store the rest of the food in Manny's pack and keep hiking.

Manny assures us the remaining path will be clear and easy. "We will reach the doorway by nightfall," he says from a few paces ahead.

Eimear has lagged behind again, picking leaves and flowers like a child playing in a meadow. But she stays within sight and sound of us, her cloak billowing whenever she races to catch up.

"And after that?" I ask Manny.

"After we pass through, we will assess the environment. I have never used this doorway before. While I know the general place we will emerge in the Otherworld, it is impossible to plan for the unknown."

I tug my ponytail tighter and brush an annoying stray lock behind my ear. My clothes feel starchy, and I'm starting to think the locker-room stink I'm smelling isn't coming from the buffalo.

Pair that with a lasting headache, blisters, and a tightness in my chest that's a sure sign I could burst into tears at any moment. I'm so eager to be done walking that I've given up on worrying about seeing Cináed. I'd trade anything for a shower, new clothes, and a bed.

I stare at the back of Manny's head, where his shaggy coat gathers in a ridge that trails down his spine. I notice a small braid with a bead on the end peeking out between tufts of fur.

I've wanted to say something to him, to apologize for my words on the ship. It'd be similar to thanking a faery—they also hate verbal apologies. But then I remember the glamour pill—and the fact that Manny isn't technically fae.

"Hey, Manny," I call ahead. His fuzzy ears twitch and rotate in my direction, so I know he's listening. "I'm sorry for what I said last night."

His voice is gruff but not unkind. "Your words cannot offend me. I collected you on behalf of Cináed—he is the one who thinks so highly of you." A pause. "I watched you during the merrows' attack, when you were thrown overboard trying to save Leif."

I focus on the pebbles along the path, glad this conversation isn't face-to-face.

Manny continues, "You claim to be at odds with the fae, and yet you risked your life to save one. The question that remains is, why?"

The silence that falls between us is interrupted by Eimear's boots hitting the dirt as she runs to rejoin us. I slow down and glance behind me, sensing the moment with Manny has passed.

Although I know I can't brush aside his poignant words. They struck a deep chord, and the note echoes within my bones in a song I don't understand.

The pockets of Eimear's cloak are stuffed with twigs and leaves. Her freckled cheeks are flushed and pressed into a wide smile.

"What are you grinning about, Peter Rabbit?"

She brushes her flaming hair out of her face. "You speak in riddles, Róisín."

"The plants?" I clarify with an exasperated smile as I slow my pace, no longer trying to keep up with Manny's lumbering strides.

"Oh!" she trills. "It has been many moons since I could gather herbs. I have been at sea for so long, and our stops are so short, that I almost forgot how much I've missed this." She swings her arms wide, and I take it she's referring to the flora around us.

"Are the plants for your magic potions?"

Her smile falters. "Such is the calling of a druid." She shrugs and trails her eyes along the edge of the path, as if searching for more herbs we both know she hasn't the pocket capacity to carry.

I lift a hand to shield myself from the sun. Manny is a few yards ahead of us.

"Eimear," I begin, careful with my words as Eimear is, in fact, a faery, "I didn't mean to be rude earlier. I'm just not comfortable with all this magic stuff."

Her boots slow as she dips to pluck a handful of stems. "That is the problem with humans." She stands and looks me in the eye, her voice like a blade, steady but sharp. "You say you are *uncomfortable* with magic. But what you mean to say is that you cannot accept who we are—who *I am*."

She bites her lip and looks away, eyes shimmering. I take a step toward her, another attempt at an apology forming in my mouth.

But she shakes her head, lifting a finger to silence me. "I've heard a lot about you, Róisín. Both good and bad. But I told myself not to believe a word, to wait to form an opinion until I met you myself."

Her jaw flexes. Stray curls float on a sudden gust of wind. I hug my damp coat around me—shivering from a cold beyond the frigid weather.

"You might not be the heroine, or the god-child, that some have called you. But at the very least, don't be another bigoted, ignorant human. They are the reason we hide ourselves from the world."

Eimear steps around me and runs ahead before I can think of anything to say. I rock back and forth, unsteady as a buoy tossed by the sea.

{ 15 }

Turns out not all faerie portals are made of stone.

The three of us stand in front of a tree the width of double doors and the height of the Robertses' three-story house. Splotched bark the colors of sage and bone tattoo the knotted trunk. Ivy and moss hang in clumps from the twisted branches.

All this fades away now that I see the doorway. Not because it's anything spectacular but because it's so subtle I would have walked right past it if Manny hadn't pointed it out.

By *it*, I mean the shifting, blurry section of the trunk. It takes the shape of a wide but short doorway. As I watch the illusive glamour, daffodil-yellow fungi begin to grow along the edges of the doorway in a loose outline. They look like tiny steps or handholds the right size for Darren's brownie to use.

When no one speaks, I clear my throat. "So, uh, we going in or what?"

Manny glances at me and nods toward the side of the tree. "Come, we must not disrupt her."

I glance at Eimear and realize she's staring at the portal like a doe caught in the headlights. I let Manny pull me to the side, leaving Eimear in her entranced state.

"What's with her?"

"She is conversing with the tree," he says without fluctuation in his condescending tone, as if the answer is obvious.

I peek around the trunk at Eimear. Her face is hidden beneath her hood. I half-expect to hear her mumbling something, but the silence offers nothing except the sounds of the forest. The faint splash of the stream. The twittering of two birds overhead. The evening breeze forcing the branches to shudder against each other.

Of all the questions buzzing in my head, I choose the one that covers the most bases. "What are they talking about?"

Manny's wide, cow nose twitches, his gaze lost on something in the darkening trees. "The druid is asking permission to enter the doorway. Only when the portal accepts you can you cross realms unharmed."

I think back to when Darren and I crossed through that first portal. Cináed placed his hand on the cave wall, and within seconds, the entire thing crumbled and reformed into a stone arch. Maybe, like Eimear, Cináed telepathically asked the rocks for permission.

I rub an arm across my bleary eyes. If I hadn't seen this stuff for myself, I'd think my train of thought belonged to a crazy person. "So, how long until the tree says yes?"

But Manny isn't listening to me. He's still staring into the forest. I look, too, but my human eyes don't pick up on anything unnatural. The hairs on my neck quiver as I imagine all the things I'm potentially *not* seeing.

"What is it?"

"Move toward Eimear. Slowly."

I ease one foot across the deadfall-littered ground. I've almost rounded the tree when I hear something whiz past my ear. The tip of a smooth, black arrow wobbles in the trunk beside my head.

Manny growls behind me. "Move!"

Eimear breaks eye contact with the tree and grabs my hand. Before I can take a breath, I'm tumbling with her into the shimmering portal.

Sound rips away from me, and I'm temporarily blinded in tangible darkness before I fall on my face and breathe the musky scent of earth.

Eimear is tugging on my arm. I lurch to a knee, staring at Eimear's face just inches from mine. She's saying something, but I still can't hear. All I know is I've never seen terror in her blue eyes before, and now they're drowning in it.

I launch to my feet, and we race beside each other through the forest. Someone besides Manny must have crossed the portal because Eimear looks behind us, then snatches my hand in a white-knuckled grip. We reach an unearthly speed, nearly flying above the earth.

These trees are bigger, stubbier, their branches lower to the ground. We weave around their wide trunks. Glowing mushrooms illuminate the floor of soft moss and rich mud.

My sense of sound returns in shallow waves. First, I hear my own hard breathing. Then another noise hits me. It's both distant and impossibly present.

Manny's voice is blended with others I don't recognize. But he sounds so . . . *wrong*. I want to turn and look, but my feet are moving so fast I know I'll trip.

So I keep running. I try to lose myself in the rhythm of my heartbeats, the blood throbbing in my temples. But I can't escape those terrible sounds echoing through the forest behind us.

When the shapes of the trees blur with the night's shadows, and Manny's bellowed cries exist only in my haunted mind, Eimear finally lets us stop. She guides us to a fallen tree, and we sit in the cover of its trunk amid dirt-clotted roots.

I forgot we were holding hands until she releases mine and I wish she hadn't. The pinch of our laced fingers had kept me grounded. A deep nothingness settles on my chest like a winged beast, shrouding me in a bitter chill.

My mouth opens and closes again. I can't make myself ask what I don't want to know.

At last Eimear speaks, pulling her knees to her chest with a shudder. "He told me this might happen. I—" Her voice breaks with a sob. When she speaks again, steely rage laces her tone. "What do these murderers want? Why are they hunting Cináed's shipmates?"

"This"—I swallow to clear the thickness in my throat—"this was the merrows?"

She shakes her head once before resting it against the tree at our backs. "Merrows cannot cross land."

"So, who are they?" I growl. Hot tears cascade down my cheeks. "Why aren't we going back to fight them?"

I know what Eimear will say, but I can't imagine continuing on like this. Without at least trying . . .

Eimear's monotone response sounds robotic, detached. "I saw enough of them to know they are trained assassins. There is nothing we could have done—"

Her voice cracks, and she bites her trembling lip. "We turn back now, and Manny's sacrifice will have been for nothing. Our only chance is to reach the safety of the northern castle."

In the cold stillness, in the absence of adrenaline pushing me faster, my body feels foreign and empty. My mind is equally vacant except for the unshakable sounds of Manny, the buffalo-man, who is too huge, too stoic and strong for anything to hurt him.

"He's gone," I croak. It's not a question.

Eimear wipes a sleeve over her flushed face. The red rims of her eyes show she's also struggling not to fall apart.

"Come." Eimear stands.

I take her hand, and this time neither of us let go as we continue through the dark forest.

{ 16 }

We come across what Eimear calls a village just as the sun begins to rise. The bleak, gray dawn reveals small, hut-type buildings huddled beneath turf roofs. Smoke and fog hover over the surrounding fields, boundaries demarcated by hip-height stone walls.

From what I've experienced of the Otherworld, this modest, not-so-magical view startles me.

The forest ends at the edge of one of these fields. Our feet crunch across trampled grass hardened by icy frost as we head toward the center of town.

"It would take all day to reach the castle on foot," Eimear explains as we pass a fenced area where cattle crowd underneath a shelter. "Which is why I am going to procure us a ride."

The smell of soil blends with the tang of manure and damp straw. A mooing cow interrupts the stiff silence. I jump, stumbling over my feet.

Eimear glances over her shoulder, and I mutter that I'm fine. When she looks away, I stick my tongue out at the cow and trudge on.

After traveling all night in an eerily still wood—believing every brush of wind or flutter of wings belonged to an attacker—approaching this simple but lively civilization is jarring.

We reach the main road, and I yelp as a chariot almost runs over my boots. The driver shouts something at me and urges his horse forward. Eimear glares in my direction and orders me to stay by her side.

I want to argue that I've been by her side this whole time, that *I* was the only thing standing between her and that runaway chariot.

But beneath her glare, Eimear's eyes mirror my own pain. Like me, she's wrapped herself in sharp scales. For protection. For survival. We can't afford to break down when assassins are hot on our trail.

We wait until the road is clear before crossing the muddy street peppered with potholes and deep divots. A harmonious sizzle and clang issues from a crude, open-faced building with a display of weapons at the entrance.

Up ahead, a cluster of carts and crates blocks part of the road, and it seems the entire village is gathered there. Eimear heads that direction, and I follow, noting the smell of baked bread and savory spices.

Before entering the busy market, Eimear leans toward me and hisses, "Stay close and speak to no one."

"Can we at least buy some food?"

It's been over twenty-four hours since we last ate. Although I didn't notice until a second ago. When my mouth filled with saliva at the smell of warm food.

"Here." Eimear takes my hand, and I feel the pressure of a few coins on my palm. "This is enough to purchase soup and half a loaf of bread. Have them fill this flask with soup, and we will share it on our ride to the castle."

She places her empty flask—we ran out of spring water late last night—in my other hand. I nod and tuck the coins in my pants pocket.

I already ditched my coat, tossing it in a river to float downstream, hoping to confuse whoever's tracking us. After all, now that we're in the Otherworld, Eimear is right—the coat does stand out. Not because of the gash so much as the human-made zipper and logo.

"Where are you going?" I ask Eimear.

"To bargain for our ride. Even with the coins I gave you, we don't have enough to pay our way." Her eyes glint with determination. "Wish me luck, Róisín. This druid is about to put all her practice to the test."

After instructing me on where to meet her, she disappears into the bustling crowd. I turn toward the soup stand, cupping the coins in my pocket.

The female faery working the stand greets me with a smile that doesn't reach her vacant eyes. Like most of the villagers, her face is haggard, her clothes worn and frayed. Her fae beauty remains visible, but only after I look past the streaks of dirt and the sallow tint to her skin.

Life at Rauri's castle was a whirlwind of parties, feasts, and glamour all day, every day. Even the servants seemed well fed and taken care of. This village must be comprised of what most would call *lesser fae*. The commoners of the kingdom.

Whether I'm part faery or not, this village matches my upbringing. Worse, even. Hand-me-downs as a foster kid doesn't equal true poverty. I can count on one hand the times I went to bed with an aching belly. The hungry look in this faery's eyes tells me she knows the feeling all too well.

I point out what I want, keeping my mouth shut like Eimear instructed. If I was worried about attracting attention in that human town yesterday, the Otherworld is exponentially more dangerous. Here, humans get thrown in the dungeon. Plus, we have no clue who is behind these attacks, which makes everyone a potential threat.

The female ladles steaming soup into the flask. "That'll be two coppers."

I retrieve two coins from my pocket. They are copper colored and look identical but have no markings to show their value. I hand them over and heave a sigh of relief when she accepts them without question.

I debate giving her an extra coin, but I'm not sure if tipping is rude or if it would mark me as a foreigner.

So I leave with a lump of guilt in my gut and a warm flask in my hands. It soothes my cold, stiff fingers, and the smell rising from the open lid is enough to make me pause and take a sip. The creamed blend of veggies trickles down my throat, warming my insides. It tastes earthy, natural. As if the female dug an armful of roots this morning to make the soup.

I locate a bearded male selling fresh bread and buy half a loaf with the rest of the coins. The dense bread is rich brown and loaded with seeds. I bite off a chunk and head toward the other end of the market, scouring the crowd for Eimear's green cloak.

"You there," someone calls from my right.

I glance out of the corner of my eye, hoping they don't mean me. The voice belongs to an older female with two gray braids that end at her hips. Her body sways as she points a crooked finger at me.

"Yes, you." She waves me over. "I have something for you, child."

My pulse quickens. Sure, she's not the obvious threat I've been bracing for, but it makes me nervous that she picked me from a crowd. She's dressed in a long cloak that drowns her small frame and, by the looks of her sunken eyes, she's in even more need of food than the first faery was.

I hesitate out of curiosity and the fear that if I ignore her, she'll create a scene by hobbling after me. She holds up a finger as if to tell me to wait, then bends over and sifts through a basket of folded clothes in every earth tone imaginable.

That's when I notice a small wooden sign on the ground, propped up with a rock. It reads *WINTER WEAR* in painted white letters. I let a young couple pass between me and the elderly faery and then close the distance to the sign.

"No, thanks, I don't have any money," I say. Then my eyes grow wide as I realize I just spoke out loud.

If she notices my foreign accent, she doesn't show it. She straightens her spine and lifts a cloak for me to see. Thick, black stitches connect a patchwork of wool in shades of umber brown, pale gray, burnt orange, and caramel tan.

I'm afraid to repeat that I don't have any more money. She might not notice my accent, but someone else could. So I just shake my head.

"You cannot survive the winter without warm clothing." Her clear eyes give me a once-over, emphasizing her point.

Her concern isn't misplaced. My long-sleeved shirt and pants do little to block the chill. The hair on my neck stands on end as a breeze floats by, and I try not to visibly shiver.

But Eimear promised she would acquire new clothes for me at the castle. "Cináed will insist on it first thing," she'd said.

I blushed at her comment, but thankfully she was too busy re-lacing her soft leather boots to notice.

I shake my head again and turn my pockets inside out to show the faery I have nothing to offer.

She says in a huff, "Then take it as a gift before your lips turn blue."

The words burst from me unbidden. "I'm not taking it for free."

Before I've completed the sentence, she's sidled up to me, and her frail arms throw the cloak around my shoulders with surprising agility. The material settles around me, smelling like pine sap and warm spices. Maybe she infused the cloak with magic because I swear I already feel my body defrosting.

"There." She looks up, appraising the new me. "Now, isn't that better?"

I can't help but smile a little. It's as if her kindness is the thread that unravels me. My vision blurs as I stand there, unable to express verbal thanks without offending her and unable to offer anything as payment. Then I remember the food tucked in my arm. Without a second thought, I shove all of it at her.

"Take it," I insist, and although she voices a complaint, she doesn't try to hand it back.

The edges of her hollowed eyes crinkle into perfect crow's feet, and the corners of her mouth lift. "A suitable trade, then. Besides"—she lowers her voice and winks—"we mutts need to stick together, do we not?"

I quirk an eyebrow.

"Oh, excuse my foul tongue, child. You know, us *half-fae*."

My mouth pops open in shock. The faery flicks her wrist to shoo me away, still smiling.

"Safe travels, child. Go n-éirí on bóthar leat."

I'm about to press for more information—to ask why she thinks I'm part-faery. But a surge in the crowd forces me back a step, and in order to keep my footing, I leave the kind, mysterious faery and let the flow of the market push me along.

When I emerge at the opposite end, I see Eimear waving to me on the side of the road. I'm still reeling over the elderly female's words, and I barely listen as Eimear explains how she bartered for a ride to the castle.

"It was my first time practicing divination for a stranger." Her voice is an octave higher, and she can't seem to keep her hands and arms still. "I was more nervous than if Goddess Morrigan were perched on my shoulder, but I *felt* it, Róisín."

"Felt what?"

She rests her hands on the sides of her flushed face. "I felt, *connected*. Somehow, I knew Dea was guiding me. My master druid taught me I would, but to have it happen . . ." Her eyes brim with tears, and she shakes her head with a smile. "I am one step closer to becoming a full druid."

I smile, too distracted to respond. I glance toward the market, but the elderly faery is out of sight.

If she picked me out of a crowd as half-fae—as did Eirwen, though her opinions came with a side of chilled condescension—am I the only one who refuses to see it? Have I been resisting the obvious?

Probably.

It's no secret that my stubborn streak can keep me in the dark. But I can't be too hard on myself. I mean, this is extreme stuff: one of my parents could be a faery.

And might still be alive.

I shake my head. There are more important things to worry about right now than the constitution of my blood.

Like making sure murderers don't catch you and stain the snow red with *your blood.*

"You spent the coins on a cloak?" Eimear's question is a lifeline, reeling me back in from the depths of fresh horrors. "The cold spoke louder than your stomach, eh?"

Her chastising tone doesn't match her haggard, distant expression. I don't doubt she's teetering on the cusp of our dark memories too.

I sway in the cloak, letting the heavy material shift around me. Now that my entire being isn't trembling with chills, my stomach resumes its steady grumbling. It's hard to know whether I'd choose food over warmth if I had to decide again.

No, I correct myself, *I'd choose warmth because that faery needed the food.*

While Eimear teases me half-heartedly over my fickle desires, we climb into the back of a wagon three times the size of a chariot.

Crates fill the front of the wagon near the driver's seat. A male faery appears from around the two speckled horses hitched to the wagon. He nods to Eimear and tells us to settle in and hold on.

Eimear pulls her knees to her chest with a tired sigh. I sit across from her, snuggling my shoulder blades against the side of the wagon, glad for the comfort of the cloak around me.

The driver clicks his tongue, and the wagon pulls onto the road. I tug my hood on, and Eimear and I fall silent amid the monotonous clacking of the wagon wheels rolling out of the village.

{ 17 }

"Róisín."

I blink hard, pulling my gaze from the soft landscape of hills and shrubs. My eyes settle on Eimear sitting across from me in the wagon.

"We will arrive any moment," she says.

She sounds as tired as I feel. But thinking about sleep sets my teeth on edge. I haven't slept since the shipwreck. Nor has Eimear. Not after what happened to Manny . . .

My vision blurs, and my cold nose stings. What he did, what he sacrificed for us . . . I swallow hard, willing the gripping pain in my chest to disappear. I didn't know him all that well. But I think he was the type nobody knew that well.

Kinda like you.

A lot was lost in the shipwreck, the least being *Branna.* Leif is gone, and other crew members too. But I didn't have to listen to any of them die while I ran to save myself. First mate Manny's loss is *too* real, *too* personal.

Eimear reaches across the space between us and rests a hand on my knee. We lock eyes, both of us holding back the tears as best we can.

"I want you to know," she begins, "it was wrong of me to assume the worst of you. As a druid-in-training, I can be a bit sensitive about all I have yet to master."

Heat colors her cheeks. She removes her hand and lowers her chin.

Her sincerity takes me aback. Not that Eimear has ever come across as insincere—she just doesn't seem the type to willingly admit her errors.

A trait I understand all too well.

"For the record," I say, nudging her boot with my own, "I think your druid stuff is pretty cool."

"Cool," Eimear repeats the word like she's tasting it in her mouth. "This means *good* in your dialect?"

"Yeah."

We share a smile, and Eimear turns to stare up ahead. Her view of the horses and the road isn't blocked by crates like mine is. The wagon jostles as the wheel beneath me dips into a puddle. I hiss as my aching tailbone protests, and then I add it to my growing list of bruises.

Once I readjust myself, I interrupt the silence.

"Maybe you don't remember, but"—I pause to clear my throat—"you healed my brother last summer."

Eimear stares at me, her expression unreadable.

I continue, "A Sluagh tried to steal him, and its claws left a deep cut." My voice sounds pinched, tight with emotion. I can't meet Eimear's eyes. "I know Cináed pays you, but Darren is *my* brother."

I fall silent and stare at my fisted hands in my lap. After the last couple of days, talking about Darren—remembering when we were still together—pushes me to a new limit. My body feels like it's made of glass. But not collected and smooth like a vase. No, I'm a mess of broken shards hastily reassembled into fragile, dangerous spikes.

Eimear stares at me and nods. "I recall meeting him, your brother." Her voice has never been gentler. "You owe me nothing, Róisín. I did apply ointments to the wound. But it wouldn't have healed so quickly if not for his own glamour."

I frown, unable to respond for a few seconds. "Wait." I heave a breathy laugh. "You mean he healed himself?"

"His glamour definitely played a part. He needed no instruction from me—I only realized his abilities after redressing the wound later. So when you appeared, I expected similar results, and I wasn't wrong."

Now I'm reeling. I want to laugh, but it comes out like a choked bark.

Darren can heal himself. We can heal our own wounds. *What does this mean about us—about our parents?*

Eimear observes my reaction like a vet treating a hysterical animal. Her next words are quiet, as if she's thinking out loud. "Your level of awareness astounds me."

I could say the same about you, I think. But I ignore my knee-jerk response. It's one thing for my human jokes to fly over Eimear's red head. It's another for me to be unaware of my own magical abilities.

Another jolt of the wagon lurches us from our conversation. This time, the dips and bumps persist, and I glance behind to find the dirt road has given way to salmon-colored cobblestone.

Soon after, the landscape of rolling hills disappears. Hedges twice the height of the wagon shadow the road in green ivy. And behind the wall of shrubs, the largest cherry trees I've ever seen grow in a long line. The branches stretch above us, intertwining with those on the other side in an expansive yet delicate floral tunnel.

Then I see it. A spire, peeking between the blossoming branches. The wagon turns in a wide arc, and as we round the corner, the hedges and trees fall away, revealing the entire structure of the castle.

Rounded, gray towers glint in the sunlight beneath dusty-rose rooftops. Touches of cream trim the windows and balconies.

The wagon stops in front of the gates. Normal-sized trees line the circular driveway. Their branches show signs of early spring buds, nestled in groups of green leaves with slivers of blossoms. The air is crisp and sweet, and a chorus of birds chitter as they fly toward the surrounding forest of pines and firs.

I look at Eimear, who's smiling at my awed expression.

"Welcome to the northern kingdom."

"It's . . ."

It's like a scene straight out of a fairy tale. Not to be confused with the *faerie* tale I experienced on my first visit to the Otherworld. King Rauri's grand castle in the south embodies the bold passion of a summer storm, despite the pungent presence of corruption and death.

But the northern castle—it captures the tender, enchanting breath that lies between winter and spring.

Eimear and I hop down from the wagon and, after waving goodbye to the driver, we approach the metal fence separating the driveway from the castle gates.

The intricate metalwork forms a collage of vines, flowers, and branches, but when I reach out a hand to touch a perfect, gray leaf, a metal spike twists toward me, and I jerk my hand away.

I look at Eimear, who is conversing with one of the guards, and I'm glad no one saw me almost lose a finger out of curiosity.

"Tell him Eimear the druid is here," Eimear is saying. "He's expecting me."

He nods and leaves us with two silent guards who stare straight ahead, hands poised on the hilts of their rose-gold swords.

Eimear leans close, her blue eyes bright. "I visited Queen Caitriona's castle as a child, when our kingdom gathered for feasts. But I've never stepped foot inside."

A few agonizing minutes pass, during which I try—and epically fail—to think about anything but Cináed. Then a faery walks out the gate and hands a note to a guard. She reads it, unlocks a door in the metal fence, and tells us to follow her inside.

The front garden is an adorable maze of pebble paths, bubbling fountains, and ivory statues. We cross through the large gates, and I realize the castle's detailed interior is even more breathtaking. Every ceiling, pillar, and doorframe is carved or painted in intricate designs. Oval windows cast sunlight on the pale-blue walls and cream tiled floors.

We follow the guard down a hallway with a view of the ocean below. I hadn't realized the castle sits on a cliff, or that we're even close to the ocean. *Maybe this is an inlet.* A finger of land curving into the sea. Don't I remember Ireland having those?

Then again, the geographical structure of Ireland doesn't limit the Otherworld. After all, everything I'm looking at is technically underground. The sea, the sky, the castle—it's all created and maintained by glamour.

A fact that's just as impossible to grasp now as it was last summer.

We round a corner. As I take in the room beyond the open doorway, my breath is snatched from my lungs. And the person sitting before me is entirely to blame.

He turns his face toward us, and I watch as the words he was about to say fall from his parted lips. His sea-green eyes lock onto me, and I freeze mid-stride. I can almost hear his breath catch.

Chair legs screech across the tile as he stands and, in a blur I can barely track, crosses the space between us. His arms encircle me, burying my face in his shirt that smells like his pillow. His cheek presses against mine, and my skin catches fire where his lips trace the line of my jaw until his mouth finds my ear.

"Róisín."

Hearing Cináed say my name alters something within me. I feel both broken and healed. Cut open and patched together again.

When he pulls away enough for me to see his face, I stare into the ocean pools that are his eyes and at my tiny image cocooned within them. He blinks, and a tear clings to his long lashes. On instinct, I brush the tear away, and he smiles.

"I was so worried." His voice is low, husky. He cups the side of my face with his warm hand. "I thought you'd choose not to return."

I thought so too. *But I didn't actually have much of a choice.*

Before I can respond, I remember Cináed wasn't alone when we arrived. I become aware of the several pairs of eyes watching us. I step out of Cináed's embrace, my skin still tingling, and let him lead me through the doorway.

Three faeries lounge in a bright, circular room dotted with pastel furniture.

"Introductions, Cináed?" asks a female with coiled, blond hair.

Cináed, who seems a bit dazed, smiles at her. "Of course, of course." He closes the distance I tried to put between us, his arm wrapping around my middle. "This is Róisín Montes."

He gestures to Eimear, who hasn't moved from her spot just inside the doorway. "And Eimear, druid of the Northern Isles." Cináed faces the room again. "They are returning from a voyage, and I ask Her Majesty's blessing as they join me for the remainder of my visit."

The female nods deeply and smiles without showing her teeth, her round cheeks dimpling. "Any friend of Cináed's is a friend of mine," she says. "I am Queen Caitriona. Welcome to my kingdom."

My eyes widen, and I duck in an awkward curtsy. Based on Caitriona's relaxed position on the couch—propped with cushions, her legs tucked beside her—I wasn't expecting her to be the queen. A closer look reveals a simple rose-gold crown within her full curls.

Without looking, she motions behind her toward the two younger faeries. "These are my children. Princess Aibreann."

The female sitting on a baby-blue couch nods at us. She looks like a twenty-year-old version of her mother—which means that she's probably semi-ancient like Cináed.

"And Prince Padraic," the queen continues.

The teenage male standing beside the grand marble fireplace offers a shy smile, his shoulder-length, dirty-blond hair falling in his eyes. His demeanor reminds me of Darren for some reason, and I look away with a pang of sadness.

It's now that I sense Eimear's pointed look, reminding me that Cináed still doesn't know what happened to his ship, to the crew, to Manny . . .

Nausea roils my gut. Eimear moves a step closer while Cináed and Queen Caitriona continue speaking. I try to use my eyes to convey to Eimear that we can't tell him here. We need to get him alone.

"Or perhaps the ladies would enjoy a tour of the gardens," Caitriona's melodious voice says. "Padraic, do escort our guests to the gardens for a nice walk before supper."

Eimear clears her throat, dread written on her pale face. "Wanderer," she mutters, "we bring news of the voyage."

Cináed is about to answer when Caitriona chimes in, her eyes sparkling as she leans forward.

"What is it? What news?"

When no one speaks, the queen sighs. "Oh, do tell. My guests cannot have secrets—you know this, Cináed."

I can tell Eimear is fuming just beneath the surface. We all look at Cináed.

He runs a hand through his curls and tacks on a forced smile. "You heard the queen, Eimear. You may proceed."

Eimear swallows and mumbles, "A storm—your ship, she . . ."

"Speak up, child," Caitriona wiggles her fingers at Eimear. "I know addressing a room of royals is intimidating, but don't be timid now."

That does it. If only my glamour could strangle her royal neck.

Eimear looks panicked. I can tell she's caving to the pressure from the queen. She faces Cináed and opens her mouth. I take a step between them to somehow shield Cináed from what's next.

"*Branna* is wrecked," Eimear blurts. "We were attacked and pursued on our way here. And Manny—" She falters as tears track her cheeks.

Cináed steps around me, his face stricken. He places his hands on Eimear's shoulders and shakes her once.

"Where's Manny? What happened?" His voice sounds foreign.

Eimear's freckles are bathed in tears, but her blue eyes could slice through a diamond. "They killed him."

Cináed stumbles into me. I try to hold him, but he spins to face me, gaze pleading. "Róisín?"

If I could somehow undo the truth or craft a lie to protect him from this pain, I would. But all I do is nod.

Like a defeated cliff crumbling into the relentless waves, Cináed cries out, dropping to his knees, burying his face in his hands.

Caitriona has the decency to stay silent. I hate that they're watching him. I want to bend the universe, create a new realm, hide Cináed away. To let him grieve in peace, if such a thing is possible.

You wouldn't know. I've never allowed myself to fall apart—to feel as deeply as Cináed does.

I sink to the ground beside him and lay a hand on his trembling shoulder. His head jolts up at my touch, and his eyes belong to a wounded creature. Tears drip from his chin as he stands and runs from the room.

{ 18 }

When I wake, I first notice my dry, puffy eyelids. Then I remember how Manny's screams and Cináed's unguarded sobs haunted me through the night.

Soon after Cináed disappeared, Caitriona's guards escorted Eimear and me to our rooms. But not before Caitriona invited us to wash up and rejoin them for supper—an invitation I took great pleasure in ignoring. My guess is that Eimear also opted out of dinner. I didn't hear her open the door across the hall again after we parted ways.

I couldn't believe it when Caitriona bragged about the delegates arriving for dinner—as if she hadn't just witnessed Cináed flee the room in tears. Her lust for gossip caused the whole mess.

No. I snarl at the ceiling adorned with painted birds perched on twigs. *The instigator behind these attacks caused it.*

Whoever they are, whatever their motives, I vowed last night to ensure their deaths match their crimes.

I roll over with a groan—wishing now that I'd bathed before climbing into bed—and watch the dappled sunlight through the tall, slender windows.

On top of everything else, I hate that I didn't go after Cináed last night. Eimear insisted he'd prefer to be alone. But he's likely experiencing the worst pain he's felt since losing his sweetheart, Branna—who died from the same mysterious sickness that killed King Rauri and Queen Finnabair.

My body resists as I tumble off the bed. I glance in a mirror and cringe.

You've got to be kidding.

My eyes are swollen red from crying and shadowed with dark half-moons from lack of sleep. Also, something green is streaked across my forehead. *Do people mold if they don't shower enough?*

I can't believe I saw Cináed for the first time in months looking like this. I sniff at one of my armpits and scowl.

Despite my eagerness to make sure Cináed is okay, I decide a bath and a change of clothes is mandatory before I leave my room.

My damp hair and clean skin tingle with the scent of peppermint soap as I step into the hall. After inspecting the bedroom's wardrobe situation—and being disappointed when I can't find a single pair of pants or leggings—I decided on a loose, cotton dress and a knitted shawl.

I knock on Eimear's door and, after a full minute of silence, conclude she's not here. My bare feet follow the sound of conversation and music. I hope I can find Eimear or Cináed before someone else finds me first. I'm in no mood to chat with Caitriona right now.

I turn the corner and see the source of the noise up ahead: a room with two guards standing like pillars on either side of the closed doorway.

I pause a couple yards away, eyeing the doors and wishing I knew if my friends were inside. Before I can decide if I should risk entering, one of the guards sees me and clears his throat to get his companion's attention. Then they swing the doors wide open.

I replace my scowl with a forced smile, take a deep breath, and march inside.

Dozens of faeries dressed in extravagant gowns and jewels swarm the room. Laughter and music float toward the high ceiling, making the airy space feel hot and small.

Round tables are strategically placed throughout the room, each adorned with rose-gold dishes, white candlesticks, and gray linen napkins. A crystal chandelier hangs from the ceiling, casting tiny rainbows of light across the walls.

From my secluded vantage point, hiding beside an opal vase twice my height, I scour the crowd for Cináed and Eimear. I spot a trio of flutists playing a cheery tune in the corner, but Cináed isn't anywhere to be seen. The only faces I recognize are the royals.

The princess is standing with a drink in her hand and a tight smile on her face. She's listening to two handsome males talk animatedly about something I can't hear. I smirk as Aibreann stifles a bored yawn behind her napkin.

The prince is sitting at a table further away, eating by himself. And the queen is lounging on a couch, surrounded by several laughing faeries. She opens her mouth, and a servant standing beside her lowers a forkful of food to her pink lips.

Just in case my friends are hidden in the crowd, I decide to cross the room and exit at the other end. Leaving the shadow of the vase, I weave through tables and faeries, scouring the sea of beautiful faces.

I halt when someone's gentle but strong fingers encircle my forearm. Turning, I see Aibreann staring at me with desperation in her lavender eyes.

"Well, if it isn't . . ." She trails off, glances at the males hovering a couple steps away, and then looks back at me. She hisses in my face, "Oh, good gods, tell me your name!"

I make her wait several seconds just to see her squirm. "Róisín."

She takes a step back but doesn't remove her hand. Then she raises her voice so her companions can hear. "If it isn't my dear friend, Róisín." She smiles at the males. "You will have to excuse me. Róisín and I have much to discuss."

Both faeries bow. Aibreann's pinched grin disappears as soon as they turn their backs to us. I quirk an eyebrow at her and fold my arms. She sighs but doesn't seem sheepish at all.

"All *right*." She rearranges her layers of glittering bracelets. "We obviously have nothing to discuss. But for rescuing me from two of the most hawkish suitors in the Otherworld, you may wear one of my gowns at tonight's dinner."

"No, thanks."

Her eyes give me a once-over. "Are you sure?"

I clench my fists, itching to be rid of the princess. "Just tell me where Cináed and Eimear are, and we'll call it even."

But Aibreann's attention has wandered elsewhere. She sips her drink, and her gaze follows a couple entering the room. My patience spent, I wave an annoyed hand in front of her face.

"Hey? Have you seen Cináed?"

She blinks and refocuses on me, her auburn brows knitted together. Her tone is authoritative but not angry. "Be glad that horridly human display of yours wasn't in front of my mother." She tosses a lock of blond hair behind her bare shoulder. "Cináed was here, but he disappeared with the druid an hour ago." Then she adds, more to herself than to me, "It's a shame, really. He's one of the few tolerable males in the Otherworld."

Now I'm glad when Aibreann's distracted gaze returns to the party. My cheeks burn as I repeat her words in my head. I don't want to imagine that Cináed and Eimear could be enjoying each other's company as more than just friends. But how can I defend myself against that thought when I don't know where Cináed and I stand?

I take a step toward the doors, and the princess stops me again. "Róisín."

I meet her lavender eyes.

"You should know I am not my mother. I can appreciate what most would call *unladylike* behavior, and I find your lack of propriety refreshing."

I stare at her for a second. "Wow, that was quite the compliment," I drawl.

She grins and sashays away, off to break more hearts. I don't miss the lingering stares from several males and females as the princess reenters the party. I sense she's acutely aware of her influence—not just as a royal, but as a captivating and powerful leader. With a flick of her diamond wrist, she could command armies that would follow her to the death.

I duck my head and escape the room. I'm not jealous of Aibreann's wealth, status, or poise—although I'm severely lacking in all three areas. I'm jealous at the thought of Cináed and Aibreann as a couple. They would be ridiculously stunning—each made *more* perfect with the other at their side.

Hell, even fiery Eimear would be better—more *right*—with Cináed than I ever was, or ever will be.

I might have fae blood in me, but it'll never be enough. Not when I don't belong in the Otherworld—in *his* world.

{ 19 }

"More peas, my lady?"

I shake my head at the waiter—*servant*, as the royals would call him. I'm sitting near the end of a grand table at the dinner party Aibreann told me about.

I wish she'd thought to warn me about showing up late. Unlike at the parties I'm used to, tardiness is quite the opposite of fashionable here.

After learning that Cináed and Eimear had disappeared together—in an expansive, unsearchable castle, no less—I didn't know what to do but return to my room. By the time I gathered the nerve to look for them again, a timid servant named Fawn knocked on the door.

She mumbled something about helping me change for dinner. When I told her I wasn't dressing up, the look of panic she gave me guilted me into compliance.

Something about Fawn's delicate, wide-eyed face reminds me of my ladies-in-waiting when they first met me. I don't know if Fawn's nervousness is inspired by my humanity—that had made Lana, Fodla, and even Hafwin uncomfortable at times—or if she's naturally skittish. Either way, I took strange comfort in allowing her to choose a gown for me and to brush the tangles from my hair.

By the time she finished, I was so anxious to talk to Cináed that I held the hem of my dress and jogged down the corridor.

It was in that breathless state that I stumbled into this room and realized everyone, including Cináed, was already seated at the table.

My gaze locked on Cináed's smiling eyes as he stood from his chair. But when he didn't rush to me like before—and then the prince and the other males all stood too—my thrumming heart sank to my knees.

Even though my mind knew better, my traitorous heart wanted Cináed's formal gesture to be romantic. In that moment—when he stood there and took me in with those sorrowful ocean eyes, his lip twitching in the smallest smile—I'd imagined escaping this place together. Hands intertwined, feet running side by side. Until the castle walls fell away and we could be alone at last. Until we could *really* talk, just us. And my arms could surround him, comfort him in his grief.

But instead, whatever conversations I'd interrupted were cut off, and Caitriona exclaimed from the far end of the table, "What interesting guests you've brought into my home, Cináed." She looked at me, full lips dripping with contempt. "If our company is unworthy of your time, my dear, perhaps you should return to where you came from."

Pride stinging, I quickly found the nearest empty chair and sat like a mute, spineless eggplant.

Now, halfway through dinner, I'm still fuming, homing in on my plate, aware of Cináed's watchful stare from his seat at Caitriona's right hand.

I tune out the conversation about the upcoming winter festival as Eimear tips her chair to whisper behind the backs of two faeries seated between us.

"Where in Goddess Ceredwin's name have you been?" she hisses.

"I could ask you the same thing," I snap, not bothering to hush my tone. I reach for the bowl of steaming red potatoes and stab one with my knife. Caitriona's appalled expression gives me a little thrill of satisfaction.

Eimear shoots me a reprimanding glare, mouths, "You're being irrational," and faces the table of guests with an apologetic smile.

My nostrils flare. *Irrational?* I'll show her irrational—starting with flipping this stupid table.

What are we even doing here? This dinner, this castle—none of it matters compared to everything that happened on our journey. We need to be hunting the assassins. Searching out clues about the nature of these attacks.

Finding Manny's body . . .

I'm so engrossed in my thoughts that it takes a moment to return to the conversation.

And the only reason I do is because Cináed, who has been silent until now, starts talking.

"While I regret to say it, dear queen," he says, his tone normal but his eyes flat, missing their usual luster, "it seems that, in light of recent events, our small party will be begging your leave tomorrow."

Yes! I resist the urge to start clapping. Of course Cináed is on the same page. He lost his ship, his crew. One of his closest friends.

Caitriona raises her glass, and a servant pours a sparkling drink. I sniffed at mine already and decided to stick to plain water tonight. It smells too similar to the faerie wine I tried last summer—the most delicious, and dangerous, drink I've ever had.

According to Hafwin, my lady-in-waiting, fae wine strongly influences humans. And I guess half-humans too.

The queen looks at Cináed with glazed, heavy-lidded eyes. Maybe being a full faery isn't enough to conquer the wine's spell, either, once you've had enough.

But her tongue flows unhindered as she responds, "My Wanderer,"—I cringe at the possessive fervor in the title—"you know I cannot grant my blessing if you depart before the festival."

Cináed lowers his napkin from his lips. A vein in his forehead twitches, and subtle anger flashes in his eyes.

"I'd hoped Her Majesty would understand, after the attacks—"

"No, no, no," she titters, shaking her head of blond curls so intensely that she almost falls off her chair. A servant rushes to steady her, and she waves him off. "I simply cannot allow it."

Heat colors Cináed's tone. "Please, Your Majesty, I—"

She shoves herself to a standing position, and this time she lets the servant take her arm. "Not before the festival!"

Everyone shoots to their feet when she stands. I'm a couple seconds late, but no one notices because all eyes are on the queen. She storms away, tripping a bit in her heels but keeping her chin held high as she makes a sloshed, yet still regal, departure.

While the rest of us sit back down, Cináed remains standing. After a moment, he excuses himself under his breath and tosses the napkin on his barely eaten food before exiting out the same door. I stare after him, wondering if he's going to try to persuade the queen to let us leave.

I want to follow him, but I second-guess myself again.

What if he's avoiding you? a snide voice chimes in.

My logic provides a counterargument. *What if that's for the best?*

Indecision traps me in my seat, and I pick at my food, catching bits of Eimear's conversation with the royal siblings. The high fae between us also excuse themselves, and I'm about to do the same—to hide in my room like the coward I am—when Prince Padraic addresses me.

"Lady Róisín." His kind, unassuming smile softens me—a distinct contrast to his mother's haughty demeanor. "Your name precedes your visit to our small kingdom."

"Wait." Aibreann's dark brows disappear into her voluminous waves of golden hair. She points a jeweled finger at me. "*You* are Róisín the Shadowslayer? The girl everyone keeps talking about?"

By now, only Eimear and the royal siblings remain at the table. Aibreann gestures for the servants to bring another round of desserts. Eimear pats the chair beside her, inviting me closer. I comply, too torn and distracted to decide what to do with myself.

I respond to the princess more seriously than I intend to. "You shouldn't believe everything you hear."

Padraic gives a polite nod, and I think that line of conversation is over until Aibreann says between bites of cherry pie, "I heard you caught the eye of a marshland faery rising to power. He held the throne in his hands—he could have his pick of any bride he wanted—and he chose you."

I swallow hard, nails digging into my chair. Eimear gives me the side-eye, like she's poised to run or to dive in front of me if I start swinging punches at the princess. Padraic is watching my face, looking nervous.

And Aibreann? She's leaning toward me from across the table, her eyes spitting lavender flames.

"I heard he threatened your kin," she continues. "That he used your heart to manipulate you. And when he least expected it, your spear ran him through, and you broke his curse over the southern kingdom."

I'm on my feet, every muscle in my body tensed. A quiet space in my mind knows I'm overreacting. That there is no danger here.

But I can't reach that space. Not from where I'm now crouched, hackles raised, backed into the corner of a nightmare painted in Naoise's blood.

The princess's savage interest seems to grow as she watches my reaction. Eimear stands beside me, reaching for my trembling hand. But I can't stay. I can't sit back down and pretend Aibreann's words haven't triggered me, calling my buried demons to the surface like an internal apocalypse.

Demons that have traveled the Otherworld over—bearing my secrets, my *life*, to the public for entertainment's sake.

At last, Eimear says to the siblings, "I think Róisín should rest. We've had a long journey."

She's trying to give you an out. If I weren't struggling to pump air into my lungs—to fight against my blackening vision—I'd wrap her short, druid self in a hug.

Padraic stands, concern etched between his hazel eyes. "Of course. Let us know if there is anything we can do to improve your stay."

Aibreann doesn't move. Her calculating eyes are trained on me. When she speaks, her dismissive words feel like a cold slap.

"You are *nothing* like what I expected. Where is the dauntless, lionhearted creature we've been hearing about?" She flicks a hand at me with a disappointed frown. "All I see is a girl who resents our praise because she is unable to stomach her own deeds."

Padraic interjects, his tone low and cautious, "Aibreann, you forget yourself."

Before anyone else can say what I am or what I'm not, I push aside the panic in my chest and meet Aibreann's gaze. "You're right—I murdered Naoise." I swallow the tremor in my voice. "But I didn't do it for your praise."

I knock over a chair on my way around the dinner table. No one speaks or tries to follow as I bolt from the room.

{ 20 }

Though I'm exhausted enough to sleep for days on end, hours pass and I'm lying on the bed, staring at the ceiling, trying not to think of all the ways I could sneak out of this castle.

But I have nowhere else to go. Even my own brother . . .

I shake my head, suppressing thoughts of Darren with a mental dam.

Anyway, escaping would be silly. I made my choice when I came back here. How could I expect faeries to stop being faeries? That instead of trying to kill each other with blades or mind games, they'd suddenly learn to get along in this land of plenty?

Someone knocks on my door, and I sit up with a start.

"Róisín, it's me," Cináed calls.

I wipe my tired eyes on the nearest throw pillow and comb my fingers through my hair before opening the door.

Cináed's shadowed figure scatters a swarm of lovesick moths in my gut. He smiles, but even in the low lighting of the hallway, I see the smile doesn't reach his eyes, which have darkened several shades. As if he's half drowned, trapped in dark eddies like his wrecked ship.

"Hey." My arms ache to hug him, so before they act out, I lace my fingers behind my back.

"Hey." His smirk grows enough to show his dimple. "Have you seen the gardens?"

"What?" Has it always been this hard to understand his accent?

"The castle gardens," he says slowly, like he's teaching me to read or something. "Has anyone shown them to you yet?"

I strangle the nervous giggle bubbling in my chest and respond with a brisk shake of my head.

He tucks his hands in his pockets and tosses his chin toward the corridor. "I'd be honored to be your guide, if you'd like to join me for an evening walk."

"Okay."

Instead of stepping back from the doorway to allow me through, Cináed stands there, humor brightening his eyes.

"What?" I say again, suddenly paranoid I have food in my teeth.

"Shoes, Róisín." He glances at my bare feet. "And a coat would also be wise."

I roll my eyes and move to find my boots, but his hand grabs mine, stopping me.

"And"—he lifts his other hand to tuck a loose strand of my hair away—"I missed you."

I've thought about this kind of moment all day. And yet I pull away, leaving him at the door as I find sufficient clothing.

When I return with my cloak, he offers his arm and I take it. We wind through the sleeping castle until we reach a balcony that overlooks the gardens.

We step out the glass doors and onto the wide platform that trims the entire southern wing of the castle. Like much of the palace's structure, the balcony is made of swirled white-and-gray marble, with a tall railing and stairs cascading to the lawn below.

Under a sky of twinkling stars and a waxing moon, Cináed guides me along the garden path. Even in the dark, the diverse array of plants amazes me. Who knew so much could grow in the winter? Lilies, tulips, and shrubs of lavender and roses line the path, clustered in the snow like pieces of carefully placed art. The same ginormous cherry blossom trees shelter us with their branches of tiny pink buds.

Cináed glances at me, his tone gentle. "Eimear told me Darren remained behind."

His words unsettle me, mostly because I won't—no, I can't—talk about my brother or I might break down. How can I cry over Darren in front of someone who just lost his friend in the most significant, permanent way?

So, in as few words as possible, I explain the events leading to my decision to keep Darren safe by removing myself from the situation.

"I came here to figure out who our parents are," I say, "and why faeries are trying to kidnap me." *Again.*

He nods, watching me from the corner of his eye. "And when you find your answers?"

My throat closes, but I force the words out. "I'll go back home. I want to be in Darren's life." Even at arm's length, if that's what he wants.

Cináed doesn't press for more information, and we fall into a distracted silence.

I can tell Cináed's mind is elsewhere, that his eyes don't see the scenery around us. But questions weigh on my tongue. After a few more minutes, I ask the softest one on the list.

"When's this festival the queen is obsessed with?"

Cináed sighs, leading us around a bend in the direction of a fountain. "Five days hence."

We're the only two beings in sight, but I lower my voice when I ask, "And we can't just sneak out of here before then?"

He gives me a mirthful smirk. "Caitriona assumes the appearance of a petty hostess, but do not be fooled. Even if we managed to escape her kingdom, it would not be worth the lifetime of consequences."

"Like what? Not being invited to her next party?"

The smile I was hoping to tease from him doesn't come. Again, his thoughts have drifted away from here. I remain standing while he sits on the lip of the fountain.

Water tumbles from the mouths of dozens of stone fish carved into a sloping wave that begins in the fountain's pool and ends several feet above me. A peek reveals that the pool floor is covered in salmon-pink pebbles.

Classier than dirty pennies—I'll give Caitriona that much.

Cináed murmurs, "The sooner we leave, the sooner these attackers are revealed and brought to a deserving end."

I sit beside him and rest my hand on his. I've never been the comforting type. But despite feeling like I'm floundering in the water behind us, I want to be here for Cináed. I don't want him to face this alone.

"Do we know anything about the attackers?" I ask.

"I have few enemies. Fewer still who would pay a legion of merrows to overtake my ship. If it had been further from land, I might have guessed some foolhardy pirates mistook my vessel for one of greater value. But Eimear says they attacked with the intent to sink the ship, not commandeer her."

"But why? Who would want to sink your ship?"

He wipes a hand across his face and through his golden hair. It's grown at least an inch since I saw him last. The longest curls brush his shoulders.

"No one." He sighs again, this time from deep within. "No one being would stage this kind of attack. This was a collective decision made by faeries who wish to stop my search for the heir."

"So why don't you?" I ask. Cináed frowns but doesn't respond, so I rush to explain, "I mean, if you can't find the lost heir and none of the eligible candidates will take the throne, maybe that's a sign."

His tone hovers above a growl. "And what kind of sign would that be?"

My skin prickles, but I don't shrink from his anger. Cináed's godlike fury is intimidating but doesn't make me want to run and hide.

Unlike the terrifying, choking rage of a particular shadow faery.

I press on. "Maybe it's a sign that you're going about this search in the wrong way. Instead of chasing after rulers who don't want to rule, let those who desire it come and prove themselves."

"A competition? We used that approach for centuries. The festival games are derived from those old traditions."

Just hearing the words *competition* and *festival games* makes my gut draw tight. "I just think the right kind of ruler should want it badly enough to fight for it."

He quirks an eyebrow. "I never took you for the bloodlusting type."

I ignore the flash of Naoise's pale face, his last breath on my cheek before he died.

My small laugh is clipped, forced. "Not like, *actually* fight. Sheesh, not everything has to be physical."

I hear the words I've just said and turn crimson. Cináed's smirk returns, and flecks of gold sparkle in his eyes.

"I told you, Róisín." He nudges me with his shoulder. "The fae are physical creatures."

His tone is playful, but I can't help but hear the double meaning. We stare at each other, our faces mere inches apart. I can taste his honeyed scent from here.

No.

I turn away so he can't see the longing in my eyes, and I steer the subject to a more important conversation.

"Cináed, I . . ." I glance up to find him watching me, his brow furrowed. "I know Eimear said you want space, but if you ever want to talk about Manny—what happened to him . . ."

I trail off and stare at the ground. My emotions wrecked my delivery, but I need him to know I'm here for him.

At least until I leave again.

He matches my position, leaning forward to rest his forearms on his thighs. He stares ahead at nothing as he says, "I did tell Eimear I needed space. Those were the words of a captain."

His chin trembles, and he sniffs, shaking the curls from his face. "What I truly need is a friend. An ally I can trust."

My chest rends as I look at him—the powerful, golden being that he is—and sense how close he is to breaking. His fragility terrifies me.

Even more, it fuels my thirst for vengeance.

Whoever they are, whatever their motives, someone wants to hurt Cináed. They want to pick off his friends like flies because they know his caring, protective heart can't take it.

But these killers don't know that this fly bites back like a freaking dragon.

I take Cináed's fisted hand. "You can trust me."

Being alone with him has reminded me of what I'd fought all winter to forget—Cináed holds a piece of my heart.

And even though I tremble at the thought, I would willingly give the entirety of it—of me—to him. That is a fear I could face. And I believe I could be stronger for it.

But that isn't our story. I came here to demystify my dangerous ties to the fae and sever them for good. Possessing fae blood doesn't alter the truth carved in my bones.

I don't belong here.

When my battles are won, I need to return home. And as long as I'm here, Cináed needs a friend.

We link arms as we return to the castle. When he pauses outside my room, I peck a kiss on his cheek and close the door before my new decision has a chance to unravel.

Because if saying goodbye to Cináed hurt the first time, I know that falling any more in love with him will imprint his soul on mine. And when I'm home—making a mess of my recovery all over again—I'll never, ever be able to forget.

{ 21 }

The next two days drag by in a lonely haze. Eimear is gone visiting a childhood friend who lives within Caitriona's borders. Cináed and I share a few brief exchanges in passing before he's swept into another meeting.

I pass the time hiding in my room or wandering the gardens. Fawn, the mute maid, is the closest thing I have to companionship. She brings breakfast, tames my hair, and urges me to wear some gaudy thing every day. But I choose the dullest options for my own comfort. Besides, I'm not trying to impress anyone.

I've caught Fawn trying to throw out my wool cloak, probably because I wear it all the time.

In a palace filled with crystal goblets, velvet tapestries, and polished banisters carved into ocean waves, the crudely stitched cloak doesn't fit in.

Which is why it fits me perfectly.

On day two, I find the library and spend the entire afternoon pouring over every book written in English, hoping to learn something useful. Information about half-breeds. Faerie assassins. The difference between high fae and lesser faeries.

None of those topics are covered in the English texts, however.

I do learn more about Celtic legends of the Tuatha de Danaan—the ancient gods and goddesses who inhabited Ireland before humans forced them underground. That's when the Otherworld was created.

Humans are the reason we hide ourselves from the world.

Remembering Eimear's words makes me cringe. I get why she has serious reservations about humans.

And after everything she's done for me, I want to prove to her that I'm not some bigoted human. Or at least show her I've taken the first steps to change my insensitive perspective.

Later, I make an appearance at a fancy meal just to eat something more than breakfast pastries.

And when I exit the dining room early, Queen Caitriona comments to Cináed about the rudeness of his guest. I don't falter a single step as I walk out the door.

It's day three. Just two more to go till we can leave this stuffy palace.

I roll out of bed fully dressed, as always, and ready myself for my morning walk. But one glance out my window changes my mind.

Faeries throng the pathways, hanging strings from the trees, cleaning the fountains with brushes, and trimming the hedges.

As I watch them work, last night's dream surfaces in my mind. I dreamed that I served Caitriona a pink cake filled with a powerful laxative. I smirk to myself. At least it provided a sweet reprieve from my night terrors.

Feeling cooped up in my room, I decide to search for my breakfast instead of waiting for Fawn.

Soon enough, I come across a fantastic brunch spread. I sneak inside the room, thinking I'll load up a plate and eat in the library like a nerd.

I linger along the perimeter of the crowd, keeping my gaze detached. I don't need glamour to be invisible to the high fae. With my drab clothes and bored expression, most of them probably think I'm a servant. No one bats an eye when I pocket a napkin full of nameless delicacies and head for the door.

A pyramid of silver-colored fruit at the end of the table snags my attention. I pause a moment to watch a faery choose a fruit from the stack and take a bite. My curiosity wins out, and I turn to snatch one. But another hand is reaching for the same silver fruit.

When I look up, Vera's glistening eyes are staring back at me.

She quickly hides her shock with a sneer that reveals one of her sharp canines. Her large selkie eyes narrow to slits. She grabs the piece of fruit we were both going after and twirls it in her gray-brown fingers.

"So, you were stupid enough to return after all." Her sultry voice ripples like dark, seamless waves.

I scowl. "What are you doing here?"

I don't care about Vera's whereabouts, as long as she's far away from me. The last time we spoke, she told me my human heart wouldn't be able to handle the heartbreak of a relationship with Cináed—or, rather, the heartbreak of inevitably losing him.

And she was *almost* right.

Her smile is hungry, letting me know I asked the wrong question—one she will sharpen and use to humiliate me.

"Didn't Cináed tell you?" Her throat purrs his name. "He asked me to bring word of the political and social dealings in the southern kingdom. And to join in the festival celebrations, of course."

She watches me, unblinking, as she lifts the silver fruit to her mouth and takes a big bite. The fruit cracks when it splits, its meat white like an apple.

My hands twitch, aching to knock that apple from her satisfied mouth. "It must suck to be Cináed's messenger. When's the last time he rewarded your loyalty?"

Her smooth jaw stops chewing. The glint in her eye tells me I guessed correctly—her efforts to get back together with Cináed are still failing.

"I hear you've become a cave goblin, hardly leaving your room." She scans my disheveled appearance, her lip curling. "It shows."

She's right, of course. And her flawless siren appearance gives me nothing to criticize in return. I've lost this round, and the smirk on her oval-shaped face tells me she knows it.

Back to my goblin cave I go, then.

I make a crude hand gesture that I picked up from Cináed's crewmen, snatch a silver apple, and pivot toward the door.

"What are *you* doing here?" she says to my back.

For three seconds, I debate whether or not to indulge her. But I decide against it and leave without responding.

Bottom line, I don't trust her. And in a public setting where others could overhear us, who knows what kinds of things she might say to get under my skin or to spread more rumors about me?

Since when do I care what any of them think?

I change direction, turning down an unknown corridor. After seeing Vera, I'm too wound up to escape to my room just yet. My bare feet patter across pea-green stone as my teeth tear into the strange but delicious silver apple.

For the billionth time, my thoughts return to last summer. I was an outcast, thrown in the dungeon as a "diseased" human. Then I became known as Naoise's plaything—his pawn in the games. I had little-to-no control over my own reputation. The fae were going to believe whatever they wanted about me.

And I hated every second of it.

I answer my own question: I've *always* wanted to prove myself to the fae. I think I've always wanted to prove myself to the entire world. Not only do I care what others think of me, I care so badly that it gets me and my injured ego into trouble.

I pause beside an open doorway leading to a small balcony. Fresh air rushes in from the sea below. I step outside, filling my lungs with the scent of salt and pine. The castle sits atop a cliff, allowing me to take in the lofty, breathtaking view of the forest and the ocean beyond.

Warbling voices direct my attention to the garden pathway three stories below me. Two gardeners kneel beside a bed of yellow tulips. I catch myself peering at their ears, but they're too far for me to see any points. Chances are, they're fae. I've yet to see a human working as a castle servant.

Not that humans are spared from hard labor. I learned last summer that humans are bought and traded to fight wars, nurse and mother faerie children, and do other jobs the fae prefer to avoid.

Not to mention the demeaning, wretched things faeries make humans do just because they can. I guess they see it as payback, but that justification should have expired centuries ago.

A new voice pulls me from my dark thoughts. A noble wearing a satin tunic stands over the gardeners. The anger in his voice carries on the breeze. Even from here, I see fear in the submissive, bowed heads of the servants.

The noble flicks his wrist, and I gasp as the entire bed of tulips wilts. The gardeners balk at the brown, shriveled flowers around them.

A passing cloud uncovers the sun just as the noble grins, his teeth flashing in the sunlight. He clasps his hands behind him and meanders down the path.

My mouth works, my tongue hot with curses to shout at the cruel faery. I look at the apple core in my hand, and before a complete thought forms, I swing my arm around and launch the apple at the noble's adorned head.

My eyes widen, watching as the apple core curves in a perfect arc and smacks the faery right in his upturned nose.

I drop to a crouch behind the marble railing. The noble cries out, and I can't suppress a grin. A quick peek through the railing tells me I'm not the only one stifling a laugh. The two gardeners hide their smiles behind dirt-crusted hands.

I dare a glance at the noble. But he's not looking for a culprit. No, he's far too busy screaming profanities and using his silk sleeves to wipe the ridiculous amount of *bird poop* from his face.

I second-guess the thought, but a closer look confirms it. The white-and-black liquid is clearly bird poop. I scan the path but find no sign of the discarded apple.

Pure confusion wrinkles my brow. I come out from hiding as the noble storms off, trying to wring the crap from his hands.

How did that happen?

I'm still struggling to make sense of what I saw as I step inside the castle. A lone figure stands at the end of the long corridor. His presence isn't what startles me—this place is swarming with faeries. It's the sense of warning I feel in my gut.

I don't question the instinct. Ducking behind a life-size statue, I catch my breath before taking another look at the faery.

Nothing about his worn travel clothes or weaponless belt seems suspicious. From what I can tell, he's waiting for someone to emerge from a room. Could he be a messenger? The fae have to communicate somehow, and without technology I assume that means they send letters, probably by horse or chariot.

Then Princess Aibreann waltzes into the hallway. She doesn't seem to see the male until he addresses her.

"Your Majesty," he says in a deep voice, "I have a message for Cináed the Wanderer."

Aibreann pauses, eyeing the messenger with a small frown. "And how does this concern me?"

"I've been unable to find him. I apologize for the inconvenience." He bows his head and starts to turn away.

The princess holds out her hand. "Wait. I will deliver the message."

The messenger reaches into his leather vest and gives a sealed letter to Aibreann, who hardly waits for the messenger to disappear down a side corridor before she starts picking at the seal with her nails.

I emerge from behind the statue and walk right up to her. "That's not yours."

She barely glances up at me. The wax must be tricky to break. "Good morrow, Róisín."

My nostrils flare. "I heard the messenger. That's for Cináed."

"I do not need your permission, nor your approval. At any rate, I'm only reading it to learn if Cináed has a significant love interest. I pray he does. My mother is insistent on our union, despite the fact that I have no desire to be high queen."

My frown deepens as I try to unpack her words. *Why would marrying Cináed lead to Aibreann becoming high queen?*

Instead I ask the simpler, more burning question. "So, you're not pursuing Cináed?"

"Of course not. No amount of charm could convince me to leave my kingdom."

She sighs and stops picking at the seal. I'm surprised at the emotion swirling in her lavender eyes. "If my mother marries me off, there will be no one left to rule when she's gone."

"What about the prince?"

Her mouth softens. "Padraic may be royalty, but his gentle heart would be squashed and overrun by those who see his kindness as weakness." She smiles and stares out the window. "He is the most talented painter. I promised him long ago that I would do all I could to remain here as heir apparent of the north, freeing him to pursue his true calling."

She seems to remember who she's talking to and straightens into an elegant posture. "Not that any of this matters to you. Take my advice—do not get involved in fae politics."

I hold out my hand for the letter. "If I get it open, you'll let me take it to Cináed?"

She sighs, but I catch a mischievous gleam in her eyes. "As long as I can read it first."

I remove my pocketknife and ease the wax seal off the paper with the edge of the blade. It's only after I tuck the knife away that I realize I used an iron weapon in front of a faery princess.

But if Aibreann notices, she doesn't show it. When I unfold the letter, she snatches it away, her gaze roving the page. I fold my arms and wait for her to finish acting like a middle-schooler passing notes in class.

I study the princess's face, expecting to find either relief or disappointment. Again, my traitorous heart gives my feelings away. But I ignore the longing as Aibreann practically tosses the letter at me.

"Time wasted," she calls as she walks away, her golden curls bouncing against her hips.

I grip the paper in both hands, stuffing my wild heartbeat back down my throat, and scour the letter.

Cináed,

Word of your extended stay in the northern kingdom has inspired me to write this letter. While I know you are hoping to convince one of Caitriona's offspring to take the high throne, I encourage you to return here, where you are truly needed.

In your absence, the castle falls further into chaos. I do not know how much longer I can persuade the remaining advisors to support your quest to find a blood heir.

Again, I implore you to desist. Return home, Wanderer, before it is too late.

Lady Orla the Gray

{ 22 }

The next morning, Eimear finds me in my room. I'm standing in front of the clothes rack, searching for something to wear that isn't loaded with jewels or extremely revealing—or both. She greets me, sits on my bed, and starts eating from my breakfast tray.

I roll my eyes but only in feigned annoyance. I already ate my fill of the sweet green melon, warm toast with pear jam, and tiny round pastries filled with chocolate cream.

Humans who partake of faerie food or wine can't pass through portals anymore. But now that I know fae food doesn't affect me—because I'm only part-human—I can fill my belly on all the dishes I missed out on last summer.

I'll admit, when Fawn brought in that breakfast tray and the first chocolate pastry melted on my tongue, the thought of being stuck here forever didn't seem too horrible, anyway.

"How was your visit?" I ask Eimear. I swallow a comment about how embarrassingly lonely I was in her absence.

"My friend is well. She shared news of home, further north where we were raised."

Her voice trails off. I glance at her, noticing she's forgotten the pastry in her hand. Her blank eyes stare out the window.

"Eimear?"

She jumps and shakes her head. A tight smile replaces her drooping frown. "I came to tell you I'll be out again today. Aibreann or Padraic are around to keep you company, at least during meals. Apparently, the queen has Cináed trapped conversing with delegates and advisors, and neither of them will have time to eat."

She must have had better luck finding Cináed. He wasn't at dinner last night. I wandered the halls early this morning hoping to catch him, but still nothing.

I want to give him Orla's letter. I also want to see him again, but that part of me holds no sway. My mind is made up.

You keep telling yourself that, my heart putters in response.

I ask Eimear, "Are the meetings about Aibreann or Padraic taking the high throne?"

She shakes her head, her mouth full. I return to perusing the clothes as she responds.

"Caitriona hopes that if Cináed is praised enough, if he feels he's supported by enough high fae, he will accept the nomination as high king and take Aibreann as queen."

My jaw slackens as I turn to stare at Eimear. She pauses between bites of toast and lifts an eyebrow.

"You didn't know? Everyone has been practically begging Cináed to take the throne ever since you"—she cringes—"well, you know. But he refuses to accept it, saying he's not the rightful heir."

Confusion and understanding course through me like two converging streams.

Well, my *understanding* is more like a trickling spring. At least my conversation with Aibreann makes sense now. But with it comes a river of questions, roaring in my ears, sweeping my feet out from under me.

Eimear goes quiet, then says apologetically, "I thought he told you."

I turn my back to her again, hiding my burning blush. I have more questions to ask, but I tuck them away for now. I've been side-tackled by this news and need a moment to recover.

To change the subject, I ask Eimear where she's going.

"I'm visiting a sacred site, a holy well. Within Caitriona's borders, of course."

She doesn't have to explain. Neither of us are eager to leave the safety of the castle's lands, at least not alone. Not while assassins could be lurking just outside its protective boundaries.

Safe or not, the thought of sulking around the castle another day makes me sick. "Can I come?"

She pops the last pastry into her mouth. "Aye. But if Cináed asks, I tried to make you stay behind."

My brow furrows. "Why does he care if I go?"

She stares at the ceiling and sighs. "Great goddess," she mutters. "Just dress in something warm, fit for riding horseback, and meet me at my door."

After some searching, I find a replacement for my tattered boots in a side closet, where spare linens and several pairs of shoes are stored.

I scan past the dainty slippers and select a sturdy pair of boots. They're a bit snug when I pull them on, but at least they won't take on water if we hike through snow.

My wool cloak hangs beside the door. I shrug into it, never tiring of the heat that tingles through my skin at its touch.

I enter the hall as Eimear emerges from her room. She's wearing her forest-green cloak with a long skirt and knitted sweater underneath, her red hair tied into a curly bun at the nape of her neck.

We leave the warmth of the castle, heading in the direction of the stables. Faeries bustle around the gardens. I see someone attempting to corral a flock of white swans toward a small pond, while others tend to rows of vegetables and herbs.

"How do things grow here in the winter?" I ask Eimear as we pass the gardeners.

"The same way we do everything else it takes to survive in the Otherworld—with glamour."

I remember the gardeners' shocked expressions when the tulips wilted around them. The way the noble seemed to use his glamour to kill the flowers—it was as if the gardeners were powerless to stop it.

"Do some faeries not have glamour?" I ask.

"We all do. But lesser faeries, well . . ." She glances at me, then stares at the ground, her expression pained. "Most don't have the ability to use glamour for more than simple tasks. To turn invisible or play a harmless trick on humans. Only the high fae and gifted lesser faeries can use glamour to protect or sustain themselves."

The unsettled feeling in my core shifts. I think about the village we visited. All those half-starved faeries . . .

I'm now wishing I'd been practicing glamour all this time. If I'm capable of creating food with glamour, I could have done something to help them.

We step inside the stable, and while Eimear chats with the groom, I meander down the aisle, admiring the horses in their stalls.

I hope Sona, the maroon horse I trained with last summer, is being fed as well as these horses. Their plump bellies and contented snorts distract me from my anxieties about the struggles of faerie poverty. At least for now.

A toffee-colored mare with a white mane and tail nickers at me, and I pause at her stall.

"Hey, there." I reach out a tentative hand. She nudges my palm, probably searching for food. I scan my surroundings for a bucket of oats or an apple and see Eimear walking over.

"Good, you've been chosen, then," she says.

"What?"

She nods to the mare, who's watching us with dark umber eyes, similar to Sona's.

"The mare chose you as her rider today," she says simply, as if talking about how to microwave popcorn. "The one that chose me is being saddled."

I recall a similar discussion when I met Sona. Fae horses can bond closely enough with their riders that they can hear each other's thoughts. When I left Sona, it seemed he was able to understand me, but I often still felt like I was talking to a brick wall.

Our horses are saddled and led to the other end of the long, wooden building. Eimear assures the groom that the horses will be returned tonight.

When Eimear mounts her horse with notable grace, I fear I've forgotten everything I learned about horseback riding. But when I mount my horse—whose name is Imelda—and she tosses her toffee head and paws the frozen earth, excitement shivers through me. I didn't realize how much I've missed riding.

Muira, the horse that chose Eimear, has the coat of a snow leopard and different-colored eyes—one ice blue, the other jet black. They take the lead as we find the forest trail and enter the speckled shade of the moss-coated branches.

I set aside my angst over everything from Cináed to faerie hunger and decide to enjoy this beautiful day.

Several minutes pass in comfortable quiet. Only the steady footfalls of the horses in the entangled undergrowth break the silence.

The trail winds uphill over thick roots, rocks, and snowmelt springs that tumble down the mountainside. Birdsong blends with the burble of running water. The smell of pine needles and wet earth tingles in my nose. My breath dissipates in the growing heat as the sun travels into the sky, warming the frosted earth and my ponytailed head.

We pause at the top of a particularly rough incline and let the horses drink from a pool of clear water while we sit astride their sloped backs.

"Why do you want to visit this well, again?" I ask Eimear.

She removes her green hood, her hair catching the sunlight like fervent flames. "Druids are called to visit sacred sites for many reasons. This holy well has not been visited all winter, as the snow was too deep to make the journey. I hope to restore its healing and psychic energies with a renewing spring ritual."

I make a face, letting her words sit in my mind. "A ritual?"

But she doesn't hear me because Muira starts clopping along again. Imelda and I settle into steady pace behind them, and I try not to freak out about Eimear and I performing some ritual in the woods.

The further we climb, the more the scenery transforms. Mossy boulders and roots become a haunted winter wonderland. Sparkling snow coats the earth, and I have to duck beneath tree branches heavy with jagged icicles. One sharp point grazes the back of my cloak like the lick of a knife.

Imelda high-steps through the deep patches of snow. My stomach, back, and leg muscles work to follow the horse's movements and keep myself from falling off whenever she bounds over something or trudges up a steep slope.

I see Eimear ahead, her horse stopped on the trail. The druid waves at us and calls out that we've made it. I can see her grinning from here.

While a knot of dread forms in my gut, I urge Imelda over the last ridge. We crest the slope to find a portion of level ground. Despite the bite in the air, the earth is untouched by snow.

Eimear stands a few paces away, holding her horse's muzzle in her hands, speaking words I can't hear.

I dismount and scan the wilderness of knotted tree branches blanketed in dense moss, searching for the holy well through the layers of white mist curling across the rich, hard-packed earth beneath my feet.

This place might have evaded the harshness of winter, but this landscape feels frozen—not with ice, but with a timelessness that grounds me. An otherworldliness that keeps my pulse racing.

My vision blurs as I step into the mist. It's like I'm being pulled by an invisible rope tied around my waist. I resist it and glance back at Eimear, who is removing her bag from the saddle.

Imelda snorts a gray cloud and stomps a hoof. I hear—no, I *sense* that she wants me to keep going. So I leave Eimear and the horses behind without a word and enter the wall of fog.

A strange humming vibrates in my ears, seeming to come from everywhere at once. I pull aside a curtain of vines and moss, and that's when I see it.

The holy well, centered in a small glen of glowing clover.

{ 23 }

The well is round and short, built from dark-gray stones speckled with age and sprouting fungi and tiny blossoms.

The hovering mist lingers outside the glen, and so do I, afraid to cross some unseen barrier around the well. I don't wait long. Eimear arrives with her satchel slung over a shoulder, her blue eyes glowing brighter than ever.

"You found it," she says, her voice just above a whisper. "Must have heard its song, then."

I start to tell her I didn't hear a song, but she ducks under the curtain of greenery, her gaze locked on the well. She hesitates at the unseen line around the glen, then gingerly steps through it. When nothing happens, I follow her.

She kneels in front of the well and lowers her forehead to the ground. I glance at the well, then at Eimear. With a grimace, I mimic her position, lowering my face into the plush carpet of emerald clovers.

I hear Eimear muttering a prayer and mentally offer one of my own.

Hey there, fae gods. I didn't mean it when I said I hated faeries before. Just wanted to clarify that in case this ritual takes a bad turn.

When Eimear stands, I follow but keep my distance as she leans to look into the well. The humming has intensified to the point that I wonder if I'd hear Eimear if she spoke again. The sound is a combination of a human voice and a chime, both singing the same clear note.

I'm torn between leaving to wait with the horses and watching what the druid will do next. And I won't lie, something else is urging me to stay. The invisible rope that pulled me here feels more like a chain now, anchoring me to the well.

Eimear pulls items from her satchel and sets them on top of the stones that cradle the pool of water. First, a tiny bowl, then a white unlit candle on the opposite side, a dappled feather furthest from us, and a rose-colored stone the size of my palm in the last spot.

When she steps back, she looks at me and says in a clear, soft voice, "The ritual requires silence and openness from the participants. You may sit and allow your mind to be guided."

I stare blankly at her, my tongue itching with smart-ass jokes. But she looks so genuine, I cannot tease her. I lower myself to the clovers, finding a comfortable cross-legged position, and try my best to silence my thoughts. Which I soon realize is beyond my skill level.

Eimear pulls her hood on and faces the pool, so all I see of her is the back of her green cloak. It sounds as though she starts humming the same note that hovers in the air. Both voices shift slightly, then again. As she hums along with an unseen chorus whispering through the trees, every hair on my body stands on end, my spine like an iron spike, my senses on alert.

In a movement too fast to follow, the candle's wick bursts into a tiny orange flame. Eimear, who hasn't moved from her statuesque position, stops humming.

I inhale, my blood chilling. A fervent breeze tosses the clovers and tugs on my cloak and hair, moving across the glen and fading as fast as it came.

The forest goes silent. I know I'm still breathing, but even my heartbeat seems to have stilled. An unbidden peace drenches me, and all of the tight fear in my chest dissolves.

Eimear sinks to her knees and whispers another prayer. Then she reaches for the bowl and lifts it to her mouth. When she turns to me, her eyes dance with elation. She hands me the bowl.

"Drink. Goddess Brigid grants her blessing and wishes that we both partake of this sacred water."

I take the bowl in both hands. Sure enough, it's brimming with clear water, although I swear I didn't see Eimear fill it in the pool. My skin tingles as I take a sip and swallow a cold mouthful that has the softest floral aftertaste.

Eimear places the bowl in its spot and sits where she can lean against the stone wall. Her freckled cheeks are flushed, and I can tell she's making an effort to stay serious. When she looks at me, she smiles with a breathy laugh.

"Is that it?" I ask.

She nods, looking dazed. It's as if the spell on this place has broken into a million bits of stardust and we're drunk on the wonder of it.

"Gosh." I lean back on my hands, my head too heavy for my body. "I was worried you were going to sacrifice some woodland animal."

Eimear collapses onto her side on the ground. "Not for this ritual. And, anyway, blood sacrifices are above my level of training."

Her tone is so matter-of-fact and my senses are so fuzzy that I can't stop from exploding into a mess of giggles. Eimear laughs, too, her hair tangling with the clovers like a forest fire. I'm on my back, tears dripping from the corners of my eyes.

I'm not sure I should have drunk that water. But, then again, what do I know? I can't even remember how we got here.

The world tilts and blurs around me. This space feels good, so I tell myself not to worry.

The trees, or maybe it's Eimear, start humming again. Oblivion finds me before the laughter dies on my tongue.

I blink, and I'm in a different place. I'm still lying on my side on the ground, watching seaweed-green water lap at gray sand.

Blink. I see a curved spine and a wet fin sink beneath a retreating wave.

Blink. A pair of emerald irises ringed in gold stare down at me. A hauntingly beautiful melody tickles my ears. A child's fingers curl around a lock of auburn hair.

Róisín.

I stir, sensing myself waking up. I resist it, longing to hear the words of the woman's song.

Róisín.

The woman shakes my shoulder. No, someone else is trying to rouse me. I reach for the woman, alarmed when the hands above me appear to be those of a child.

"Róisín."

I gasp and sit upright, then nearly topple over again with dizziness.

The glen, the holy well, the entire forest has transformed under night's dark embrace.

A waterfall of stars lines every twisted branch in a soft glow. My breath comes out in puffs of white mist, and my body trembles from the drop in temperature.

I rest my aching head in my palm, my jaw clenched. Something moves behind me, and I spin on my knees.

Eimear. She's sitting with her hands propped on her thighs, staring at me. Fear pollutes her eyes.

I heave a steadying breath to calm my pulse. "What the hell happened?"

Her tone is dismissive, distracted. "I do not know."

I peer at her. "Excuse me? You're the one who performed the ritual. All I did was fall asleep." I point at the obsidian sky. "For *hours*."

She looks away and says in a bit of a sheepish drawl, "Holy water has a habit of putting you to sleep . . ."

I stare. "*And*?"

She glowers, but I sense it stems from something other than anger. Maybe guilt or fear. "And I thought you would be forced to face whatever dreams you've been avoiding."

So she found a way to put me to sleep after all.

She cuts off my noise of protest. "As I slept, I was given a psychic dream, as I expected." The sting melts from her voice. "Only I was *not* expecting the message I received."

Another series of chills scatters over me, erasing my frustration. Eimear is more than a little shaken up.

My voice is gentle as I ask, "What did you dream, Eimear?"

She bites her lip and shakes her head. Then hides her face between her knees. I crawl closer until I sit in front of her.

I open my mouth to tell her about my dream—hoping it might coax out hers—but I decide against it. I feel like I was just given a tender, delicate blossom. Speaking my dream aloud would force the flower open before its proper time. I don't know what to do except to hold it in a safe space in my mind, undisturbed for now.

Eimear lifts her face, eyes shimmering. "We need to find Cináed. Then I'll tell you my dream."

I nod and help her to her feet. My fingers pick something green from her hair as she gathers her belongings.

I hold the stem in a beam of moonlight. It's a four-leaf clover.

I clasp it in my fist, sensing Eimear's foreboding dream has to do with all of us. And that we will need all the luck we can get.

{ 24 }

I toss a handful of sticks on the fire and watch the trail of sparks flicker and disappear into the night.

Eimear and I stopped the horses just short of the castle and found a secluded clearing to wait for Cináed.

When I asked her how he'd know to meet us here, she told me to build a fire. I almost laughed, astounded and excited. *No way is she sending smoke signals.*

She didn't, though, and I'm still bummed.

Instead, she whistled a little tune, and after a few seconds, a green will-ó-the-wisp darted through the dark trees. The same one I saw on the ship, perhaps? Has it been floating nearby this whole time?

Eimear whispered something to the glowing orb, and it flew away again.

That was fifteen minutes ago. Eimear hasn't spoken since, and I don't press her. My mind is busy mulling over the day—with the news about Cináed as prospective high king at center stage.

I kick a stray coal into the fire and turn from the flames to stare into the blackness where Cináed should appear at any moment. My eyes adjust in degrees until orange flames no longer dance in my vision.

I expected to feel angry that Cináed hadn't told me the news himself. Our evening walk would have been a prime opportunity. But, for whatever reason, he kept that significant detail from me.

And it hurt to be told by Eimear instead. It hurts to think he doesn't trust me. But there's not a drop of resentment in me. And I think it's because there's a blinding truth floating above the pain.

Cináed and I have never shared complete trust. Our bond wasn't forged by it. We came together like hot metals. But when we cooled, we did so on separate continents, in separate realms.

And as we cooled, a ridge formed between us. A hardened, unflinching spine. And I pray—for the sake of my patched-up heart—he doesn't attempt to scale it.

***

The moment Cináed enters the clearing—slow and lithe, his face and curls warming in the fire's glow—I shoot to my feet and step toward him.

But I pause and choose a less possessive greeting. A pinched smile and an awkward wave.

He watches me, too, and seems to hesitate. Then he sees Eimear, sitting on the cusp of shadow outside the firelight. And he passes me by to approach her.

"I came as quickly as I could," he says, sounding drained. I note the half-moons beneath his green eyes—still void of their usual luster.

I pluck out the thorn of misplaced jealousy in my chest and close the distance to Eimear.

She sits like she did at the well—her knees tucked to her chest, arms wrapping herself in a hug. She looks so small like that. Her cloak spills around her and blends into the earth.

"Sit, both of you," she says, her voice hoarse.

Cináed and I share a worried glance and obey. We sit cross-legged on the ground, the fire at our backs, Eimear before us. I'm aware of every inch of empty space between Cináed's knee and mine.

Cináed nods at Eimear in a silent invitation to begin. Her eyes swarm with keen fear. She swallows and stares at the fire as she speaks.

"I dreamed I was flying high above the Otherworld in the form of an owl. The beauty I saw consumed me with gladness . . . the land, the fae, every living thing." She licks her lips and wipes a stray tear. The wonder in her voice vanishes on the next breath. "Then a patch of darkness grew, covering the trees, obliterating a village, dissolving everything to ash.

"Everyone was fleeing, or so I thought. I flew closer and saw the darkness was *alive*—it was an army of faeries. And the ones they were hunting—" Her jaw clenches as her gaze flickers to me, then away. "They were half-breeds. Faeries with mixed blood."

My muscles tense as a chill settles beneath my skin. I frown and shake my head. "It's okay, Eimear. That's not going to happen."

I look to Cináed for confirmation, for him to pat Eimear on the head and tell her it was just a bad dream. Nightmares are awful, but the one solace is that they aren't real. I remind myself of this every morning.

But Cináed isn't looking at Eimear or at me as he asks, "And you were given this dream at a sacred well?"

Eimear nods. "Just after partaking of the holy water."

Cináed hisses through his teeth and stands. I don't miss the quick look he gives me or the concern in his eyes.

"I appreciate that you shared this, Eimear." He wipes a hand across his haggard face. "We will continue this conversation soon. Vera is meeting us with news of the southern kingdom. Then we must return, as Caitriona will surely miss our absence at supper."

I would clarify that she surely wouldn't miss *my* absence. But I'm too salty over the thought of Vera showing up at any moment.

Cináed helps Eimear stand, then he turns to me. I take his hand, deciding it would be weird not to. I stand and quickly tuck my hands into my cloak.

Eimear glances between the two of us with a quirked eyebrow. "I will gather more firewood." She shuffles into the trees, muttering something under her breath.

Cináed gives me a tired but genuine smile and steps to the edge of the fire to warm his hands. This is the second time we've been alone since my return. I remind myself to breathe and act normally.

"I have something for you." I step beside him and remove Orla's letter from my pocket.

His body remains still, but his eyes rove toward me. "You wrote me something?"

I pray the fire's glow masks my red face. "Um—no, I—" I shove the letter at him, and he takes it. "It's from Orla."

"Oh."

His gaze falls, as do his shoulders. *Cináed wants you to write him?*

I shrug deeper into my cloak, wishing I could tear out my racing heart and be done with its nonsensical antics.

His fingers tear the letter at the top, bypassing the cracked seal. I study his face as he reads, noting each wrinkle that forms in his forehead and every speck of fear that taints his expression.

He folds the letter and tucks it in his trouser pocket. It's now that I notice he's not wearing his cloak. His fitted leather pants and embroidered tunic tell me he must have come straight from an especially important meeting.

Seeing him tormented by the letter makes me scramble. I rush to explain how I got the letter, even though it doesn't matter. Nothing matters to Cináed as much as Rauri's kingdom.

"I heard a messenger asking Aibreann where you were. She intercepted the letter and"—I pause to skip over the princess's confession, not ready to delve into that topic—"anyway, I couldn't find you yesterday. But now you have it, so . . ."

So now what? I count the days on my hand and realize the festival is tomorrow night. Which means we could leave in twenty-four hours.

"Who else has read this?" he asks. So he *did* notice the cracked seal.

"Aibreann. And me."

He tucks his hands in his pockets and widens his stance with a loud sigh. "I will be home soon enough. Until then, I pray Vera's news won't worsen this grim letter."

I huff and roll my eyes. *Since when has Vera ever brightened anything?*

"You do not like Vera."

Cináed is looking at me. I erase the scowl on my face, but my reaction already gave me away.

This is uncharted territory for me—we've never discussed his past relationship with Vera. And I've never maintained a steady boyfriend long enough to deal with talk of exes.

"We're not besties, if that's what you mean," I say.

His lips twitch into a small smile. "Humans have the most interesting words."

When he says nothing more, I take a deep breath and ask what I've never dared to before. "I know you guys were a thing. Why did you break up?"

Because she's obviously still into you, I add silently.

Cináed glances toward the unseen trail through the trees, where Vera will appear soon. His tone is low. "When Branna died, I swore off the idea of lasting companionship. Vera and I shared that opinion for a time. Our impermanence was natural, as was our ending."

He looks at me, and his smile grows just enough to reveal his dimple. Then his mouth falls again. "Róisín, I—I've sensed a change in you since you arrived." His earnest eyes gaze into mine. "A change . . . between *us*."

Self-preservation urges me to escape, to sprint into the trees. This is exactly the kind of conversation I want to avoid.

But my traitorous heart pummels my willpower, leaving me panicked and motionless.

He goes on, "You are mourning many losses, as am I. Which is why I have tried to give you space, as you did for me." He lifts a tentative hand, and I hold my breath as he traces a finger down my cheek. "But if I am to show restraint, I must hear the order from your lips. Tell me what you would have of me."

Curses grate against the melody of my sputtering heart. I say nothing for several seconds, not trusting my mouth to obey.

At last, I manage to blurt a few words—each full of desperation and air and lacking a single trace of conviction.

"Space. I need space, please."

He stares at me. I feel like he's sifting my soul, searching for some buried proof that what we had last summer was real. I know that endeavor all too well.

He opens his mouth to say something when Eimear and Vera step through the trees.

"I've never seen so many wild turnips in my life." Eimear pauses when she sees us—I notice her arms are completely empty of firewood—and Vera almost collides with her.

Eimear shoots us an apologetic look before entering the clearing, Vera following. Vera observes Cináed and me like she's an investigator at a crime scene.

The private moment they interrupted feels like a burnt-out ember. I sense it go cold, and I move to stand near Eimear, putting as much distance between Vera and me as possible. Eimear hands me a dirty root, telling me to eat.

"Our strength is low, after the well."

I take the turnip and try brushing the dirt off with my cloak. Cináed's lingering stare warms my cheeks. When he looks at Vera, my chest loosens in a painful sigh—my heart aching like it's been used as a punching bag.

"Tell us your news, Vera," Cináed says.

Vera shoots Cináed a stunning smile. Then her expression hardens, and her tone grows serious. "The advisors spend every waking hour arguing over who will rule. Most of them campaign for themselves. Only three of the thirteen members advocate finding a blood heir."

Cináed paces, running his hand through his curls. "Only Barlow, Quinn, and Tilly? What of Roan?"

"He was recently swayed by Orla's supporters. She has been the top candidate for the throne for an entire moon cycle."

What about Orla's letter?

Fresh confusion invades my tired mind. I try to catch Cináed's eye, but shadows mask his expression as he stares at the ground.

"Orla?" Eimear asks. "The one who vied for Naoise's crowning?"

Vera nods to Eimear, and with a pointed look at me, she rounds the firepit to stand near Cináed. I crunch on the turnip.

Cináed shakes his head with a deep frown. "Orla has no interest in ruling. Manipulating the crown, yes, but not wearing it herself."

Vera tosses her white hair over a shoulder. "You underestimate her if you think she doesn't lust after the throne."

I remember Orla's reaction after I stabbed Naoise, frazzled but almost gleeful. Eirwen's warning rings in my ears with new understanding: *Naoise left Orla the Gray in his shadow.*

"Vera might be on to something," I say, and everyone looks at me with surprise—especially Vera. "Orla visited me that night after the games. She was clearly thrilled about what had happened."

That I had done the dirty work for her, perhaps?

"Of course Orla was thrilled to have Naoise gone," Cináed says curtly, still pacing. "All of us were. She might have supported him at first, but she must have realized her mistake."

I track Cináed's movement as I respond with equal shortness. "Or she was glad to have Naoise out of the picture so she could step in."

"He had appointed her as his closest advisor," Vera adds. "Maybe this was her plan all along. To use Naoise to gain political status and then take his supporters—and his crown—for herself."

Cináed looks like he's been hit over the head, talking more to himself than us as he murmurs, "She has been a lifelong friend of the royal family. She wouldn't do this."

But even he is beginning to sound doubtful. As if to allow Cináed time to process, Eimear asks Vera why she's continuing north from here instead of returning with us.

"I have some loose ends that"—she pauses and bites her bottom lip like she's searching for the right word—"need to be knifed in the back, so to speak."

Eimear raises her eyebrows. Vera smiles to herself, no doubt picturing whatever dark dealings she has planned.

Cináed—who seems to be far away—says, "Let us rendezvous again tomorrow. If Caitriona suspects our secret meetings, she will demand to know everything before we leave her kingdom."

Then he walks into the trees without another word, leaving the three of us staring after him in collective silence.

We put out the fire and erase all signs of our presence from the clearing. At least, Eimear and I do. Vera disappears as smoothly as she arrived.

"Time for supper, then." Eimear brushes the dirt from her skirt, and we mount our horses, heading down the trail.

But once I catch sight of the castle gleaming through the trees, I pull back on the reins.

"Hey, Eimear?" I call to her. "You go ahead. I'm not hungry."

Muira slows, and Eimear turns her head. She frowns, and I brace myself for an argument. But instead, she nods. "I'll have Fawn bring a tray to your room."

I hope she can see my grateful smile in the dark. While she continues toward the stables, I veer Imelda into a shallow ravine, following the sound of the ocean.

I find Vera on the other side of the off-white sand dunes, facing the muted horizon where gray water blurs against a grayer sky.

While it wasn't my intention to search for her, seeing her makes me realize I want to speak with her in private. I tie Imelda to a tree and make tracks across the moist sand.

Vera doesn't acknowledge me when I stand beside her. A wave hisses toward our feet—the only sound for miles of empty beach.

Moonlight captures Vera in its soft beam, illuminating her dove-gray leggings and tunic and the collection of knives glinting from the straps on her plum-colored vest and belt. Her black, knee-length boots stand just out of reach of the waves' gentle kisses.

"Why are you really here?" she says, giving me a sidelong stank eye. The moon shimmers in her stare and glows against her gray-brown skin. "Do not tell me you are foolhearted enough to return because of the Wanderer."

Bitter, much? But I let her venom slide off my shoulders. Despite my initial reaction to her appearance, I realize Vera isn't my enemy. Granted, I wouldn't trust her to tie my boots—but Vera will always deliver blunt candor. Which is just what I need.

I respond as I kick a pile of sand into the next wave. "The fae were still targeting me in the human realm, so I left to protect someone I care about."

"You expect me to believe you risked it all to save your brother and then left him because the fae scared you off?"

I didn't think she knew that much about Darren. This discussion is verging on *too* personal. But I have my own questions for Vera, and if I want solid answers, I know I'll have to deliver on mine.

"Darren has adopted parents." I clear my throat. "They're moving to a different state, far away. He's safer with them than with me."

She stares at the horizon, seemingly satisfied with my response. For the first time, I wonder if Vera left anyone behind when her selkie skin was stolen and she was forced to remain on land.

"Your turn," I say. "Why are you continuing north?"

She gives a wry, bitter smile. "As you know, I enacted my revenge on the monster who stole my skin. I was so blinded by rage at the time that I did not recognize he might be the one soul who knew the whereabouts of my skin." She pauses and sighs. "Not until he had drowned beneath the waves."

I remember this story vividly. It still makes me shudder like it did the night I first heard it. She tosses her head of silky white hair, her casual demeanor a bit unsettling.

I doubt I could ever retell the moment I stabbed Naoise without revealing the lasting trauma it caused me.

Vera continues, her tone sharpening with anger. "I recently became aware of a trade circle specializing in rare items—one of many contraband markets in the Otherworld. I believe my skin was smuggled through this chain. I assume some faery lacking in morals and overcompensating with coin owns it by now."

I didn't know anything was illegal here. The fact that Vera's skin—part of her being—could have been sold like a prize . . . it makes me sick.

"Is there anything I can do to help?"

The moment the words leave my mouth, I long to pull them back. Vera is just as shocked as I am, her voice layered with ice.

"If you are mocking me, I swear—"

I hold my hands up in a gesture of peace. "I'm not. I was serious." Although she's not the only one having a hard time believing in my sincerity.

Me, wanting to help Vera. I almost laugh, but one glance at Vera's slitted eyes sobers me.

"Why would you want to do that?" The venom in her tone is replaced by pure confusion.

I pause, staring out into the endless expanse of water. The answer arrives with the deliberate grace of the softest wave. "I know what it's like to not belong."

She watches me, as if searching for the smallest sliver of dishonesty. At last, she purses her lips and nods, her doe eyes distant as we face the ocean.

"It's true that I have been prisoner to this land far too long," she says. "This journey is one I must travel alone. But if there comes a day that I need a favor, I will take you up on that offer."

I nod, almost fearing what Vera might ask me to do. But I have more questions.

"What do selkies look like?"

Vera's soft mouth puckers into a frown. "Why?"

I realize she might be thinking I know something about her lost skin, so I rush to say, "When Cináed's boat crashed, something saved me from drowning."

Her shoulders sag just slightly, but she asks, "What did the creature look like?"

The memory replays, blurred and sparkling like a fractured light fixture. A naked spine leading to the curvature of a scaled backside and an iridescent fish tail. I tell this to Vera, and she nods.

"Merfolk. Although why they would be so far from their waters, I do not know."

So I was right—a mermaid saved my life! I suppress the urge to freak out until I'm alone and won't get made fun of.

"What do you mean, their waters?" I ask.

"You were attacked in merrow territory. The merfolk rule the eastern sea, the opposite shore. While sea-beings can cross borders, it's unsanctioned and dangerous. Especially where merrows are concerned."

Vera looks at me, her gray-brown skin pinched around her black eyes. "Do you know of any reason one of the merfolk would put themselves in danger to save you?"

I bite my lip and shake my head.

Vera seems to think it over. "To answer you, selkies look similar to the creatures you call seals. We can shed our selkie skin, our seal skin, to appear like this." She gestures to her body, then adds with a vengeful gleam in her eyes. "If you see anything akin to a seal pelt, you let me know."

"I will." I inhale a steadying breath. "I'm actually looking for someone too. How did you put it—a faery with no morals but loaded with coins?"

Vera quirks a white brow. I can sense she's grown bored with me. So I talk faster.

"Someone paid the merrows and a group of assassins to track down Cináed's allies. I want to find out who."

She sighs, sounding a bit exasperated. "And you came to me. Why?"

I lick my dry lips. "Because you're one of the most fearsome beings I know. You know what it's like to need revenge."

Vera stares at the waves. I steel myself for her dismissive response. She locks her iridescent eyes on me. "I do not know how to help you."

My mouth pulls into a line, and I nod.

Then her lips curl in a smirk. "But I know a place that might have your answer. If you are *fearsome* enough to join me."

As she speaks, my concern festers into true fear. My protective instincts are squealing at me: *run, hide, this isn't your fight.*

But my instinct to protect the ones I care about screams the loudest of all*: you are more than your fears.*

I don't shrink. I rise up. "Join you where?"

That wicked gleam returns to her eye. "Tonight, we journey to Mouth of the Beast—the largest forbidden market in the Otherworld."

{ 25 }

Nothing but wild desperation could get me to agree to a girl's night out with Vera.

And as desperate as I am for answers, I still almost talk myself out of it as we find Imelda.

I expect some pushback when I sit in the front of the saddle. But Vera says nothing as she skirts around the horse, her eyes bulging, nostrils flared.

"You don't like horses?" I ask.

She hisses—at me or the horse or both—and gets a running start before launching onto the saddle.

We follow a side road to avoid other travelers. With Vera's guidance, we exit through a smaller gate used for deliveries of food. And the guards standing watch—slouched and dozing through their night shift—hardly notice us trotting past.

The dirt road follows the cliff away from the castle. When the path veers toward the coastline, Vera tells me to break away from the road and head straight for the trees.

At her words, I yank back on Imelda's reins so hard that Vera and I almost flip forward off the saddle. A less patient horse—like Sona—would have thrown us.

Vera's head knocks against mine from the unexpected stop, and she shoves me with a snarl. "What is wrong with you—"

I cut her off, glad she can't see the renewed fear on my face. "You didn't say we were going into this forest."

These are the trees that have been plagued by Manny's dying cries. His final screams will live forever here, trapped between the twisted branches and moss-coated deadfall.

Vera's tone bites through my panic. "If you cannot brave the forest, you won't survive Mouth of the Beast."

I force myself to take a shuddering breath. The dark spots in my vision remain, but at least they stop growing.

"The assassins—" I swallow hard. "This is where they killed Cináed's first mate."

Vera is silent for a moment. Then I hear her sigh. "They are long gone by now. Besides, you traveled here from a doorway, correct?"

My hooded head nods.

"Our path takes us further north, away from the nearest doorway." The absence of frustration in her voice surprises me. Then she adds, "You have three seconds before I abandon your cowardly ass and journey the rest of the way on foot."

Exhaling through my teeth, I grip Imelda's reins and click my tongue. She stops nibbling the grass beside the road and clops forward at a gentle trot.

Sorry about that, I mentally apologize to the horse.

We settle into a steady stride, and I focus my gaze on the dark, misty trees ahead.

I don't bother apologizing to Vera.

We cut through the pathless forest, but we make good time. At least, I guess as much from where the moon sits in the sky.

But I don't care about time or the moon—only Imelda's steps and my breath. I sink into the simple rhythm and use it as a shield against the haunting memories that are trying their best to crawl to the surface of my mind.

Somehow, I manage to keep them from worming their way into my sanity.

I know we've reached a landmark only because Vera tells us to halt. She dismounts and takes three swift strides away from Imelda, searching.

My limited focus widens to take in our surroundings. All I find is an unassuming body of trees, huddled in their lichen-and-moss coats like sleeping giants—the same view we've seen for miles.

But Vera seems intent on something. She's distanced herself even further, wandering between two thick roots that bubble up from the earth. I dismount—mentally telling Imelda to wait for us unless a monster tries to eat her—and rush to join Vera before she leaves me behind.

She ignores my presence, her gaze sharp and intent.

"What are we looking for?" I whisper.

Her lip curls in a silent snarl. "I am not *looking*. This is the place." She doesn't bother lowering her voice, and her bravado startles me. "Few know the entrance. I killed the faery who told me of it."

I trip on a stick and catch myself before I crash into the undergrowth. "Why? Is that the rule?" Keep the secret or be killed for it—that would definitely decrease the number of shoppers in your illegal market.

"No." Her face turns just enough for me to catch a flash of her vicious grin. "I killed him for practice. I want to be ready when I meet my true victim."

A nervous laugh huffs through my teeth. Vera eases beneath a low branch, and I follow, reminded once again of her vengeful prowess.

How far would you go to reclaim what's yours?

Darren's face brightens my mind's eye. For him, I would do anything. I proved that at the end of the games.

Or, at least, I told myself it was for Darren. But if I were to face the bloodstained truth . . . I'd know better. Darren was already free. I had already secured his and Cináed's safety.

I killed Naoise to reclaim myself.

Maybe I'm more fearsome—more *faerie*—than I thought.

Vera and I have almost made a complete loop around a large tree. I'm about to risk my neck to ask if we're lost when the trees, the ground, the air itself starts to shimmer like ripples on water.

I place a steadying hand against the tree and blink hard, but the vibrations quicken into a dizzying blur.

Vera pauses, too, and we watch as the earth beside us quakes open like a gaping mouth. The packed soil cracks as it peels wide until it shudders to a stop above our heads.

Exposed roots dangle in clumps from the lip of dirt. *They look like teeth*, I realize. *Layers of teeth on an earthen maw.*

It's the entrance to Mouth of the Beast.

{ 26 }

Within the mouth—breathing hot, musky air right in our faces—is a tunnel leading into shadow.

I peel my wide eyes from the entrance to glance at Vera. She brushes a strand of white hair behind an ear. Then she straightens, puffs out her chest, and marches right in.

"See," she shouts to me without stopping, "I told you I knew where it was."

I roll my eyes but save my snarky reply for a less *earth-rending* moment. I do, however, allow myself a small smile at my attempt at humor.

Then I square my shoulders and charge after her.

As soon as my feet cross the threshold, the earth trembles. I think the tunnel might collapse, so I sprint deeper into the dark.

The mouth slams shut behind me. I peel around the corner and find Vera standing at the other end of the tunnel.

And my panting breath is stolen from me at the sight of the dimension living *beneath* the underground world of faeries.

Just like the Otherworld, this realm creates the illusion of a night sky, adorned with a milky stream of emerald and citrine stars. An indigo river snakes along a shore of trees dipping their branches into the current of water.

It's a scene that shouldn't be able to survive under volumes of earth. A place that could never exist in real life.

Scratch that—it couldn't exist in *my old life.* At this point, claiming these magical experiences aren't real simply because they're beyond human comprehension would be juvenile.

Vera and I seem to spot the lone faery at the same time. He's bent over, dragging a small wooden boat from the river and onto the shore of charcoal-gray sand.

When Vera walks toward him, I scurry after her, fist closed around the iron knife in my cloak pocket. I will defend myself against any unprovoked attacks. Otherwise, if someone must die, I'll let Vera do the honors.

My boots dodge a series of scattered stones glowing in neon shades of yellow and orange. A sharp contrast to the dark sand.

The male straightens and spots us. Even in the shadows, I see his eyes narrow as we approach. He's young, or at least he appears my age. Brown hair swooshes off his forehead and behind his pierced ears.

Vera strides right up to him, halting a yard away. I hover beside her, my gaze darting in all directions to make sure nothing takes us by surprise.

Vera addresses the male with unflinching authority. "Do you offer passage within?"

The faery folds his bare, toned arms and scans the two of us. "Within?"

Vera rolls her eyes and growls. "You're actually going to make me say the code?"

When the male gestures with an expectant hand, Vera says in a deadpan voice, "Grant us passage within, for we are solitary, lawless creatures, unbound by court and kingdom."

As Vera speaks, I notice how the male's gaze lingers on the full curve of her right hip, jutting out in an exaggerated stance.

"The unsanctioned trade circle welcomes you," he says with a smile. Then he turns to me. "And you? Got your tongue sliced out for your unspeakable crimes, is it?"

"I speak just fine," I retort.

At the same time, Vera says coolly, "She's a solitary—a human mutt. And she's with me."

The dark-haired male lifts his brows. "Welcome, then. It's been a decade since we have had a human visitor." With a wink at Vera, he adds, "At least of their own choosing, anyway."

Vera's annoyed frown deepens, and she shoves past the male, heading for the boat. "I'm not paying for your chatter, faery. Take us to the market."

Vera and I sit in the back of the boat while the faery guides us down the dark river, seemingly oblivious to Vera's mounting annoyance at his attempts to charm her.

"And that's when I told her," he says, flexing his biceps with each rotation of the paddles, "that she might be a powerful high fae, but I only take *solitaries* for lovers."

When he turns to gaze down the river, Vera looks at me and pretends to gag herself.

The air tastes humid and muggy here, reminding me of the time I ran away from my foster home and took a bus to

Florida. My child self thought I'd be alright if I could make it to Disney World.

It wasn't the first—or the last—time I confused freedom with temporary escape. Running from my life never changes what's waiting for me when I go back.

I thought I was done running. I thought I'd find that freedom in my new life with Darren.

The boat floats beneath a looming tree. A curtain of drooping branches brushes my skin, bringing me back to the present.

"What's our plan again?" I ask Vera.

We went over the basics on the ride here, but my nerves didn't allow much to stick.

"Stay close, and for the love of Lí Ban, speak to no one."

That's not really a plan. But I remind myself that I'm not here to be babysat by Vera. I'll do whatever it takes to gather information about the assassins and get out alive.

The knife in my fist suddenly feels three times heavier.

Up ahead, the river curls and widens. The view beyond the branches becomes clear as we round the bend.

Long docks line both sides of the river. Wooden shelters crowd the docks horizontally as well as vertically, like stacks of toy blocks building on each other. The layers of the market stretch above the trees in a constructed hill. Floating will-ó-the-wisps and the occasional torch illuminate the night in flickering colors.

The sketchy workmanship—the way each floor and roof precariously balances against the next—tells me that only glamour keeps the entire thing from toppling over.

Our guide brings the boat alongside the front of the market and leaps onto the dock. He lowers a hand to Vera with a grin. "Just so you know, I accept a variety of payment options—"

"Coin only," Vera snaps, ignoring his hand as she withdraws a small satchel from her vest.

She hands over the money, and I follow her from the boat.

The male brushes his hair back, maintaining his charming smile despite Vera's rejection. "If I don't have the pleasure of meeting you again, I offer you both this blessing: may we ever be free to speak, deal, love, and kill as we so choose."

"May we ever," Vera drawls and strides off.

We enter the throng of shoppers and traders. I stick with Vera even if it means pushing through conversations or cutting someone off. Without money of my own, she's my literal ticket out of here.

I'm glad I took my cloak off in the boat to hold in my arms. The humid air is warm and sour in the mass of bodies. Not to mention we're floating on pillars of damp wood on a stagnant river.

I guess glamour can't hide everything.

But despite its abrasive smell and crude appearance, the underground market boasts a unique wildness, even for the Otherworld. I've never seen such a diverse gathering of creatures. The horns, the tails, the wings and fangs.

My attention ping-pongs between the displays of magical objects for sale. I overhear a goblin ordering a serving of maggot tarts from a shop called *Wicked Delights*. Around the corner, a female faery barters for a vampire tooth.

I spot Vera cutting between two shops and jog to catch up. By the time I pass through, she's climbing a rope ladder into a tall tree. A rope bridge connects that tree to another, where a wooden hut perches like a fat bird.

As I climb, Vera tiptoes across the bridge and steps inside the hut. The air up here smells fresher, and the noise of the market fades into the background.

Pausing outside the hut, I read the sign painted in shimmering pink letters above the door.

Blood and Piss Tattoo Parlor.

Catchy, but random. What does this have to do with the assassins? Or Vera's selkie skin?

I duck inside and see Vera talking to a female near the back of the shop. My ears tune in to their conversation as I observe the art covering the wooden walls. Strings holding single candles hang from the ceiling boards, which have gaps wide enough to reveal the strange stream of colored stars in the sky.

Vera's voice is smooth, absent of its usual edge. "When I heard you spend your winters here, I could not believe it."

I look away from a painting of a dragon in shimmering green ink. Vera is holding hands with the female. I notice her long hair—pulled into tight braids down her back—is white like Vera's. And her flawless, ebony skin has a distinct gray undertone.

The female's voice is rich and full. "My time here is my choice, which is why you cannot understand. I visit the land as I choose—as should always be our way."

Vera releases the female's hands and turns, holding her arms around her. Shadow darkens her expression, but her pained stance says it all.

The female frowns, her large eyes filled with concern. "I am glad you came, Vera-selch. I know to whom you must speak. A vile, infamous mixed-breed and trader of rare furs. If anyone knows of your selkie skin, it's him."

Vera seems to remember my presence and casts all vulnerability aside as she straightens and gestures to me. "Cora, this is Róisín. A half-fae from the human realm."

Cora rests her eyes on me, her gaze intense and discerning. "Greetings, Róisín. I take it you are not here for a tattoo."

I glance at Vera, unsure what to say. Or if I should say anything. Is Cora someone I can trust, and if so, how much information do I share?

Vera responds for me as she peruses stones and shells on a table. "She's looking for assassins."

Cora's white eyebrows lift. Her voice is spiced with surprise. "And who might the unlucky soul be? Did a lover cross you?"

Confusion muddles my mind. Then realization hits me. "Oh, I'm not looking to *hire* them." More like have them fired. From life. Permanently.

Understanding softens Cora's full mouth and high cheekbones. "I will brew us some tea. I sense you have a story to tell."

{ 27 }

Cora invites Vera and me to sit on a bench behind the counter. Then she crosses the one-room hut to the door and bolts it closed.

"Now, explain what you are searching for," she says to me while she digs through a cupboard tucked inside the counter.

So I tell her everything I know about the assassins. Which, once I spill it all out, is even less than I realized. And I omit several details for Cináed and Eimear's safety. The last thing I need is to get them in trouble because I entered an illegal market.

I fall silent and wait for a response from Cora, who's busy holding a full kettle over a candle. It must be a glamoured flame because steam pours from the kettle's spout within a few minutes.

"The terrible truth," Cora says as she pours hot water into three clay mugs, "is that Mouth of the Beast specializes in selling the physical parts of magical creatures. Not in hiring out mercenaries."

I take the mug Cora offers me and stare at the slatted floor, feeling deflated. *You shouldn't have gotten your hopes up.*

Vera inhales the steam from her mug and says with nonchalance, "Well, I know of another market swarming with assassins."

"Close by?" I ask.

She sips the tea and smacks her lips with delight. "If you consider a three-day swim into the sea close by."

My shoulders sag. "Seriously, Vera?" I snap.

Her eyes seem innocent enough, but I catch her smirking behind her mug. Cora must take pity on me because she sits beside me in a chair and rests her hand on my knee.

"How about that tattoo, then? No cost for a friend of Vera-selch." Up close, I notice her sharp canines as she smiles at me. "It might help you feel your visit was not in vain."

When Cora calls us *friends*, Vera chokes on her tea.

But I happily ignore Vera as I ask Cora, "Are you a selkie too?"

Her smile widens. "Did my fish breath give me away?"

I laugh and shake my head. *Gosh, why can't Vera be this awesome?*

Cora sobers as she leans back in the chair, pulling her chunk of white braids around her shoulder.

"To tell you truthfully, living in a place like this—if only for the winter—wears on my conscience. I take pride in my work, but I loathe sharing my art with those who would steal my pelt if they had the chance."

"Why not be a tattoo artist outside the market?" I ask, lifting the mug to my lips and taking a gulp. The taste of seaweed makes my throat close, and it's all I can do to not gag.

Cora and Vera share a knowing look over the sound of me coughing into my fist.

Vera's tone is bitter. "The high fae do not appreciate diversity. And most everyone else spends their limited resources on basic survival."

Cora's wide nostrils flare. "Although, if I ever did practice elsewhere, it would be nice to do away with that barbaric title." She tosses her head toward the door.

My burning throat opens enough for me to squeak, "The blood-and-piss sign?"

Cora's laugh is as full-bodied as her speaking voice. "You noticed it. The message is misleading, but I had to play to the market's demeaning standards to fit in."

Vera downs the rest of her tea and stands to pour another cup. "Using a little bodily fluid is not a crime, Cora-selch. It all depends on the creature you take it from."

Cora meets my eyes and pulls an exaggerated face of disapproval. I stifle a giggle as Vera sits down and Cora continues, "Well, I keep my ink strictly plant-based. It is a blend of my own creation, using algae." She winks with a satisfied smirk. "The best part is that they glow in the dark."

Vera swirls her mug, her eyes glinting. "Well, if you ever come across someone with a stolen selkie skin, tattoo a glowing target on their forehead for me."

Vera and I say goodbye to Cora and climb down the ladder into the frenzied market below.

We agree to find the fur trader Cora referred us to and then get out of here on the next available boat.

But not three minutes in, I lose sight of Vera in the throng. My heart skips a beat, my gaze searching for her white head of hair.

"You there! Take a look at these rare furs."

I spot the male trying to wave me down. He's standing behind a booth laden with pelts. His soft, short body appears human except for the small tusks poking out from his unkempt beard.

When he sees he's caught my attention, he amps up his sales pitch.

"Rarest furs and skins around! Much finer than what you have there." He gestures to the wool cloak in my arms, and I clutch it closer with a protective frown.

Based on the directions Cora gave us, this isn't the top fur trader. *But what if Vera's skin is here?*

I take two steps, closing the distance to the table. "Do you have any selkie skins?" I ask in a hushed tone. This might be an illegal market, but shopping for a part of Vera's body makes my stomach squirm.

The male tries to hand me a fur coat from a rack behind the table. "No, I don't. Haven't seen a selkie skin in ages."

My heart sinks. I turn to leave, but my gaze snags on something impossibly familiar. A bundle of thick brown fur with a dark ridge trailing up the spine.

Nausea overtakes me to my core. My hands shake. I hold my breath as my trembling fingers lightly brush the fur.

It can't be.

As if from a world away, the male's intrusive voice bellows in my ringing ears.

"You have an eye for treasure. Traded for it just this morning, and it won't be long before it's snatched up." He leans across the table, spittle flying from his bearded lips as he whispers, "That there's a genuine minotaur pelt."

As the words leave his mouth, my fingers wrap around a small braid tucked in the fur. *Manny.*

In a movement too fast to be my own, I dive over the table, spilling furs to the ground. The full weight of my body pins the male to the floorboards.

His small eyes bulge, and he releases a startled yelp. But I lean toward his pudgy face and press the edge of my knife against the soft flesh of his neck, silencing him.

"Who did you buy it from?"

His legs squirm as he tries to get free. I dig my knee into his thigh, and he yelps again. Then he falls still. By now, I sense onlookers gathering closer. Soon enough they'll find us behind the table.

I press on the blade until a sliver of blood drips down his neck. "Tell me!"

"T—two faeries!" he sputters. "A male and female!"

My voice climbs to a shrill scream. "What are their *names*?"

He pales even more. "I—I don't know!" he cries. "They didn't say!"

"*Liar!*"

My vision goes dark, then returns like a gray pulse. Two creatures enter the booth from behind me. I hear myself screaming as they grasp my arms, pinning them against my back.

Pulse. Darkness. Pulse.

They drag me off the male. I flail my feet, searching for a foothold, for any kind of leverage.

My boot upends the table. Furs scatter everywhere. *Which one is Manny's?*

Pulse. Darkness. Pulse.

They're dragging me away. Away from Manny's skin, being *sold* like a prize. Away from his degraded remains, lying like scraps on the floor.

Pulse. Darkness . . .

My vision doesn't come back. Instead of losing consciousness, I spiral inward with keen awareness.

And what I find there—buried in the depths of my being—opens like a bottomless well of untapped potential. Glamour. So much of it that, for a second, I think I might burst.

Burst. Yes—I can do that.

Rough hands are still dragging me away, and my vision remains black. But I'm not afraid. I know exactly what to do. To make them pay, to make sure none of them can ever place their greedy hands on Manny again.

I gather as much glamour as I can carry. And I unleash it all.

Even without my sight, I feel the ground, the air around me, being cut open. And my throat—it feels like I'm breathing fury. Like a raging beast is clawing up my chest. And then it explodes from my mouth.

What feels like seconds later—when my vision returns, pulsing gray—I find myself on my knees, alone at the bottom of a simmering crater.

My mouth tastes of ash. I blink against the smoke curling around me. The forbidden market, the world beneath worlds, is nowhere to be seen.

Then, river water spills down the side of the crater. I fall on my back, drained and unable to move.

I blink up at the milky sky of emerald and citrine stars. I hear the water hissing closer. But a consuming darkness finds me first, and I sink into oblivion.

{ 28 }

Notes of music fall on my ears like drops of rain. The melody is sweet, calm, restful.

Everything I am not.

I turn away from it, retreating back to the dark void in my mind. But it's too late. I'm waking up, and all the hurt is waking with me.

My eyelids squeeze tight against the soft sunlight. My throat swallows uselessly—my tongue is a mountain of sand in the desert of my dry mouth.

"You are safe, Róisín."

Cináed's voice is so close. I squint one eye open and find him sitting beside my bed. His familiar wooden flute rests in his hand. *Explains the music.*

But my tattered memories don't explain how I got back to the castle.

My head pounds, and I close my eyes again. "Wh—" I cough, but it doesn't soften the gravel in my voice. "What happened?"

"Well, that is a solid question." Cináed sounds concerned but also angry.

I peek at him again. His polished, glowing skin doesn't mask the lines on his forehead, between his eyebrows, around his frown. And in his eyes, I find a lightning storm of emotions.

"What happened?" I ask again. Then I sit up with a start. "Where's Vera?"

My head spins, and Cináed supports me as he props pillows behind my back. "She left right after she delivered you here. I spoke with her briefly"—his gaze bores into me—

"before I had to carry your limp, injured body inside."

Shame hits me like a wall. I bite my lip, still wishing I could crawl back to that dark, consuming void and never return.

"Cináed, I'm so sorry. I wanted to find the assassins."

"What good would that do if it left you dead, Róisín?" His voice grows in strength, sharpened with fear. "I've sent three guards to the location where Manny . . ." He clears his throat. Grief hardens his next words. "Not one of them has returned. *Not one.*"

I shudder, not from his anger but from my own inner torment. *What was I thinking?*

The answer, and my surprise, arrives at once. *I was tired of playing the victim.*

Cináed goes on, not releasing me from his stare. "Then Eimear knocks on my door at some godless hour of the night and tells me you are missing."

The last words crash together like broken waves. But something has shifted inside me. Cináed's pain rocks me but stops just short of my innermost self.

The self that chose to enter that mouth of teeth—to prove to the fearful side of me that I don't have to run. That I'm not too broken. That I can still fight.

Then I remember the crater and gasp.

Cináed's anger short-circuits as concern floods his face. "What is it?"

"Was anyone hurt?" I ask.

In those blurry moments, all I wanted was to gather the skin shorn from Manny's body and put it to rest somewhere safe. Somewhere it couldn't be displayed or purchased by anyone. I wanted to bury it so deep that no one would ever find it again.

And so my unchecked power blew a giant hole in the middle of a crowded marketplace.

I almost wish I could say it wasn't me. I'm terrified to learn I have that potential. Me—the reckless, stupid one who's never been known for making rational decisions.

But it *was* me. I can still feel the energy, the *glamour*, sizzling beneath my soot-covered skin.

Cináed's frown deepens, but he looks confused. "Vera and the horse are fine. Was someone else with you?"

A lightbulb clicks in my head. *Vera didn't tell Cináed about the market.*

As a faerie politician, he might not know it exists—or at least he's likely unaware of its location. Vera's his messenger, but I'm learning she doesn't answer to anyone unless it serves her purposes.

"What did Vera say, exactly?" I ask.

He speaks slowly, as if suspicious. "Only that you fell off the horse as you were riding. She mentioned you hit your head on a rock and would likely not remember anything."

Clever, Vera. Insulting, but clever.

Before I can decide the least destructive way to come clean about the truth, someone knocks on the door.

Cináed sighs and gives me an exasperated look before he says, "You may enter."

A faery I don't recognize opens the door and steps halfway in. He bows to Cináed and nods to me, looking flushed and out of breath.

"Lord Cináed, Her Majesty requests your immediate attendance in the council room."

Cináed faces me so the messenger can't see him silently groan. I offer a sympathetic smile. I get the impression he was expecting this kind of interruption, but that doesn't change how annoying it is.

They both leave—Cináed promising we will continue our conversation soon—and I stare at the painted ceiling while my pounding head tries to sort through this mess.

After a few moments, I convince myself I need a bath and fresh clothes. Maybe then my brain will function.

I drag one leg from the bed. Something crinkles in the pocket of my loose skirt. I dig out a folded paper and open it. Scrawled cursive slants across the page.

You fool. You'd better have a good reason for destroying an entire corner of the market.

Since I know your erratic human feelings will want this information—you injured several, but no one was killed. Faeries who actually know how to use their glamour were there to lessen the damage.

We are both prohibited from ever returning.

And on the doubtful chance that you haven't already told the Wanderer everything, I remind you of your previous offer to help me. Keep your stupid mouth shut.

Bathed and dressed and feeling the tiniest bit less terrible, I emerge from my room.

And see someone standing across the hall, in front of Eimear's door. I recognize his stooped stance from behind. It's the messenger who delivered Orla's letter to Aibreann.

I must have startled him because he jumps back from the door, his hooded eyes darting from me to the empty hallway around us.

On instinct, I reach for my knife even though I know it's gone. I couldn't find it in my clothes, and I'm hoping it's in Imelda's saddlebag.

The male gives a curt nod and makes a hasty departure down the hall. My gaze tracks him until he disappears around the corner.

Strange.

I knock on Eimear's door. Within seconds, Fawn peeks her head out. Her timid eyes brighten when she sees me.

"Lady Róisín," she says in her hushed voice. "I just finished changing Lady Eimear's bedding."

While she speaks, my attention returns to the hallway. I ask Fawn if Eimear is in her room.

"No, my lady. She left this morning and said she would not return until this evening for the celebration of Imbolc."

That word captures my attention. "The winter festival?"

"Aye, my lady. The festival will commence at sundown in the south gardens." She ducks her head and smiles. "I—I have been sewing something for you to wear."

I can't bring myself to return the smile, not when I have no interest in attending the festival. I have plenty to worry about without adding a faerie party to the mix.

"You really didn't have to do that," I say to Fawn as I follow her back into my room.

"But my lady made it quite clear you do not approve of the other gowns." She walks to the rack of dresses and removes one from the end that wasn't there before.

I scan the dress in her arms, battling my guilty conscience. Under other circumstances, I wouldn't let an unwanted gift sway me. I don't need a dress, and I *certainly* don't need another night out.

Fawn must mistake my hesitation because she continues, "It's a wondrous celebration, my lady. With feasting, dancing, divination readings—"

"Divination? Like people who can read your fortune?"

"N-not precisely, my lady. They offer insight on your life's journey." She watches me, holding her breath.

I groan through my teeth. Since last night was such a disaster, I might as well have my cards read or whatever. Between finding clues about the assassins and learning more about my fae parent, I need all the help I can get.

"I'll go." I hold up a hand before Fawn can speak. "But only if you come along."

She hides her blushing smile with her hands, but she nods. I wish Hafwin, Fodla, and Lana were here. I actually enjoyed getting ready for Lughnasa together.

I take the dress from Fawn, admiring the way the blue-sage suede pricks against my fingers when I stroke upward and melts like butter when I smooth it down. Embroidered flowers decorate the two triangles of cloth meant to cover my chest. The skirt will reach the ground, but my shoulders and back will be totally exposed.

"It's beautiful. But I might get cold." I doubt Fawn would let me out the door with my cloak draped over this dress.

Fawn's smile grows at the praise. "Not to worry, my lady. The festival grounds will be as warm as a summer's day."

But of course. Whoever makes the plants grow in winter must now be working to heat the entire garden for the party.

"Well, then, this dress is perfect." To properly thank her, I point to the rack of gowns behind her. "Take your pick and wear it tonight."

"But, my lady . . ."

I step around her and reach for a dusty-rose dress. "Here, try this one on."

Fawn's deep blush returns. "B-but, my lady, I am merely a servant—"

Before she can protest again, I look into her timid eyes, my tone firm but kind as I say, "Look, I'm no one special, and I'm definitely not a lady. You deserve to wear a fancy gown more than I do."

Fawn's wide stare drinks in the sight of the dress like it's the first gift she's ever received. For all I know, maybe it is.

She seems to remember I'm standing there, and she nods at me.

"If it pleases my lady, I am honored to wear it tonight."

I smile, but the expression feels strained and unnatural on my beleaguered face.

Fawn doesn't notice, though. She's beaming and giggling as she scoops up the hem of the dress and steps into the bathroom to try it on.

I sit on the bed, and my aching muscles sigh in thanksgiving. My sore body wants nothing more than to spend the day right here.

But I feel restless, useless. I came to the Otherworld with an agenda, and I have yet to cross anything off the list.

Not that you could get much done cooped up in Caitriona's castle.

But after Imbolc, we will be free to leave. The information I gained last night isn't much, but it's something to start with.

Maybe I can find Cináed at the festival so we can plan. More than anything, he needs to know about Manny. Vera will have to cash in her favor some other time. I can keep a lot to myself, to a fault at times. But not something this important.

I decide to tell him tonight. And to follow him, as his trusted ally, wherever our searching takes us.

{ 29 }

The garden I know so well has been transformed into a starry evening carnival.

Soft, twinkling lights are strung around every tree and shrub and hang in lines above the walkways. Booths and seating areas cluster the paths. The occasional ice sculpture or gurgling fountain parts the constant flow of the crowd like boulders in a stream.

I wait at the edge of the scene, observing the festival from a safe distance. A few paces away, a female faery stands behind a table laden with small glass bottles. Passersby stop to read the labels or to smell the bottles the female opens for them. I can't read the sign hanging above the table, but the bottles remind me of Eimear's herbal tinctures.

Someone waves at Fawn, who's standing beside me, wide eyed and petrified. I don't know why she's so scared. With her thick hair let down and the pink dress fluttering around her like soft petals, she blends in better than I ever could.

The faery waving at her must be an acquaintance. I watch as Fawn takes a deep breath, visibly gathering her courage, and wishes me well before leaving to join her friend.

Ditched in the first five minutes. I don't blame her, of course. We're practically strangers. Besides, I'm not here to socialize.

I enter the garden path and let the current of faeries guide me along. The more I observe the guests, the more I realize that everyone seems to be high fae—nobles with power and money, as Sovereign Eirwen taught me.

From what I can tell, the only "lesser faeries" in attendance are serving food and drinks or working the carnival booths.

My thoughts go to Manny. Would he have been a guest tonight? I try to imagine him meandering through the gardens with everyone else, his minotaur horns reaching two heads taller than the average faery.

I've never seen goblins or furry creatures like Jarlath or Manny within castle walls, let alone acting as members of the High Court.

Soon, the magically heated air feels suffocating. I shove past a group of faeries clustered around a drink table and ignore their shouts of protest as I dart down a smaller, shadowed path.

A circular pool shimmers in the moonlight—which seems brighter without the strings of lights overhead. I sit on the edge of the pool and catch my breath.

"Can I interest the lady in a rune reading?"

Looking up, I notice a single table, warmly illuminated by two torches, nestled between the shrubs. The male who spoke stands behind the table, his sepia-brown skin and bronze cloak glowing in the firelight.

Why is his table isolated from the others?

I clear the emotion from my throat. "That depends. Can you answer specific questions in a reading?"

A brief smile flashes across his face. "That depends."

Intrigued, I stand and approach the table. His simple display lacks the flashy advertising of the other booths. The only thing on the table is a maroon cloth with a white line down the center, and a black drawstring bag the size of my hand.

I keep a pace between myself and the table and meet the male's gaze. His polished skin belongs to a thirty-year-old, and his deep brown eyes remind me of Darren's.

"Well, I'd like a reading," I say.

Humor tugs on his mouth, but his tone holds no mockery. "Wonderful. I will explain the process. Simply hold a question in your mind—no need to share it out loud—and when you are ready, I will toss the sticks onto the line."

He empties the black bag into his hand to show me the polished white sticks, each the length of a finger. "Then I will ask Goddess Brigid, Sovereign of Imbolc, to bestow her wisdom, and will interpret the runes accordingly."

I've been mulling over what to ask all day. Several pressing questions have vied for consideration. But in this moment, all else falls away—like sifting a pebble from the sand—and one thought stands out above all the others.

Who is my fae parent?

I nod to show the reader I'm ready. His large hands—covered in white chalky marks—cup the sticks, and he gives them a couple shakes. His eyes close, and he mumbles something incoherent.

Then, his eyes reopen, and he tosses the sticks onto the table. They clatter as they fall, but nothing else happens.

I glance from the sticks to the reader, but his gaze is trained on the runes. I notice that he only seems interested in the two sticks that fell across the white line in the cloth.

Just when I'm about to break the silence, he leans back on his heels and clicks his tongue.

"Insightful," he says, meeting my eyes. "This is the Luis rune, correlated with the rowan tree and the transition from winter to spring. She aids those who are crossing realms. This rune carries the element of fire, of rebirth, and a warrior spirit. You can stand your ground, knowing you have what you need to complete your journey."

I let the words sink in, trying to hide my disappointment. I was hoping for a simple name—not a vague, feel-good pep talk.

While part of me feels like I got scammed, I mentally store the reader's encouraging words to unpack later.

"So, how do I pay you?" I ask.

Instead of responding, the reader holds up a finger, his face lifted to the sky, his eyes half-lidded.

I look around the empty path, grateful for the seclusion. A year ago, I wouldn't be caught dead in a situation like this. If any of my former friends could see me now . . .

The male clicks his tongue, bringing me back to the present. "There is a second reading for you. Something you must know for your journey."

His hands gather the sticks, and after a single shake, he tosses them onto the table.

The instant they land, the torches on each end of the table are extinguished with a muffled hiss. The reader opens his eyes, and I see my own shock mirrored within them.

I lean in and whisper, "Is that supposed to happen?"

He shakes his head and rolls his shoulders, as if to wriggle free of the strange energy around us—like a bug in a spiderweb.

"In all my time as a seer, that was a first for me," he says with a little laugh. Then, like he's remembering his role, his expression goes somber. He places his hands on the table, staring at the sticks.

All five of the sticks cross the line. But the eerie part is that they're all parallel to each other. I wouldn't believe sticks could assemble themselves with perfect symmetry if I hadn't seen it happen myself. I bite my lip as I wait to hear what this means.

The male's eyes flicker up to me, then back to the sticks. "This rune is Ruis, or the elder tree. It symbolizes courage, transformation, and death." He pauses to glance at me again. "She inspires all to embrace their inner shadow side. Only then can you truly overcome your obstacles."

I don't say anything for several seconds. As if sensing my need for silence, the faery wordlessly goes about lighting the torches while I stare at the ivory sticks. The thought crosses my mind that they might be bones. A shudder trembles down my spine.

"Why are you all the way out here?" I gesture to the secluded, empty space.

The faery gathers the sticks into the bag. “My kind are not embraced by the high fae.” His smile is rueful. “But I prefer to read the runes in a more peaceful setting, so I don’t mind the isolation.”

I frown. “Can I ask what *kind* you are, exactly?” Then I add, in case my question sounds rude, “I’m still learning about all the different types of faeries.”

He smooths the cloth on the table. “The trouble is, I am not a faery. My father was merfolk, my mother human. Thus making me a true fish out of water, as they say.”

While his smile holds, his voice is laced with bitterness. I’m reminded of Vera—banished to the land, unable to return to the sea without her lost skin.

“How did you end up in the Otherworld?” I ask.

“Because of her fragile mortality, I outlived my mother decades ago. The human realm held nothing but grief for me, and I cannot breathe underwater, so I took refuge here.” He shrugs.

I hug my arms to stave off the chill. While the warmth of the festival beckons me, I’m not looking forward to reentering the loud, frenzied crowd. Especially with the reading fresh on my mind.

Without thinking, I remove the gold earrings Fawn picked for me to wear and place them on the table. The half-merman, half-human starts to object, but I wave it off.

“From one outsider to another,” I say, “I hope you find the refuge you’re looking for.”

He nods his head deeply, almost a bow. "Your kindness will not be forgotten, my lady. May Brigid's blessings follow you on your journey."

{ 30 }

Music and laughter embrace me as I return to the main path. I bump into a table glittering with tall champagne glasses and catch one before it topples over. The golden liquid bubbles, smelling refreshing and sweet.

I shrug and down the glass in two gulps, noting the citrus flavor and subtle burn that lingers in my throat. Now that I've had my runes read, I might as well enjoy myself while I wait for the long night to end.

I let the crowd guide me along again, remembering the true potency of fae drinks as my frayed nerves go numb. I stumble from the path, steadying myself against a tree.

"Róisín?"

I lift my head and see Eimear sitting on a cushion on the grass. A couple relaxes on a nearby blanket. Will-ó-the-wisps bob overhead, and lit candles drip white wax onto the ground.

She waves me over to sit on the empty cushion beside her, and I shuffle to the pillow, sitting down without too much effort. I notice the grass around her is littered with open books and scrolls. *She's seriously doing homework at a party?*

"Is this your first time drinking faerie wine?" Eimear eyes me like I might fall off the pillow.

"No," I say, willing my body to stop rocking back and forth.

"Then I won't waste my pity on you." Eimear lifts the top of a scroll and rolls it up. "You should have known better."

"What, so you don't drink?"

She tucks the scroll into her satchel and gathers her books. "I do. But the wine is easier on faeries."

"Well, I'm half-fae," I blurt. "That's got to count for something."

"Good to hear there's one thing you're being honest about."

I rest my head between my knees and sigh. Of course—she's upset I played hooky last night and she had to tell Cináed. I knocked on her door several times to apologize, but she was gone all day.

I lift my head and meet her flaming blue eyes. "I suck. Tell me what to do to make it up to you."

Eimear's stare flickers with mischief. "Alright, then. Tell me why you never sleep."

She got you there.

I rub a hand over my face. "The short answer? Nightmares."

She smooths the hem of her sunflower-yellow gown. I've never seen her dressed this nicely. Fawn must have helped her too.

"And the long answer?" she asks.

I stare at a candle's dancing flame. I've never confessed this to anyone. "After the summer games, I thought I'd escaped the Otherworld for good. Darren moved on—he can cope as a human with the Sight. But no matter how hard I tried, I"—I shake my head—"I don't think I ever really left the Otherworld. In dreams, I'm forced to relive the worst moments."

"With Naoise," Eimear says.

I nod and hug my knees closer.

"Is that what you dreamt at the sacred well?"

Her question takes me aback. I swallow and look up. I sense the time to keep that dream private has come to an end.

"No, that wasn't a nightmare. I think . . . I think it was a dream of my mother." The last word snags in my throat.

"Oh." True surprise widens her eyes. "Have you had dreams of her before?"

"Never."

I can't imagine what this dream would have meant to me as a child—before I gave up on my parents ever returning.

After a moment, Eimear shifts forward and places a hand on my knee. "As a druid, part of my studies includes dream interpretation. I am happy to help however I can."

The sincerity in her face moves me, and I blink back fresh tears. "Why? I hardly deserve it."

She owes me nothing. Her loyalty is to Cináed, and as far as I know, he hasn't assigned her to be nice to me.

She rises to her feet and offers her hand. "Friends fight for each other."

I look at her freckled fingers and wipe my eyes. Then I take her hand and stand beside her.

"Have you tried the lemon pastries?" she asks.

I shake my head. "Are they as good as the chocolate ones?"

She grins. "Better. Come on—I saw a tray of them near the fire dancers."

Eimear and I make our way around the festival, trying snacks and watching the performers. My full stomach bulges, and my head feels light with winter air and cheerful music and the effects of the wine.

I stop trying to track the time. Partly because I get the sense that glamour is sustaining the full moon's steady position in the sky. Partly because I find I'm enjoying myself more than I thought possible.

The only other festival I've attended was Lughnasa, the summer feast. Naoise's presence pollutes most of those memories. Plus, the celebration kickoff ended in chaos and bloodshed—when Cináed's band of performers was punished for speaking out about Princess Aisling's long-lost child. The heir of the high throne.

Looking back, I remember how Orla disappeared during the performance. Not five minutes later, the guards showed up and killed the narrator of the play in front of the audience.

I'm pulled from my thoughts by someone calling my name. Eimear has wandered ahead of me in the crowd. But the voice is coming from behind me.

I turn and find Fawn rushing toward me, blushing more than ever. The panic in her eyes grounds me, and I leave the main path to meet her halfway, beside a giant shrub shaped like a dolphin.

The pink ruffles on her dress tremble along with her entire frame. I steady her arm with a firm hand. My one glass of wine has worn off into a gentle buzz, and it's nice to have my senses alert again.

"What is it, Fawn?"

Her lips pucker like a fish until she finds her voice. "I—I was summoned by the q-queen herself, my lady. She—she demands you join her at once."

My mouth pops open. Now it's my turn to be speechless.

"My lady?" Fawn trembles harder. "Oh, please say yes, my lady."

I understand now that I'm to blame for Fawn's panic. She's terrified I'll ignore Caitriona's demands and that she will have to relay that news to the queen.

And it's for this reason—even more than my baffled curiosity—that I smile at Fawn and ask, "Will you take me to her?"

Relief softens her face, and she nods until I think her earrings will fall off. She guides me down a trail toward the castle. I hear a shift in music as we leave the fast-paced drums and flutes behind, trading it for an elegant blend of harp strings.

A secluded clearing appears between tall hedges. Overhead, cherry trees are in full bloom. But a long table set with fine dishware and silver bowls of food steals my attention. Not because of the decadent food—I'm too full to eat another bite.

It's because Caitriona is sitting at the head of the table. And when she notices me, she waves me over with a pleasant smile.

My muddy boots—hidden beneath the floor-length dress—carry me past the couple dozen dinner guests toward Caitriona. One by one, the faeries fall silent as they turn to stare at me.

Their collective attention makes me squirm. But what's worse is when I spot Cináed, sitting at the queen's side. His perplexed, wary expression tells me he's just as clueless.

Which I take as a clear warning to be extra careful.

I reach Caitriona's seat—a plush, high-backed chair the size of a throne—and offer a small curtsy.

Her bright eyes twinkle up at me beneath long lashes. Sparkling blush adorns her eyelids and apple cheeks, and pink butterfly clips nestle within her full curls.

One of the butterflies closes and reopens its perfect wings. *They're not clips, then.*

"Róisín the Shadowslayer," Caitriona purrs in her boisterous voice. "So glad you could join us."

I have to stop my mouth from popping open a second time. *Did she just call me* Shadowslayer*?*

Caitriona turns her shimmering face toward the rest of the table. "Several of my guests asked about you, and I grew tired of convincing them you're really here."

Her gaze scans the audience, her tone sprinkled with playful reprimand. "Take heed, doubters, and be jealous that your festivities have yet to entice the Shadowslayer."

I catch myself before I visibly cringe. The way she says it—*Shadowslayer*—makes me hate it all the more.

I glance at Cináed. He's silent and still, watching me like a golden lion—all his previous concern crushed under the weight of his intense, acute observance.

He hasn't looked at me like that since last summer.

I stare at the ground and try to ignore the hot embers in my core—sparking and spitting back to life against my will.

An unfamiliar male with a trimmed beard and a handsome smile addresses me. "It is a true pleasure to meet the legendary heroine." His smile grows. "And what a relief to know our dear Caitriona is still reigning queen of hosting the most reputable guests in the Otherworld."

Caitriona's full lips pinch in a coy smile. "Much to your dismay, Lord Kallen."

The guests laugh, and someone makes a toast to the queen's fine taste, or something like that. I'm not listening anymore.

I made an appearance for Fawn's sake. As a result, my ridiculous title was used to bolster Caitriona's reputation and feed her ego. She didn't care about me until tonight, when my presence served her needs.

My legs ache to carry me as far from here as possible. I lean forward in my boots and take a fist of skirt in my hand, poised to make a wild getaway through the trees.

Just imagining the reaction of shock and disapproval around the table makes my lips twitch in a tiny smirk. They wouldn't think I'm such a reputable guest after *that*.

But my ears tune back into the ongoing conversation, and I hesitate.

Princess Aibreann faces the other side of the table a few chairs from where I'm standing. Her polished demeanor seems to be cracking as she responds in a tense voice to an older female across from her.

"Correct me, but it sounds as if you would deposit *our most valuable warriors* at the southern castle's gates."

"You are correct, Majesty. Their advisors have asked for our support." The female's gaze shifts, as if searching for someone to back her up.

But Aibreann's tongue moves faster. "And support them we shall, but at a manageable cost. To send our finest warriors leaves the northern kingdom vulnerable."

It's clear from the strained silence around the table that a lot is being left unsaid. I expect Caitriona—the perfect hostess—to intervene and reroute the conversation. But when I look at her, I realize she's distracted.

By Cináed.

The intoxicated queen is pressing herself as close to Cináed as she can without sitting in his lap. And Cináed, face flaming, is evading her as well as he can at a crowded dinner table.

We share a brief glance. Torn between laughing and gagging, I settle for a sympathetic frown.

Lord Kallen's broad smile wanes. "I think what Lady Isla means is that our focus is serving the high throne. And if all we can do is send our small army, we are obligated and honored to do so."

Aibreann turns to Kallen, allowing me to see her face for the first time. The full force of her burning lavender eyes makes Kallen shift in his seat. Venom drips from her pink lips as she says, “Pretty words do not mask resentment, Lord Kallen.”

She stares down everyone brave enough to meet her gaze. “I will not take the high throne, and neither shall the prince. Our prime focus will always be the *northern* kingdom. And it is in your best interest to agree before I’m forced to see your opinions as treason.”

My eyes widen, and I resist the urge to applaud. Aibreann wasn’t lying when she said she appreciates unladylike behavior.

The silence lasts three breaths. Then Cináed shoots to his feet, forcing Caitriona’s lingering advances to an abrupt halt.

“A toast!” he says, lifting his glass. “To Princess Aibreann, future queen of the northern kingdom.”

Like obedient children, the other guests scramble to stand and raise their glasses to the princess. Her face is hidden from me, but her chin is held high, posture unflinching.

I commend her choice, but I can’t help thinking what a good fit she’d be for the high throne.

I steal Caitriona’s empty glass from the table—the queen has dozed off in her chair—and lift it up.

“Cheers to Aibreann.”

{ 31 }

As the dinner party disperses, Caitriona wakes up enough to bid the guests farewell, blowing kisses and bestowing blessings of safe travel.

I sink into the now-empty chair across from Cináed. We need to talk, and this seems like the perfect time to sneak him away from the queen.

But as I open my mouth, a messenger approaches the queen with a note. It's the same messenger who delivered Orla's letter and who I caught standing outside Eimear's room.

He bows and offers the letter to Caitriona, and after a nudge from Cináed, the queen notices and snatches the paper between two glittering nails.

"Enough messages!" she screeches. "Can I not have a single night of uninterrupted celebration?"

The messenger looks startled, unsure if he should respond. Aibreann turns from saying farewell to a guest and dismisses the messenger.

The male bows again and catches my eye on his way from the clearing. I resist the instinct to flinch away from the darkness I find in his stare.

"Oh, Mother." Aibreann sighs as she takes the unopened message from Caitriona, who has been using it to fan her flushed face.

The queen doesn't seem to notice or care—she's resumed the art of making eyes at Cináed, whose chair has been moved just out of her reach.

By now, we are the only ones left at the table. I watch Aibreann's face as she reads the letter. Her eyes widen, then narrow to slits. She hands the paper to me.

"Read this, both of you. I may not be queen yet, but I can delay your arrest if you leave at once."

Cináed stands with a frown and walks toward us, making a wide circle around Caitriona's chair. "Arrest? What the hell are you talking about?"

Aibreann gestures to the letter. Her snippy tone doesn't match the concern in her lavender eyes. "Do not speak to me as if I'm the enemy. Read the decree."

I hold the paper up to a candlestick and scan the message. Cináed leans close, reading over my shoulder.

To Her Majesty, Queen Caitriona of the northern kingdom, and her loyal subjects,

The individuals named below are traitors and criminals of the most dangerous nature. Do not house or protect them, lest your name be associated with theirs. If they are spotted, contact the royal guard—defenders of the high throne—immediately.

Cináed the Wanderer

Róisín the Shadowslayer

Eimear of the Northern Isles

You have been warned.

Cináed straightens. His expression flickers from dazed to outraged. "This decree is unfounded. It has no authority without the high throne's seal."

My voice is quiet as I stare at the letter, trying to make it make sense. "Does that matter? There isn't anyone on the high throne."

Cináed snatches the paper from my hand and holds it to the flame. His voice is tight. "This is unbelievable. The council knows of my unfailing loyalty to the crown."

"Your character is not in question, Cináed," Aibreann retorts, already crossing the empty clearing, her hip-length hair bouncing behind her like a golden cape. "Your enemies want to end you—innocence be damned. Now, leave before it is too late."

I sprint to the stables, unable to gulp in air fast enough to feed my burning lungs.

When I stumble through the open door, I see the groom sitting beneath a single torch, mending a halter.

He looks up, and his eyebrows arch. Probably startled at the sight of a frazzled girl in a gown storming in here in the deep-blue hours of early morning.

I manage to speak between panting breaths. "Three horses. Saddled. Now."

He nods and sets aside the halter. I point out Imelda and Muira, and also Cináed's horse—the forest-green mare I would recognize anywhere. Without a word, the groom gets to work saddling the horses.

I help myself to the saddlebag hanging on Imelda's stall door. My knife is here after all, but I'm too terrified to feel relief.

Cináed told me to prepare the horses while he finds Eimear. We have to get away before word spreads. Who knows who else was given a similar note by that sneaky messenger.

Aibreann is right—the authenticity of the note doesn't matter. There are those who would leap at the chance to arrest Cináed and thwart his search for the heir. Sometimes I think he's the only one standing between the high throne and a mob of Naoise-esque monsters thirsting for power.

Each second that passes is pure agony. I keep my hands busy by strapping rolled blankets and tarps to the saddles. But no amount of distraction prevents my mind from imagining the worst.

That Cináed and Eimear will be caught before they make it here.

Caitriona might ignore an order from the southern kingdom. But I get the sense that Lord Kellan and Lady Isla speak for the majority of nobles who obey the high throne always.

"The horses are ready, my lady."

The groom's voice makes me jump. I turn from the open doorway and stare at my half-dressed body, wondering how I'll pay him. I already gave away the only jewelry I allowed Fawn to put on me.

Bending over, I take a fist of skirt and tear the hem off my dress, where the sage-blue material is heavy with an embroidered design. Knowing the fae, every thread is pure gold and sure to be valuable.

When I toss it at the groom, he catches it in one hand, his eyebrows lifting again.

"To pay you for your help." I give him a pointed look. "As well as your silence."

He bows his head, seemingly astounded. "Aye, my lady. You have my discretion."

He leaves the stables with the end of my dress tucked in his pocket. I use an empty bucket to extinguish the torch, and the stable is cast in shadow. Each of our horses stands tied to the outside of their stalls. There is nothing to do now but wait.

I grip my knife and press my back against the wall beside the open door. I've counted to one hundred and seventy-three when my pulsing ears hear footsteps.

Please be them.

The feet stop short of the doorway. Then a pair of boots appears, followed by the rest of Cináed's cloaked body. Behind him, I catch a glimpse of Eimear's glowing eyes.

I step from the shadows. I'm so relieved that I want to throw my arms around them. But my sudden movement startles Cináed. In a breathless moment, he swings me around and pins me to the wall.

The motion knocks the wind from my lungs. Our eyes are inches apart, and I see the recognition transform his fear to relief. His arms swallow me in a brief but warm embrace.

When he lets go, I'm coughing too much to speak. So I gesture to the horses.

Cináed hurries to untie them, and Eimear removes my wool cloak from her satchel.

"Thought you might need this."

I left it in my room before the festival. "How did you—"

"I'll explain later." She squeezes my arm and finds her horse.

Together, the three of us exit from the other end of the stables and urge the horses into a trot down one of the trails leading away from the castle.

The moon has finally been freed to travel the sky, inviting a peach-cream dawn to warm the cold outline of trees and hilly terrain.

I hug my cloak around me and look ahead at Cináed and Eimear. A sudden rush of gratitude startles me. It surpasses the fear and anger I've been feeding ever since I read my name on that wanted poster.

We might be faerie fugitives, but I want no one else at my side.

{ 32 }

We ride until high noon, keeping to the coastline between sandy hills covered in long, yellow grass, and the dense forest that snakes through the middle of the northern kingdom.

When we stop to let the horses drink from a freshwater stream, I slide to the ground and stretch my muscles.

Ever since Mouth of the Beast, my body aches in ways it never has before. I assume it's a result of expending so much glamour in one go. I didn't use it up, though. That night taught me my glamour potential is limitless.

But I'm so tired. I feel like my insides are painted in bruises that only time can heal.

I watch Cináed pull something from his saddlebag. He hasn't spoken more than a few words since we left. None of us have.

We're still in disbelief. *Who would condemn us?*

"Where are we going?" I ask no one in particular.

Eimear is speaking in low tones to her horse.

Cináed answers me as he crouches by the stream to refill our water pouches. "To Rauri's castle." Then he adds with a quick glance in my direction. "We will journey near a portal on the way. Whether you choose to cross into the human realm or continue on with us, do not make the decision lightly. Either way, I cannot promise your safety."

I swallow the sour bile in my throat and pace beside Imelda. “Those can’t be our only options. Is there no way to figure out what’s going on without knocking on the castle doors?”

Eimear pipes in, her tone somber. “I sensed a dark presence lurking in the castle. Which is why I dedicated the day before Imbolc to divination and simple spells to gain clarity.” She shakes her head, her voice catching. “And still, I failed to see this coming.”

Her face disappears into Muira’s neck. Cináed stands and crosses the distance to us.

“We know next to nothing about these threats, and that is not a reflection on any of us.” He places a hand on Eimear’s arm, offering her a leather pouch dripping with water. “Whoever is behind this has hidden from view beneath an army of ants.”

My pulse quickens as I imagine shoving a stick of dynamite into an anthill and watching the whole thing blow up.

Eimear angrily wipes her eyes with her sleeve before accepting the water. Cináed approaches me with the pouch.

I remember his lion’s stare from last night. It warned me that the ridge between us isn’t as impassable as I thought. Which means I need to be more careful.

I reach to take the water pouch before he can get too close.

With the world crashing around us, we need to be diligent. Bonded by our shared endgame—to punish the spineless monster behind these attacks. Our enemy has made it clear they won’t stop until the three of us are dead.

On top of that, my explosion at the market has made me realize I need to take control of the vehicle that is my life. To stop waiting for others to offer me answers. Right now, I need my line of sight to be clearer than ever. And my emotions . . .

Well, they fog up the car windows.

We stop to camp in a shallow valley where a quiet, half-frozen river eases through tufts of grass and boulders decorated in lichen.

A cluster of evergreen trees hides us from view, and dead leaves and pine needles soften the ground we'll be sleeping on tonight.

The fading glow of the sunset brightens the sky enough to see by, but in less than an hour the land will be cloaked in darkness. So I get to work helping Eimear unroll our tarps and blankets. According to Cináed, we're still too close to the northern castle to light a fire, so we'll all be sleeping side by side for warmth.

He goes to find something for us to eat while Eimear and I make sure the horses are tied within reach of edible grass, without being visible to anyone searching for us.

I try not to think about whoever might be following us, but any movement or sudden sound from the landscape makes me jump in my skin.

I should have trusted my instinct about the messenger. And now it's too late. No doubt he's escaped the castle and informed his employer that we're trying to run.

And what about the queen? The princess believed we weren't guilty, but what if they get bombarded with false evidence against us?

Eimear murmurs something to her horse as she scratches its neck. Imelda snorts and nudges my arm as if insisting she deserves the same treatment. I smile and pat her coat, matted with sweat and dirt from our ride.

I ask Eimear, "Is now a good time to ask how you knew to grab my cloak and fresh clothes from the castle?"

During our last water break, I changed into the flexible cotton dress Eimear had brought for me. Traveling for days in the torn blue-sage gown would have been so uncomfortable. And miserably cold.

Eimear hands me a brush, and we both comb the grime from the horses.

"After we split up at the festival, I saw three geese fly overhead. I sensed it was an omen that the three of us would be traveling soon. So I returned to the castle and gathered a few things. Cináed found me soon after."

Her matter-of-fact explanation amazes me. What would it be like to have her connection to nature?

Curious about Eimear's upbringing, I ask, "Are the Northern Isles far from here?"

"Two days' ride, then you pay for a raft or boat to cross the inlet. Why?"

"That's where you're from, right?"

"It was my home, but no longer."

The tension in her stance and tone warns me to tread carefully. "How long has it been since you left?"

"Thirteen years." The response is immediate, like she's kept track. Before I can press for more information, she says tersely, "Look, Róisín, I have a lot on my mind. The last thing I wish to be reminded of right now is my past."

I back off. "Yeah, of course."

Cináed's appearance through the dark trees steals my attention. His finger hooks through the gills of a dead fish. I have no idea how he caught it. He left his spear with us.

"I'd like to inspect our surroundings a bit more before we try to sleep," he says, sounding as tired as I feel. "Would you join me, Róisín?"

His luminous green eyes hold my gaze as I battle between a handful of responses, none of which are ideal.

"Um, sure," I say at last.

No big deal. I've proven I can handle being alone with him.

Eimear takes the fish from Cináed's hand and mutters something about preparing supper. I make a note to smooth things over in the morning, doubting anything I could say now would help. If she'd tried to pry into my past tonight—after the long, stressful day we've had—I would have been annoyed too.

Darkness has taken hold of the valley, transforming the peaceful river and rocky hills into a scene shrouded in moonlight.

I pull on my hood to protect my stinging ears from the wind. We crest a jagged slope. Cináed leads as we serpentine through the rocks and shrubs. I can't tell if he wants to talk or not, and since I guessed wrong with Eimear, I decide to stay silent and let him speak first.

After a few minutes of walking, he stops and points at a bend in the river up ahead. “I think this spot is shallow enough for the horses to ford tomorrow.”

I nod and rub my hands together. I hope this sudden drop in temperature is from our proximity to the river. Otherwise, sleeping without a fire will be impossible.

Cináed looks at my hands, then at my face. I see him work something over in his mind, and his sudden seriousness makes me tense.

Distance, you idiot! Distance!

But my muscles ignore me, and I don’t move. Then, in a way that’s both soft and deliberate, Cináed lifts my hands to his mouth. I stare at him as he blows hot air onto my aching fingers. A touch of honey and wildflowers fills my nose—his very breath carrying with it the essence of summertime.

When he lowers my hands, he asks, “Better?”

I swallow. “Better.”

He releases me and continues walking. The place where his lips brushed my palm pulses like a tiny heartbeat. I shake my head and take a deep breath before following.

“The portal is not far from here,” he says after a moment.

I know he wants me to understand that I have options, that I’m not forced to stay. And after everything that’s happened with the fae—and even my life in foster care—his concern means a lot. My desires have often gone ignored, and I tend to get myself into trouble just to be heard.

Cináed got a taste of my old habits last summer. I felt trapped by the games, by Naoise, and it reawakened a wildness in me.

But the longer I'm here, the more I realize my wildness isn't an issue. In fact, it has saved me in many ways—not just from Naoise, but from human demons throughout my childhood. When the weakest parts of me have cowered in fear, my wildness has given me the courage to fight back.

If I had a dollar to my name, I'd bet the Otherworld is as good a place as any to strengthen my relationship with my wild side.

My response to Cináed is resolute. "I'm not interested in crossing through the portal. I'm coming to the southern castle."

He stops and turns, searching my eyes. When he seems to find whatever he was looking for, his wary frown pulls into a dimpled, sidelong smile. It hits me that I haven't seen him smile so genuinely in ages.

For a moment, I let myself imagine his warm lips lowering to mine, kissing me with longing and fervor the way he has before. I can taste the golden drops of sunshine the kiss would leave on my tongue.

He points at something behind me. "Look, Róisín."

I turn around . . . and suck in a breath of wonder.

The entire sky is blanketed by gray clouds, but a pocket has opened up in the curtain, revealing an ethereal display of stars. They seem to swirl and dance like fireflies against a midnight stream. I swear if I stood on my tiptoes, I could snatch one of the burning orbs straight from the heavens.

"It's beautiful," I whisper.

"It is."

His voice is closer than before, and when I turn to look at him, our cheeks nearly brush. I see him glance at my mouth, but this time I'm the one to step back.

To shift us away from what just happened—or more like what *didn't* happen—I broach the truth I've been needing to tell him.

"Cináed, there's something you should know about the night Vera and I were missing."

His frown returns, and he waits for me to continue.

I shudder and blurt it out like I'm tearing the bandage from a fresh wound, "I found a part of Manny—his . . . his fur."

Every drop of blood drains from his face. His voice is barely audible. "Are you certain?"

My mouth moves and words come, but like the day I learned this godless news, my mind has retreated far, far from here.

"A fur trader was selling it. He said it was a minotaur pelt. But I—I didn't believe it till I saw the braid. The small one Manny had on his neck."

Cináed clutches his mouth and moans.

I step toward him, thinking he'll either pass out or vomit. Instead, he stares off into the distance, shaking his head in horror.

Standing witness to Cináed's crushed heart is unbearable. I do what I can to combat the feeling of uselessness and rage storming inside me before it leads to another crater in the ground.

It takes three long breaths to stop my vision from spotting. Then I touch Cináed's arm and wait until he looks at me, green eyes shimmering.

My voice is colder than stone. "Whatever it takes, we're going to find these bastards. And we're going to end them."

Cináed and I share a steely gaze for several seconds.

"That we shall," he says at last.

{ 33 }

All growing up, I rarely left the house without my backpack full of emergency supplies.

But that stopped the night Darren got snatched by the shadow demon, the Sluagh. When I chased my brother down, I left my pack behind. We set sail for the Otherworld hours later with nothing but the clothes we were wearing.

It's ironic, really. For years, I carried a pack with provisions that I rarely used. And when I needed those supplies most, I didn't have them.

Now I'm journeying again with next to nothing, living day to day. The Otherworld has taught me—often through cruel lessons—that I am more than the tools I carry in a backpack.

After another long day of riding, we find a secluded glen in the late afternoon and prepare to make dinner. We haven't been able to light a fire until now, and my mouth waters at the thought of eating a hot meal.

Cináed strides over to me, handing me a brimming water pouch. "Here, Róisín. You did not drink enough today."

I obey while Cináed muses, "We are likely being followed. But all the same, I relish putting distance between us and that suffocating castle."

Eimear smirks. "No wonder, since Caitriona made you her constant companion. Tell me, did that include sharing more than dinner conversation?"

I choke on a gulp of water, spewing half of it out my nose. I expect Cináed to turn red or get angry. But his tone is neutral, his hands occupied with retying the saddlebag.

"I've journeyed the world over, and yet I never witnessed anything so dreadful as Caitriona attempting to seduce someone."

Eimear shrieks and doubles over, laughing so hard she slips and lands in a snowbank. I have to sit down, tears pricking my eyes, holding my aching stomach muscles.

Cináed chuckles as he goes to help Eimear. But when they link hands, her foot gets caught on a root, and she takes Cináed down with her into the pile of snow.

When they emerge, Cináed locks playful eyes on me. I squeal, sensing his next move. I scramble backward on my hands as he crawls toward me.

By the time my fumbling feet push me upright so I can run, Cináed swoops me into his arms. I scream and kick as he carries me with little effort to the snowbank and drops me in the deep end. I plunge into the powdery snow.

My head pops out. "You're gonna get it," I holler at him.

He's laughing too hard to form a response.

Then I see Eimear beside me, sitting waist deep in snow, grinning wickedly.

"Eimear no," I say, using my hands to shield my face, "no, no, you're on my team! Girls against boy—"

A thick clump of snow pelts me right in my open mouth. Eimear's bright laughter sounds like a horse's whinny. I spit the snow out and leap onto her.

The two of us brawl until we realize Cináed has disappeared. A bubble of panic overtakes my throat as my eyes scan the empty campsite. *Did something take him?*

A little whistle brings our attention to the tree overhead.

Specifically to the golden-haired faery perched on a branch, suspending a huge snowball between his hands.

Eimear gasps. “He wouldn’t dare.”

But we both know better.

I stretch one arm up before the snowball hits. It coats our hair and faces in soft powder. Eimear and I look at each other, and I burst out laughing at the sight of her—hair slick, face dripping, mouth wide—because I know I must look the same way.

And in this moment—throwing snow and trying to catch my breath—I feel swallowed up in an unbelievable, otherworldly happiness.

For the next four days, we ride by daylight and camp near streams at dusk. Sleeping in the cold doesn’t bother me like I thought it would.

Each morning, I open my eyes and stare at the soft sunlight warming my cocoon of wool blankets that tickle and scratch my face and wrists. When I emerge, I inhale the fresh scent of the forest—pine, frozen soil, a blend of complex aromas I can’t begin to pick apart and describe.

And each morning, Cináed is already awake, preparing a small breakfast for us over the coals from the previous night's fire.

He brews tea with the herbs Eimear collects, and we satisfy our stomachs with roots, berries, and an occasional hare or bird.

Cináed always skins and guts the animals away from camp, and then he carries the carcass, covered with a large leaf, to Eimear. She places her hands on the leaf, closes her eyes, and murmurs some sort of prayer. Then and only then does Cináed cook the meat.

On the second night of this routine, I ask Eimear what it means. Her gaze follows the rotating meat on the makeshift spit.

"Do you know what it means to be a druid?"

I bite my lip. *That you make potions and talk to nature?* "No."

"It means I have a solemn responsibility to protect and honor this land. I use my abilities to serve everything Goddess Dea has created."

I nod to show I get how big of a deal Dea is, and Eimear continues.

"The Tuatha, the fae, have many gods. We honor them, and all living things, through our festivals, rituals, and prayer."

I didn't have a reason to care about God until foster home #5 taught me I needed to pray for forgiveness or I'd be cast into hell. But sitting here beside Eimear, hearing her low mumblings as she gives thanks for a rabbit's life, I remember the prayer I offered in the cemetery—at Branna of the Harp's grave. Only later did I learn Branna was Cináed's lover. The prayer surfaced in a moment of panic, rising from a forgotten place inside me. Darren thinks I learned it from our parents as a child.

The first words of the prayer take form in my mind. I get up and walk toward the horses, feeling strange and jittery. I want this unexpected energy from my past to leave me alone.

But another part of me wonders—if I embrace the discomfort, will it unleash the suppressed memories of my first seven years of childhood?

I pet Imelda's neck as her pink lips nibble at me. *The same pale pink of Darren's toes as a baby.*

I shake my head, startled at the sudden image of my brother's infant feet, eye level and standing inside a tall, sky-blue crib.

That's how I know it's a memory from before our parents left. After that, Darren slept in a white crib.

A soothing voice undergirds the memory, but I can't see who's speaking. Still, I've never remembered something from those years so clearly.

I rest a hand against the horse's shoulder to steady myself. My ears ring as I blink against the blurred edges of my vision. My sense of control, my grip on reality, wavers.

Those are symptoms of my anxiety, of the panic attacks I experience. But the suffocating dread that usually wraps around my lungs is absent. And in its place, I feel a rush of anticipation.

"Róisín?"

Cináed appears behind me and turns me around. His arms encircle me, more secure than the walls of any castle.

The urgent whisperings of the memory fade as I breathe in Cináed's familiar scent and relax into his chest. When he pulls away to look at me, the jitters have quieted.

"Are you alright?" He cups my chin, his fervent gaze shifting between my eyes.

"Y—yeah." I lick my dry lips and take a step back. "Just lightheaded."

And experiencing sudden, vivid flashbacks.

His mouth is a thin line, his eyes a dark sea-blue. "It is my fault. I pushed for us to travel at an unsustainable pace, and you are not getting the rest you need."

"I'm sleeping better than I have in weeks." I don't know if it's my confession to Eimear or all this fresh air. But I haven't had a nightmare since we left the northern castle.

Cináed's concerned expression softens, and his eyes sparkle. "Well, I had us stop a bit early today, anyway. There is something I wish to show you."

At his insistence, I mount his horse and wait while he settles in the saddle behind me. For a fleeting instant, I'm reminded of riding in front of Naoise on his black horse.

I shudder, and Cináed must mistake it for a shiver because he winds an arm around my middle, wrapping me in the long tails of his cloak.

So much for distance.

We don't speak as he clicks his tongue and the horse starts forward, navigating over rocks and roots. Frost-kissed trees shroud us in soft blue shadow, and the whole world is blanketed in the hushed silence of hibernating animals and the promise of snowfall.

I duck under a low-hanging branch, and Cináed's face rests against mine as he follows my lead. When the branch passes, I sit upright. I might have caved to the idea of letting him hold me, in this practical sense, but I try not to relish it too much.

"What exactly are you showing me?" I ask.

A branch snaps, and both our heads turn. A tuft of brown fur darts across a bough and disappears around a tree trunk.

"Only a squirrel," Cináed says, patting my leg to reassure me. But I feel his chest loosen in a sigh.

Considering our enchanting surroundings, it might seem silly that a squirrel could make our hearts skip a beat. But both of us know we have every reason to be on guard.

"To answer your question," Cináed begins, shifting us forward in the saddle before the horse bounds over a rotting log, "you will simply have to wait and see."

I frown and preoccupy myself with scouring the scenery for potential threats.

After about fifteen minutes, Cináed makes a sound, and the horse settles, snorting a cloud into the early evening air.

Cináed dismounts and pats the horse's neck. "Good girl," he murmurs to her. Then he says to me, "We will continue on foot—the path ahead is too treacherous."

I remember the first time I saw Cináed's horse. They had entered the horse race because Cináed wanted to help Sona and me win. And we still managed to lose.

Looking back, nothing but years of training could have earned me that victory. A truth that was impossible for my thick skull to comprehend at the time.

"What's your horse's name?" I ask.

"Glasraí."

I slide from the saddle and stroke my fingers through the mare's dark mane. "What does it mean?"

"Green vegetables."

I stare at Cináed, waiting for him to admit he's joking. When he circles around Glasraí and motions for me to follow, I can't help the laughter that bubbles up in my throat. Cináed glances back at me, looking confused as he pauses between two boulders on the sharp incline.

"You named your horse Green Vegetables?" I exclaim. "What, was Broccoli already taken?"

He furrows his brow and extends his hand down to me. "I don't care how well you are sleeping—you clearly need more rest."

I stomp up the hill toward him, still chuckling. "Don't play coy with me. I know you well enough to tell when you're trying to tease me."

He turns and continues walking. "We will see how well you know me after this."

My boots falter, and my face grows hot. "What the hell is that supposed to mean?"

But he doesn't answer, and I jog to catch up, mind whirring.

Please don't do something romantic. And, for the love of everything, don't take me to another holy well.

We hike the remainder of the slope, and Cináed tells me to stop and rest a moment. He takes in the thickening trees and large rocks around us, and I use his distraction to observe him the way I rarely give myself the liberty to do.

I've never met anyone with a more expressive face. But in this moment, it's not his expression that captivates me. It's the lack of one. No creases line his forehead or pinch his eyes. The corners of his mouth sag just slightly, but not in a frown. It's like the weight of his full lips makes them bend into the softest, most supple little arc.

I feel like I'm seeing the real Cináed, the person beneath his bright, intense energy. And the sight of it hurts in a beautiful kind of way.

Cináed ushers me back to earth again. "Close your eyes, Róisín."

"Why?"

His dimple appears as he looks at me. "Forget to be stubborn, and indulge me, please."

I scowl at him, but I obey. His warm fingers intertwine with mine as he leads me along.

After about a minute, a strong floral smell fills my lungs. I almost peek, but I know how disappointed Cináed would be if my impatience ruined this. He stops and lets me go, and I hate how sad my hand feels.

I can hear the excitement in his voice as he says, "Alright, open your eyes."

I blink at the sunlight reflecting off the . . . *the sea of flowers*. I gasp, and again my senses are invaded by the heady smell permeating the air.

Tiny winged creatures flitter around us and perch on the blossoms. I can almost hear Darren's dictionary voice in my mind, explaining this species of pixie, or whatever they're called.

The warm temperature makes it seem like this periwinkle-blue meadow was stolen from spring and placed in this harsh winter wonderland just for us.

"Wow," I whisper.

Cináed watches me, his lips melting into a perfect smile. "I told you once that the Otherworld is full of more wonders than you could imagine." The smile fades again, and he looks away. "That promise went unfulfilled at Lughnasa. But no longer."

He steps into the thick carpet of bright petals. I tiptoe along, not wanting to crush the delicate blossoms with my boots.

But one glance behind us quells my worry. Not a single stem is smashed. No flowers are bruised. We might as well be clouds, and our passing shadows are the only evidence we were ever here at all.

"I want to show you the Otherworld as I wish it to be," he says. "How I hope it to be once again, if enough of us are willing to do our part."

I remember the castle guards who swore their loyalty to Cináed, even when Naoise was the prospective king. The crew members who sacrificed their lives for the cause of their captain. The way Caitriona, a *queen*, made a fool of herself to get Cináed's attention.

"You have more people who believe in you, and in your dream, than you might think." I hesitate, then ask, "Is it true the High Court wants you to be the next king?"

His shoulders droop. "Caitriona and some of her court have been encouraging the idea. But there are far fewer supporters of me as high king than she likes to admit."

"And what do *you* want?" I ask. Eimear told me already, but I want to hear it from him.

He shrugs and tucks his hands in his pockets. "I want what's best for the Otherworld and for the fae. And I still believe a rightful heir exists out there. Someone who shares the same bloodline as King Rauri."

"But we know Aibreann and Padraic don't want it."

"And I respect their decision." His lips tighten. "But they aren't the only viable heirs."

I restrain myself before I roll my eyes. "Aren't you worried all this waiting is putting the kingdom at risk?"

Frustration colors his tone. "And electing a corrupt leader won't put us in jeopardy?"

I take a deep, floral-sweet breath through my nose. "You say that anyone who isn't Rauri's kin will be corrupt. But by holding out for someone who might not even exist, I think you're allowing the thing you fear most to happen. Leaving the throne empty invites power-hungry wolves to come hunting."

"Like Naoise."

The name stops me cold. We haven't spoken about Naoise since I stabbed him.

Cináed stares at a pixie floating between us. I get the sense he said Naoise's name to gauge my reaction. Which, of course, doesn't help me recover any faster.

"I saw what his presence did," I say at last. "To the kingdom, to everyone."

Cináed's expression is unreadable.

I take a steadying breath. "All I'm saying is that waiting for the best option puts us at risk. Until this heir is found, there has to be a decent substitute."

A hint of a smile brightens his solemn features, and he shakes his head at me.

"Don't laugh at me," I bark, ready to dive into another round of debate.

He shakes his head again. "You said *us*."

Now I'm truly perplexed. "What?"

His eyes glimmer with amusement. "Just now, when you were talking about the fae. You said *us*."

I open my mouth to protest but give up as his smile widens into a grin.

Good gods, I groan, *I can't get myself out of that one.*

"Come." He extends his hand. "You need to rest before we continue riding toward *our* kingdom."

I shove his shoulder as I start down the slope. His laughter trails me the rest of the way to the horse.

{ 34 }

The closer we get to the southern castle, the further I feel from Darren.

I knew what it meant when I turned down the chance to pass through the nearest portal. That was my best shot at contacting my brother. And I didn't take it.

The reasons I recount in my head help clarify my choice. I want to help my friends. I want to find answers about the faerie blood in my veins. I want to finish what I came here to do.

But beyond the logical facts—deeper than my consciousness can understand—lives a nameless resistance. Its roots weave through the sinews of my core instinct.

Throughout our journey south, I've felt this *sense* expanding. I hear it whisper to me.

What if . . .

What if Darren isn't my only family anymore? What if I stay here longer than I'd planned?

What if . . . I could *belong*?

I never entertain these thoughts for long. Cináed and Eimear make for wonderful distractions from my identity crisis—their good humor and companionship lighten my somber moods.

Our trio of horses travels in a line, and Imelda and I usually end up in the middle. I roll my eyes at Eimear's snarky jokes and snort at Cináed's playful banter.

Bare branches splay across the muted sky, bark glittering with the night's frost. The horses' steady breaths waft clouds from their wide nostrils.

Despite the serene experience of traveling an unused winter trail day after day, I can never fully settle in to the quiet lull. We have yet to glimpse the smallest sign that someone is tracking us. But our collective energy remains on full alert, just in case.

Dusk blurs the finer edges of the forest. My ears pick up on the first sounds of evening—scattered crickets, a low hoot, the tangible hush heralding a cold night.

Cináed's horse comes to an abrupt stop ahead of me. Thankfully, Imelda was watching the trail—not the trees like I was—and she halts on her own.

A jolt from behind tells me Eimear's horse wasn't so lucky.

"What is it?" I ask, then wish I hadn't.

Neither Cináed nor Eimear speak. Their wide, glowing eyes are trained on the shadowy woods to our left.

Cold sweat trickles down my spine. I don't need to see like a faery to know we're in trouble.

Without taking his gaze from the trees, Cináed gestures for Eimear and me to turn back the way we came. But we've stopped on a rocky section of trail that slopes down to our left and up on our right. Meaning our horses have to spin in a tight circle with little room for error.

Eimear and I use our reins to steer the horses around. Muira picks up on the message. Imelda, however, seems to have turned into a statue. Other than her twitching ears, she remains motionless.

I'm about to dismount, to try leading Imelda by her halter, when a mob of toddler-sized creatures bursts from the undergrowth, wielding weapons that glint like icicles above their heads.

They scream as they swarm us, clawing at our calves with their brown fingers. Cináed manages to fight a few of them off with his spear, but their numbers overwhelm us, clogging the trail and making it impossible for our horses to bolt in either direction.

"Run!" Cináed shouts at me, swinging his spear at the creature climbing Imelda's neck, while two others cling to each of his boots.

I decide to leap from the saddle, hoping to catch hold of a branch overhead. These monsters are only about two feet tall—maybe I can climb out of their reach.

But as I lift my legs to stand on top of the saddle, Imelda rears. She launches me upward but not toward the branch.

I go flying to the left, tumbling down the rocky slope. And right into the mob of attackers.

"Róisín!"

Cináed's cry is muffled by my own screams as I'm swarmed by little arms holding me down from all sides. Cold metal clicks around my wrists and ankles.

Before it occurs to me that I'm being captured—and not impaled—the creatures hoist me above their heads and carry me into the brush.

Cináed's voice fades, as do the sounds of our panicked horses. I try to twist my head to see if Cináed fought them off or if Eimear escaped in time. But the movement is followed by a quick jab to the ribs that makes me gasp in pain.

So I grit my teeth and think of a plan, before I'm offered as dinner to the monsters' queen. Or whatever it is these little hellions have planned for me.

You could use glamour.

But I hesitate to entertain that thought just yet. I don't know how to control the level of damage I inflict. I need to see if there's a less catastrophic way to negotiate my release.

From the way they glide along the forest floor like a stream and the smell of earth that clings to their crusted, brown fingernails, I take it they're forest dwellers. We shouldn't be more than a day's journey from the southern castle. Maybe my captors were loyal to King Rauri and would be willing to strike a deal?

After all, faeries love deals.

I clear my throat and ask, "Can I interest you in a trade?"

None of them answer me, but at least I wasn't jabbed again. I stare up at the trees passing by, gathering another dose of courage, and try again.

"Release me, and I'll give you whatever you want from my satchel."

That's when I see my satchel isn't around my shoulder. In the growing shadows, I catch a glimpse of it being carried alongside me by a creature with a smug look on his wide, lipless mouth.

Well, I heave a long sigh out my nose, *there goes my leverage.*

"Could someone at least tell me if you understand what I'm saying?" I exclaim.

This time, I do get jabbed. Although not as strongly as before.

"Silence, intruder," a voice barks from below my shoulder blades.

Intruder?

I bite back my rebuttal, doubting it'll do any good. I wish I could ask Cináed what these things are. Did we piss them off because we intruded on their part of the woods? Or is the high king supposed to own this forest?

If it's the latter, maybe these creatures have claimed this territory in the absence of a ruler. It's been over half a year, in human time anyway, since the king's and queen's deaths. If I had to bet on it, I'd guess an Otherworld without governance soon devolves into total faerie bedlam.

Whatever sunset might have been goes unseen as we travel deeper into the trees. Once darkness falls, I stop searching for Cináed or Eimear. They could have escaped. They could be waiting for the perfect moment to rescue me. Or they could be somewhere behind me, being carried as captives in chains.

I take comfort in the fact that neither Eimear nor Cináed are the quiet type. If they were captured, they would have made themselves known to me.

After what seems like twenty minutes, the little demons dump me on the ground. My back feels like a slab of tenderized meat.

"What's this?"

A low female voice speaks from behind me. I start to roll over but realize one of the imps has a tiny spear held to my throat.

"Intruders, traveling by horseback on the ridge trail," says the creature with the deep, barking voice.

"Intruders? I see one—where are the others?"

I'm thrilled to know the others got away after all. *But that voice* . . . I swear I've heard it before.

I glare at the creature holding the blade and get my first real look at its face.

The wide, lipless mouth seems to be a trend. It has a pointed nose, reflective eyes like small glass beads, and burnt-orange skin like the smooth bark of a sapling. I scan the creature's short body—twiggy limbs, rotund middle, oversized feet—and decide it's not wearing clothes.

And my face is inches from its ungirded loins.

The creature seems to notice my disgust and smirks down at me. I snarl and look away.

"We captured another," bark-voice is saying. "A powerful faery. We hold him with two horses beside the trail. The third faery escaped."

The female groans, and footsteps thud closer. Wait—limping footsteps. Could it be?

As she stalks over to me, the female shouts, "What did I say before, Hemdim? If you aren't positive you can capture the whole lot, don't attack. You risk jeopardizing our entire—"

A hard boot tips me onto my back. Markie stops mid-sentence, her mouth agape, dark eyes wide.

I peer up at her, not sure whether to laugh or yell profanities.

"You've got to be joking," she says at last.

{ 35 }

"You going to stare all night or help me up?" I growl.

But when Markie's mouth pulls into a grin, I can't keep the smile off my face. I feel nothing short of utter relief—and complete confusion—to see her orchestrating this madness.

She orders the monsters to unshackle me, and once the metal clicks open, she extends a hand and heaves me up.

"I can't believe it." She shakes her head. "Tell me you have good reason to be here, Róisín. Who were you traveling with?"

I roll my bruised shoulders, wincing. "I'm with Cináed and a druid named Eimear. Your minions must have caught Cináed, but I think Eimear rode off." I meet Markie's gaze, my eyes flashing. "Get me a horse and someone who's not a walking sapling to take me back to the trail."

She studies me for a moment and then barks an order. One of the creatures hurries away.

I notice her tanned skin has lost its sallow tint since I last saw her, when we escaped with the other imprisoned humans. Her thin brown hair hides beneath a kind of war helmet. The same style of armor covers her torso and upper thighs. A sheathed sword rests on the belt of her pants.

Seeing her dressed like that makes me eager to trade my skirt for the comfortable sparring outfits I wore during the games. I briefly wonder if any of my leggings and tunics are still tucked away in that armoire.

"If the tree elves are trying to detain the Wanderer . . ." Markie wipes a hand down her face. "The sooner we reach the trail, the better. And what of this druid? I can't have word of our location spreading."

"Location of what, Markie?" My tone is equally severe. "Last I knew, I left you with a group of humans in the forest, and now I find you running some secret camp with a bunch of . . . tree elves?"

Just then, an elf returns leading two unfamiliar bay horses by their reins. Markie waves a hand of dismissal at me as she strides toward a horse, favoring her left leg only half as much as she did when we sparred together in the dungeon.

"The other humans are here too. But there will be time to explain after we fix this mess."

We each mount a horse, and Markie takes the lead through the trees, urging her horse to a trot. I hesitate to match her pace, not trusting my horse to keep its footing on a dark path littered with brush and rocks. But without my consent, the horse speeds up, forcing me into a forward crouch.

I catch sight of the tree elf with the barking voice, Hemdim, in a side pouch on Markie's saddle. His twig arms swing, and his hairless head bounces with each jolting stride.

I hear the chaos before we arrive at the trail. Markie's horse races faster toward the sound, and this time I'm glad when mine follows suit.

Several elves are gathered in a clearing beside the trail. I don't need to see through the brush to know that all the action is happening right here.

Frenzied brown and burnt-orange bodies swarm over each other in a faery-sized heap. My horse halts next to Markie's, and she jumps to the ground with a shout.

That's when I see him.

Cináed is inside the elf mass. He's trying to fight them off—somehow still managing to walk while elves cling to every inch of him. He looks like a lava monster, completely unrecognizable except for his glowing green eyes.

"Cináed!"

His eyes find me, and he pivots in my direction. Markie reaches the throng and starts tossing elves aside like they're bags of apples. Hemdim's voice is shrill as he orders the elves to stand down.

I dodge the flying elves—each one shrieking as they sail overhead—and reach Cináed while the last assailants are removed from his body.

Even in the dark, I can tell their claws left slashes in his clothes and up his neck. Three slivers of blood dribble down his forehead.

Markie talks so fast that Hemdim struggles to keep up with the translation.

I turn my back to all of them and take Cináed's hand, reaching for the cuts on his face.

He pulls me to him and wraps his arms around me, holding me tight for several seconds. I feel the fear, the relief, in him—not for his own life, but that I'm alright. He steps back but still holds my arms, somehow steadying me despite the fact that he was the one in actual danger.

"Good gods," he says, a bit breathless, "what is going on?"

"You remember Markie of the Strong-arm? Apparently she's the leader of a secret club of elves."

Cináed opens his mouth and looks at Markie and then at the shamed elves gathered below her. He closes his mouth again. Pure confusion is written in every line of his face.

"Eimear?" I ask.

He looks in the direction of the trail. "I saw her shapeshift into an owl and fly off. Hopefully she hasn't gone too far."

My eyes bulge. "She can do that in real life too?" She mentioned she'd transformed into an owl in a dream, but I had no clue that skill carried beyond the subconscious.

Markie turns from the elves and sizes up Cináed with a single glance. "From what I know of you, Wanderer, you could have annihilated these elves. I'm glad you chose to spare them, though I hardly understand why."

We both stare at Cináed, who observes the cluster of elves with a bitter chuckle. "As vexing as an unprovoked attack can be, they are the guardians of the forest."

Hemdim stands apart from the rest, and he and Cináed share a low nod.

I stare in awe at Cináed a few seconds too long. I've seen him run faster than humanly possible and use glamour to appear human or turn invisible. But I've yet to see the kind of powers that could *annihilate* someone.

Then I remember the missing third of our trio. I say to Markie, "We're going to find Eimear, but we'll be back."

Cináed responds, "You stay, Róisín. I will fetch Eimear."

I begin to protest, but he silences me with a kiss on my cheek. "Please, Róisín," he whispers to me, "I have lost enough already."

Then he strides to our horses—the elves must have tied them up after they mobbed us—and mounts Glasraí.

"Keep her safe," he says to Markie.

"Aye." She nods.

He gives me one last glance that manages to say so much more than any words. I feel like my body doesn't have the capacity to hold the emotions being passed between us.

Emotions I've suppressed—for reasons that don't seem to make sense anymore.

Then Cináed and his horse vanish through the brush.

I've moved more times than I like to count—although I have counted every single one. And despite being continuously thrown into new social situations, it hasn't done much for my friend-making skills.

But I'm not thinking about all my failed friendships as I follow Markie back to camp. I'm thinking about how I never thought I'd get to see these humans again. The people who shared a dungeon cell with Darren and me. And I can't help the excitement hopping around my chest like a happy rabbit.

Markie throws aside a draped cloth acting as a makeshift doorway, and I step under the cover of a long, narrow structure with a sloped ceiling. Before my eyes fully adjust to the light of the firepit, one of the shadows in the back corner moves closer.

Esperanza crosses the distance between us, throwing her arms around my neck with a small cry. I return the embrace, forced to bend forward because of her height. Her black hair smells like smoke and pine, and when she pulls away, her dark eyes glisten.

"Róisín, it is wonderful to see you again. Is Darren with you?"

I shake my head and smile through the sharp pinch in my chest. Esperanza's black eyebrows knit together. But she seems to sense my pain and doesn't press for more information.

Several humans are sitting against the walls or lying together on mats. Sterling steps up beside Es and extends a hand.

"We will never forget what you did for us." Instead of releasing my hand, he rests his other one on top, his blue eyes fierce with emotion. "You gave us more than our freedom. You gave us hope."

Es places a hand on her middle, drawing Sterling's full attention toward her. He looks at her like she's the moon and he's an orbiting asteroid.

The visible connection they share makes me a bit uncomfortable, as it did when I met them in prison. I've rarely witnessed such pure love between a couple, and it feels too sacred a thing for someone like me to observe. I love Darren more than life itself, but I've never experienced romantic love before.

The last look Cináed gave me flashes through my mind. I blush and tuck the thought away like a note to read later, in private.

"We may not be able to return to the human realm"—Es smiles at Sterling—"but with our freedom we can make a new future, right here."

Unlike Darren and me, these humans can't cross through the portal and return home. They've all eaten faerie food, which doesn't help their odds. But they've also been held captive in the Otherworld much longer too. Their bodies would instantly age however many human years they've been gone. For people like Sterling and Markie, stepping through a doorway would be suicide.

And if by some miracle one of the younger kids managed to survive the instant aging, that doesn't mean their transition back into human life would be easy, or that their human families would still be alive to greet them.

I look around at the other humans and imagine Darren among them. This would be our reality if not for one thing: the faerie blood we both share.

People I recognize, and some I don't, begin to approach me. They thank me, asking to shake my hand. One girl simply smiles at me while tears trickle down her soft cheeks. Her twin braids jog my memory—she's the one who can translate ancient fae texts into English, and she's also the girl who had a crush on Darren.

As if reading my mind, the girl with braids asks about Darren.

A lump sticks in my throat, and I look at my hands. "He's at home. He's safe."

I excuse myself, eyes burning from more than just smoke, and find Markie outside. I wait until she's done speaking with Hemdim, who passes on her words to two other elves. The three elves leave together, walking in stride.

Markie glances at me as I approach. She continues retying the ropes of a simple shelter. "Had enough of being worshiped?"

I clench my teeth and fold my arms, hating the aching pressure in my chest. Hating praise when I couldn't be more undeserving. Hating that my brother, someone whose opinion holds serious weight with me, isn't here.

"Give me something to do."

Markie must hear the desperation in my voice. She stands with a grunt and brushes her hands on her pants. "Not tonight, kid. If you're traveling to the castle with the Wanderer, there are things you both need to know. I'm calling a meeting—"

Maybe she sees the panic in my eyes, because she adds, "Only Sterling and Es. Strictly business, as it were."

I nod, unable to deny the importance of whatever information they can offer. I force aside a wave of exhaustion and agree to wait while Markie gathers the others.

When I'm alone, my thoughts return to Cináed. *Did he find Eimear yet? Are they okay?*

I inhale and gaze at the milky display of stars visible through the interwoven branches. Silly as it might sound, I could really use a shooting star to wish on right about now.

The instant I think the words, three stars flash overhead. Their white tails blaze and vanish as soon as they appear, leaving me awestruck.

In that moment, two things cross my mind: how fitting it is that Esperanza's name means hope. And how strange that the trio of stars reminds me of the three slivers of blood streaked across Cináed's brow.

I take the liberty of making three wishes and then sit on a fallen log to wait.

{ 36 }

The four of us gather inside the smaller shelter, sitting on blankets on the frozen ground. A circular pit in the center holds a bed of coals and warms the space between us.

Then Sterling tells me everything that's happened since all thirty-six humans were freed from the castle dungeons.

After Darren and I left the Otherworld, the rest of them wandered through the forest for several weeks, looking for a safe place to settle. They considered leaving the forest—not exactly the most welcoming place—but feared they would be recaptured and enslaved by the first faeries they came across.

"That's when we found the tree elves," Sterling says.

Markie snorts. "More like they found us."

Sterling nods, his faint smile filled with chagrin. "Tree elves protect this forest. You could say they are the keepers of the trees. Some even inhabit a certain tree, bonding with it in such a way that if anything hurts the tree, the elf feels the wound as if it were his own."

"A noble choice." Es tucks her black hair behind her ears. "Because of this, the trees bestow their blessing on the elven race. The forest protects the elves as the elves protect the forest."

I note how Markie rolls her eyes but stays silent. Sterling continues, his gaze distant as he stares at the glowing coals.

"We formed a pact with the elves, you could say. We help them keep the forest free of thieves, unwanted settlers, or suspicious travelers"—he gives me an apologetic look—"and as payment, we receive shelter, food, and protection from the fae and other threats."

Markie adds dry sticks to the dying embers, coaxing the lazy flames back to life.

"Sterling manages supplies and tracks our weapon and livestock count," she says. "Esperanza has the most patience, so she's become a sort of mother figure for the annoying kids we've been stuck with."

Es nudges Markie but smiles at the compliment.

"And I," Markie says, "am co-commander of our warriors. Hemdim is our translator and the chief of this elf village. I work alongside him to protect this place as best we can."

"Have you been successful in avoiding contact with faeries?" I ask.

Sterling and Es share a look, and Markie answers, "We have, yes. But evading recapture is the least of our worries these days."

I stare at each of them in turn, my blood chilling despite the warmth of the fire. "What happened?"

"More like what *is* happening," Sterling says. "Living among the elves has broadened our perspective. Humans have long forgotten the intelligence of nature. But the fae, especially the tree elves, hold deep respect for the land."

Hearing this makes me feel bad for calling the elves *little monsters*. But not *too* bad. They did pulverize my entire back with their tree-protecting, land-respecting fists.

I refocus on Sterling, sensing he's about to explain this meeting's purpose.

"We've learned that, like all intelligences, the trees of the forest commune with each other. They speak in a language few understand. Over the centuries, the tree elves have mastered this sacred tongue and safeguard it as a priceless treasure."

Again with the talking trees.

As if sensing my doubt, Sterling continues, "None of this matters as much as what the trees are saying, the messages they've been spreading throughout the forest for many months. There is a great disturbance in the Shadowlands—the southwestern corner of the Otherworld that the worst of the Unseelie Court have claimed as their unofficial kingdom. The woods there are teeming with horrors, and we *all* have great reason to fear what's coming."

"What is it?" I lean forward as anticipation grips me. "What's coming?"

Everything I know about the Shadowlands, I learned from Naoise. He was raised in the Western Moors, but he was abandoned as a newborn in the Shadowlands.

I've never been there in person. But Naoise showed it to me by transporting me into his memories.

That was all it took for me to know the Shadowlands will never be on my list of places to visit.

Sterling shakes his head, a stray lock of blond hair loosening from his low bun and falling in front of his face. "That's the problem—the elves are unable to decipher the specifics of the message. But one thing is clear: this dark energy is shifting closer, building in a way that can only mean death in mass numbers."

As he talks, the hair on my neck and arms stands straight, and a ball of dread curls in my gut. Right now, rulers are busy pushing their self-serving agendas, and "lesser" creatures suffer while a throne sits empty. I can't imagine what an all-out war would do to this place.

What kind of world would be left after that?

Esperanza rests a hand on the subtle bump beneath her linen dress. "What we are saying might sound . . . strange, unbelievable." She places her other hand on my knee. "But, please, Róisín, heed our warning. You will be at great risk when you enter the castle. The High Court is corrupt. We don't know what's happening behind closed doors."

"Just watch your back, kid," Markie says.

Markie's eyes are shadowed beneath the lip of her helmet. Her cold cynicism often resonates with me. It's sobering to see her take these tree-talking rumors seriously.

The three of them ask a few questions about what's happened since they last saw me. I give the shortest answers possible. It doesn't take long for Markie to notice I'm not in the mood to talk about Darren or home.

"We should call it a night." She stands and slaps my shoulder on her way out. "Es will show you where you'll sleep."

I follow Esperanza to the main shelter, half listening to her explain all the different types of forest food the tree elves have taught her to prepare. We enter the sloped structure, and Es points out a mat for me.

She kneels by the firepit and feeds the embers. I lie down on my stomach to favor my bruises and turn my face to the wall of branches joined with ropes.

I know Es is warming some dinner for me. But my tired, itchy eyes fall shut, and I'm asleep within seconds.

I jolt awake with a gasp. Esperanza kneels beside me, hands rocking my shoulder. "Róisín, Cináed has returned."

Faint light paints the canvas door in a muted gold. People lie asleep on the mats around me. Without a word, I follow Es from the shelter, feeling anxious but taking Cináed's arrival as a good sign. He must have found Eimear.

Elves cluster at the side of the clearing, and Markie is speaking with Cináed. But my excitement dims when I see Eimear.

She's sitting on the ground beside Esperanza, who is in the process of wrapping Eimear's right arm in some kind of cloth. Eimear's face is drained of color and clenched in pain.

I race over to her. "What happened?"

Eimear's eyes flicker to mine, but as she opens her mouth to respond, Es cinches the bandage. Eimear bites her lip to keep from crying out.

Esperanza's hands fall still as she apologizes to Eimear. Cináed appears beside me. His hand brushes mine like the subtle, natural touch of a leaf in the wind.

His tone is low. “Her arm—or rather her wing—hit a tree as she flew, which is why the injury will be difficult to treat without the advice of another shapeshifter.”

I cringe as Eimear yelps and pulls her arm away from Es, who looks torn between giving up and finishing her task by force.

“Do you know where to find one?” I ask Cináed.

He glances at me with an unreadable emotion in his eyes. “A druid and trusted ally lives in Rauri’s castle.”

I furrow my brow at Cináed, silently asking what’s wrong. But he isn’t looking at me as he says, “I have some things to discuss with Markie and Hemdim before we depart.”

As he walks away, Esperanza stands from the log and dusts off her long skirt.

“I will prepare something for you to eat on your journey.” She offers Eimear a kind smile, shoots me an exasperated look, and leaves us.

Eimear seems lost in her own world. I take Es’s seat, exhaustion dragging me down. At least I managed a few hours of sleep. The evidence of Eimear’s long night shows in the droop of her shoulders and the bags beneath her eyes.

“I didn’t know you could turn into a bird in real life.” I wonder if she can hear the underlying question in my words, if she knows I’m asking if she meant to abandon us like that.

She grimaces, brushing a small curl from her face. “Neither did I until last night. I meant to use a spell on our attackers, but then I saw they were tree elves. Instead of striking them, I tried to transform the three of us into birds.”

She shakes her head. "I should have known I would fail. I'm lucky I didn't cause any of us serious harm."

"Well, at least you were able to shapeshift yourself, right? Cináed said you flew off to find help."

She shakes her head again, her cheeks burning. "In dreams, I can transform and still maintain my current consciousness. With physical transformation, the animal instincts are stronger than I'd anticipated. The owl's form sensed danger and forced me to flee."

I nod. "Which is how you hurt your arm." *Flying into a tree.* But I leave that part out.

She sighs and glares at her arm, bandaged and tied in a crude sling. "It was dark, and I am unused to an owl's night vision. When my wing broke and I fell to the ground, I was finally able to regain control and shapeshift into faerie form."

"And that was all worth it?" I gesture to her arm. "Just to keep from harming the elves?" Also known as the butt-naked, oh-so-sacred little hellions.

Her glare narrows in on me, but then she chuckles. "You are such a human sometimes, you know that?"

"Well yeah—you won't let me forget it." My exasperated tone makes her laugh harder, but then her smile falters and she looks away.

"There is something else you should know."

My ears tingle as I wait for her words. She peers around the clearing, as if checking to make sure no one can hear us.

"It's Cináed. He . . . he wants to leave you here when we continue to the castle."

My eyes narrow. "What? Why?"

"He wants to keep you safe, Róisín. He knows you would protest being left behind, which is why he asked me not to tell you."

My temper sizzles just below a boil as I remember how often Cináed has forced me into a cage—quite literally one time—to try to *keep me safe*. After everything we've been through, I thought he was done treating me like a helpless human child.

But beneath my pride, I feel hurt that he would rather ditch me than have an honest conversation.

Without another word, I leave Eimear and trudge through the camp.

I find Cináed sitting with Sterling and Es around a smoking firepit. Sterling tips his head back and laughs. Cináed's smile holds when he sees me, but as I get closer, I watch it fall in concern. He sets his bowl of food on a tree stump and stands.

"Róisín, what—"

"You were going to leave me behind without telling me." My voice is sharp, injured. I stop in front of him, holding my arms around myself like it might keep all this pain from leaking out.

For what it's worth, Cináed doesn't try to lie. He reaches for me, but I retreat a step. I'm aware of Sterling and Es pretending to be engaged in their own quiet conversation.

Cináed's tone reminds me of someone soothing a screaming kid, which only upsets me more. "Not for long. Just until I can get a sense of the danger at the castle." His voice grows bitter. "Things have worsened since I left, and I will not put you at risk."

I hear the emptiness at the end of that sentence, where the word *again* should be. He has long since apologized for leading Darren and me into Rauri's castle just after the High Court decided to blame all humans for killing the king and queen.

While I appreciate his raw sincerity, it doesn't fix the fact that he tried to trick me. "Why didn't you tell me?"

The flash of sheepishness almost goes undetected beneath his words. "Would you have listened to me if I had told you the truth?"

I work my jaw. "Well, yeah, I'd listen. But I won't go along with something I disagree with."

He throws his hands out as if to celebrate his victory. "Then forgive me for not being transparent with you, but you can hardly blame me for that, Róisín. Your stubbornness forces my hand at times."

"Stubborn? Look who's talking!" I hate how juvenile I sound. I should have prepped for this fight instead of marching straight into it. "I've messed up plenty. I know that. But I got us all here, didn't I?"

I might not be a heroine worthy of the legends being told about me. But I want to believe that the fact that we're all standing in this tree-elf sanctuary means I might have done something right for once.

"You help me by staying here," Cináed responds after a moment. "Your friends need you here too."

The way he says it reveals the underlying truth he still won't admit—he doesn't want me to ever return to the castle. He wants to make sure I'm protected and useless.

Sterling stops pretending he can't hear us. "It's true, we could always use more helping hands—"

My glare silences him, and Es takes the message to clear out. Once the two of them walk away, I feel that ugly wad of emotion crawling back to the surface faster than I can wrestle it down.

"You"—I swallow hard, willing my voice to sound more like steel and less like Play-Doh—"you still don't see me as an equal, do you? I've always just been a human kid to you. Someone you have to chase down and clean up after." I'm babbling now, barely listening to myself.

"Róisín, hear me out—"

"No, *you* hear me. Caring about someone doesn't give you the right to control them." My heart aches as Darren's face flashes in my mind. "If you really care, you let them live their life. Even if you lose them."

Cináed stares at the ground, subdued. It occurs to me that he might be remembering Branna, and what it meant to lose her.

I leave him standing there—knowing that pain isn't something I can mend—and wander off to lick my own wounds.

{ 37 }

I find Esperanza inside the small shelter when I go to tell her goodbye. Then I plan to wait by the horses until Cináed and Eimear head out. I don't know if Cináed will still try to ditch me, but I won't chance it.

"For what it's worth, I think you had every right to be upset with Cináed," Es says to me. "He should not have kept that from you."

I nod, wishing her validation could ease the barbed wire wrapped around my chest.

"Thank you for everything." Then, with a small smile, I add, "Wow—it's been a while since I've been able to say that."

Her beaming smile brightens her raven eyes. "Human courtesies are always welcome here."

As I step out of the shelter, she says my name. I see she's resting her hand on her stomach.

"I hope my child fights for what's in her heart the way you do, Róisín."

The afternoon sun and blue sky create the illusion of spring, but a vengeful winter chill nips at my exposed face and hands, seeping through even the faithful warmth of my cloak.

Cináed rides in the lead, with Eimear in the middle. I chose my place at the rear. I need some distance before we reach the castle.

We've been silent since they found me waiting astride Imelda. I entertained the thought of leaving before them—to spite Cináed—but I don't know the way to the castle from here.

I use the reins to slow Imelda until Cináed's head of bouncing curls—glowing warm in the orange sunset—vanishes around a bend.

I remember last summer, standing in the Dublin airport. Cináed showed up like a knight in golden armor. But instead of taking control, he pushed me to solve our problems myself. He inspired me to embrace what I'd been too terrified to consider—that I had fae blood in me, and that I was capable of much more than I realized.

I used glamour for the first time that day.

Where is *that* Cináed? The one who believed in me when I didn't believe in myself?

The barbs around my chest squeeze tighter.

If Cináed thinks I'm going to hide in the woods while he fights for what we both care about, he doesn't know me at all.

Traveling behind the others makes me jumpier than I'd anticipated. Every rustle in the brush or howl of the wind seems to belong to an assassin. I catch a glimpse of the horses up ahead and resist the urge to close the gap between us.

That is, until I realize the horses are stopped. Eimear is on her feet, scratching her horse's neck. And Cináed is gone.

Eimear sees me approaching but doesn't acknowledge me. Imelda comes to rest beside the other horses and snorts happily as she starts munching on the grass peeking through the snow.

"What's going on?" I ask.

Eimear responds without looking up, her voice tight. "Stopping for water before we complete the journey."

I hop down and face Eimear's back, quirking my eyebrow. "Eimear, what's wrong?"

Her hand—on her uninjured arm—stops brushing Muira's speckled neck.

"You did not have to ride alone."

I frown. "I wasn't avoiding *you*, Eimear."

She faces me and tosses her head with a huff. I squirm under her petulant gaze.

"Well, the Wanderer is not the only one you punish by choosing to travel alone through a dangerous wood, Róisín."

I blanch. "I—I'm sorry."

"Cináed made a mistake. But you do not prove yourself to anyone by putting your life at risk. You may have survived as a lone wolf before but not anymore. You belong to a pack now. And packs take care of their own."

I nod, my throat thick. "Okay. It won't happen again."

She nods too. Then she bites her lip and turns back to her horse.

The last stretch of the journey proves uneventful. The three of us ride within sight of each other. Silent as the grave, never speaking. But aside from the suffocating tension smothering us, we reach the edge of the forest unscathed.

Cináed's horse stops short of the rolling pasture surrounding the castle. Eimear guides her horse up to his, and I halt mine beside hers. As soon as the view beyond becomes visible, my breath shoots from my lungs with the force of a punch to the gut.

The southern castle is almost unrecognizable.

The same peach- and honey-colored walls form the base and towers. The same blade-like spires pierce a misty, evening sky. But every turret, archway, and distant windowpane looks dulled, lifeless, half-dead.

Like an abandoned mansion. All the more haunted because of the life that once brimmed within. Tainted by the memory of what it used to be.

I swallow to wet my dry throat. "What happened?"

Eimear shakes her head slowly, her vacant stare locked on the grim view.

Cináed says numbly, "It is even worse than when I left."

The look on his face mirrors the expression of grief, fear, and anticipation he had the day Darren and I first arrived here. Before any of us knew King Rauri and Queen Finnabair were dead.

Ever since I returned to the Otherworld, I've been holding out for a sign—some proof that I did the right thing in stabbing Naoise.

Last summer, rumors that he'd caused the castle's visible decay spread like wildfire. Cináed agreed that Naoise's presence eroded the castle, and the kingdom.

I whisper, "I thought—I thought things would get better."

Cináed looks at me. His eyes tell me he understands, that he feels it too—the agony of wasted hopes.

Then he dismounts and unstraps his pack from the saddle. "Your horses can find their own way to the pastures. Glasraí is too recognizable. She knows how to hide until I return for her."

I don't miss the significant glance Cináed sends my way. *She knows how to hide until I return for her.*

My answering frown of defiance goes unseen as he removes a twig from Glasraí's brown tail.

Sorry to disappoint, Goldilocks, but I'm not your horse. But I bite back my sharp retort for later. Cináed and I can resume our childish fighting after we survive tonight.

Who knows what awaits us inside the castle. The arrest order is a total scam. But will anyone else be able to cut through the lies with the same precision as Aibreann? Or worse, will they even *want* to see the truth?

Both Eimear and I drop to the ground and remove our personal items from the saddlebags. Or I should say, my personal *item*, my pocketknife. Other than my cloak, even the clothes I'm wearing are all borrowed.

"How will we get inside the castle?" Eimear asks.

"There is an entrance at the base of the western tower, near my personal quarters."

He pats Glasraí's green rump, and she trots into the trees, blending into the forest faster than should be possible. Eimear and I walk alongside our horses as we follow Cináed into the rolling hills that embrace the castle walls like waves around an island.

But before we approach the castle, we veer toward the pastures. We pause above the dip of earth that retreats into the expansive bowl of trampled grass. My gaze falls on the distant outline of the stables. I think of Sona and wish it were safe to go greet him. *Soon, hopefully.*

At Eimear's encouragement, Muira and Imelda crest the bowl and meander into the pasture.

Eimear voices my concern as we watch them go. "By tomorrow, the grooms will notice their presence and their riderless saddles."

Cináed starts toward the castle. "By tomorrow, either we will have silenced this lie against us or been imprisoned."

Moonlight paints us in a gray-blue glow. Clouds swirl overhead, seeming to gather above the castle. I smell the promise of a winter storm in the breeze. The skin on the back of my neck tightens, and I pull the hood of my cloak over my head.

I expect to feel the strange shifting of the grass around the castle. I remember how the grass used to lift my feet, making me move faster than I could on my own.

Today, however, the limp blades barely shudder in the wind, as lifeless as the castle they encircle.

Cináed's tower overlooks the grounds near the pasture. With stealth and quick strides, we soon reach the outer castle wall that blocks our access to the tower.

"Now what?" I whisper.

Cináed appears to set aside the bad blood between us for now, because he smirks at me and his eyes sparkle in the dark. "This castle holds many secrets. For example . . ."

He kneels on the ground and rests the side of his face against the wall. If I weren't watching, I wouldn't notice his mouth moving with inaudible words. Moments later, what once was a solid wall wobbles and fades, and an arched doorway appears.

My jaw drops, and Eimear's eyes grow wide.

Cináed grins at our astonishment. "Hidden doors are rumored to exist throughout the castle. I only know of this one because I installed it myself. It opens to my voice alone."

His dimpled smile disappears as he strides through the blackened doorway. Eimear walks right in after him, while I have to duck my head beneath the shallow entrance as I step into the stone tunnel.

A pale-orange will-ó-the-wisp hums above Cináed's head, lighting the way when the doorway closes behind me and casts the tunnel in darkness.

I'm unsure of our exact location. But when the glowing orb flies ahead to reveal a narrow, winding set of steps, I recognize the enclosed stairway of his tower.

We start climbing, and when I look back, the tunnel we used to get here is gone. Stairs trail beneath us, no doubt leading to the main tower of the castle.

Cináed's quarters are separated into three levels. We enter the bottom floor—the small sitting room with a couch, a fireplace, and cluttered shelves gathering dust whenever Cináed is gone. Which I know is more often than not.

He kneels by the ashen fireplace, his nimble fingers constructing a balanced pile of kindling. Eimear plops onto the couch with a sigh, and I end up beside the shelves, too anxious to sit.

"What happens now?" Eimear asks.

This stagnant air is even colder than the outside. Or maybe it feels that way now because I'm standing still after running like a bandit. My veins freeze up like unused water pipes.

"There must be someone we can talk to," I say, shuffling closer to Cináed as the first flames lick their orange tongues over the kindling. I'm not quite ready to make peace with him, but I long to dull the deep chill in my bones.

The subtle warmth leaks through my stiff cloak, easing the sting of the cold. When Cináed faces the room, he avoids direct eye contact with any of us. His voice sounds foreign, detached.

"Both of you will remain here. Open the door for no one but me or Hafwin"—his gaze flickers to me, then moves on like a restless moth—"whom I will send with fresh clothes and warm food."

Just hours ago, Hafwin's name would have lightened my mood. But watching the heaviness pressing into Cináed's shoulders, seeing the grief etched into his subtly glowing skin—it numbs my senses to anything but a desire to help.

Hoping to convince him, I soften my words. “Let us come with you, please.”

I expect Eimear to protest too—I’m banking on it, actually—but she stays silent. Her obedience baffles me until I remember he’s her employer. They might be allies, but she depends on his funds.

“Well, I’m coming,” I say.

Cináed is halfway to the door. I follow, but my boots falter when he spins around and pierces me with blazing eyes.

He growls through clenched teeth, “No. You. Are. Not.”

I shudder under his wrath, but I stand my ground. “You don’t have to do this alone, Cináed. Don’t trap us up here all night.”

But my words bounce off his back as he crosses to the door and closes it behind him with a quiet but resounding *thud.*

{ 38 }

An hour passes in which I construct, tear down, and reconstruct an internal argument about whether I should go searching for Cináed. One of the reasons I stay is Eimear's vow that she will kill me herself if I'm foolish enough to leave.

She wandered upstairs to bathe a while ago. How she can soak in a tub right now is beyond me. I feel like my skin will burst from all this agonizing worry.

He's been gone too long. Something's happened.

A knock on the door interrupts my endless pacing. I grip my pocketknife in my fist and press my ear to the door.

"Who is it?"

"Hafwin, my lady."

I inch the door open, peek through the crack, and then pull her inside. Her heart-shaped lips pucker at the corners, worry creasing the porcelain skin between her amber eyes.

"Ambaiste." Her hands tremble as she unloads a tray of food and a basket of clothes onto a shelf. "The Wanderer told me you were here, my lady, but I did not dare believe it until now."

Without thinking, I throw my arms around her. Her stiffness melts in our quick embrace. When I step back, I lift one brow with a chastising smile. "What did I tell you about calling me a lady, Hafwin?"

At that, her lips widen to reveal a glossy smile. "I have missed you, Róisín. You look well."

"Well, we've been traveling for days, so all this"—I gesture to the crackling fireplace and tray of warm food—"couldn't be more appreciated."

She sets a steaming bowl of roasted vegetables and potatoes on the coffee table and gestures for me to sit. "No, it is more than that." She hands me a cup of warm milk, her touch lingering on my arm in a comforting way. "There is a brightness about you that I did not see before. You are more at home within yourself."

Her honesty takes me aback. I sit on the couch and sip the milk. The heat from the mug warms my chilled fingers. Not knowing how to respond, I change the subject.

"How are you? Do Lana and Fodla still work here too?"

"They do, and they will be thrilled to see you." I notice she bypassed my first question. Her eyes pinch, and her hands pick at a loose thread on her purple blouse. "Lord Cináed asked me to keep your presence a secret. Is it unsafe for you to be here?"

Her fear is a tangible thing. I sense it circling her head like a vulture. A flash of shame and anger tears through me, knowing that—both last summer and in this moment—I played a part in her torment.

I gesture for her to sit across from me. "We're safe. But more than that, we're here to help."

She nods, and her smile returns as she sits in the armchair with a tired sigh.

I bite my lip, debating my next question. But I want to hear her perspective. I respect Hafwin's advice—I grew to rely on her in many ways during the summer games.

"How have things been since I left?"

As if remembering her role, she stands and fusses over the food. I've told Hafwin she's not my maid, she's my friend. The only reason I was ever assigned maids was because Naoise ordered it. But the class divisions run deep here.

"All is as well as can be expected," she says. "I doubt the kingdom will be at peace until a ruler is crowned."

I nod and sip the warm milk. "Do you have a preference?"

She glances at me, her posture stiff and nervous. "I truly cannot say."

My frown deepens. "Hafwin, you can be honest with me. I'm sure you have an opinion about who should rule."

Her lips pucker as she shakes her head, busying herself with dusting a bookshelf. I'm about to ask her to tell me what's really going on, but Eimear walks down the stairs and into the room. Her damp hair is braided, and a large blanket consumes her small frame.

"Eimear, this is my friend, Hafwin." I emphasize the word *friend* to make a point, but Hafwin curtsies without making eye contact with either of us.

Eimear offers some pleasantry, then falls silent as she notices the food. I swear I see her pupils dilate.

She nods toward the tray. "That is all for us?"

I turn to smirk at Hafwin. "Like I said—we really appreciate this."

But Hafwin stands near the door, her fingers resting on the handle. “I must bid you goodnight. I will return tomorrow if I can.”

I stand with a protest forming on my lips. But she curtsies and whisks out the door in a flutter of skirts.

I’ve been walked out on twice in one night. And man, does it sting.

Eimear steals my seat on the couch. She pops her good arm out of the blanket and uses it to dig into the food, muttering prayers between every bite. I roll my eyes, grab what looks like my change of clothes, and head upstairs.

Eimear calls out to me with her typical feistiness. “Once I’ve eaten, I need your help. Apparently, my injury hinders my ability to clothe myself.”

“Only if you admit I’m not a bigoted human after all!” I shout back as I climb the stairs.

The second floor is Cináed’s bedroom and adjacent bathroom. I notice the recently drained tub where Eimear bathed. My nerves still don’t have the patience for that, so I wash off with a rag and change into the outfit Hafwin brought me.

I pull on the clean cotton tunic and tighten the drawstring across my chest. Then I step into the pair of comfortable leather leggings and feel my body relax into the familiar clothes.

I’ve missed this.

Once, I tried to recreate this outfit with human clothes. But it couldn’t compete with the tactical versatility of a finely made faerie sparring outfit.

I glance out the window, checking on the storm. My reflection stares back at me, catching me by surprise.

Have I really changed so much since leaving the northern kingdom? During Lughnasa, my tawny hair grew several inches, my olive skin turned a bronzy tan, and a faint glow often flickered in my brown eyes.

Peering at my reflection now, it's clear these changes have not only returned but increased exponentially.

I let my hair down from its ponytail. Sure enough, it rests against my collarbone, whereas mere weeks ago it barely brushed my shoulders. This is the longest my hair has been since I can remember.

I tuck a strand away, pausing to smooth my finger along the rounded bend of my ear. At least no faerie points have sprouted. *Yet.*

And what if I wake up next week with pointed ears? Would that be so terrible? My identity continues to shift around me like the mist outside. Whenever I think I know who I am, the next breeze changes everything.

I'm a foster kid. But maybe not an orphan like I thought.

And while I'm not a faery, I'm also not a human. I'm a mixed-breed, a misfit who doesn't belong in either world. A mutt, to use the old faery's words.

As I gather my hair into a ponytail and walk downstairs, I can't help but smile ruefully.

I've struggled my entire life to belong somewhere—anywhere. It only seems right that, by definition, I'm incapable of blending in with any single group. My lines are too messy for that.

When a knock reverberates through the room, both Eimear and I jump in our seats. Cináed announces himself through the door, and Eimear lets him in.

At his jovial smile and the bound in his step, my mouth falls open in shock. We've been waiting for hours, expecting the worst.

"Good news?" Eimear asks when Cináed strides past her.

Cináed brushes loose curls from his forehead and plops onto the couch beside me. His closeness startles me. We've barely made eye contact all day. The way he sighs, relaxing deeper into the cushions, tells me he might be too relieved to care.

"Not the best news but far better than I'd dared to hope," he begins. "I spoke with a trusted guard. While it is true there are nobles vying for the throne, we are far from anyone trying to take it by force."

"Even Orla?" I ask.

Cináed props his feet on the coffee table—the picture of perfect lightheartedness. "I met with Orla briefly, long enough to learn the letter is a hoax. No one has even heard of it. Some traitorous fool must have forged it."

I release half a sigh, relieved that we might not be fugitives. But too cautious to celebrate anything yet.

"And?" I press him. "What did Orla say about wanting the throne?"

His mouth falls in a hard line. "Nothing. She could not speak long, but she invited me to tea tomorrow to hear of our travels. I plan on confronting her then."

Eimear and I share a poignant look, and Cináed catches it.

"Enough worry from the both of you. You can join me tomorrow to hear out Orla yourself."

He rests his arms on the back of the couch. His hand is inches from my ponytail. My imagination bombards me. What would it feel like if he ran his fingers through my hair?

"And the search for the heir?" Eimear asks.

Her question pulls me from my ridiculous daydream. I sit forward on the couch to put distance between me and Cináed's tantalizing fingers.

"Our search for the rightful heir continues," he says, some of his carefree luster turned gray. "I have several groups scouring the land for information. But we are not sitting idle as we wait. I plan on unmasking the culprit behind these attacks."

This time I won't accept his dismissal. "What can we do?"

I can see the tension return to his shoulders. "I need you to stay safe. Now that I've done some research, you can leave this tower as you wish. But you should always be prepared. Carry some sort of weapon."

I turn to Eimear. "Can you give us a minute?"

Both of them look at me, but Eimear nods and skirts around the couch before disappearing up the stairs. I wait until her retreating footsteps fade away.

I can tell I've provoked Cináed's curiosity because his agitation melts like snow in the rain. He stares at me calmly, waiting for me to speak.

"I understand why you tried to leave me behind at the camp."

His eyebrows disappear into his frazzled curls. I take a deep breath, itching to pace the room while I talk but forcing myself to sit still.

"Until we find out who's behind these attacks, we won't be able to protect ourselves or fight back," I say. "We won't be able to stop them or keep our friends from getting hurt."

He squirms and looks away, but I continue.

"But it doesn't have to be like this. We want to help because we care about you and because you aren't the only one who lost someone." My voice cracks, and I swallow. "I understand you want to protect us. But every time you push me away—even for my own safety—it makes me feel useless. And even worse, it gets in the way of us solving anything."

As I speak, it feels like all my wound-up tension unravels and falls to my feet in a heap. The pressure between us eases and—even as I brace myself for his reaction—I'm glad I've released these festering emotions into the open air.

Cináed stares at a spilled spot of milk on the coffee table. He exhales so loudly that I wonder how long he's been holding his breath.

"How . . ." His Adam's apple bobs, and he looks down, turning from me. "How could this have happened? All this chaos and corruption. I cannot tell you how many times I've wanted to seek Manny's counsel, only to remember . . ."

A breath shudders through him. "I—I have not slept in days." He sniffs and wipes a forearm across his eyes.

I've seen him cry once before, but we weren't alone like this. I stiffen and feel a touch of panic. Can I comfort him without it coming across as flirting?

As soon as I think it, I shove the thought away, frustrated that my mind would even go there. None of that matters as much as Cináed's friendship. And friends are there for each other no matter what. I'm reminded of Eimear's outburst in the woods—how she said we were a pack.

Besides, now that it feels easier than ever to make a decision to stay in the Otherworld, would it be so terrible if I came across as forward?

My stomach flutters. I scoot closer to Cináed until our legs touch. Then I reach for his hand. His fingers glide between mine and fit snugly, effortlessly.

We sit like that until the fire resolves to coals and snowflakes fall outside the darkened windows.

{ 39 }

The sound of a door clicking shut wakes me the next morning.

I lurch up with a start, my eyes darting around Cináed's empty living room. Soft buttercream light warms the snow on the windowsill. The fireplace simmers.

We must have fallen asleep on the couch. *Together.*

Nothing happened, of course. But wanting to console Cináed is a very different thing than spending the night with him. And I don't know how I feel about it—or even what to feel.

I spot a small paper beside me where Cináed had been sitting. In a few words, the note tells me he will meet us for tea in the afternoon.

I feel my stomach constrict. I'd almost forgotten about today's agenda: confronting Orla.

The last time I saw her, she'd found me in Cináed's tower and told me to leave the Otherworld before one of Naoise's allies killed me. I didn't have to ask a follow-up question to grasp the underlying warning—someone would kill me if *she* didn't do it first.

Yet here I am again, sitting in that same room. In confronting her today, I'll defy her threats. But I could also compound them.

With a frown, I peel myself from the couch and move closer to the fireplace. I rub a fist across my eyes and roll my neck around—soothing the muscles that are tight from sleeping on Cináed's shoulder.

My breath catches. The full memory surfaces.

Late in the night, delirious with exhaustion, I rested my head on Cináed's shoulder. I fell asleep seconds later, but not before I felt him ease a careful arm around me, holding me close.

"How is it still so cold?"

Eimear's voice snaps me to attention. She steps from the stairwell but lingers at the edge of the room. The same thick blanket swallows her, and her red hair floats around her face in frayed wisps.

I'd forgotten I sent Eimear upstairs. I cast her a sheepish look. "You found somewhere to sleep?"

Her nose wrinkles, and she shrugs. "Cináed's bed." She doesn't step closer as she purses her lips and scans the living room. "I would have thought you would prefer his bed, but it is rather small . . ."

My brows knit together as she rambles. But then, like a slap to the face, it hits me. Heat crawls up my neck, and I wave my hands at her.

"What? Hold on!" My high-pitched voice sounds like a shrill bird. "It's not like that, Eimear. Nothing happened."

She stops examining the room and rolls her eyes. "There's no need to lie. I have been traveling with the two of you, enduring the ceaseless exchanges of advancement and denial. It was high time you quit that nonsense."

I swear my face has caught fire. Urgency colors my words. "Nothing happened! And don't even think about mentioning this to Cináed."

She dips her chin, staring me down with a half-smirk. "Keep your secrets, then, if it means that much to you."

I toss a crude gesture her way and strut toward the door. "I need to get some air. Unless you and your wild accusations want to keep each other company, go get dressed."

"Wait!" Eimear cries. "You know I cannot dress myself with my lame arm!"

I fold my arms and stare her down. "Promise me first that the teasing ends here and now."

"Alright, fine!" she huffs. Then she waggles her eyebrows at me. "It's just as well. I doubt your human ears could handle a faery's version of a *wild accusation*."

The heady scent of straw and manure tingles in my nose as I step inside the stables. Eimear and I just finished a morning ride, our horses kicking up the fresh snow that blankets the pastures in a white, sparkling coat.

Sona bumps into my side while we walk to his stall. I nudge him back, happy to be reunited but also feeling a bit salty after our ride. My backside throbs. Sona, the horse who wants to walk one second and lunge into a gallop the next.

Eimear clicks the stall door shut and scratches Muira's dappled nose. I tug on Sona's halter, but instead of entering his stall, he starts eating the oats from another horse's trough.

I groan and throw my hands in the air, and Eimear laughs.

"Make fun all you want," I say. "But you have an easier horse."

She walks to Sona and pats his maroon neck. He snorts amiably, his snout buried in the oat bucket.

"Actually, he is quite fond of you. He says you remind him of his first rider."

I peer at Sona, taken aback. I remember the day Sona and I met, when Orla told me he had belonged to Princess Aisling. Before she married the prince of the merfolk, anyway.

My mind tries to picture the princess, and how she no doubt handled Sona's mood swings with unwavering grace.

Out of nowhere, my pulse quickens, and my hands tremble with the same jittery feeling I had before the flashback to my childhood.

Someone enters the stables at the opposite end and distracts me long enough that the out-of-body sensation evaporates. Breathless and disoriented, I lean against a stall and blink as the familiar face registers.

Irvin—the faery who saved my life last summer. If his knife hadn't intercepted a guard's swinging blade, I would not have survived the games.

Shaking my head to clear the last remnants of dizziness, I wave to Irvin and stride his direction. "Hey, Irvin! What are you doing here?"

His dark, shaggy hair and soft, handsome face haven't changed at all. Irvin's the type who I hope never changes.

He beams at me and lowers a bucket of apples to the ground before pulling me into a hug. When he steps back, his kind eyes take me in with obvious surprise.

"I have employment as a groom. Now what are *you* doing here?"

Not in the mood to unpack that question, I pretend to be distracted by Eimear, who smiles at Irvin before helping herself to an apple.

Irvin, however, is genuinely distracted by Eimear. The prominent scar on his face crinkles when he smiles back at her, but she doesn't notice. Irvin's lingering stare follows her as she saunters over to the horses.

I bite back a smirk. "That's my friend, Eimear of the Northern Isles. She's a druid."

Irvin swallows and peels his eyes from Eimear. "Oh?"

"Come on, I could use your help." I take an apple from the bucket. "Maybe you can convince Sona to choose his stall over those oats."

Irvin's easy laugh lightens my mood, and I'm reminded of how much fun we had at the Lughnasa feast. There was no one else I'd rather have had with me on my first night trying faerie food and wine.

He helps me guide my stubborn horse into the stall and feeds Sona the apple while I struggle to comb his black mane.

Stubborn, stubborn beast.

Sona snorts like he heard my thought. Which he probably did.

I speak loudly enough for Eimear to hear. "Hey Irvin, why don't you join us for a ride tomorrow morning?"

"I would be honored." His gaze flickers to Eimear, who is busy reorganizing the reins hanging on the wall as best she can with one hand. "Seeing as not many of the nobles get outside in the winter, I know the horses would enjoy the extra company."

He gives a shy wave at Eimear as we leave the stables and head toward the castle.

A flurry of perfect snowflakes swirl at our feet as we cross the frozen garden and step inside an archway.

And I realize with a start that it's the archway where Cináed and I shared our first kiss.

I trip and catch myself but not without Eimear noticing. She glances back at me, but when I press on, she does, too, hopefully mistaking my furious blush as cold-flushed skin.

The familiar golden marble halls and bright windows hold no warmth. It's clear that the grim shroud hovering outside the castle has infected the interior. Or maybe the poison originated within—while Naoise was here—and leached outward.

I smell the food before we round the corner to the great hall. My stomach growls and my tongue tingles when I think of the breakfast spread waiting for us through the open archway. There's no denying that the fae know how to eat.

A few steps short of the great hall, we intersect another corridor, and I collide with the armored belly of an oncoming faery.

"Oh!" I exclaim, stumbling back.

My neck cranes back to take in the full height of red-beard, a familiar opponent from the games. Eimear gawks a bit but quickly snaps her mouth shut.

Then Cináed appears from behind red-beard's looming form.

I gasp and almost swallow my tongue. After last night, I'd planned to take the entire morning to prepare to face Cináed. My blush flares with renewed intensity.

"Gravest apologies, my lady," red-beard says to me. His thunderous voice almost startles me more than our collision.

I nod to the giant of a faery. When I glance at Cináed, I see his eyes are fixed on me. He looks away, his torn expression softening into a polite smile.

"Eimear, Róisín, this is my dear friend, Gerard."

Gerard bows as far as his armor will allow.

"I saw you during Lughnasa," I say. "In the sparring competitions."

"I still thank the gods I never had to spar with you," Cináed says.

I frown. "But I thought you two fought each other." *I watched Cináed hand Gerard's ass to him*, I add to myself.

Gerard chuckles. "You must mean my twin brother, Rupert. We've been near identical since wee lads." He peers down at me, hand resting on the sword by his side. "But you and I crossed paths in the final round, the day you broke the curse and saved our kingdom."

My eyes bulge as Gerard takes a knee, lowering his shaggy head until his face is hidden beneath a red curtain.

"I prayed we would meet again, my lady, that I might pledge myself to your service."

Cináed stares between Gerard and me, eyes wide, the hint of a smirk on his lips. Eimear nudges my side, reminding me to say something.

"I—uh—I appreciate your kind offer," I stammer.

Gerard seems satisfied because he stands and beams at me. One look at Eimear tells me she's seconds away from bursting into a fit of laughter. Her hand barely covers her wide grin.

I wish I could find some humor in this. But I just watched a faery pledge himself to a half-breed based on rumors that aren't true. An honest look around the castle makes it clear I didn't break any curse.

I excuse us and take Eimear's arm, and we enter the great hall. Eimear giggles as she swipes a glass of red wine from a table.

"I have never seen a warrior pledge to anyone other than a High Court noble. Your reaction was hilarious!"

My furrowed brow deepens. "Glad you thought so."

She waves off my words, setting her glass down to reach for a gold plate. I watch as she loads it up with food.

We both pile our plates to the sound of murmured conversation and harp music. Eight long tables fill the room, and we find one with only three faeries and sit at the opposite end.

We have yet to experience any hostility—which makes me wonder if Orla was right about no one knowing who wrote that decree. But all the same, Eimear and I have agreed to steer clear of most interactions just to be safe.

Eimear sets her fork down on her plate with a subdued expression. “Gerard vowed to serve you because you are a symbol of hope.”

That’s what Esperanza said.

“I don’t know why.” I look away, staring at my food. “I’m no hero, Eimear. Anyone who really knows me would see that.”

“You have been blessed with fame. You can ignore it, or you can rise to the call.” She lifts a forkful of food. “It matters not whether you feel deserving. It’s how you choose to wield your power.”

{ 40 }

We return to the tower to lounge until teatime. A light knock on the door rouses Eimear from a nap and me from my nagging, insistent daydreams about Cináed.

Eimear yawns as she stands and shuffles to open the door.

Hafwin curtsies as she enters, her arms full of clothes. "Good morrow, Lady Eimear. Lord Cináed asked that I prepare you both for tea with Lady Orla."

I stand, wishing Hafwin would meet my gaze so I could get a better sense of where we stand. *Is she mad after last night?*

"Prepare us?" I ask. "It sounds like we're going into battle."

My attempted joke fails to lighten the weight of anticipation sitting on my chest.

But it does tease a brief smile from Hafwin, which she tries to hide as she gestures to the clothes in her arms. "Not today, my lady. Lord Cináed mentioned you do not have gowns to wear."

"Oh." She's here to play dress-up. *How boring.*

Eimear winks at me. "You will learn the ways of the fae soon enough, Róisín. Our females fight and win the most important battles every day—often with only a gown for armor, our words for knives, and our smile as the sharpest weapon of all."

"Make haste, ladies, or you will be late," Hafwin scolds us. But I catch her smirking as she glides past us to attend to the fire.

Eimear and I are dressed and primped for an elegant war—her wild hair swooped in a stunning updo and my lips painted the color of blood.

A knock on the door silences our light conversation.

Hafwin stands behind me, wrapping a small braid around the top of my head in a circle. Our eyes meet in the mirror before us, and I see her fear matches my own.

Even after walking the castle halls without being arrested, I still won't allow myself to fully believe we are welcome here.

A tight smile brushes Hafwin's lips like a passing shadow. "Lord Cináed, perhaps?"

But we both know Cináed said he would meet us at tea. Wanting to be cautious, I hold out an arm to motion that I'll check the door.

"Who is it?" I call out.

A clear, familiar voice reaches my ears. "Aimsir, the bard. Cináed told me a certain young druid might be here?"

Eimear leaps to her feet, her eyes wide. She crosses to the door in three strides, her ruby skirt floating around her ankles. I step out of her way as she swings the door wide and welcomes Aimsir into the room with a swoop of her good arm.

I remember the wise bard well. She helped me train for the storytelling competition. Her auburn hair, streaked with gray, is gathered in a long braid, and her keen eyes brighten as she nods to both Eimear and me.

Eimear's cheeks flush, and she wipes her fidgeting hand on her dress. "Lady Aimsir, it is an honor to meet you."

Aimsir offers a soft smile, retaining her stoic demeanor. "Good morrow, Róisín. And you must be Eimear of the Northern Isles. I just spoke with Cináed, and he asked that I introduce you to Ovid the Watcher."

Eimear swallows a gulp of air. She nods, hustles over to the couch, and starts digging through her satchel.

I turn to Aimsir, feeling a bit unsettled that Eimear is being summoned now, right before our face-off with Orla. "Who is Ovid, exactly?"

"A lifelong friend of mine and a known recluse." Aimsir's eyes sparkle with humor. "Which is why I imagine I was asked to make this introduction, since Ovid has not left his quarters since last Beltane."

Eimear returns, wielding her wand in her white-knuckled fist. Her eyes blaze with a terrified but determined energy. "Lord Ovid is the shapeshifter Cináed said might be able to heal my arm. He's also the greatest druid in the Otherworld."

"Don't go telling him that." Aimsir winks at Eimear. "He has been given enough praise to sustain him well beyond this life cycle."

Eimear nods and sets her jaw in a firm line, seeming to take Aimsir's joke too seriously.

"We will not be long," Aimsir says to me. "I know where Orla takes her tea and will deliver Eimear there shortly."

I nod and say goodbye as they close the door. When I sit down, Hafwin resumes braiding my hair.

We linger for a while after I'm ready, and she doesn't urge me to leave until I know I'll be the last one to arrive.

Hafwin and I walk side by side down the empty corridors. I hear nothing beyond our shoes pattering across the reflective floors.

The fact that the castle isn't swarming with guards and nobles should be a relief. All day I've hesitated to trust we aren't considered criminals here.

But the eerie vacancy feels wrong. As if the castle was abandoned overnight.

"Where is everyone?" I ask.

Hafwin's lips disappear in a tight line. "Nearly half the residents are gone."

"Gone where?"

She pauses and casts a quick glance behind us. "Fled. The castle is not safe." Her voice drops to a low mutter. "Especially for those without power."

It's no secret that between the royal family's deaths, Naoise's arrival, and the throne's uncertain future, the castle has become an inhospitable place.

It already seemed half empty last summer, at least until the competitors arrived and the games began.

To see that things have worsened so much since then . . .

We turn a corner, and Hafwin slows. She dips her chin toward two guards standing like pillars beside closed double doors.

"Here we are," she says.

I pause, steeling myself for whatever lies beyond those doors. Knowing Orla, it'll be more than just tea.

I touch Hafwin's arm in silent gratitude. Her amber eyes sparkle as she whispers, "Keep your smile sharp."

The guards swing the doors wide, and I enter the room.

Glass panels enclose the far wall and the ceiling of the circular room. Shriveled vines and frosted thorns vein across the outside of the glass like spiderwebs.

An unexpected memory disarms me. This reminds me of a place I hid as a child—the neighbor's greenhouse behind foster home #2.

I take a deep breath to ease the painful recollection. A table in the left corner catches my eye, and I turn, expecting to find everyone waiting for me.

But Orla sits alone, facing the wall of windows.

Her straight spine runs parallel to the back of her chair, but her neck leans forward, her attention on three piles of papers organized in small stacks. A tiered tray of desserts and a porcelain teapot wait untouched at the far end of the table.

She hasn't noticed me yet. I spin on my heel and take two steps toward the closed doors. The sound of laughter stops me cold.

I turn my head. Orla must have heard me, and she's twisted around in her chair.

The polished structure of her face is disrupted by the unnatural lines that pinch her mouth and eyes. Her laugh is equally off-putting. The noise falls hard on my ears like two hands clapping a practiced staccato rhythm.

Warning sirens scream at me to run. But her reaction to seeing me is so baffling—so opposite of the wrath I expected—that my curiosity wins out.

"What?" I snap.

She goes quiet. Her parted lips frame her straight white teeth, her mouth still pinched in an odd smile. Her voice is colder than I remember. Pitiless and mirthful.

"I cannot believe it." She shakes her head, and not a single graying hair shifts in her tight updo. Her steel eyes lock onto mine. "Cináed mentioned the trouble he faced on his journey. And now it all makes sense."

As she speaks, my frown sharpens into a scowl. I know she's mocking me. But in a way I don't understand. Which only worsens my embarrassment.

I cross my arms. She must sense my impatience because her face returns to its usual condescending expression.

"*You*, idiot girl, are the reason. You did not think you could escape punishment for murdering Naoise, did you?"

Her words don't register, and she notices. I didn't think it possible that she could sound any ruder, but she figures it out.

"*I* might have let you leave the castle alive. But I do not speak for Naoise's supporters bent on avenging his death."

Realization clicks in my head. A mountain's worth of dread crushes me to my core. The blood drains from my face until I feel like my head will topple from my shoulders.

It's all your fault.

Moments replay in my mind, each cast in a horrifying new light. Falling into the hole in the park. Fighting the merrows as they wrecked Cináed's ship. Finding Manny's fur.

Eirwen, the Sovereign of Winter, was right about one thing: I caught the attention of faeries who wanted to capture me. But it has nothing to do with the blood in my veins—and everything to do with the blood I spilled last summer.

I double over, resting my hands on my knees as bile claws up my throat. Cináed said the attacks were related to his search for the heir. And I believed him—I swore to help him.

I blamed everyone but myself for the destruction in my wake.

Orla watches me while I struggle to breathe. Annoyance colors her next words. "We will know soon enough what threats you've led to the castle. And after all the time we spent cleaning up your mess."

My vision blackens until all I see is a spot of dead vines on the glass. *Dead, dead, dead. So much death—because of me.*

I become aware of Cináed and Eimear beside me. The ringing in my ears must have muffled the sound of their entrance.

Someone's hand rests on my arm. But all I see is Orla, standing, a dismissive frown on her face. I should have listened to her the first time. I should have never come back.

A few minutes ago, I was planning to confront her about the threat she posed to the crown. When all along, the worst threat was me.

I gather enough awareness to stumble from the room. My numb legs pump hard, and I gasp air into my seizing lungs.

I don't get far before Cináed catches me. His strong hands spin me around and force me to stop. The lines on his forehead tilt upward when he sees my face.

"Mother Dea, what happened to you?"

I want to shove him off me. I want to scream until he lets me go for good.

But one glance at the concern in his sea-green eyes, and I know that even the truth—that I am a monster worthy of total exile—might not scare him away.

So I let his hands guide me out a door to an enclosed patio. He sits me down on a small bench and kneels in front of me. His nearness makes me cringe.

But I swallow my screams and force my breathing to slow. Because there is a way to ensure he lets me go and never comes looking for me again.

Cináed smooths my hair behind my ears. His soothing voice feels like a slap on my traitorous cheek.

"Róisín, what happened? Did Orla say something?"

I inhale, clearing away the last dark spots in my vision, and craft a heartrending lie. I stare at my clenched hands, unable to meet Cináed's kind, imploring gaze.

"No, this isn't Orla's fault. She just reminded me of something I already knew. Something I've been ignoring for weeks."

I take a deep breath through my mouth to lessen the comforting smell of warm sunshine wafting off Cináed's skin.

His gentle, firm fingers encircle the bend above my elbows as he waits for me to continue.

"When you asked me why I came back here, I didn't tell you everything. Darren asked me not to come. He wanted me to move to Maine with him."

I dare a quick glance at Cináed's eyes so he can see the fire in mine. Because he needs to believe that *I* believe my own lies. "I don't belong here. And I don't want to be here anymore. I need to go home."

Cináed doesn't move or speak for several seconds. Then he releases his hold on me as he rocks back on his heels and stands up. I stare at his shadow on the ground—shortened by the angle of the sun—that almost reaches my dress shoes.

His voice sounds the way my heart feels—like it's been hit with a debilitating blow, left exposed and desperate.

"We will contact Darren. I can convince him to join you here."

I'm shaking my head before he finishes speaking. "Darren wants to stay with his new parents."

Cináed throws his hands out. "We will find your fae parent, who is likely still alive and *here,* in the Otherworld. Then Darren will want to be here too."

I infuse every remaining drop of willpower into my shattering voice. "Even if Darren wants to be here, *I don't.* I'm leaving, and I'm not coming back."

Cináed's mouth opens and closes like the most beautiful goldfish. Raw pain shimmers in his eyes. I bite my tongue until I taste blood. Then I force myself to become a steel pillar—cold and unwavering to the core.

"I already know how to cross through the nearest portal and get to the airport. I'll leave in a few days."

He tucks his hands into his pockets, and his head hangs until long curls drape over his eyes. His voice is so small. "You will let me know before you leave?"

"Yes."

His curls bob as he nods once. "Our most trusted guards will escort you. And you will be given any funds or provisions you need."

My trembling arms push me to my feet. I turn to step back inside when his question stops me.

"Is it because of him?"

I pause and look at Cináed. The pain in his eyes has hardened like deep-blue ice.

I clear my throat. "My brother needs me."

Cináed's jaw works. "Not Darren. Is it because of Naoise?"

The tightness in my face—from keeping my emotions at bay—wavers as true shock hits me like a side tackle. "What?"

Anger heats his voice, deepening his faerie glow. "You have changed since Lughnasa. Since *him*. Do you"—he seems to second-guess the question for a moment—"do you regret killing him?"

My eyes widen, but I have to turn away because the brightness of Cináed's fury stings my eyes.

He thinks I cared for Naoise enough to mourn his death.

And in those few seconds, as I regain myself, I realize something. And it makes me hate myself all the more.

This. *This is the lie that will break him, enough to make sure I can't hurt him again.*

I become steel once more as my mouth utters the most horrific lie it's ever told. "I do."

When I step inside the castle, Cináed doesn't follow me.

{ 41 }

I make a quick stop at Cináed's tower to change into brown leggings and a loose, black blouse. I strap on a leather vest and tuck my pocketknife and a small dagger inside. Then I don my patchwork cloak and close the door behind me.

I keep my head down and don't stop walking until the castle walls are behind me. The gardens, the sky, everything has fallen under a grim sheet of ice gray.

I told Cináed I'd leave in a few days. But I can't risk my friends' lives. Orla was right. Soon enough, the threats that followed me here will attack again. And I plan on being far away from everyone I care about when that happens.

The lifeless grass shudders beneath my feet. I feel it inhale, stirring from sleep and rising to propel me forward. With the earth softly rolling beneath me, I reach the forest's edge in seconds.

Trees block the clouded light, chilling the forest air. I move silently, deliberately, putting as much distance between myself and the spires that are still visible between the bare branches.

I don't know where I'm going. All I know is I don't belong in that castle.

I don't belong anywhere.

My body moves as a detached entity, my mind too distracted to feel the moss give beneath my boots or to hear the wind stirring the last brown leaves clinging to the giant oak tree overhead.

If it weren't for the animal snare—the same kind I saw Cináed make to catch rabbits—I might have walked right past the campsite.

But seeing the snare in my path jolts me from my thoughts. I pause, nostrils flared and ears keen on the sounds floating over the next slope.

I crawl across the incline and peek around a tree. At the bottom of the hill, a simple tent is propped next to an extinguished fire. Two horses are tied nearby.

No faeries in sight.

"If that were true, we wouldn't be freezing out here, waiting for permission to move."

A female with a gruff voice appears from somewhere behind the horses. She's dressed in layers of leather and fur, her dark hair tied into a short braid.

Whoever she's talking to is hidden from view as he says, "We wait until she gives the word. Need I remind you she pays handsomely?"

The female squats by the tent and starts riffling through a pack. "Not till we complete the order, she won't. We've been tracking them for nearly three weeks, and I've yet to receive a single coin. Didn't you tell her we already killed one of them?"

I spot the male by one of the horses, his face hidden beneath a hood. He begins brushing the horse, and when he speaks, his tone is chilled.

"I sent the message. I've sent three messages, in fact. Either they were intercepted, or she changed her location for safety. You know how heated things are in the castle."

The female mumbles something incoherent. Then she curses and tosses her pack aside, standing and facing the male.

"I don't care who my clients are, as long as they pay. Make excuses for her all you want, Bane, but I didn't risk my neck to bring down that minotaur for nothing."

I clamp a hand over my mouth to contain the scream of rage and pain clawing its way up my throat.

She killed Manny. *The assassins.*

"What do you want me to say?" Bane's voice sounds like it's reaching me from underwater. Are my ears ringing? Or is the entire forest crying out at the same wailing pitch?

I'm faintly aware of Bane saying, "How about this—when we get word to move in on the next targets, I'll give you first pick. That redhead seems feisty enough to be an entertaining challenge."

The female barks out a low laugh. "And let you have the Wanderer? Nice try, but you could never hold your own against him."

Like hell will I let them have the chance. *This ends now.*

I dig my fingers into the dirt until my nails pull upward. I embrace the sharp pain, letting it ground me.

"Fine, then I get the girl." Bane's dark tone makes my skin crawl. "The pretty one they call Shadowslayer."

I breathe deep, filling my lungs with cold, numbing air. Then I formulate a plan.

If I unleash my glamour again—let myself tap into the raw power stored within me—I could explode and blow up their campsite. The potential destruction burns like magma in my core, awaiting a simple invitation. It would be as easy as breathing.

And gods, would it feel good.

But I check myself. The assassins could still escape, injured but able to run. And I still don't know how to control that power before I'm left drained, seeing stars, slipping into unconsciousness.

The female says, "Pretty or not, the Shadowslayer didn't become an overnight legend for her looks. I'd wager she puts up a worthy fight."

"A safe bet, seeing as neither of us has any coin to lose."

Hearing them talk about me gives me a new idea. *The Shadowslayer didn't need glamour or explosions. She killed Naoise with a simple spear.*

And the element of total surprise.

I crouch beneath the tree, gripping my pocketknife in one hand and the dagger in the other. The female is squatting by the tent again. The male, Bane, is still hidden behind the horses. Their conversation falls quiet, and the female pokes her head into the tent, seeming to be searching for something.

My gaze narrows on the tree beside me. The trunk arches over the slope. And one of the branches stretches above the tent.

I tuck my knives into the vest and climb. Straddling the thick branch, I ease my way across it until I sit directly above the female. The image of Cináed grinning in the tree as he dropped the huge snowball flashes in my mind.

This is for you, Cináed. This is for everyone I love.

The female ducks out of the tent, and I choke on a gasp, praying she doesn't look up. But she just takes a tarp from her bag and pops her head back in the tent.

A tight sigh spills from my flared nostrils. I pull my iron pocketknife from my vest and grip it, blade facing down.

Then I jump.

I planned to land on the assassin and stab her in the same motion. I manage the first part—landing on the female's back and crushing the tent around her.

But my dagger misses its mark, cutting through layers of cloth. The wind gets knocked out of me on impact, and I roll over, gasping but unable to breathe.

The female's unmoving body is half hidden beneath the tent. The sound her spine made when I landed on her tells me I might have broken something.

Then she moans. Her legs bend, and her upper body shifts, as if she's trying to get free.

Panic swells in my throat. I act fast, sinking the knife into her lower side. She topples over with a howl.

Blood spurts up my arm. I stab twice more to be sure the iron-poisoned wounds won't heal.

The female is quiet and still. I back away and heave until I can think through the suffocating smell of blood.

I know Bane heard the noise, and maybe saw the tent collapse. Only a few seconds have passed since I jumped. But he doesn't race over to investigate, like I'd planned, so I lurch to my feet in time to see him mount a horse and take off.

I grab the female's spear as my second weapon and sprint after him.

In a leap, I mount the other horse and kick my heels into its side. We give chase, and right away I know Bane chose the faster horse. Already they've put significant distance between us.

I urge the horse faster, pleading with it both verbally and mentally. Then I readjust the spear in my fist, holding it horizontally beside my head.

Bane makes the mistake of veering into a bramble. His horse stumbles and slows enough for me to catch up. His cloak tail flaps behind him, almost within reach.

Boiling hatred pulses up my arm and through my fingers, still wet with blood.

I cry out as I plunge the spear into Bane's lower back. The motion knocks me off balance in the saddle.

We reach a cluster of roots, and the horses rear. Both Bane and I are thrown, and we land hard on the frozen earth.

I choke on air that smells of blood. The sound of the horses galloping away nearly drowns out the injured gasps of the assassin.

I scramble to my hands and knees, finding my pocketknife beside me. Bane grasps at each breath like it's his last. The rasping sound grates on my frayed nerves.

One thought keeps time with his breaths and my heartbeats. A haunting drumroll I long to erase but know I never will.

You stabbed someone. You stabbed someone. You stabbed someone again.

My hands shake so hard I'm forced to drop the pocketknife and bury my fingers beneath a layer of dirt. Bane's body lies in a crumpled, contorted heap across a gnarled tree root. The angle of the root pushes his chest up higher than the rest of him.

On my third attempt to crawl closer, I finally convince my trembling muscles to obey. Bane's face appears from bottom to top, so that I see his eyes last. But once I do, full recognition floods me.

It's him—the messenger I saw in the northern castle.

His dark stare bores into me, and I bite my left fist—the one not caked in blood—to keep from screaming.

It's one thing to stab someone. It's another to stab someone and then watch them slowly bleed out and die. The difference between the two, I realize, is enough to make me wish I were dead too. Oblivion would taste sweeter than witnessing the finality of a murder I've committed.

But I have to finish this. I have to make sure he never hurts my friends again.

"Shadowslayer, isn't it?" He coughs, and blood drips down his chin. "Minx was right not to underestimate you."

Bane's head turns, and he blinks at the sky—a sunset the color of an orange-cream popsicle. Darren's favorite flavor.

I become aware of the tears streaming down my cheeks when I lick my lips and taste salt.

Then I plunge my knife into the assassin's chest.

I stay until his eyes glaze over and his pulse flickers out. I don't know how I manage it, but my legs somehow continue to carry me deeper into the darkening forest.

Time is irrelevant. I run until I trip on a log or a root, and then I gag until my gut aches. Some unseen beast howls in the distance. But these black trees and ink-blue shadows don't scare me tonight.

Nothing is scarier than what I've done.

I cup some snow in my palms until it melts and use the icy water to wash my face and hands. I make sure to scrub every drop of blood from my skin and my knife.

Finally, I rise to my feet. And my eyes rest on the stone archway of a portal. Not just any portal, but the exact doorway Darren and I crossed through.

I approach it slowly. How did I come across it by accident?

Like always, a handful of will-ó-the-wisps float nearby. Their glowing colors cast the archway in gold, cerulean, and crimson.

I shiver in my wool cloak, exhausted but hyperalert. Aware of the birds flying high above the trees. Detecting the subtle scent of mildew from the cave beyond the portal.

I came here thinking things would somehow be different. But all this place has brought me is more pain, more loss. I can never belong here, or anywhere.

Naoise is gone. But now I know he will make me pay for my freedom every day of my life.

I rest a hand on the stone archway. When Darren and I escaped, Sterling opened the portal for us. A skill he'll never be able to use for himself.

The stones vibrate under my touch. I focus inward and am surprised by the clarity of the connection I feel to the portal. When I ask permission to pass, the answer is immediate.

I blink, and the empty archway fills with the scene of the ocean cave. My boots carry me through. I hear the stones reassembling behind me, barricading the passage.

I don't look back.

{ 42 }

Traveling through the quiet cave and entering the loud, jarring land of humans makes me glad for night's shadows. The darkness softens the cement buildings and the speeding traffic and makes this realm more bearable for me now.

Which, in and of itself, is an unbearable thought. To think I left the only world I've ever known, and on my return, I feel as much of a foreigner as I did in the Otherworld.

The gas station lights flicker as I step inside. The convenience store is empty except for the cashier. When I ask if I can borrow his phone to make a call, he glances up from his comic book and tells me to use the pay phone down the street.

But I quickly explain that the number I'm calling can only be reached with WiFi, and he finally consents. "But do it here so I know you're not stealing it."

My nose wrinkles as I watch him remove his phone from his back pocket and hand it over. But I accept it and log into my messages.

Most of the unread messages are from coworkers asking where I've been, saying I'll lose my job soon. Those stopped a few weeks ago.

I scroll until I find several messages from Darren, each sent a few days—or weeks—apart.

Hey Raisin. I got a new phone, and the speakers actually work. So call when you see this because I won't miss it this time.

We just bought the new house in Maine and guess what. I HAVE MY OWN TREE HOUSE. You may now call me Master Commander of the Birchwood Starship.

Manny's guards are still here. Yesterday Thomas and I tried to prank them, but it didn't work. I don't think they have a sense of humor. Juliana and Howard still don't know about them.

Juliana asked how you're doing today and I had to lie because I don't know. Is everything okay in the Otherworld?

Raisin, I miss you. Master Commander out.

I wipe my eyes. Comic-guy is staring at me, probably wondering why I'm crying instead of making a call. I turn to face the window, watching my reflection in the dark glass as I press the phone icon and wait.

"Raisin?"

Fresh tears spring to my eyes, and I fight to keep my voice steady. "Hey, Darren. How are you?"

"Hold on," he says. I hear footfalls, then a door slam. "Okay, it's safe to talk now. I'm in my room."

I smile. "So, you like the new house?"

"It's so cool. There's a theater in the basement, and my tree house is in the backyard, of course. Did you see my message about the tree house?"

"Yes, I did, Master Commander. So, you're safe? No more . . . incidents?" I glance at comic-guy, but he's returned to his reading.

Darren sighs, and I imagine him lying on his bed with his feet against the wall. "We're totally safe. Manny's guards never leave. Once I tried to watch them all day, and they didn't even eat or pee or anything."

I lean against the counter, overwhelmed with relief. "Really?"

"Yeah, it's freaky but awesome. Are you going to visit soon? You've been gone three and a half months. I've been keeping track. It's almost as long as the first time we were gone."

I already guessed the time I've lost from the dates on the messages. But I don't have the energy to think about it now.

"I'll visit soon. Don't worry."

The lie tastes like ash in my mouth. I hope Darren won't pick up on it over the phone. There's a pause, and when Darren speaks again, he sounds tentative.

"So . . . what does that mean, exactly?"

My vision blurs as the tears return hot and fast. My raw emotions won't be subdued much longer. I sniff and clear my throat. "I shouldn't have come here. But I can't come back home just yet."

Not until I find every last assassin, every last threat, and end them all.

It could take months, years even. And until then, I will have nothing—no one. I'll wander the earth as a dangerous, lonesome outlaw.

"What happened?" Darren asks. "Did you figure out who our parents are?"

"No. I've been busy with other stuff." Like sabotaging the lives of everyone I care about.

"Did you and Cináed, you know, break up or something?"

I shake my head, glaring at comic-guy, who seems to be eavesdropping again. "It's not just him. It's literally everything. I don't belong here."

My brother sighs loudly, making the phone speaker crackle. "This is my fault. I tried to make you go because I thought you'd like it there. At least, better than you like living here."

"You mean"—I swallow to ease the lump in my throat—"you weren't just sick of having me around?" My tone is light, humorous, but I feel neither of those things.

"Are you kidding me?" Another pause while he exhales. I think he might be pacing now. "Why do you think I made Juliana and Howard buy a house with *three* bedrooms?"

His exasperation makes me smile, but his love soothes my heart like a balm. "I have a bedroom?"

"Yeah, and it's right next to mine, so I hope you stopped snoring in your sleep."

"I've never snored!" I exclaim. Then I realize someone is behind me buying gum. Both the customer and comic-guy shoot curious glances my way. Grimacing, I turn my back to them.

I can hear Darren's smile in his voice. "You'll have to prove it. When will you get here? I'll ask Juliana if we can pick you up from the airport. She'll totally freak out when I tell her."

I take a deep breath. The gas station, the nosey locals, everything fades away, and for a moment it's like I'm standing alone with Darren, and nothing else exists. I wonder how much he's grown in three and a half months—if hugging him would be different now because his head won't fit under my chin anymore.

My free hand reaches into the pocket of my cloak. The patched material smells like woodsmoke, frost, and rich earth.

The kind half-faery who gave it to me flashes in my mind, followed by Cináed, Manny, Eimear, Jarlath, Esperanza, Hafwin, Gerard, Irvin . . .

All of them different, each with their own story.

I feel physical pain at the thought of leaving them, deserting the castle like so many others have done.

Shame worms its way into my heart. If I'm a threat to my friends, why do I feel like I'm running away? *I always run when things don't go according to plan.*

Bits of the assassins' conversation filters through my mind. When I overheard them, all I could think about was ensuring they never hurt anyone again. Now, my instinct tells me I missed a major detail.

The assassins were hired by a female in the castle. A female who pays handsomely. Who doesn't just want me gone—she wants Cináed and Eimear gone too.

What if . . . the person who wants to punish me for killing Naoise is the same person who wants to get rid of Cináed and his supporters before they find the heir?

I swear under my breath, not yet ready to believe my theory. But I know I cannot leave without absolute assurance that I'm wrong. My hands shake as I hold the phone closer, wishing I could hold Darren too.

"Actually, I'm not coming home just yet. I'm not finished here."

He sighs again, and I steel myself for his disappointment.

"This means I can say *I told you so,* right?" Now I'm sure he's grinning. His smugness practically leaks through the phone.

"You punk." I smile, relieved at his response and reeling at the sudden pivot I've taken. "You know this doesn't change a thing between us, right?"

"What do you mean?"

"You're still my favorite brother. I'm still your favorite sister. And I expect that spare room to be safeguarded until I visit."

"As Master Commander of the Birchwood Starship, I give you my word."

{ 43 }

I decide to run, not walk, on my return through the faerie forest. The faster I distance myself from the portal, the less chance I'll psych myself out and turn around.

A few hours ago, I was certain that if I left, I would take the threats with me. Now, I don't know how to prove myself wrong without endangering anyone. But I have to see this through.

My feet carry me with newfound agility and lightness. Other than my steady breathing, I make no sound as I travel at a personal-record speed.

As I cut around a sharp bend in the trail, my cloak snags on a bough. My momentum rips the branch from the tree with a loud *crack*. I keep running, and my pulse thunders in my ears as I pray nothing carnivorous heard me.

The sound of flapping wings directs my attention to the branches up ahead. A red barn owl flies closer, hooting several times. I smile warily, slowing my pace.

"Eimear?" I whisper, feeling silly addressing an owl. Has her arm/wing been healed already?

The owl hoots again and dives at my head. I duck with a yelp, feeling her claws tug on my hair before she flies off. My hand massages my smarting scalp as follow her lead along the moonlit path.

Now I have no doubt that this bird is Eimear. And that she's pissed at me for running off on my own.

We reach the forest's edge and enter the rolling pastures near the stables. I see two faeries on horseback galloping in the direction of the moors. Eimear flies off in their direction, and I'm about to follow when I catch sight of another rider.

Cináed is by the stables, mounting his green horse. Even from half a mile away, when he turns the horse around and faces me, I sense the exact moment he sees me. I can feel the air between us shift—a lurch that echoes from my stomach to my chest.

His horse leaps into a sprint, tail raised. Cináed crouches low on Glasraí's bare back. I don't have to tell my body to move—my legs start running again on their own.

We reach each other at an inhuman speed, me barreling to a halt and him jumping from the horse without slowing it down. He lands before me, catching me in his arms, pulling me to his chest.

I feel his heart racing through his thin shirt. It's nearly freezing, and he's out here in just a tunic and pants. As if someone woke him to tell him I was gone. As if he ran from his tower, not stopping to find a cloak or even put on a pair of shoes.

His face is buried in my loose hair, his voice low, raw. "I thought you left. I thought . . ."

I pull back to meet his eyes. Emotion surges within them like turbulent waves. He cups the side of my face with his hand, his touch warm despite the chill. When I don't speak, he continues, glancing behind me at the trees.

"You were running. Moving as swift as the wind, like a . . ."

I give a small smile. "Like a faery?"

He stares at me, a million stars dancing in his eyes. He lowers his hand from my face but remains close, one arm wrapped around my middle. "When I heard you were gone, I feared you meant to leave the Otherworld this night."

"I was going to."

My mind lingers on all of the things I'm not saying. The assassins' conversation. My swift vengeance that left two more stains on my murderous hands. The phone call with Darren.

Things I will share with him tomorrow, but not tonight.

Cináed's question is hesitant, like he doesn't want to scare me away again. "And why did you return?"

"I changed my mind." For reasons I still don't fully understand.

His lips tighten, but he doesn't press. Instead, he says, "So, at least for now, you have chosen to stay."

"You're stuck with me for now." As soon as I hear my own words, a hot blush creeps up my neck. I'm not ready to discuss the terms of our relationship. Not until I confess the string of lies I told him in the name of his own safety.

But his smile, dazzling and dimpled and belonging to a sun god, stuns me into silence. For a moment, I think he might kiss me. Then horse hooves shake the ground, and I see Irvin and Gerard riding toward us, with Eimear flying overhead. Gerard leaps down, hand on his sword.

"My lady," he pants. "Were you captured? Where are your pursuers?"

I shake my head, removing myself from Cináed's embrace. He drops his arms but stays locked to my side.

"I'm fine. I took a walk and forgot to let someone know first."

Irvin's rigid posture softens with relief. After we share a wordless smile, he drops to his feet and starts leading the three horses to the stables. Gerard stares at the forest a moment longer. When he seems satisfied that no one is about to attack us, he follows Irvin.

Eimear swirls overhead, reminding me that she won't be letting me off the hook so easily. She hoots once more and flies toward the castle.

Cináed watches me, waiting within arm's reach. "By now I should know better," he says at last.

"What?"

His smile is rueful as he runs a hand through his mess of curls. "That I can have every intention of coming to your rescue, but you do not need my chivalry." He meets my gaze, his humor replaced with reverence. "You save yourself better than I ever could."

Without thinking, I take his hand. I've missed how easy, how right, it feels to be with him. We walk across the frosted grass, his bare feet beside my worn boots.

The castle windows wink at us as we approach, and the sky softens into a blue dawn. A sliver of sun scorches the horizon, haloed by wispy clouds that trail the sky like smoke.

I halt on the steps in Cináed's quarters. He stops and looks down at me. "Róisín?"

I stare at our intertwined fingers. "I need to sleep in a separate room. Alone."

His hand tenses, but he doesn't let me go. I realize how this sounds—what he must be thinking. And it makes me sick.

Good intentions aside, I used Naoise to push Cináed away. And I sense the wedge it formed—like a spike jammed between converging branches.

But he'll never let you sleep alone if he knows the truth.

He'll defend me, keep me locked in his tower, shield me from danger at his own risk. He said he knows I don't need saving. But his actions have yet to align with those words.

Before Cináed can respond, Eimear peers around the bend in the stairwell above us. Her nose wrinkles.

"Tell me you aren't wearing the face off each other in the stairwell. Let me pass, and I will find a room of my own . . ."

While Cináed's face is turned toward Eimear, I shake my head at her with wide eyes. She falls silent, brow furrowing.

I speak before she can say anything else. "No need. I was just leaving to get my own room." I release Cináed's hand, and my chest squeezes as he watches me with injured eyes.

"You are certain?" he says just above a whisper.

I bite my lip and nod. The numbing shock of the day is beginning to wear off. *Too much—this is too much pain in a single day.*

He looks at the ground. "When you leave the tower, you will find empty rooms in the second corridor on your right. I had Hafwin and the other servants move to this wing since the rooms were deserted."

Of course Cináed had the servants move to nicer rooms. I try to smile, but my face feels broken. "Okay. Goodnight."

I descend the stairs and tell myself to focus on finding an unoccupied room with a lock on the door. I'll worry about cleaning up my long list of messes in the morning.

Another wave of exhaustion hits me as I take the second right down the darkened corridor. The unlit sconces on the walls and the chilled air tell me the entire hall is probably abandoned.

I knock on the third door in, and when no one answers, I peek inside. Sure enough, the room is empty. By the looks of the king-sized bed, grand fireplace, and sapphire chandelier, I'm sure I scored a noble's room.

I slip inside and lock the door. I've just found the basket of kindling by the fireplace when I hear a knock.

I freeze and stare at the door. Have more assassins found me already?

A voice hisses. "Róisín, it's Eimear."

My chest loosens in a sigh. I stand and move toward the door, my tongue itching to give Eimear a lecture and turn her away.

But the second I open the door, Eimear points a finger at my chest.

"Tell me everything. And don't you dare try to lie to me, Róisín. Your little story about a walk in the woods might have fooled those dense males, but I know you are hiding something."

I sigh again. "Not tonight, Eimear."

"Something happened to you." The anger in her voice softens. "Multiple somethings."

Delirious with exhaustion, I move to the empty hearth and kneel to start a fire. Though I doubt anything will warm my bone-deep chill. I only hope that, with time, I can begin to heal from what I've done.

"Lock the door and sit down," I tell Eimear.

She obeys, sinking into an armchair beside the hearth and drawing her legs up beneath her cloak.

Once the first sparks catch the kindling, I move to sit in the opposite armchair. I stare at the tiny flames while I explain everything that happened. From my conversation with Orla, to finding the assassins in the forest. I leave out the call with Darren, unwilling to share something so personal.

When my story sits like a heavy cloud between us, I rest my head on the chair. "Now you know why I need to be alone. I won't put you and Cináed in danger."

Her brow furrows. "She *lied*, Róisín. We are in danger because we are *all* a threat to Orla. That's why she wants to be rid of us. I would bet she had that letter delivered to the northern castle in the hopes that we would be arrested. If she can stop Cináed from finding a rightful ruler, the throne is hers for the taking."

I sigh through clenched teeth and pinch the bridge of my nose to stave off my growing headache. "You think it's always been her? The merrows? And Manny? It was all her?"

She hugs her knees closer. "After speaking with her at tea today . . . she encouraged us to leave on another quest. To continue our search for the heir, ostensibly. She must have known those assassins were waiting for us the moment we entered the forest."

Eimear pauses. Then her tone sharpens. "So, yes, I do believe it has been Orla from the start. And today—the way she manipulated all three of us with her lies—she proved she will do whatever it takes to win."

I nod, sensing the truth in Eimear's words.

She glances over at the closed door. Her voice drops. "Do you think Orla would try to kill us while we're inside the castle? You know her better than I."

I pick at the loosened threads where the branch caught on my cloak. After today, Orla doesn't scare me half as much as she used to. What scares me is the thought that Cináed and Eimear could have entered the forest and been killed like Manny. But by sheer, wild luck, I stumbled across the assassins first.

"I think she'll wait us out," I say. "She likes to use others to do her dirty work. As long as we're in the public eye, here in the castle, she won't risk getting caught."

Murderers like her can afford to keep their own hands clean.

Several more minutes pass, and I almost forget Eimear is sitting there until she asks me when I'm planning to tell Cináed what happened.

"Tomorrow morning."

Eimear's spine curls in a feline stretch. "It *is* morning. But he meets with the advisors at dawn, so you will have to wait. We should try to sleep for a few hours."

"You can't stay here."

She rolls her eyes. "I don't care how dangerous you think you are. I am not knocking on Cináed's door now when the only person he wants to see is you."

While Eimear rises from the chair and shuffles into the bathroom, I stare at the fire, broken in ways I can't explain. As beaten down as I am, I doubt I'll be able to sleep a single minute.

{ 44 }

Morning sunlight warms the honey-marble walls as I search for Hafwin's new room. I still haven't seen Lana and Fodla, and I'm hoping the three of them are together as they usually are. My torn cloak sits tucked beneath an arm in case I see Fodla—she's the best at mending clothes.

Eimear had a lesson with her new mentor, Ovid the druid. We agreed to meet for lunch in our room.

But before that, I need to find Cináed and tell him everything. My stomach roils at the thought of admitting my lies. And coming clean about my conversation with Orla . . . I haven't firmly concluded that her accusations were untrue.

I'm so consumed in my thoughts that I almost walk right past a familiar voice that reaches me through an ajar door. I step closer and press my ear to the gap.

"It is only a matter of time before she succeeds," Fodla says, sounding smug.

I almost knock, but something stops me.

Fodla continues, "She is the one to bring peace to the kingdom. I've already offered her my support in secret."

"But isn't that dangerous?" Lana asks, her voice nervous. "If she loses, you could be banished from the castle—"

"Better to lose everything for the Reclamation than stand by as humans and mixed-breeds infest our home."

I suck in a breath, not wanting to believe what I'm hearing from someone I consider a friend.

"Fodla, you are scaring me."

"We've forgotten our own strengths, Lana. In fear we've relied on humans, on impure races to fight our wars, nurse our young, and grow our food. It's time we reclaim what's ours. With Lady Orla leading this movement, we will purge the Otherworld and restore the Tuatha de Danaan to our former glory."

"I—I don't know."

Fodla's response is agitated and flippant. "Are you not tired of being a servant?"

"I suppose so, but—"

"Well, Orla has promised to dissolve the lines between high fae and lesser faeries. That means status and class will no longer matter. We are purebloods, Lana. We deserve to be treated as such."

"But everyone who isn't pureblood has to leave? What about Róisín?"

I hold my breath, straining to hear. No one speaks for a few seconds, then Fodla sighs. "Róisín is kind to us. But she is not our friend." Her tone is stern, unwavering. "Everyone knows she's mixed, like Naoise. We are better off without them and their kind."

I stumble back a step. I think Lana is approaching the door as she says, "Do not speak that demon's name. I must go. These sheets need washing."

Scrambling, I barely make it around the corner before the door opens. I pick a random direction and speed walk away from what I've just heard.

If supposed friends will betray me so easily, who knows who I can trust.

I grind my teeth and tell myself not to jump to conclusions. When I first arrived in the Otherworld, all humans were thought to carry a faerie-killing disease. In the end, even superstitious Lana saw that was false.

But if Orla heads this movement, this plot extends far beyond me. Orla would get rid of every human and mixed-breed. Cináed needs to know her true intentions, even if it ends in Fodla's banishment.

Worry for Fodla tumbles through my gut. There has to be a way to give her a second chance.

We might need Fodla's testimony if we put Orla on some sort of trial. Would Fodla confess to avoid banishment?

I frown to myself, realizing I'm hypothesizing about criminal punishment when I don't really know how things are done here. More than ever, I wish I had a better grasp on faerie politics.

"Lady Róisín."

Hafwin approaches from down the hall, and I wait for her. Her full, heart-shaped lips sag, and her smooth skin pinches with worry.

Does she know about the Reclamation?

I decide to keep my mouth shut for now until I have a chance to tell Cináed.

Hafwin reaches for my arm and glances around the empty hall as she whispers, "Come to my room where it is safe to speak."

We link arms and continue down the hall until her bedroom door closes behind us. Her pale face looks ghostly white. I wait in pained silence, fear paralyzing my tongue. She moves to her bed, and I sit beside her.

Her words sound hushed and loud all at once. "As servants, we overhear things we should not. Court gossip of all sorts. But ever since the deaths began, first with two servants, then young Prince Tiernan, the rumors darkened into terrible accusations. When the king and queen died, I heard the most atrocious things . . ."

She wipes the back of her hand over her upper lip, her voice choked with emotion. "Things I did not dare repeat because I feared for my life. I did not know who I could trust." Her gaze finds me. "But I heard something last night that I cannot keep to myself. I know I am merely a servant—"

I open my mouth to protest, but she holds out a hand to silence me. "But you have always treated me as a friend, an equal. Which is why I pray I can trust you with this."

I bite my lip, pausing to let this sink in. "I won't promise I'll keep your secret if it's too big for either of us." I rest my hand on hers and meet her eyes. "But I swear I'll never reveal your identity. You can trust me on that, Hafwin. No one will trace this back to you."

She nods, swallows, and leans closer. "There are those who believe the royal family did not die from an illness, human-inflicted or otherwise. They—they were poisoned.

Slowly and carefully, over a period of time." A tear trails down her cheek. "And last night, I heard who did it."

My ears burn, and I hold my breath. I think the name the same moment Hafwin speaks it aloud.

"Lady Orla."

My head spins like a windstorm collecting scattered items and swirling them together. Sovereign Eirwen's voice pierces through the mental noise.

Those who claim to serve the crown are often the ones who lust for it most.

Out of thousands of questions, I ask the one that steps forward first. "Has Orla always lived in the castle? With the royal family?"

She licks her red lips, amber eyes wide and distant. "Aye. Lady Orla came to the castle before I was born. She was Princess Aisling's governess. It was Orla who swayed King Rauri to arrange the union between Aisling and the prince of the merfolk."

My eyebrows arch. *Orla was Aisling's governess?* "But why did Orla want the marriage?"

Hafwin smooths a stray hair from her face with a trembling hand. "The merfolk govern the eastern waters, and they were attacking and sinking our ships. Since the alliance, we have sailed in peace.

"But that is not the reason I heard from the mouth of an advisor himself. He was entertaining a noble from the north, and he forgot I was filling the bathtub for them in the other room. He said Lady Orla's intentions were not as pragmatic as they appeared, that she had fooled the king into the alliance.

At that point, Princess Aisling was already married, and I tried not to think about the advisor's words. A fortnight later, the strange deaths began."

More tears drip from her trembling chin. I rest a hand on her back, lost in my own thoughts.

"Will you tell anyone?" she murmurs.

"I have to." I meet her shimmering eyes. "But no one will know it came from you."

Her taut shoulders sag a little, and she wipes her tears away. "I have lived my entire life within this castle. My mother was a nursemaid for Princess Aisling and Prince Tiernan. She and my brother's family live just south of here."

A lightness softens her voice as she speaks about her family. I ask why she's living at the castle and not with them.

She sighs ruefully. "That is a complicated story, my lady. One I will share with you someday."

"I'd love to hear it. But only if you stop calling me a lady."

She smiles and is about to say something when the bedroom door bursts open and Fodla steps inside without looking up from the large stack of clothes in her arms.

"I mended Lady Tilly's linens if you want to return them to her—"

She glances up and jolts at the sight of me, almost losing her grip on the clothes.

"Oh!" she gasps, then pivots toward the dresser on the opposite wall.

From the line that appears between Hafwin's eyes, she seems confused about Fodla's reaction. I stand and remember the torn cloak on the bed.

Asking Fodla to mend it is out of the question now. Thankfully, Hafwin follows my gaze and sees the cloak—the frayed material facing upward.

"I will make sure it is mended for you," she says.

We share quick smiles, and she mouths to me that we will speak later.

With Fodla's slanderous words fresh in my mind, I'm surprised when I hesitate to leave. This is the first time I've seen Fodla since I returned. We should at least acknowledge each other.

Since her back is to me, I mutter a small greeting and call it good. As I'm closing the door, she turns her face toward me.

Waves of bitter loathing seem to roll off her skin, shooting red-hot lasers from her slitted stare. I know without a doubt that—somewhere between Lughnasa and now—Fodla decided to hate me.

{ 45 }

I stroll down the wide corridor leading to Cináed's tower. A pattern of windows and pillars create blocks of color on the ground. Sunflower, dark honey, then bright yellow again. Counting the steps between each window and pillar soothes me, giving my tired mind something tangible to focus on.

If only everything could be so simple.

Thoughts tumble in my head like wet clothes in a dryer—Hafwin's confessed secret and Orla's ulterior motives. And my place in all of it.

Despite how completely wrong it is that I've been made out to be a faerie heroine, I can't deny the truth in what Eimear said about my *gift of fame.*

What matters is how you choose to wield your power.

Last summer, I failed on so many levels. My pride got me locked in the dungeons or in my room and didn't do me any favors in the games.

I know I'll never deserve the misplaced praise of those who see me as a savior, a curse breaker—but I want to fight for them, and for the betterment of the Otherworld.

And maybe the key is to find a way to use my platform to my advantage. I can speak out against corruption. Be a spokesperson for fae without a voice. The impoverished, the shunned, the mutts that Orla and her followers want to banish from the Otherworld.

I'm so overwhelmed by my thoughts that I don't see or hear Cináed walking toward me until we're a few paces apart.

Startled, I lurch to a stop. Again, I sense the wedge of tension between us like a physical barrier. Built from the dozens of secrets I have yet to tell him—the lack of trust on both our parts.

His bare feet, rolled pant legs, and loosely buttoned shirt remind me of our first encounter. His hair is tussled, no doubt from running his hands through it too many times this morning. The half-moon shadows beneath his eyes tell me I wasn't the only one who had a sleepless night.

He removes his hands from his pockets, opens and closes his mouth, and tucks his hands away again. At last he speaks, his voice low and groggy.

"You found a room, then?"

I nod, tossing my hair behind my shoulder. I swear it's grown another inch.

He pauses, glances out the nearest window, then back at me. "And are you alright?"

The question surprises me. As does the sudden lump of emotion in my throat. I almost nod out of instinct, but I catch myself. "Actually, no, I'm not alright. Can we talk . . . in private?"

A cautious kind of hope flickers in his eyes. "A horseback ride, perhaps? I have been trapped in meetings far too long."

I manage a small smile, trying to ignore my growing nausea. "Sounds perfect."

Sona and Glasraí sway beside each other in a gentle walk as we ride away from the stables. I've never noticed how Sona's maroon coat, paired with Glasraí's green-vegetable color, create a unique Christmas-y vibe.

Something that could only happen in the Otherworld, where horses come in every shade imaginable.

As usual, the pastures are empty under a frigid winter sky. I had to borrow one of Cináed's cloaks and soon realized it retains heat only half as well as my wool cloak.

I'm still gathering the courage to begin my confession when Cináed clears his throat and glances over at me.

"Róisín, I . . ." He swallows. "I want us to trust each other. To communicate freely. I apologize if my reactions have ever influenced your ability to tell me how you feel."

Please don't be referring to my feelings about Naoise. I stifle a gag. That lie needs to die before I lose my breakfast.

He stares ahead at the horizon, where a pale sky holds the sun, the color of a juicy peach. Light caresses his face, adding to his faerie glow.

I remind my heart to keep beating, and I lick my dry mouth before responding.

"It's true that I've kept things from you. Which is why I wanted to talk to you."

After speaking with Hafwin, I've decided the only information I'll withhold from Cináed is the rumor that Orla poisoned the royals. This detail seems the most unprovable.

But more than that, if Orla masterminded the "kill the royals and blame the humans" ploy—that means she might have poisoned someone else too. Someone who supposedly died from the same mysterious sickness that killed the king and queen.

Branna of the Harp.

And that is a detail I need to be absolutely certain of before I share it with Cináed. I cannot imagine what that news would do to him. He would kill Orla himself before we could uncover the rest of her plot.

Cináed's voice pulls me from my horrifying speculations. "I want to hear everything you have to say. But there is something I should have told you yesterday."

His nostrils flare as he exhales. When he speaks, his voice aches with untamed resolve. "I will not bow to Naoise's lingering hold on your heart. I have waited, and I will keep waiting for you, Róisín."

I'm taken aback, overwhelmed by the weight of his affection. No one has ever fought for me, unveiled their heart for me to do with as I please.

How can anyone deserve that kind of love? I wouldn't know.

Tears flood my vision as I stare ahead at nothing. "I don't understand. Why?"

Cináed halts his horse, and Sona stops too.

He seems to wait to respond until I turn and meet his fervent gaze. His voice is low and thick with emotion. "I have only felt this way once in my entire lifetime. And if there is the smallest chance you care for me, too, I am not giving you up."

Tears track across my cheeks. Words rush from me in a jumbled mess.

"I—I let you believe I had feelings for Naoise so you would let me go. I had to leave the castle—leave the Otherworld. Orla told me the attacks were my fault. Retribution for Naoise. They still could be. But I want to fix this the right way. I won't put you in danger anymore."

When I fall quiet, he dismounts and nears my horse. His lithe body moves like a graceful lion. But his eyes are different—they watch me with a foreign emotion—something I've never seen staring back at me.

I command my tear valve to shut off as I hiccup and hastily wipe my nose. Cináed reaches out a hand. I take it and dismount Sona.

Cináed's gentle fingers hover at my waist. Sunlight glints off the moisture clinging to his long, blond lashes.

"Hear this now, Róisín." His voice is soft but firm. "You have never been, or will ever be, to blame for what happened. None of us are. All we can do is continue to act in accordance with what we know now—what we believe to be right. How others react is out of our control."

A silent pause floats between us. Sona's brown tail flicks the air. I inhale and bite my lip.

"So, you aren't mad at me? For lying?"

He chuckles and shakes his head. "If I am being transparent, I am too relieved to feel anger. Besides"—he winks at me—"you are not the only one of us who has mistakenly withheld information for the other's safety."

I shove his arm in jest but sober as I return to my long list of confessions. "When I told you I needed space, I thought I had good reasons. But yesterday, I realized I've been running from you—from us. When something is real, it scares me. And I run away before I can get hurt."

My voice catches. I've never been so vulnerable with someone—I didn't know I could feel so small and so blown open at the same time.

"But more than anything," I continue, "I need you to know that I *do* feel the same way about you. I want this. I want *you*."

I break eye contact to stare at the small spot of ground between us. Every inch of my skin trembles, and my stomach is dizzy from flipping over and over.

Cináed lifts my chin with two fingers, and our eyes meet. Both of us shift closer, and our warm lips find each other.

The gentle kiss swells with intensity. My veins tingle as electricity courses between us. I realize with awe that it's magic, faerie glamour. Not just his, but mine too.

He pulls away, and our cheeks press together. He whispers in my ear, his breath carrying the sweet scent of his tongue—the honey flavor lingering on my lips.

"Keeping my distance from you all this time . . ." He breathes deep through his nose, like he's smelling me. I shudder with pleasure at the thought. "I cannot tell you how difficult it's been, feigning my complacency when my feelings for you are anything but that."

I nibble at his bottom lip. He smirks, revealing his dimple. I could waste the day like this—sharing kisses and laughter while the barrier between us crumbles to dust at our feet.

And someday we will. But not today.

"Let's take the horses the long way back," I say. "There's a lot more you need to know."

{ 46 }

Naoise's old quarters—his lair, as he called it—have remained untouched since Lughnasa. Hafwin told me the entire wing has been abandoned for months, that servants refuse to step foot there to clean or heat the rooms.

Which means it looks and feels just as haunted as ever.

By the time I reach the end of the corridor and step silently into Naoise's quarters, not even the warmth from my mug of soup can stave off the fierce chill.

The small front room, lighted by three tall windows, is as much of the quarters as I've ever seen thanks to the choking purple mist Naoise summoned.

Now I notice a grand fireplace made of obsidian, bordered by two tall mirrors in black frames. On the opposite side, a hallway curves and disappears behind the corner, probably leading to his bedchamber.

I shudder and move to light a fire. When I find no kindling or turf logs, I decide it's for the best. The less attention we draw, the longer we can use this place for our meetings.

An idea came to me this morning.

After I told Cináed about the assassins and the theories Eimear and I have about Orla, he returned to his meetings with renewed determination to keep Orla's power in check. We agreed to rendezvous tonight to share information.

Whatever our plan, we need to act soon. If Orla is as cunning as I believe she is, we will have to use supreme caution.

I'm concerned that no one is coming—that they got held up or simply chickened out—when I hear sturdy footfalls approaching the open doors. Gerard peeks in, his red hair framing his cautious eyes. I wave, and when he sees me, his broad shoulders relax.

"You found it," I say, keeping my voice relatively quiet. We're so far from the nearest occupied wing that we can speak freely, but these halls carry echoes, so it doesn't hurt to be careful.

Gerard matches my quieter tone. "The others?"

"Should be here any moment."

He nods, crossing the threshold, his eyes fixed on the rounded corner. "I'll do a quick surveillance, my lady. Before they arrive."

I smile, grateful I don't have to do that myself. Though I know Naoise is gone, it feels like yesterday when I stood in this room, alone with the shadow faery, pulse racing, panicked but somehow entranced by his attentive presence. Hating the power he held over me. Hating his claims that we were similar—and that, deep down, I sensed he might be right.

An unsolicited inner voice whispers, *Naoise saw you for your strengths. He wanted you to be high queen.*

But Naoise used manipulation and mind games to control me. He wanted me to be his fearsome, muzzled pet—obedient to his every whim, with an insatiable thirst for power to match his own.

Hafwin and Eimear arrive—Eimear in the lead and Hafwin tiptoeing behind her, her skin so pale it glows like the moon.

Irvin shows up as Gerard returns unscathed from his investigation. The five of us make do with the three chairs and a few cushions. I try to ignore Naoise's distinct, tantalizing scent of midnight and honeysuckle, preserved in the furnishings.

In the end, I opt out of sitting, giving my chair to Irvin, who protests but obeys once I start pacing in front of the group.

"Before I explain my plan, I need to confirm where we all stand. We need to trust each other, which means we need to be on the same page."

Blood pulses in my temple, and hot fear curls in my gut. *Time to get the hardest part over with.*

"Some of you might know about a secret movement called the Reclamation."

Irvin cuts in, his tone icy. "The hate-movement for elitists? I know of it. And I turned down the prejudiced pricks who invited me to join."

I pause, relieved by his response but not wanting to move on without hearing everyone's views.

To my surprise, Hafwin speaks next. "The Otherworld is a home to creatures of all kinds. And I believe we are stronger together."

When both Eimear and Gerard confess they don't know about the movement, Irvin dives into an impassioned explanation. His sermon about the way the current leaders use fear to control their subjects reminds me of a similar conversation he and I shared last summer.

"True, we are far from the paradise the Tuatha de Danaan intended for their posterity," Irvin says. "But we must look inward to solve our problems, not blame everything that isn't purely fae."

When I told Cináed what I overheard from Fodla—and he realized with horror just how conniving Orla has been all along—he explained why the Reclamation is so attractive to faeries like Fodla.

High fae come from elite bloodlines. They hold positions of power in the three kingdoms, occupying the High Court and the advisory table.

Those who work in the castle—like Hafwin and Irvin—and those who become druids or warriors—like Eimear and Gerard—are almost always pureblood faeries too. But because of money or their family's status, they are considered to be low class. Lesser.

These are the faeries Orla is marketing to. They have the most to gain from the Reclamation.

Which is why—when Eimear and Gerard add their voices in a unanimous vote against Orla and her secret movement—it means that much more.

"Now that we are in agreement," Gerard says, "what is this plan of yours, Róisín?"

I nod and resume pacing. "Some members of the High Court know the truth behind all this corruption." I catch Hafwin's eye, sensing her keen awareness. "But one wrong move, and even the nobles could be banished, stripped of their titles."

I look at each of them in turn, this group of unlikely allies.

"None of us hold official titles. Some of us have been overlooked and underestimated. I think this gives us an advantage."

"Use our insignificance as a weapon," Irvin says. His scar pinches as he smiles. "Clever."

Gerard sets his sword on the ground with a *clang* that makes all of us jump. Hafwin yelps. He ignores our skittishness and stares me down until I squirm.

"Lady Róisín has spoken with the heart of a warrioress. I will follow you to the end, my lady."

I clear my throat, more than a little uncomfortable with the gravity of his words. "Your support is appreciated," I say to Gerard. *Especially since you haven't even heard my plan yet.* "But the point of this is to keep us safe."

"How?" Hafwin asks, her brow furrowed. "I assume you want to reveal our information to the public. But I was raised in this castle. If you speak out against the high fae, you suffer the consequences."

"That's why I'll be the one to speak out. Once I have a solid statement, I plan to address the advisors and High Court." I add with a wry smirk, "I can't get into any more trouble than I'm already in."

"I will stand with you, whatever the cost," Eimear says in a clear voice.

She's been quiet till now, which isn't like her. She senses my lingering stare and shoots me a look. *Later*, she mouths.

My attention returns to the group as everyone but Hafwin verbalizes a willingness to speak out against corruption. My chest burns with gratitude. The thought of any one of these allies beside me boosts my courage.

"Until then," I say, "we will be the ears and eyes of the castle. Any information we collect, we will share at these meetings. If something is urgent, bring the news straight to me."

Hafwin raises a tentative hand. "I apologize for the interruption, but do you mind if I open the curtains? I can hardly see your faces in this terrible place."

Why didn't I think of that? *Maybe because you're more used to the encroaching darkness of this room.* I shudder in my cloak.

"I will open them," Irvin says.

He stands, but Eimear throws out her arm. "Wait! I want to try a spell I learned from Lord Ovid the Watcher."

Irvin freezes at Eimear's touch, his gaze following the freckled length of her arm. Eimear removes her hand to withdraw a smooth stick from her emerald cloak.

I hold my breath at the sight of the wand, praying to any listening fae gods that she doesn't blow our cover.

Gerard seems wary, too, as he rises to a low squat, holding his sword. Eimear's eyes are lidded, focused on the windows. Her hand rises, and she mutters incoherently. Three heartbeats pass in strained silence. Then I hear it.

The wind.

It rushes through the gaps between glass and stone, tumbling around the room, fluttering our clothes and hair.

The disturbed air calms, leaving behind pillars of floating dust. I brush my hair back to see that the curtains have been shoved aside, allowing white moonlight to spill like milk across the dark floor.

We all turn to Eimear. Her eyes are wide open, looking as surprised as I am that it actually worked. Irvin congratulates her, and she flashes an unguarded, beautiful smile in his direction. I smirk at Irvin's stricken expression, his longing stare that lingers on Eimear well after she turns away from him.

When the secret meeting disperses, Eimear and I stay behind.

"What's going on?" I ask her.

She sits on the windowsill, bathed in moonlight, while I stand near the cold fireplace.

Her vacant eyes stare at nothing. "Remember the dream I had at the sacred well?"

My brow furrows. "The one with you as an owl flying over the Otherworld?"

She meets my gaze. And understanding hits me like a blow to the chest.

"The half-breeds," I whisper. "Being chased out by an army of faeries."

"Not chased out, Róisín." Horror seems to almost suffocate her voice. "They were being *exterminated*."

I hold my arms around me and pace. "What does this mean, exactly? Do your dreams come true because you're a druid?"

"The dream is prophetic because it was given to me at the well. That is why I reacted so strongly."

I pause and stare at her, no longer doubting that Orla lied to me about everything being my fault. But in the same breath, a heavier dread crushes me, like the ceiling has fallen on my shoulders.

The Reclamation isn't just a hate movement. It's a massacre.

"It's Orla," I say with equal parts shock and rage. "She means to kill everyone who isn't a pureblood faery."

Determination hardens Eimear's bright eyes. "Not if we stop her."

{ 47 }

Two staffs collide with a loud *thwack* that echoes off the stone walls of the courtyard. I retreat a step, panting hard. I take in Gerard's experienced footwork as he circles me, forcing my exhausted, trembling legs to keep moving.

We've been sparring for what feels like hours. The winter morning air cools the sweat dripping off my face and down my back.

A small group has gathered to watch us from behind the open archways. Gerard's relentless pace makes it impossible to search for familiar faces in the crowd. I tell myself that it doesn't matter who's watching. *Just focus on training.*

Which is easy enough as long as I ignore the dark glowers, the lips curled into sneers. Turns out my fame has a shadow side, awarding me a new list of enemies.

And a new list of reasons to watch my back in the castle.

I pace the ring of trampled earth as Gerard and I circle each other. Whenever I retreat too far, white frost crunches beneath my muddy boots.

Gerard's teaching style differs from Cináed's. Instead of pausing the fight to fix my position or to instruct me on my next move, Gerard never stops and rarely speaks. He only slows his movements for me to better mirror them.

Whenever he bests me by pushing me to the ground or sending my spear flying from my hands, he waits for me to regain my composure, and then he shows me what I did wrong by acting it out.

The one time I manage to outmaneuver him—knocking him off-balance so he's forced to take a knee—his small eyes twinkle beneath his red mane of hair.

My heavy breathing is sounding more and more asthmatic, and he must take pity on me because he plants his spear in the dirt and reaches out a hand. I go to shake it, but he locks his meaty fingers around my forearm instead, and I do the same. He pats my shoulder once with his free hand before breaking away.

"Now I know why you made it to the final round in the games." He grins beneath his sweat-darkened beard.

Whenever I think about that day, everything is swallowed in the haunting memory of stabbing Naoise. But this time, I rewind back to before I consciously knew I would try to kill the soon-to-be high king.

I remember entering the field in my armored leathers. Staring down the other competitors—including Gerard, who I mistook for his twin brother at the time. Despite my fears, I put on a brave face that day.

Gripping my spear in one fist, I follow Gerard off the lawn. He hands me a water pouch from the table along the courtyard wall.

A group of spectators steps onto the lawn and approaches us. Gerard eyes them while he drinks water. He shifts enough to place himself between me and the faeries.

If the approaching faeries notice Gerard's protective stance, they don't show it. Their eyes are trained on me.

The female in front is high fae. A noble in the High Court. Since they all wear fighting clothes, class distinctions are harder to detect. But I'm learning how to spot even the subtle differences between the high fae and everyone else.

Their skin glows brighter. Their eyes hold an iridescence akin to a cat's. And there's something powerful about the way they move—a warning that they can outrun, outfight, outperform any human or lesser faery nine times out of ten.

Who's to say whether I have traces of high fae blood flowing in my veins, as the Winter Sovereign believed. But it's hard to remind myself of that when I'm being singled out and approached by one of them.

The female halts in front of me, while Gerard looms to the side. Her straight black hair, pulled into a tight ponytail, cascades over her shoulder to her hips.

Her voice is deeper than I expected, alluring, husky. "We enjoyed your sparring. You are Róisín the Shadowslayer?"

"Call me Róisín." I see the staff in her hand, the leather armor hugging the strong curves of her lean form. "Looks like we had the same idea to start the day right."

Her sidelong smile seems sincere, but it gives her a feral look that chills my blood. "Seems we did. I am Sorcha from the western kingdom, and these are my travel companions."

I pick up on the casual omission of her full title. When the fae greet each other—especially upper-class faeries—using a title is a sign of pride. A way to parade your tail feathers, so to speak.

So it seems a little weird that Sorcha left hers off.

"And what brings you south, Lady Sorcha?" Gerard asks. His spine is no longer rigid, but his hand still hovers near his sword.

She takes in red-beard's full stature, her lips twitching in a small smirk. "I would rather witness the action firsthand than hear it told in legends."

I frown, observing her three groupies with new eyes. The way they fan around her, shielding her from all sides like bodyguards. Sorcha's not just a noble lady—she holds significant political power.

"You're referring to the question of the throne," I say, my ears burning with cautious intrigue.

All humor falls from her stunning, angular face. Her sapphire eyes flash, and her low voice makes me tremble. "Nothing concerns me, or the western kingdom, more than who we appoint to the high throne." Her tone softens with suppressed emotion. "The Otherworld holds its breath, awaiting our next ruler. I pray to Dea we choose the most deserving of us all. Someone who can unite us—*all of us*."

"Me too," I say, sobered by her words.

Is she telling me she rejects the Reclamation movement? Maybe Sorcha realizes that to appoint Orla would be to choose war. Outright carnage.

"Then may our desires be fulfilled," Sorcha says.

Sorcha nods to Gerard and me and leaves the courtyard with her guards close behind her.

My body aches with every step as I enter the great hall for a late breakfast.

The soreness from my daily horseback rides with Eimear and Irvin, followed by intense sparring with Gerard, brings a soreness to my muscles that hurts in the best of ways.

I can't help but laugh a little when my legs protest as I sink onto a bench. I've missed the empowerment of training for the games. Challenging my body, strengthening me to my core.

All classes of fae have begun to share meals together, partly because of dwindling numbers, partly because of Cináed's announcement that anyone willing to stay through this madness deserves the best that castle life has to offer.

I can only hope these kinds of changes will help those like Fodla to see that equality can be attained without the Reclamation.

I dig into my bowl of porridge and wild berries, feeling hungrier than I have in days. Someone sits beside me, and I glance up to see Lana's blue eyes staring back at me.

In a whisper I can barely hear over the noise of the great hall, she says, "I saw you outside the door, listening to what Fodla said."

Oh crap. I inhale a blueberry and cough into my fist.

Before I can formulate an excuse, Lana continues, "And I want you to know, I've tried to tell Fodla she's wrong about you. I . . ." She shakes her head, butterfly lashes blinking rapidly.

I regain my voice and rasp, "It's okay, Lana." *At least she's not ratting me out to Orla.*

"But that's the thing. It is not okay," she says with a frown. "I don't want you to be banished, Róisín. Despite what Fodla says, I consider you to be my friend."

Her chin trembles, and tears brim in her eyes. I pull her into a quick hug—taken aback by her sincerity and recognizing her fear.

Seeking me out like this took guts.

"You're my friend too," I say with a smile. "After you eat something, I could use your help with a wardrobe project."

Her tentative smile grows wide. "Given how you despise your wardrobe, I suspect it's for the best that I join you."

{ 48 }

Lana's laughter fills the room, the sound like the most enchanting, tinkling bells. These vacant quarters are meant for the high queen. They were meant for me—before I killed Naoise.

We're clearing out my old wardrobe, still here from last summer. The outfits are mostly gifts from Naoise.

Which is one of many reasons why they must go.

I sit on the grand bed—where I slept just once—and hug a satin blanket closer, already missing the familiar comfort of my patchwork cloak. Hafwin asked another seamstress to mend it for me.

I push aside painful thoughts of Fodla as I watch Lana emerge from the bathroom wearing a dandelion-colored dress with shimmering thread running through it. I believe she's laughing at the layers of tulle ballooning from her hips into a wide skirt that ends above her knees.

"This design has not been in style for decades!" she squeals, twirling before the tall mirror.

I honestly can't tell if she likes it or not, so I ask her.

She spins to face me. "I love it, of course! Think of the dancing I could do without a heavy skirt trapping my legs!"

I tip my head back and laugh. Lana dances around the room, twirling and leaping like the world's most talented ballerina.

A light knock precedes Hafwin's entrance. She sets aside the tray of food she's carrying as Lana bounds to her, takes her hands, and swings her in a circle.

Hafwin's expression turns from surprise to pure happiness, and soon all three of us are laughing so hard we can barely breathe.

Hafwin finally releases Lana's hands and sinks onto the bed, using the bedpost to steady herself. Lana's dancing feet carry her to the pile of gowns we've heaped on a small couch.

"Are you sure you do not wish to keep any of these?" she asks, gathering them into her arms.

"Positive. You sure you don't want them?"

"Just this and the pink one." Only her glittering eyes are visible above the ball of fluff in her arms. "It's as you said, we should give all we can to those who are truly in need."

I smile and watch her leave with the clothes. My exact words to Lana when I told her why I was cleaning out my wardrobe were, "I know others can get more use out of these than I can."

I was referring to the impoverished villagers I saw up north. I have no doubt that bejeweled and embroidered dresses could be sold for a good price—that a dress I'd wear once here could feed a family for weeks.

So while Lana might be envisioning the villagers wearing the gowns instead of selling them, her choice to only keep two dresses and donate the others means a lot.

With Lana gone, Hafwin stands to lock the door.

I sober. "What have you heard?"

It's been a week since we put the group's plan into motion. And while Hafwin hides her nervousness with polished poise, I've caught glimpses of her true fear behind closed doors.

Her clue that Orla poisoned the royals is hands down the most incriminating information we'll ever gather. Maybe that's why she feels she has the most to lose if this plan gets exposed.

Hafwin clasps her hands. "Irvin told me he saw Lord Hagan arriving this morning. Only he was alone."

Lord Hagan—the advisor with the beard that looks like black cotton balls. He deserted the castle a while ago, taking his family and servants with him.

"He isn't the first to return by himself."

Hafwin frowns. "At least a dozen nobles—and half of the advisors—have done the same. When the political balance in the castle collapses, I assume they want to seize as much power as they can without putting their families at risk."

I want to commend Hagan's attentiveness to his family. But I also remember that he was sitting in the tent with Naoise before my first horseback-riding lesson.

Anyone who glued themselves to Naoise's side last summer is only loyal to themselves. They smelled power and followed it like hungry dogs, willing to do anything for Naoise's scraps.

"Anything else?" I ask.

"Not yet." Hafwin retrieves the tray of food and glides closer. "With the weather being as it is, there is a terrible draft in the great hall. So I thought you might prefer your supper in here by the fire."

As if on cue, the turf log in the fireplace crumples under the heat of the flames, sending a puff of sparks into the warm air. The smell of earth blends with the mug of spiced cider Hafwin hands to me.

When I blink and glance out the window, flames burn on the backs of my eyelids. Eimear is practicing spells on the small balcony. I don't know how she stands being outside on such a bitterly cold day.

But I guess she doesn't have much choice. After she accidentally flooded our bedroom during one of her rituals, Hafwin made it clear she's not allowed to practice magic indoors anymore.

"Oh, I almost forgot." Hafwin glides to the door and fetches a bundle I didn't notice was there. "Your cloak is mended."

I grin and take the wool material in my hands. Hafwin ladles soup into two bowls. I know without asking that the second bowl is for Eimear.

Despite the fact that Cináed's orders have helped to disable the social structures in the castle, some still struggle to accept the changes. Hafwin being one of them.

"Dinner in here is a great idea," I say. "But it's missing something."

Hafwin sets a bowl down, her brow pinched in concern.

"You and Lana join us, and then it'll be perfect."

The wrinkle between her eyes disappears. She sighs, but I see the smile she tries to hide. "As you wish. I think there are extra bowls stored in the hall."

I stand and cross to the door before Hafwin can beat me to it. "I'll get them," I say, winking at Hafwin's exasperated look as I step into the hall. She calls to me from the open door, telling me where the bowls are.

My cloak shifts around my bare ankles as I walk to a hall closet tucked between two bedrooms. I find a couple of glass bowls, painted green with gold-leaf rims, and smile. Hafwin will protest when I tell her these bowls are for her and Lana to eat from, but I'm even more stubborn than she is.

When I reenter the bedroom, Hafwin is singing to herself, bending over the fire to add another log. The melody floats to my ears and, without warning, I come to an abrupt stop.

That song . . .

Hafwin notices I'm standing by the door and frowns at the bowls in my hands. "Let me guess, you want Lana and I to use those."

I look at her, feeling like I'm standing on the grass outside. Like the ground is moving out from under me. "What song was that?"

Her eyes light up, and she brushes her soot-covered hands on her skirt. "A lullaby. My mother's, actually. She wrote it when Princess Aisling was born."

I swallow and take a deep breath to keep my vision from darkening. An image from a dream fills my head—my tiny fingers lifting to grasp at a hand above me. The hand of the woman with the beautiful voice.

"I—I know that song," I whisper.

Hafwin's lips pucker. "Perhaps you heard me sing it before. My mother only sang it for me, and for Aisling when she was her nursemaid."

It's as if I'm hearing Hafwin from the end of a tunnel. I know my hands are shaking because I'm faintly aware of the glass bowls clinking together. I can't tell where the dream—no, the *memory*—ends and where my current reality begins.

The woman's stunning face smiles down at me. She's singing Hafwin's mother's lullaby. *My* lullaby—the song she always sings to me. Her voice sounds like spun sugar, like spring rain on a bed of soft blossoms. A lock of her auburn hair tumbles forward as she leans closer, cooing at me.

"I love you, Róisín, my little faerie rose."

Weight falls from my hands, followed by the sound of shattering glass.

It's me.

"Róisín!"

Hafwin is in front of me, holding my empty hands. Green and gold shards cover the ground, sparkling like the woman's eyes.

"Róisín, are you well?"

I look at Hafwin's concerned face.

"It's me."

Hafwin's frown deepens. "What are you talking about?"

"The lost child. Princess Aisling's daughter. It's *me*."

I burst through the door of Cináed's living room. He's standing with Gerard and a golden-cloaked guard. Their conversation falls quiet, and Gerard takes a step toward me.

"My lady, has something happened?"

I shake my head—actually, my whole body is shaking. I just stare at Cináed, unable to speak. Knowing if I start, I'll say too much. He must sense I want to talk in private because he asks the other two to give us a moment.

As soon as the door closes behind them, I exclaim, "It's me, Cináed. It was me all along, and I can't believe we didn't see it before."

He reaches for my hand and leads me to the couch. "What are you saying, Róisín? What happened?"

I tug my hand back and start pacing in front of him. My words burst out like water from a busted fire hydrant.

"I thought I had no memories of my childhood. At least, nothing important. But then I had that dream, and then Hafwin's lullaby, and—and I finally know who I am!"

Cináed's eyes are wide in cautious observance. When he speaks, his words sound hopeful. "And who are you, Róisín?"

I toss my hands in the air. "That's just it! It's so crazy I don't want to say it out loud!" I face him and point at the couch. "You should sit, though, before I tell you."

He stares at me, unmoving.

"Seriously, this is big."

He sits without breaking his gaze. I'm starting to feel super nervous, so I blurt it out before I get cold feet.

"I'm Aisling's child."

Cináed looks like he's been slapped. He sits and says nothing for three agonizing seconds.

Then he leaps from the couch so fast that I don't see it happen. All I know is his arms are around me, swinging us around, his laughter like warm honey in my ears.

"Of course you are!" he cries, kissing my hair as we twirl.

I stiffen and pull back from his embrace, my head spinning.

"You knew?" I screech.

His brow knits together. "What? No! I was agreeing with what you said—that we should have seen this before."

He steps back with a sheepish shrug. "I mean, I suppose I entertained the idea once. But you said you were born across the ocean, and I did not think Aisling ever left the Otherworld."

I suck in a deep breath through my teeth. "Okay, I guess that makes sense." *What am I saying? None of this makes sense—does it?*

He takes a half step closer, eyes pleading. "I know this is a lot to process. But I want you to remember something you told me that night in Caitriona's gardens. That a true ruler does not have to be persuaded. They should *want* to lead, to help the kingdom and its subjects. You still have the freedom to choose, Róisín. Your birthright does not supersede your decision of whether or not to make the Otherworld your home."

I take a moment to let his words sink in. When I open my mouth to respond, the door bursts open and Gerard barrels in.

"My lady, Lord Cináed, forgive the intrusion, but we've just heard from our loyal guards standing watch in the north wing."

Cináed and I both face our red-bearded friend. The look in Gerard's eyes tells me something has gone terribly wrong.

He takes one ragged breath. "It's Lady Orla. She has barricaded herself and her followers in the throne room. We believe she means to crown herself high queen tonight."

{ 49 }

The entire north wing is eerily still. I find myself mirroring Gerard's fighting stance—my fist clenched around a bladed spear—as he and I follow close behind Cináed.

The way Cináed's agile form prowls ahead without making a sound reminds me of a cat on the hunt. He also carries a spear, along with a vest of daggers on his torso.

Gerard said there's already been a brawl in the servants' hall. A group of castle workers began rioting, and instead of arresting the servants, the guards reacted with their swords.

At my insistence, our trio made a stop at my room. But my room and Hafwin's room were both empty. The best I could do was leave a message for either Hafwin or Eimear to find, instructing them to get Lana and meet Irvin in the stables so the four of them can ride to safety.

My mind goes to Fodla, who might be risking her life tonight for Orla's sake. I have no doubt Orla would never do the same for any of her followers. She would let this whole place burn—heck, she'd light the match herself—to save her own neck.

Cináed pauses in an alcove, just a corridor away from the throne-room entrance, and peers around the corner while Gerard and I wait against the wall. When he motions us forward, I creep past several open doorways, past the room where I sat for hours, memorizing a scroll for the storytelling competition.

Gerard is a looming giant at my back, consuming my shadow in his own. I readjust the staff in my hand. In the silence, I pick up on the muffled sound of drums. The steady rhythm courses through my veins.

Cináed rounds the corner ahead. When I follow two seconds later, he's gone. Air whooshes from my lungs as I leap into a dead sprint, Gerard close at my heels.

I make it a few strides before a hand snatches my tunic and pulls me through a doorway. I open my mouth, but a hand clamps over it before I can shout. Gerard stumbles into me, and I'm forced to fall onto whoever grabbed me. We collapse in a heap on the cold marble.

Eimear rolls onto her knees, having cushioned my fall. Her eyes flash in annoyance, but I ignore that and pull her into an embrace.

Will our friendship change once she knows? I never want Eimear to not get mad at me—to treat me differently—just because I'm royalty.

Royalty. I stifle a deep groan. How in all heck am *I* supposed to pull that off?

Aimsir the bard is here, standing close to Cináed against a wall of scrolls. They seem to be sharing information in inaudible tones. Aimsir maintains the same severe expression she used when she trained me to memorize that long-winded legend—an expression that tells me the gravity of our situation.

A shadow falls on the room. I turn to see Gerard standing guard, blocking the doorway with his body.

I feel Aimsir staring at me, and when I meet her steady gaze, I instinctually know Cináed just told her who I am.

I'll admit, knowing that someone as wise as Aimsir didn't put the pieces together before me softens my stinging pride just a little.

It makes me wonder if Gerard suspected it—if his loyalty was inspired by my royal blood and not the "broken curse" or the title of Shadowslayer.

Cináed helps me stand, and the four of us gather near the back wall as he rushes to explain.

"A series of glamoured barriers have been placed in the hall leading to the throne room, to stave off any intruders. If we make it through those, there's still the barricade blocking the doors."

"Can she really do this?" I ask. "Lock herself up with a handful of followers and still be made queen?"

Aimsir and Cináed share a look. Aimsir answers, "It has never been done. The Reclamation has won Orla numerous supporters, but it should not exempt her from our sacred traditions."

Cináed nods, his tone severe. "The high kings and queens have always been crowned before the entire Otherworld, on the Hill of Teamhair." I don't miss the pointed glance he gives me, its significance anchoring me to the floor. "Orla's decision is disgraceful, but it ensures success. And now I see that is all Orla cares about."

Protective rage boils in my core. The feeling is both foreign and intrinsic—as if it were there all along, waiting to be awakened.

Orla is trying to steal my *crown.*

The weight of that thought threatens to send me to my knees. I need time to process this, but that's a luxury I won't have today. Or maybe ever.

Grounding myself in the present, I ask, "How long do we have?"

"I say we have an hour to breach those doors," Aimsir says.

"An hour?" I can't imagine a rushed ceremony taking that long.

Aimsir's tight mouth curls in a small smirk. "Orla the Gray is as clever as she is arrogant. She might have orchestrated a secret ceremony, but it will last as long as she likes. And her blind pompousness will be her downfall tonight."

"Eimear, rally the other trusted druids," Cináed says. "Tell them to unleash everything they have on those blockades."

Eimear's frazzled hair matches the flames in her blue eyes. She nods, and her cloak billows behind her as she sprints from the room.

Cináed continues, "Gerard and I will find something to break down the doors."

Hearing his name, Gerard tosses a response over his shoulder, "Already found it, my lord. One of the pillars from the gardens has a crack in it. Shouldn't be too difficult to remove."

There's no time to dwell on the mental picture of Gerard hefting a marble pillar through the castle.

"I have an idea that might help," I announce. "Start without me—I'll be back as soon as I can."

I turn, about to squeeze past Gerard when Cináed reaches to take my arm. I flinch, dreading the orders he's about to give me. Commanding me to stay put, to stay safe and out of harm's way.

Instead, he tugs my hips close until our bodies align. His warm mouth finds mine, lips parted, hands roving across my back. My hands tangle in his wild hair. I fall into him, giving myself to a kiss that demands time itself to stop.

We break apart, and my pulse slows to a steady thrum. I become aware of our spectators, trying their best to give us privacy in such a small space.

Knowing that an audience witnessed our make-out session should mortify me. But not today—not when we have no way of knowing how this will end.

I drop my arms from his shoulders and loop them around his hips.

He whispers, "Whatever you choose, Róisín, choose it for the right reasons."

I nod, and we share a brief kiss before I take my spear in hand and run out the door.

{ 50 }

I find Hafwin in one of the darkened corridors that branch off the great hall. She's not alone—a cluster of faerie children follow close behind her.

I've never seen a fae child before, and I'm taken aback at how beautiful they all are. Even with their terrified expressions and simple clothes, compared to human kids, these children are almost laughably flawless. Like miniature gods and goddesses, with delicately pointed ears peeking through their hair.

"Hafwin."

She looks up from the toddler whose hand she's holding. I sense her urgency, so I step into stride with the group.

"Hafwin, I need to know if there's another entrance to the throne room."

We pass an alcove where two bodies lie dead, their golden cloaks stained in blood. They must have turned on each other—one supporting Orla, the other supporting the royal family. I hold my breath.

It doesn't matter whose side any of the fae choose—both lead to death. All this time, I thought the quest to find a rightful ruler was the worthier cause. But how I can think that amid so much death?

And even more than that—whichever one died for the royal family . . . died for *me*.

I grip my side as nausea wracks my body.

"I heard Orla has barricaded the doors," Hafwin mutters at last, frowning at the sight of the guards.

She calls behind her for the children to keep moving. I snatch a stray kid before he tumbles down a stairwell, shepherding him back into the herd.

"There is a secret entrance to the throne room," she continues. "But there is a lever one must hold open while another passes through."

"Can you tell me where it is?"

She glances at me with a strange look in her eye. "It is rumored to only allow royal blood to pass through unharmed. It was created centuries ago, by a high king who possessed a druid wand."

"That won't be a problem," I say, catching the same straying kid's arm before he veers into an intersecting hall. "Where is the entrance?"

Shouts echo from behind us, and I jump at the sound of clashing metal. Unprodded, all of the kids increase their pace to a jog.

"I will come with you," Hafwin says.

I gesture to the children. "What about them?"

"Lana will return soon from escorting another group. She can bring these ones the rest of the way to our safe place behind the pasture's tallest hill."

"You don't have to do this. I can find Cináed or someone else to help me get through."

Her jaw tightens, amber eyes glowing as she meets my gaze. "For too long I have stood by and watched this castle suffer. I want to fight for my home." Her mouth softens in a faint smile. "*Our* home."

We cross the last corridor to the gardens. Sure enough, Lana is there to greet us.

"I've delivered the elderly to safety," she says. "Are these the last of the young?"

"Yes," Hafwin says. "You must take them now. I am going with Róisín."

Lana's eyes fill with tears. She looks pointedly at my sparring outfit and the spear in my hand. "Hafwin, you are not a fighter. Come with me, both of you."

I lower my head, biting my tongue. I also want Hafwin to change her mind, to run to safety with Lana. But if I want others to respect my decision to fight, I have to allow my friends the same freedom.

"This is what I must do, Lana," Hafwin says. Her voice is kind but unwavering. "Take the children, and stay hidden until someone comes for you."

Lana must know she's not winning this argument because she throws her arms around Hafwin with a small cry. After their embrace, Lana turns to me, her rosy face glistening with tears.

"Take care of her. She might be the oldest, but she has never wielded a weapon in her life."

I nod, and we both ignore Hafwin's noise of protest. Then Lana leans in, pecks my cheek, and begins leading the young faeries out of the castle walls.

The last kids are still shuffling away as Hafwin and I turn around and silently sprint through the archways in the direction of the throne room.

"You are certain, my lady?"

I'm standing before an impassable stone archway in some forgotten tunnel that connects the northwestern corner of the gardens to the throne room. The only light comes from the cracks in the earthen hatch above. Hafwin and I forced it open to reveal a stairway shrouded in cobwebs and musty gloom.

"I'm ready," I say to Hafwin. "And I'm not a lady, remember?"

She's behind me, hands poised on the lever she has to push down until the archway opens and I pass beneath it.

That is, if the lever is still functioning. And if I have enough royal blood in me to make this work. I thought about asking Hafwin what happens to any non-royal who tries to cross through, but I think I'd rather not know.

"I'm afraid I do not agree, my lady." I can hear the smile in her voice, the respect and the lighthearted teasing. "You will have to get used to being called much more important titles soon enough."

I go to roll my eyes at her, but I'm forced to brace myself against the sudden onslaught of emotions rushing through me. I can't imagine being called *high queen*—even the thought triggers my gag reflex.

But does that mean I should walk away from my birthright? Abandon the throne left to me by my mother?

For the first time in years, I come face-to-face with a deep longing for her. I wish she would appear and tell me what to do. Hell, I wish she would show up so *she* could become queen.

But if things were so simple, Cináed would have found a way to bring Aisling home long ago.

Like countless times before, I shrug off all thoughts of my parents and the childhood dream of being rescued by them. They aren't here. Aisling isn't here. *I have to do this on my own.*

At my signal, Hafwin heaves her weight onto the lever. She grunts, and the solid stone archway before me wobbles, raining dust and loose earth from the ceiling. The platform I'm standing on shifts, and I teeter before catching my footing.

"Do not move from the platform until you reach the other side!" Hafwin calls.

I shout that she could have told me that sooner, but my voice goes unheard when the stone slab beneath the archway shudders open.

The tunnel seems to continue through the archway, leading to another set of stairs and what I assume will be a floorboard hatch that opens somewhere in the throne room.

"Róisín!"

I turn my head to catch sight of Hafwin, struggling to keep the lever down. Just then, the platform jolts forward, and I have to grab the archway to keep from falling.

Hafwin's voice reaches me over the rumbling earth. "Róisín, I will wait here for you!"

I can't turn around on the tiny platform. The archway passes above me as I shout, "I'll be alright! Go tell Cináed that I'll stall the ceremony!"

I know I could end up trapped in the throne room with no way out. But I won't flee. Nothing will change my course now.

The platform stills while the archway groans. I hear Hafwin call to me one last time before the barrier slams into place, isolating me in total darkness.

I pause, waiting until the tunnel stops raining dirt from the ceiling. Then I take a careful step from the platform and pause. When nothing happens, I remove my other foot and use memory alone to find the invisible staircase.

My nose itches in the stale, dusty air. I almost trip over the first step, and crawl up the rest. I give a tiny squeal when my fingers touch something slimy. I hope it was a harmless toad and nothing more.

My head brushes the ceiling, and I pause again, straining to hear anything through the floor above me. Empty silence greets my ears. I hold my spear between my knees and use my fingers to trace the outline of the hatch, surprised to find this one is circular, not square.

One hard shove jostles the heavy floorboards and spews dirt onto my face. I cough and lower my head, leveraging my shoulders and back against the ceiling. Then, with my hands on the stairs beneath me, I shove upward again.

There's a soft suction sound, and fresh air fills my nose. I try to ease the latch open but realize there isn't a hinge. The entire section of compacted earth must be lifted and removed for me to crawl through.

Making as little noise as possible, I try lifting it high enough to see into the room above. My eyes blink in the soft darkness.

This can't be the throne room, teeming with Orla's followers.

I shift the circle of earth and get one hand through the opening. My hand stops, pressed against what feels like smooth marble. Shaking under the weight of the earth, I let it fall back into place, breathing hard.

Crazy as it seems, I'm pretty sure this tunnel leads to a hollowed-out marble pillar within the throne room. There must be a way to get out of the pillar—maybe another secret doorway.

I grit my teeth and lift the compacted earth once more, this time pushing it at an angle so it falls beside me, allowing me to stand up inside the pillar. Sure enough, there's a distinct cutout in the pillar. Light from the throne room glows in the cracks, just bright enough to allow me to make out the words carved into the stone.

My heart plummets as I peer at the foreign language. I can't read a single word of it.

I try using my nails, jamming them into the slit of light to pry the stone open. When one nail bends enough to break, I wince and suck the blood oozing from my wounded finger.

I reach for my spear to use as leverage and see something smudged across the symbol of swirls carved beneath the unreadable words.

I lean closer, peering at the dark swaths and drip marks. It almost looks like paint, layers of it that dried at different times.

My fingers burn, and instinctively I brush a careful hand over the symbol. Some of my blood smears the carving. The symbol brightens as if held to the sun. I gasp, wide-eyed and frozen, as the rectangle door soundlessly glides open.

{ 51 }

I hold my breath and duck as far as I can into the circular cutout in the floor, pressing against the back of the hollow pillar. The view beyond shows an empty corner of the throne room, with no fae in sight.

I blink several times, adjusting to the light from the glowing torches on the wall. I've never entered the throne room before. I've only seen it from the doorway when Darren and I first arrived, so I struggle to orient myself.

I tune in to the voices filtering through the pillar's tall, slender opening. Murmurs, mostly, but a single voice carries across the room, seeming to come from my right.

"For too long we have bowed under the weight of our past." It's a male's voice, high-pitched and nasal. I think it's Lord Hagan, with the cotton-ball beard. "For too long, we have lived with the battle scars of wars we never fought. But no more! We are entering a new era! This day, we crown a high queen who will lead us into a brighter future!"

Stomping feet and roaring cheers send vibrations through the stone floors and walls. Suddenly, the sliding door begins to close. I squeeze sideways through the opening before it's too late, pressing myself against the pillar as it resumes its ordinary disguise. From the outside, the seams of the doorway are invisible, making it look like every other marble pillar in the castle.

I have no plans of misplacing this pillar. I also know that the whole point of sneaking in here is to stall the ceremony. But in the rush to get here, I didn't come up with any worthwhile ideas.

I peek around the left side of the pillar. The edge of the room is lined with an attentive audience all the way to the main entrance. I imagine Eimear with the other druids, trying to break through the glamoured barriers while Cináed and Gerard prepare to bust down the doors at the first possible moment.

The crowd is facing forward and to my right. I peek around the opposite corner to find the object of their attention. Where two empty thrones once stood at the head of the room, only one remains. And on the top step of the dais, Hagan, and two other advisors I recognize as supporters of Naoise, face the audience.

"We present to you, our soon-to-be high queen, Lady Orla!"

More cheers erupt as the advisors step down from the raised dais. I inch forward a bit further to see into the middle of the room, where the crowd is parting in a glittering wave.

Orla walks down the aisle, head held high, seeming to glide across the floor in her silk, charcoal-gray dress. The sequined gown accents her curves, and a tuft of tulle floats behind her, drawing the eye to her twisted updo and the glittering black headdress I assume she'll replace with the crown.

Keep the tiara, Orla. It's the closest thing you'll ever wear to a crown.

I hear soft murmurs from someone on the other side of the pillar. “Look at her. She’s been waiting the better part of our lifetimes for this day.”

Another voice adds, “I heard she was old enough to be Finnabair’s mother when King Rauri chose his bride.”

“And he overlooked her, the same way everyone has overlooked her all these years.”

The voices pause as Orla takes the three steps to the top of the dais and turns to face the room.

“Her history is something she will not soon forget,” one of the voices says.

I can hear the dark humor in the reply. “Or let anyone who’s done her wrong forget, either.”

The entire assembly falls into a hushed silence as Orla lifts her hands. She smiles—a forced, vicious gesture like that of a hawk closing in on its prey. Her face resumes its natural severity as she begins her speech.

“Fellow members of the High Court, and every pureblood faery who shares this moment with us today. We celebrate your loyalty, vision, and dedication. Together, we are purifying the Otherworld and laying claim to what is rightfully ours!”

I retreat to the other side of the pillar as the audience cheers. With everyone’s eyes locked on Orla, I’m at liberty to get a better look at the entrance.

Sure enough, the doors have been blocked by wooden beams. And there . . . along the edges of the doors. It’s faint, but the subtle shimmer tells me the doors are also sealed with glamour.

Similar to the glamour barrier surrounding ice-queen Eirwen's safe house. The one I was able to pass straight through. Does that mean I could do the same thing here? Or even reverse the barrier's magic altogether?

It's worth a try. The fewer blockades, the faster the others can break through.

Then I remember what I'm wearing—fighting clothes. Even if I walk on the shadowed side of the pillars, I'll stick out like a sore thumb in this crowd of saccharine gowns and gold-trimmed tunics. I need to blend in if I hope to reach the doors unnoticed.

A guard in the crowd catches my eye as she raises a fist to cheer. If only I could snag one of those gold cloaks . . .

I glance at the patchwork cloak draped around me. Closing my eyes, I recall the way I used glamour to transform our passports. When I open my eyes, I can't help but smile. The ragtag material has transformed into silken gold. I shift, letting the cloth sway.

The glamour wobbles, revealing sections of the true cloak beneath. I focus harder and try again. This time, the magic holds.

Taking a deep breath through my nose, I tug the hood on and brace myself before stepping out from behind the pillar. I keep my gaze forward and gait purposeful, holding the spear like the guards do, in front of me like a walking stick.

Orla's voice continues, "As high queen, I make a solemn vow to expel any foreign presence from our lands. The journey to peace will be long, unforgiving, and painted in blood. But nothing will stand in the way of the Reclamation!

Together, we will return the Otherworld to her original state—a thriving sanctuary for the true descendants of the Tuatha de Danaan!"

I reach the entrance and finally let myself breathe again, careful not to let the glamour slip. My position at the rear of the crowd protects me from the majority of suspicious gazes. But a few advisors—and Orla herself—face the entrance.

I plant myself against the edge of the doors, head lowered so my hood shadows my face. Tuning out Orla's sickening speech as best I can, I search for the soft vibration of magic humming through the doors. I rest my free hand right where the seam of glamour runs strongest. It flickers beneath my touch, almost as if it senses me.

Unlike the shimmering barrier surrounding Eirwen's house, this wall of glamour is dotted with holes. Whoever created it must have been in a hurry. Their sloppy work should make mine easier.

I try to silently banish the glamour. It flickers and wobbles, pulsing against my hand like rippling waves. I try again, and while I sense the wall weakening, I already feel drained. It will take too long and sap all my energy.

I close my eyes, observing the magic through my mind's eye. The vibrations almost seem to be whispering to me, a lilting song I struggle to understand.

My eyes fly open. *Energy can be rerouted.* I need to give the glamour something else to do.

With a whispered command, I order the magic to unlink from the doors, but instead of sending it into the throne room, I tell the glamour to travel through the wood and into the hall.

And then I instruct the magic to clear out all the other glamoured barriers in the corridor.

A *clang* and several loud *cracks* sound through the closed doors. Orla's speech cuts off, and I feel the eyes of the room turn toward me.

Without lifting my head, I retreat two steps from the doors and stand in the shadow of the nearest pillar. My heart races in my throat, and I wait in pained silence for someone to point me out, to call me a traitor for trying to stop the ceremony.

"Do not fear!" Hagan cries, waving his hands to redirect the attention away from the entrance. "Try as they might, nothing is getting through those doors!"

I heave out a sigh, leaning on the pillar for support. *No one saw me.*

Orla shouts above the commotion. "Friends, calm yourselves. Opposition howls at our doors, but when have we ever fled from conflict? Never!"

Cries of agreement ring out, and with horror, I watch as the crowd parts again. An elderly faery in plum robes glides toward the throne. He carries a crown.

A collective hum builds into a terrifying chant. The crowd stomps their feet in unison. A sickening chill shivers over my skin.

I return to the door and press my ear against it, but I don't hear anything over the growing roar.

Were the barriers destroyed? Are Cináed and Gerard about to break down the doors? At the thought, I jump back, not wanting to be impaled by splintered wood.

I feel useless, frantic. The old faery has almost reached the dais where Orla waits on the throne. Her hands grip the armrests, gaze locked on the approaching crown. Her hawkish smile returns, and the hunger in her eyes makes my stomach squirm.

No. This can't be happening. We need more time.

My feet carry me into the swaying throng. I'm swallowed in the sea of haunting chants I don't understand. No one notices me, not in this intense moment.

I press against the other faeries, forcing my way forward, panic rising like bile in my throat.

I break free of the last line of defense between me and the carpeted aisle. The maroon rug trails across the center of the room like a river of blood. It leads straight to the dais, the throne, and Orla.

My feet stumble toward her. My mouth opens.

"*Stop!*"

{ 52 }

The eyes of the audience narrow in on me, their stares laced with venom. I take another step down the aisle. Anyone standing on the carpet jumps aside, clearly not wanting to be seen standing close to me.

The instant Orla's sharp eyes find me, it's all I can do to hold the weight of her stare and not dissolve on the spot.

Lord Hagan takes one step onto the dais and points at me. "You—how did you get in here?"

My mind spins wildly, grasping for a plan. Any moment now, I'll be arrested and removed from the scene. Orla nods at someone in the crowd, and I see faeries shuffling aside to allow a pair of golden-cloaked guards through.

"Stand back!" I shout, swinging my staff in a wide circle.

Anyone within range leaps away. One male shrieks and knocks several faeries over as he scrambles to the side.

"Stand back, or meet the same fate as Naoise!" I call.

Orla shoots to her feet. Her expression is emotionless, but I know her well enough to catch the annoyance in her tone as she addresses the room. "Calm yourselves. It is only the faerie mutt, Róisín." Her eyes slice into me like iron blades. "You gained our attention, girl. But your futile attempt to thwart the ceremony has failed."

The tangible shift in power takes my breath away. The energy of the audience sharpens, their eyes glittering with wicked humor.

Orla continues, knowing she has control over the situation. "As you can see"—she extends her arms toward the room—"you are outnumbered."

Laughter ripples through the crowd. Just then, the guards reach me. I face them in a fighting stance, feeling like an animal trapped in a cage.

Shame flares hot beneath the anger. *They think I'm a joke. None of them will believe I'm Aisling's daughter.*

The female guard strikes first, aiming low. I block the spear with a quick swipe, barely bringing the staff up fast enough to stop the second blow from the male guard. They circle me on the rug. Everyone taunts and cheers as they gather around the fight.

I toss my glamourless cloak aside, and the nearest faeries cry out in dismay as they dodge it like it's a dirty rag. I ignore all of them, focusing on my two opponents.

The male strikes at my front in the same instant the female aims at my side. A low duck sends both their spears into an *X* that grazes the top of my head in a clash of sparks. Using my spear as a pivot, I swing my leg around and manage to knock the male to the ground.

But the female hops over my leg and strikes at my exposed chest. I hold my spear close and roll to the edge of the crowd. Her spear slices the carpet beside my head.

I jump up, but my opponents hesitate to strike with the spectators so close behind me. It allows me to catch my breath and plan my next move.

I don't know how much longer I can fend off two guards like this. My training with Gerard has saved me thus far. But my lungs are already burning, my vision spotting from lack of oxygen.

The guards stride closer while the faeries behind me disperse. I glance at the doors, wishing I could see into the hall beyond. *What's taking them so long?*

"Enough dallying," Orla calls like a ruthless crow. "Kill her, and be done with it."

The guards nod at their leader and face me with renewed determination. I toss my ponytail behind a shoulder and resume my stance. Despite the adrenaline pumping hot in my veins, a cold swell of dread crashes over me.

This is it. This is the end.

I unlock my jaw enough to flash a fierce grin at Orla. "You have a habit of underestimating people. And it's going to come back to bite you—right in your arrogant, traitorous ass."

Her eyes widen, and for a moment, the rage in her face makes her look more her age.

Before she can summon a response, both guards lunge at me. I shout and raise my staff to meet them.

The second our spears collide, an earth-shattering explosion erupts through the room.

I go flying, landing face-first on the carpet. My ears ring so loudly I can't hear myself think. I try to stand, but another faery has landed on my back. A lancing pain pierces my left leg.

I'm aware of the commotion in the room. Sounds bubble around me, unintelligible and heavy. I probably have a concussion from the explosion.

Then I remember the doors—my friends on the other side—and I shove the faery off me, peering through layers of floating particles until I find the entrance.

The end of a marble pillar skewers the doors—or at least the spot where the doors used to be. The gaping hole surrounding the pillar is so huge that only the remnants of door hinges remain intact. Even parts of the stone wall have been blown to bits.

Others are beginning to stir, their moans filling my pounding head as my hearing returns. I crawl over one of the guards, then yelp at the pain in my leg.

I glance at it and wish I hadn't. The entire bottom half of my legging is dark with blood. A broken spearhead lies between me and the unconscious female guard. She must have unwittingly stabbed me during the explosion.

Something moves at the entrance. I look up to see Eimear standing atop the pillar, red hair splayed around her, a simmering wand in her hand.

She hops into the room, followed by Gerard, Cináed, Irvin, and a number of guards and servants I recognize and others I don't. I lose count of their numbers as they spill through the opening.

Cináed starts toward me, shoving faeries out of his way. I finally find the strength to stand by using my staff to support my leg.

Our tribe is fresh, ready for battle, while a third of Orla's followers lie in heaps on the floor. The rest are injured, still reeling from the explosion. Their haughty glowers and the fancy clothes that intimidated me before now look silly compared to the gritty demeanor of our ragtag group.

Cináed reaches me and circles a strong arm around my waist.

Then Orla's voice rings out above the din. "Well played, Wanderer." She sits on the throne, unharmed by the explosion except for the white chalk smeared across her crazed, maniacal face. "But you are too late." She lifts the crown from her lap and sets it on her askew hairdo. "I have been crowned high queen, and all of you will be banished from the Otherworld for treason."

A quick search shows the old faery at the bottom of the dais in a crumpled pile of purple robes. My eyes narrow in on the crown. She must have snatched it from his cold fingers.

Cináed calls, "Your reign will not last. Your subjects will overthrow an unworthy ruler. Which is why you were forced to perform this ceremony behind closed doors in the first place."

The surviving advisors, guards, and other faeries begin to gather at Orla's feet. Although dazed and mostly weaponless, they are a force to be reckoned with. And we are still outnumbered.

I know Orla sees this. Her rigidity softens as if she realizes she is untouchable. She responds to Cináed, her voice coy.

"Then to appease my subjects, I dedicate my first act as high queen to you. I will give you a head start before I send my guards after you. I suggest you hurry if you wish to reach the nearest portal with your heads intact."

Our small party flocks to us. Gerard nods at me before facing Orla with his sword in his fist. Eimear and Irvin stand beside Cináed, their stone-cold gazes locked on Orla.

Some of the High Court cluster along the edges of the room, either too injured or too afraid to stand with their queen.

I search their faces for Fodla, praying she's among them—alive and willing to surrender.

But I don't see her standing with them, or with those gathered beneath Orla.

My gut clenches, and tears prick my eyes. *Please don't be dead.*

Cináed looks at all of us, silently asking if anyone wants to run while they still can. When no one moves, he faces Orla again. "It appears your first act is a waste, as will be the entirety of your limited reign."

Orla's snide smile disappears. She straightens on the throne, crown tilting on her head. "Then you, Wanderer, will die with the rest of the leeches polluting our lands. The Otherworld will be purged, and there is nothing you can do to stop it."

"You weren't crowned," I say.

Everyone looks at me. Orla's momentary shock is replaced by an icy glare.

"How dare you speak to me," she spits.

"You're lying!" I continue, my voice building. "I was here the whole time." I point at the unmoving form of the old faery. "He was supposed to crown you, but we broke through the doors before he completed the ceremony!"

From the look of stupor on her face, I know I'm right. She stands from the throne. "Silence! I am high queen!"

"You are nothing!" I scream back, pointing my spear at her.

The faeries around Orla shift anxiously, glancing between us. Her voice drops to a low hiss. "You have damaged our kingdom long enough with your lies, you worthless mutt. Who do you think you are?"

A familiar melody brushes my mind—my mother's voice. I take a step forward on my good leg, squaring my shoulders as I look right into Orla's condescending eyes.

"I am Princess Aisling's daughter, the missing child and rightful heir to the throne. Now remove that crown before I knock it off your head."

{ 53 }

Orla's shrill laughter slices through the throne room.

No one else moves or makes a sound. Her followers continue to watch me, but their hardened gazes shift with confusion. Some of the guards share long looks.

"Another brazen lie." Orla shakes her head once, then reaches to catch the tilting crown before it falls. "You might have manipulated your way into Naoise's heart but not mine."

I sense Cináed's presence behind me, and the rest of our group flanks me, their support giving strength to my words. Instead of speaking to Orla, I look into the faces of her followers. "I speak the truth, but I don't expect any of you to believe me just like that. I must earn your trust, the way any ruler should."

My gaze locks onto the pillar on the far side. At the edge of Orla's faerie blockade.

"I can prove who I am." I point my spear at the pillar. "If you let me, I will show you I'm speaking the truth."

I hobble forward, aiming to pass between the two groups. Cináed fuses himself to my side, half-carrying me while I use my spear as a walking stick.

"I assume you have proof?" Cináed whispers in my ear. His gaze never stills as he keeps watch for any attackers.

I nod, trying to carry myself with some degree of poise despite the pain in my leg and the terror rattling my bones.

"Kill her!" Orla screeches.

A few faeries move but only to follow behind me in slow silence. The air hangs heavy with cautious hope and wary disbelief. Every eye tracks my journey to the pillar.

"What are you doing?" Orla stands from the throne, pointing a long finger at me. "Kill her! Kill them all!"

We reach the pillar, and I give Cináed a look. *I need to do this alone.*

He takes a small step aside. But he faces the group of two-dozen onlookers with a dagger in each fist. Out of the corner of my eye, I see that Gerard mirrors him—sword drawn and ready—to guard my other side.

I meet the eyes of Orla's followers who stand closest to me. Most of them are guards in golden cloaks, wielding spears and observing me with intrigued expressions.

Realization softens my frown. Most of them probably protected King Rauri. *As his guards, did they learn about the secret passage?*

I'm surprised by my commanding voice. "I was asked how I entered the throne room. This is how."

I sink my weight into my good leg and reach a hand down to my wound. I want to be sure this works, so I dig two fingers into the tear in my leggings and press them against the gash. I bite my cheek to keep from crying out and withdraw my scarlet fingers.

Once I've controlled my pained expression, I look up and brandish my dripping fingers high above me.

"There's a doorway in this hollow pillar. It opens at the touch of royal blood. And it opens for me."

A few gasps disturb the stagnant, chalky air. I turn to touch the pillar's glossy exterior, but pause.

Oh shoot.

If blood opens it from the outside, the marble would be streaked with dried markings just like on the inside. Right?

No time like the present to test it out. I hold my breath and press my bloody fingers to the marble.

Nothing.

"It did not work!" someone cries. "Liar!"

Cináed—the ever-charismatic diplomat—steps forward. "Wait a moment. We are all aware that blood spells can be precarious."

My frame trembles, and I fight to contain my fear before it shows on my face. *Maybe I'm wrong. Maybe I'm not royalty.*

I shove aside my doubts. More blood—I need more blood. I grit my teeth, about to use my spear to slice my palm open.

When I think of something.

While arguments break out between groups—and Cináed shouts above the chaos to try to maintain some order—I lean close to the pillar and begin to sing.

I sing my mother's lullaby. In my pitchy voice, leaving out the words I still don't remember.

And the throne room falls silent, listening as the song builds to the chorus. I hear myself singing words in a language I don't understand.

But I trust the melody that awakened me to who I am, letting it flow from deep within me.

As the chorus ends, I dare a glance at the silent onlookers. Gerard exclaims, "You did it, my lady!"

I spin and watch as the pillar slides open.

All the noise in the room—gasps, whispers, a few screams—blend into the background once I notice a cluster of guards dropping to their knees before me.

One in the front addresses me with his head bowed. "We surrender, Your Majesty, and pledge our service to your rightful reign."

Before I can respond, Irvin hollers, "Lady Orla!" He points at the dais just out of my view. "She's gone!"

No.

In an instant I can't catch, everything flashes white. A strange, choking smoke clogs the room, formed from the stone particles that coated the floor after the explosion.

I cough and peer through the smoke. As the white cloud starts to fade, I see that those near the throne are trying to wave the cloud away. But the throne itself, where Orla stood seconds before, is empty.

"Don't let Orla escape!" I shout.

At my command, our group scatters to all corners of the room. As we disperse, some of Orla's followers gather the courage to pick fights with us in a last-ditch effort to save their leader. Two guards swarm Gerard as Irvin dukes it out with Lord Hagan.

I dodge a flying spear, joining hands with Cináed as we race through the dense cloud toward the entrance. Red sparks fly up ahead, and I veer toward them.

Eimear's green cloak is smeared with dust, her wand pointed at Orla's back. She shoots more sparks, and Orla's skirt bursts into flames.

Orla shrieks. She stops running to tamp out the fire with her hands. Eimear reaches her, and before Orla sees what's coming, Eimear's fist hits her square in the nose.

I screech to a halt, my mouth agape. Orla drops a slender stick to the ground, stumbles back, and lands on her rear, nose dripping with blood.

Cináed duels with a faery who tries to interfere. The sound of their clashing spears joins the unseen chaos around us as they retreat to the center of the room.

Eimear snatches up the slender stick. Her rage could boil water. "Go hifreann leat! You killed a druid for this wand, didn't you?"

Most of Orla's graying hair has fallen from her updo. Her hands shield her gushing nose, and her eyes widen in panic. When she fell, she cornered herself against a pile of rubble. I stand next to Eimear.

"I should kill you for this!" Eimear cries, pointing her wand at Orla's head.

"Wait," I say, not taking my gaze off Orla.

Eimear pauses, glancing at me through her tears. "You'd best have good reason for this."

In any other situation, the bite in her tone would make me smile. She knows who I am now—and it hasn't hindered her defiant tongue.

"Orla has answers we need." I clench my teeth, willing the image of dead eyes and the smell of blood to vanish from my memories forever. "And I know what it feels like to take a life." I hold Eimear's gaze. "I'd never wish that feeling on anyone, especially a friend."

Eimear faces Orla again, wand outstretched. But her arm trembles and falls to her side. Just then, Gerard approaches with a pile of chains in his arms. Eimear walks away before I can say anything else to her.

"Here, Your Majesty." The chains drop to the floor with a loud *clang*, and he bows his head. "If you wish to take any prisoners."

By now the smoke has cleared enough to take in the battle scene. Our allies have surrounded a group of Reclamationists—some are kneeling in surrender, others are pinned down with knives against their necks.

"Yes." I cough to clear my tight throat. "Yes, gather the survivors as prisoners, and take them to the dungeon."

Irvin and the other loyal guards approach us. Gerard instructs them on how to lock Orla in chains. I leave them to it, not caring to spend an extra second in Orla's presence. Not trusting that my fingers won't start clawing at her face or choking her with my bare hands.

She's the one who killed Manny. Who threatened my friends time and time again.

And she might be the one who murdered Rauri and Finnabair. *My grandparents.*

I'll make her pay for everything she did. But not until I leech every ounce of useful information from her.

The throne is just visible through the fading cloud. The crimson rug is littered with chunks of rock and splintered planks of wood. Beneath that, I count the bodies crushed in the explosion.

And right there and then, I vow to never sacrifice the lives of my followers to save my own skin.

I remain in the throne room until all the traitors are led away in chains. I stay until only a few allies remain—to treat the wounded and start the long process of cleaning up the mess. I'm limping around, doing my best to help, when Cináed finds me.

He tells me to stop and tries to pull me into his arms. I resist his touch at first, but he refuses to let me go. With gentle coaxing, he leads me into a side room and shuts the door.

As soon as we're alone, out of the public eye, my reserve cracks open. All at once, like the barricaded door bursting wide.

I give in to the mounting pain, letting Cináed hold me as tears wet our shirts—as we mourn for all that was lost and honor all that was found.

{ 54 }

A faint floral smell wafts in from the open doors of my balcony. I imagine Eimear in the gardens below—where she's been hard at work for two days. Under her care, and with the sudden shift in weather, the rose bushes have already begun to bloom.

Hafwin smiles at me in the mirror as she finishes braiding my hair. "You're certain you do not want to wear a crown?"

I shake my head, then regret it. Even the slightest motion invites a rush of pain up my spine. After the fight in the throne room, I spent an entire day in bed. And it'll be a while longer before my numerous injuries fully heal.

Especially my leg. I wince as I stand, accepting the spear Hafwin hands me.

"I wish you would let me find you a proper walking staff, my lady. Using a fighting spear is quite unusual for someone of your status."

I smile and turn away from the mirror to meet Hafwin's concerned gaze. "I'm not a ruler until I've been properly crowned. Until then, you'll have to put up with my unconventional ways."

Hafwin smirks and huffs a teasing sigh. "Knowing you, my lady, even a proper crowning will not cure that."

I let Hafwin help me to the door. Gerard jumps to attention at the sight of me, and I have to stop myself from rolling my eyes.

"You have to eat and sleep at some point, Gerard," I say as I walk past him down the hall.

"Not until I am relieved of my post, Your Majesty. Which will take time. I do not trust the other guards, especially not the ones who were supporting Orla just two days ago."

He matches my slow pace, his hand poised on the hilt of his sword even though there's no danger in sight. A servant passes by, and with the glower Gerard gives him, it's a miracle the poor faery doesn't drop the tray of dishes clanking in his hands.

While Gerard's protective presence might annoy me a little, I can't argue with his logic. Even after I opened the secret passage in the throne room, some still doubt my legitimacy.

And I don't blame them. After this bad streak of power-hungry rulers, I can only expect them to be suspicious.

Which is why, for the sanity of us all, I appointed Cináed as my head advisor. I'm a new face—a faerie mutt whose short time in the Otherworld has been fraught with scandal and exaggerated legends.

But it's rare to find anyone with something bad to say about Cináed the Wanderer—the charming, golden-haired faery who traveled through realms on quests for King Rauri himself.

He was the late king's most trusted advisor. And he's already becoming my most trusted advisor too.

We reach the stairs that lead to the dungeon. I let Gerard enter first, blinking as my eyes adjust to the dingy gloom of the pit I know all too well.

Behind the bars of the main cell, I see twenty-something faeries chained to the walls. From what Hafwin told me, Fodla is among the captured Reclamationists. I look away before I happen to spot her in the throng.

The three guards on duty nod to Gerard and bow to me.

"Give me a moment," I say to them.

The guards nod, moving toward the stairs. I send Gerard an insistent look, and he relents, distancing himself to stand at the foot of the stairs.

I turn my back to the main cell, facing the small cage in the corner beneath the stairs. And wait until a pair of steel-colored eyes open and focus on me.

"I wondered when you would visit," Orla says coolly.

The fact that she still manages to inject any condescension into her words amazes me. Since I'm in no mood for small talk, I cut right to the point.

"You manipulated Aisling's parents into marrying her to the prince of the merfolk." It's not a question, but I wait for her to show me she's listening.

She turns her head to cough. The metal spikes are inches from pricking her sallow skin. Already the iron has drained some of her energy.

"I did. For political reasons your childish mind could not begin to understand."

I drop to her level, kneeling on my good leg. My words are sharper than the thorns of her cage. "Do not lie to me, Orla. I know you couldn't care less about improving relations with the merfolk. You got rid of Aisling for the same reason you poisoned her brother and her parents."

I peer at her, searching for the smallest sign of proof. I'll admit—I *want* it to be her fault. I want to satisfy my craving for revenge. And if she's to blame for all of it, my punishment for her will be that much sweeter.

Orla's eyes flash in the dark, revealing nothing to me. "You might have everyone else fooled, but I knew Aisling better than anyone. She would never demean herself by mating with the likes of a human. You have brought destruction on all our heads with your treacherous lies!"

She spits at me through the cage. I don't flinch as I stand and start for the stairs, making sure my response is loud enough to be heard by the entire dungeon.

"Save your energy for the iron, Orla. You're going to be spending a lot of time in that soul-sucking cage."

I reach the top of the stairs a bit breathless and pause to rest my leg. My blood simmers as I replay Orla's comebacks. Even though she lost and can't hurt anyone again, I can't ignore the fear I felt at her words.

You have brought destruction on all our heads.

Already I've been forced to punish faeries for their prejudice against me. While I envision an Otherworld free of oppressive power structures and ridiculous titles—a world where, as Hafwin said, we are stronger together—I'm terrified by the daunting prospect of turning that dream into a reality.

"Róisín." Cináed strides toward me with a paper in his hand. "This just arrived."

I take the letter, admiring the teal emblem on the front. "What is it?"

Gerard leans over my shoulder. He shares a look with Cináed. "Could it be?"

Cináed nods, eyes wide in amazement as a smile tugs on his lips.

"It's a letter from the merfolk royal family."

My heart leaps into my throat. I tear the letter open, scanning the words so quickly that I have to reread them a second time.

To Her Royal Highness, Princess Róisín,

I would be honored by your visit to our palace at your earliest convenience. I look forward to your response.

Your hopeful ally,

Prince Llyr

{ EPILOGUE }

My breath is loud in my ears. I blink, and the landscape around me begins to take shape. Wisps of mist gather at my feet, forming a grove of trees.

I reach out to touch the nearest branch and gasp as my fingers pass right through it, scattering particles of mist that swirl together again in an instant.

Everything, from the sparse grass to the bark on the trees, is gray. Well, almost everything. I glimpse my own arm and see that I'm dressed in a purple robe.

I take a step, and the mist scatters and re-forms around me. There's a small clearing in the trees. I pause at the edge, listening to the wind of my breath in this soundless place.

Am I dreaming?

My eyes lock onto the muted earth at the center of the clearing as it stirs, picking up speed until a tornado of smoke forms into a pillar.

As the pillar solidifies, my intuition kicks in.

I try to look away, to turn and run. But I can't. I can't do anything but watch as Naoise appears in front of me, looking as real as the night we met.

Like me, he's also draped in a purple robe. We stand still, the only splashes of color in a gray grove, watching each other like two forest creatures who accidentally crossed paths.

My insides scream like I've caught fire, but my frozen body still won't budge. Naoise's clear eyes scan my face. His own face, cut from the pale marble of the gods, is expressionless. His eyes glint with an emotion I can't name.

At last he says, "Hello, my traitorous rose. Did you miss me?"

I don't respond. Even if I could force my body to react, I'd rather endure countless other nightmares than converse with this all-too-real demon from the dead.

Choking silence hangs heavy between us. Suddenly, the spark in Naoise's eyes ignites in a raging blaze. His hands clench into fists at his sides. My throat constricts, and the sound of my breath goes silent.

His voice doesn't rise above a low hum, but it carries the energy of a hurricane. "I expend my strength to heed your call, and yet you remain silent."

I wade through his words, acknowledging that this is a dream while also remembering Naoise's unique abilities. He's created a place of mist and shadow before—a dimension within the mind where he showed me memories of his past. Could it be that, even in death, he's able to contact me here?

Naoise's anger seems to cool to a simmer as he quirks a dark brow. "Perhaps you are moved beyond words at the sight of me. Did you truly believe me to be dead? I thought you, of all creatures, would know better."

The gray trees wobble and blur together. Naoise removes his gaze from me to observe the fading forest.

"I must depart," he says. "Already my energy wanes. Let us meet again. Soon."

Color drains from his purple cloak, pooling at his feet like dark blood. I want to scream at him, to order him to stay away from me. But, like in most of my nightmares, I'm rendered useless. Mute and motionless.

Naoise must sense the fear I'm unable to express because, as we both scatter into tendrils of drifting smoke, the last thing I see are his lips widening into a serpent's smile.

ABOUT THE AUTHOR

Logan Miehl loves writing fantasy, camping with her husband, and reading a good book with a mug of tea. She believes in the magic of travel—whether in person or through stories—and enjoys discovering new places when she can. The Faerie Festival Series was inspired by her travels in Ireland and her studies of Celtic myth.

For exclusive book content—including soundtracks and character pronunciation videos—visit her at www.loganmiehl.com.

Made in the USA
Monee, IL
15 February 2021